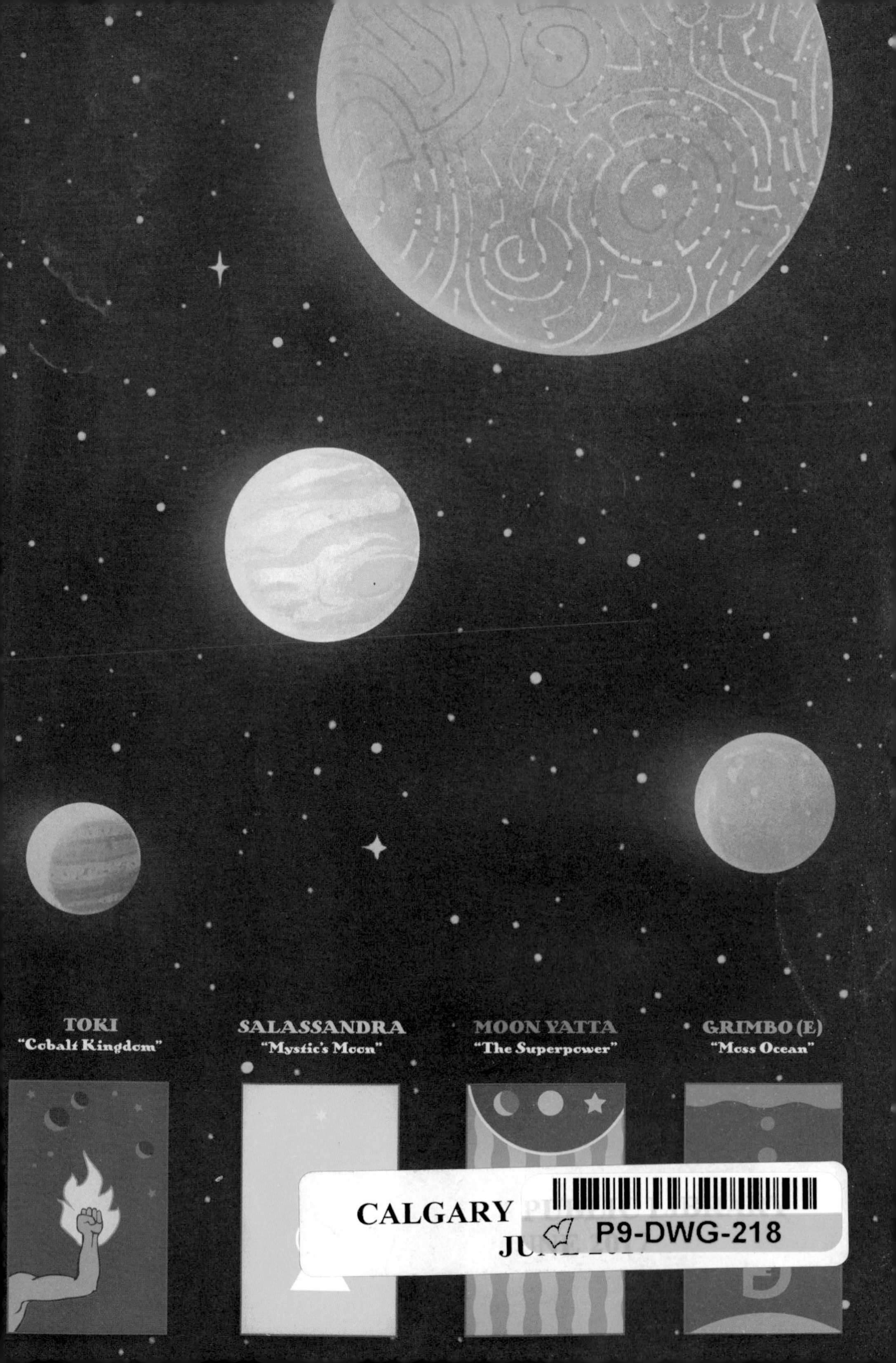
TOKI
"Cobalt Kingdom"
SALASSANDRA
"Mystic's Moon"
MOON YATTA
"The Superpower"
GRIMBO (E)
"Moss Ocean"

5 Worlds

BOOK 1

THE SAND WARRIOR

Mark
SIEGEL

Alexis
SIEGEL

Xanthe
BOUMA

Boya
SUN

Matt
ROCKEFELLER

Random House  New York

"One by one the five great Beacons
went dark and the Gods were gone.
And none would ever again light the
shining Beacons, save a Warrior of
Sand, crowned with living fire. . . ."

—FROM THE HOURS OF PRINCE FELID

Chapter 1

RUNAWAY SAND

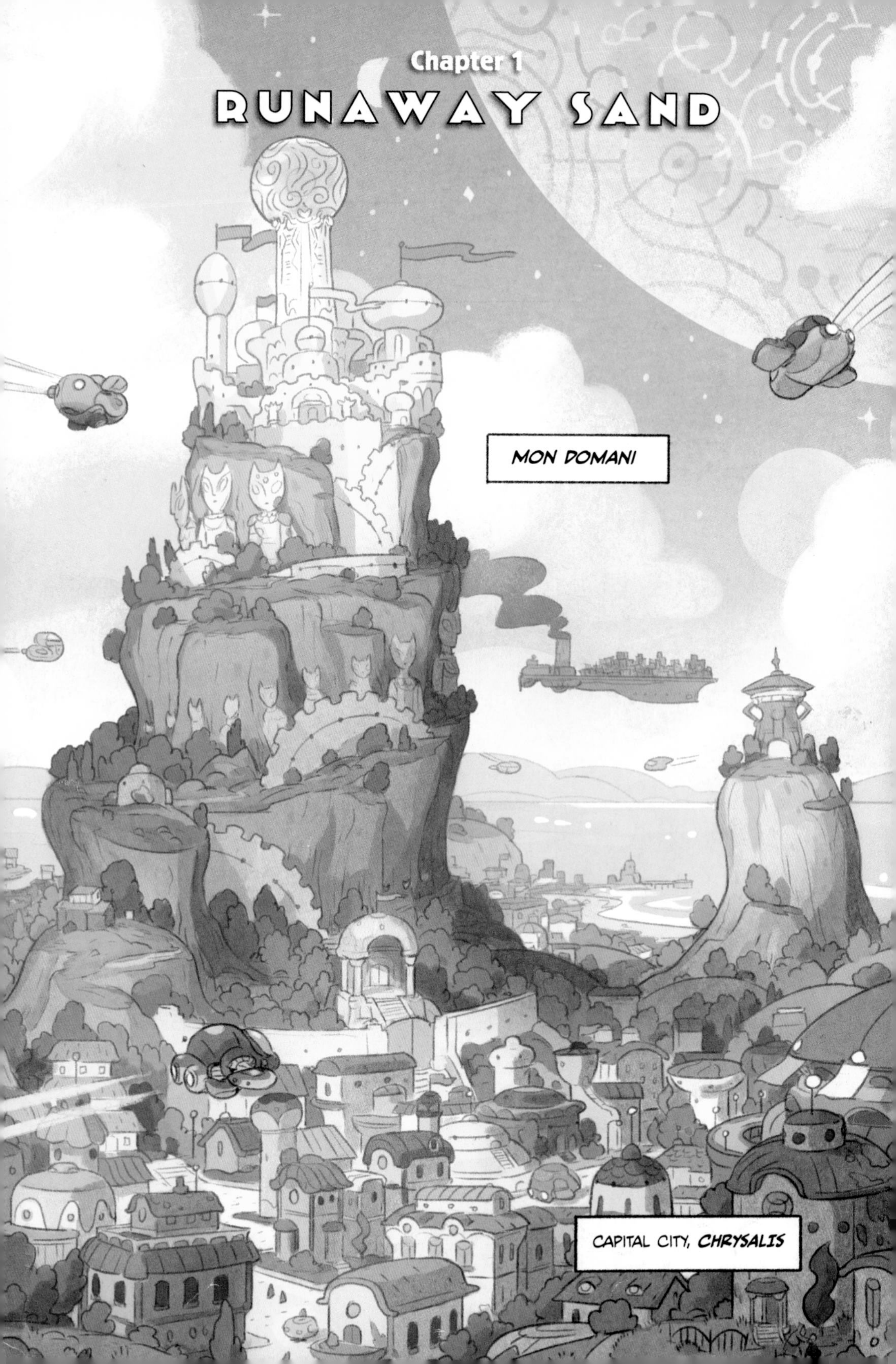
MON DOMANI
CAPITAL CITY, CHRYSALIS

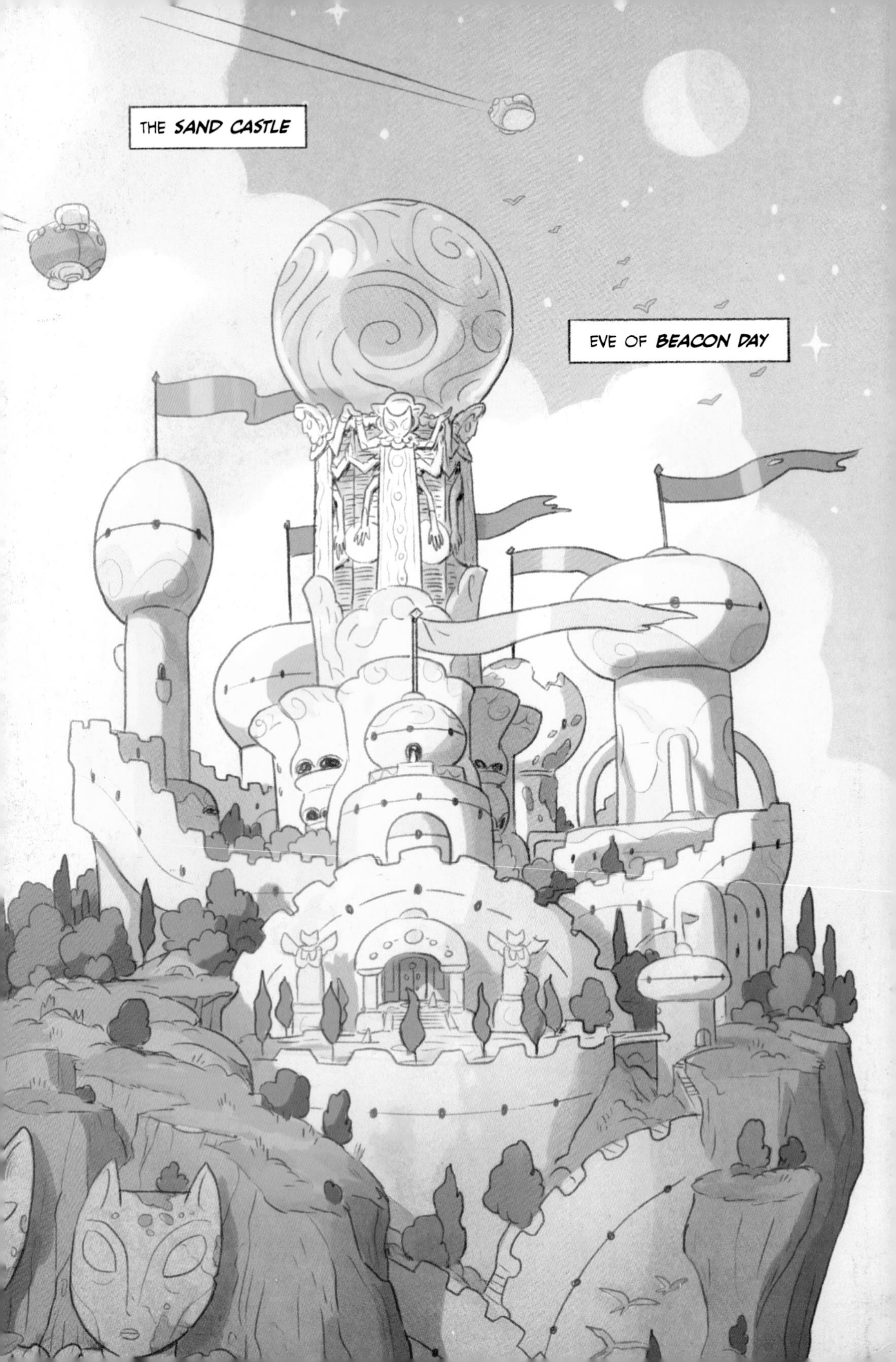
THE SAND CASTLE
EVE OF BEACON DAY

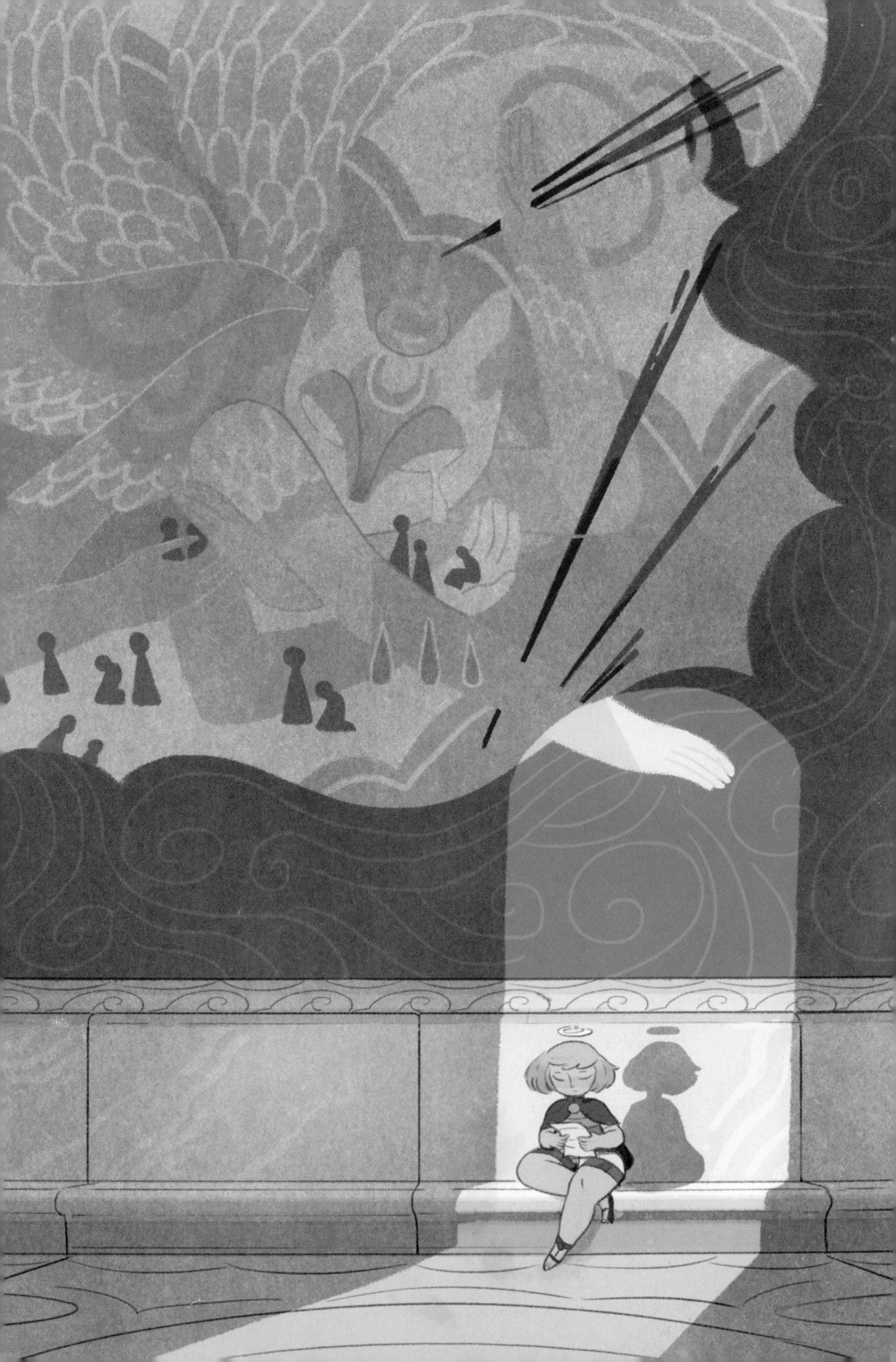

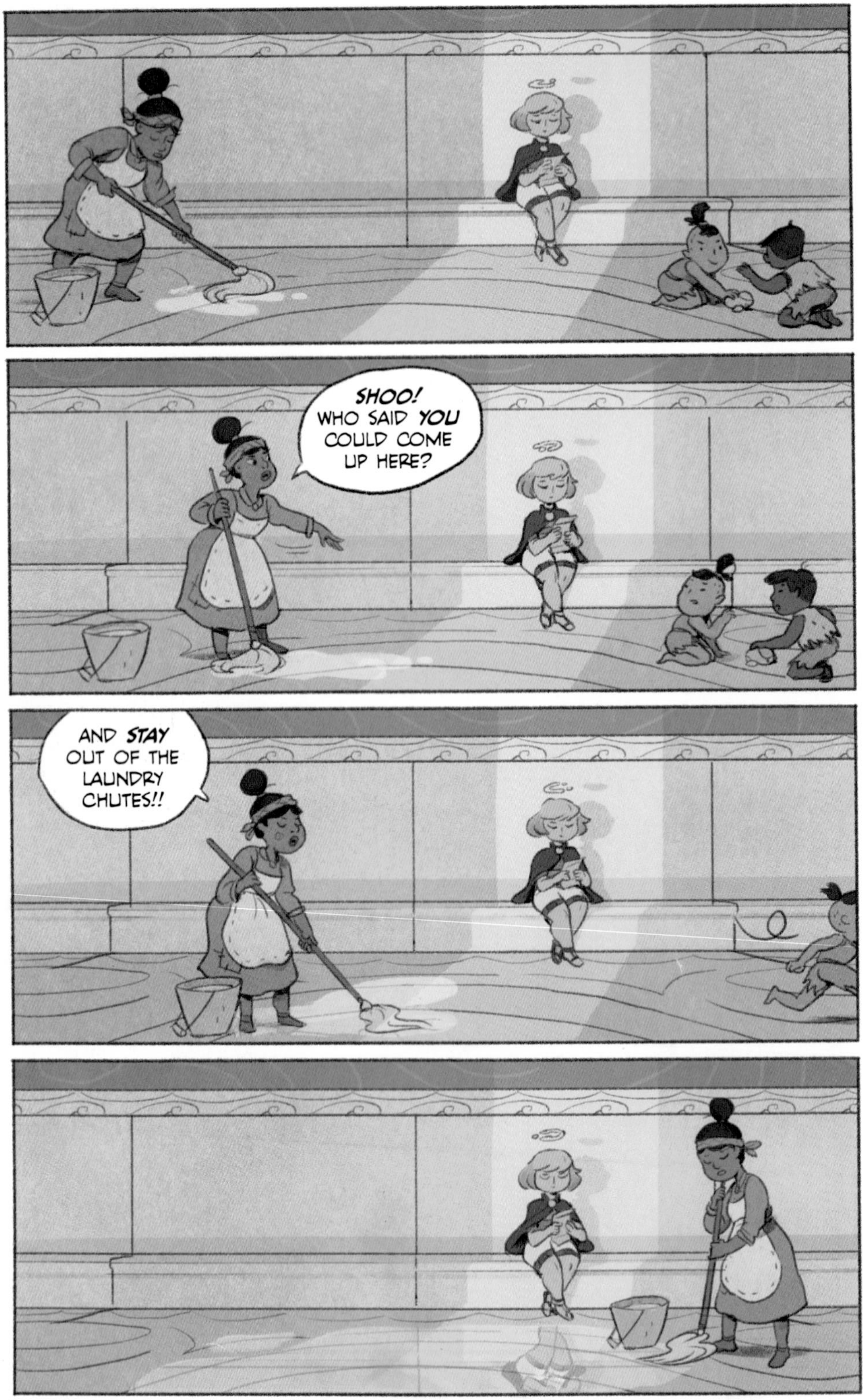
SHOO! WHO SAID YOU COULD COME UP HERE?
AND STAY OUT OF THE LAUNDRY CHUTES!!

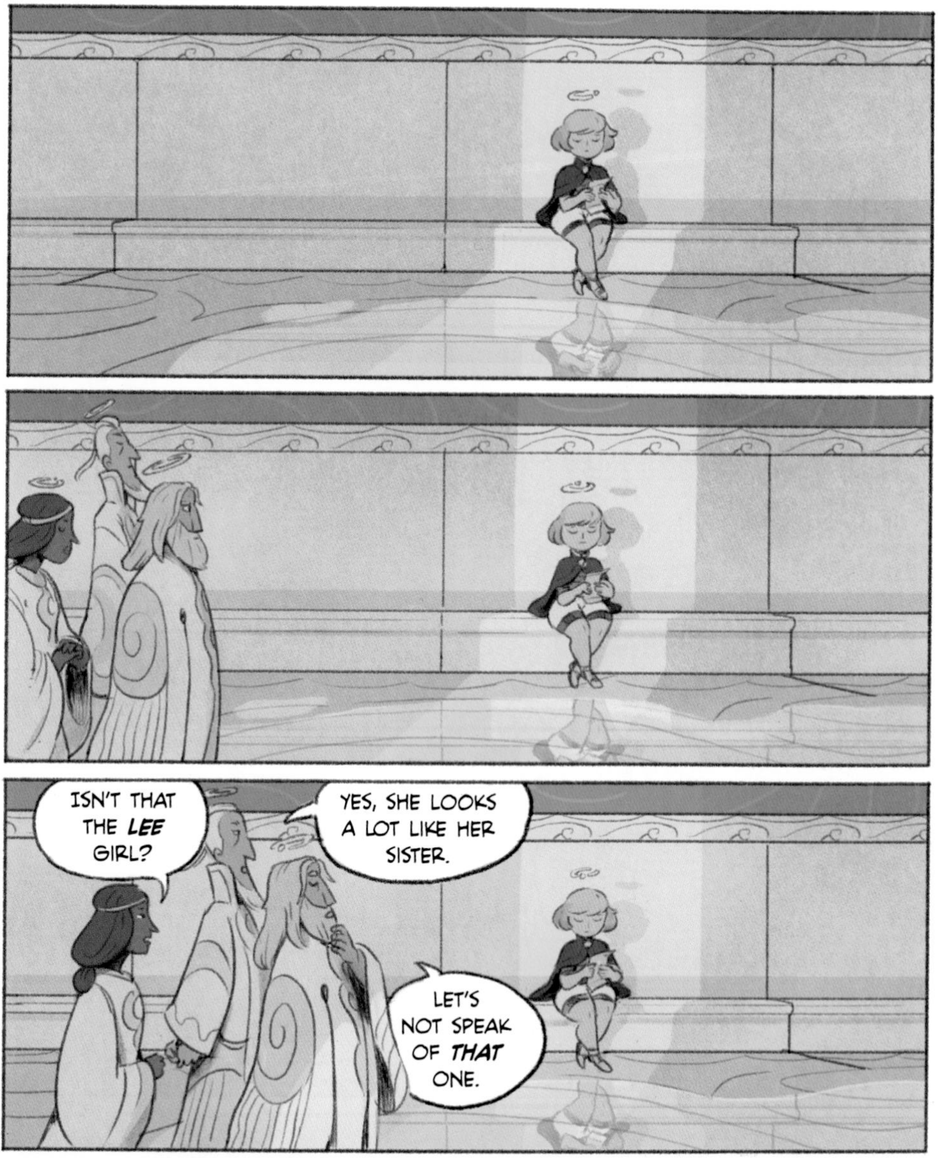
ISN'T THAT THE *LEE* GIRL?
YES, SHE LOOKS A LOT LIKE HER SISTER.
LET'S NOT SPEAK OF *THAT* ONE.
ESPECIALLY NOT BEFORE THE COUNCIL MEETING.

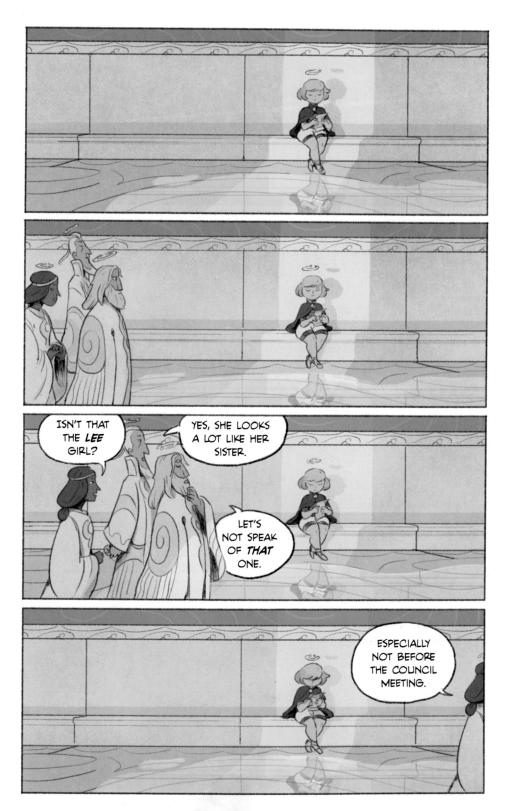

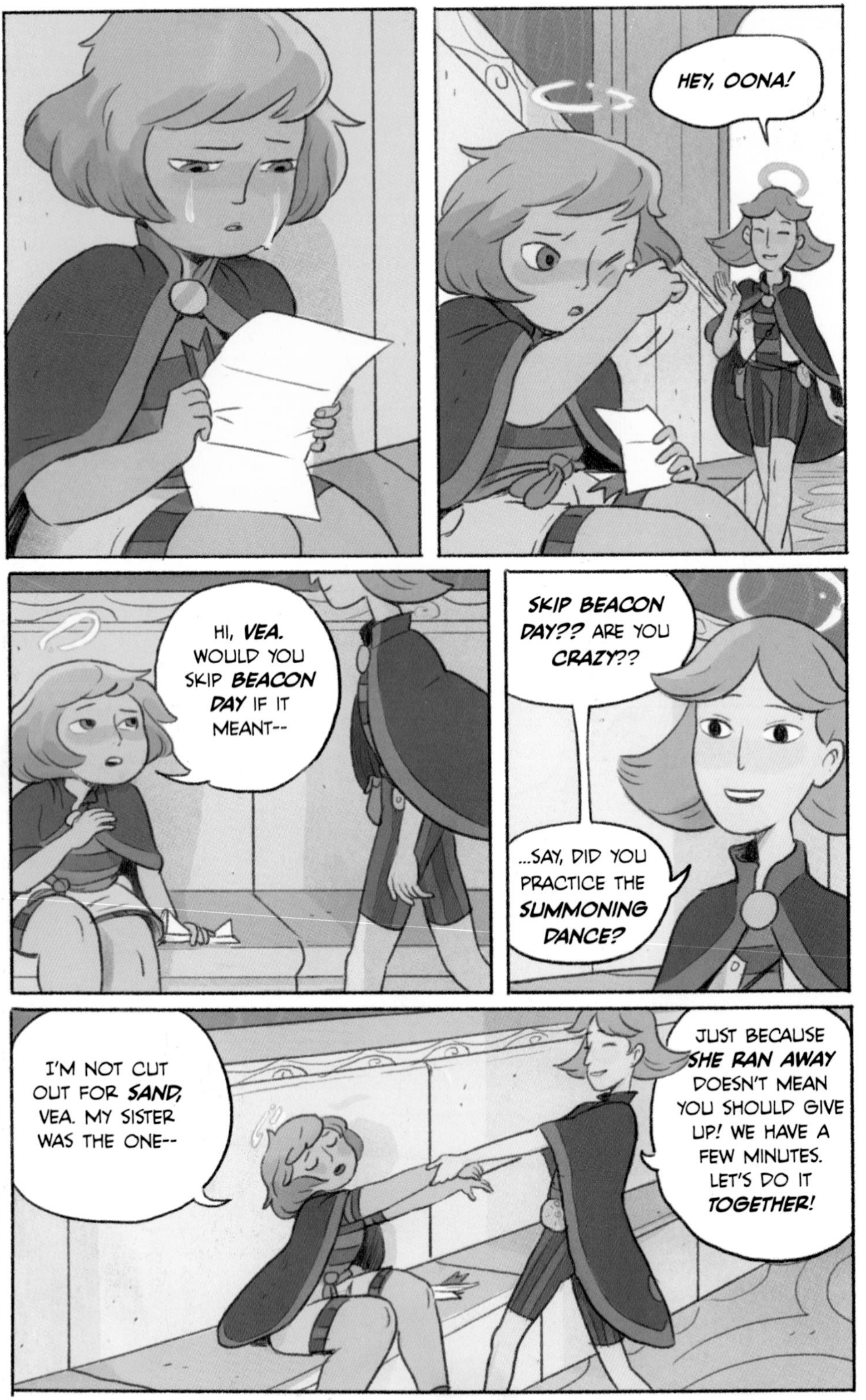
HEY, OONA!
HI, VEA. WOULD YOU SKIP BEACON DAY IF IT MEANT--
SKIP BEACON DAY?? ARE YOU CRAZY??
...SAY, DID YOU PRACTICE THE SUMMONING DANCE?
I'M NOT CUT OUT FOR SAND, VEA. MY SISTER WAS THE ONE--
JUST BECAUSE SHE RAN AWAY DOESN'T MEAN YOU SHOULD GIVE UP! WE HAVE A FEW MINUTES. LET'S DO IT TOGETHER!

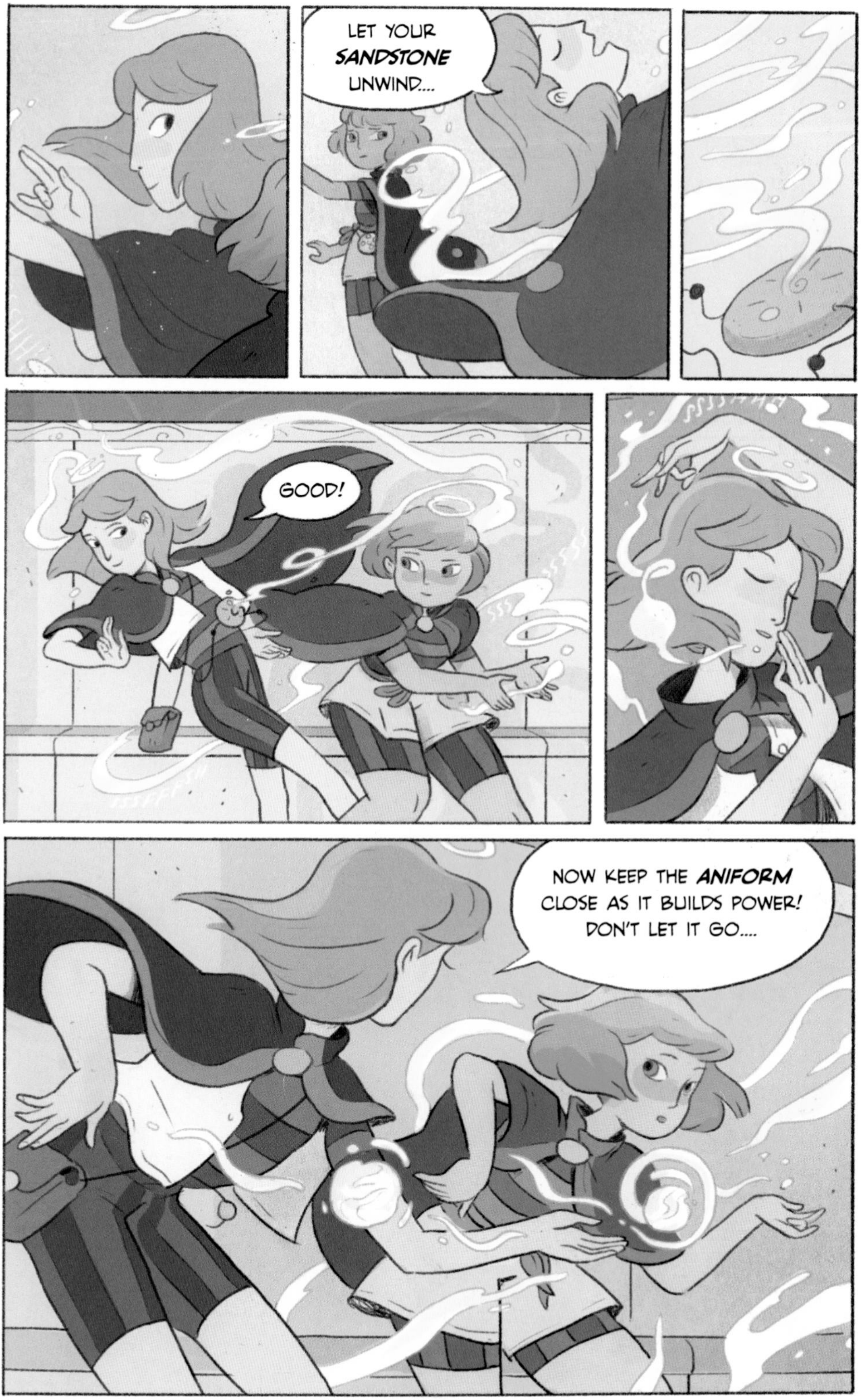
LET YOUR **SANDSTONE** UNWIND....
GOOD!
NOW KEEP THE ***ANIFORM*** CLOSE AS IT BUILDS POWER! DON'T LET IT GO....

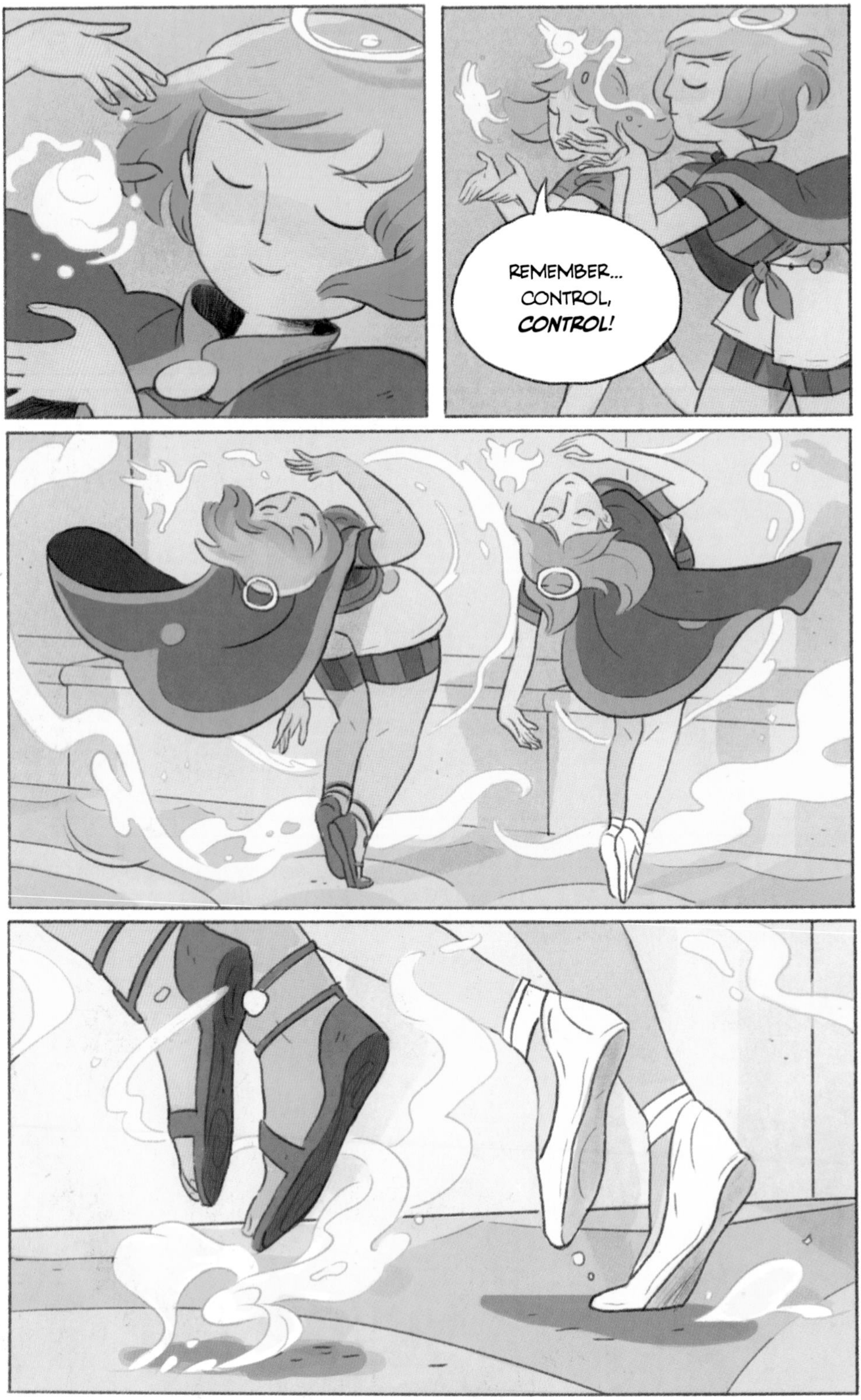
REMEMBER... CONTROL, **CONTROL!**

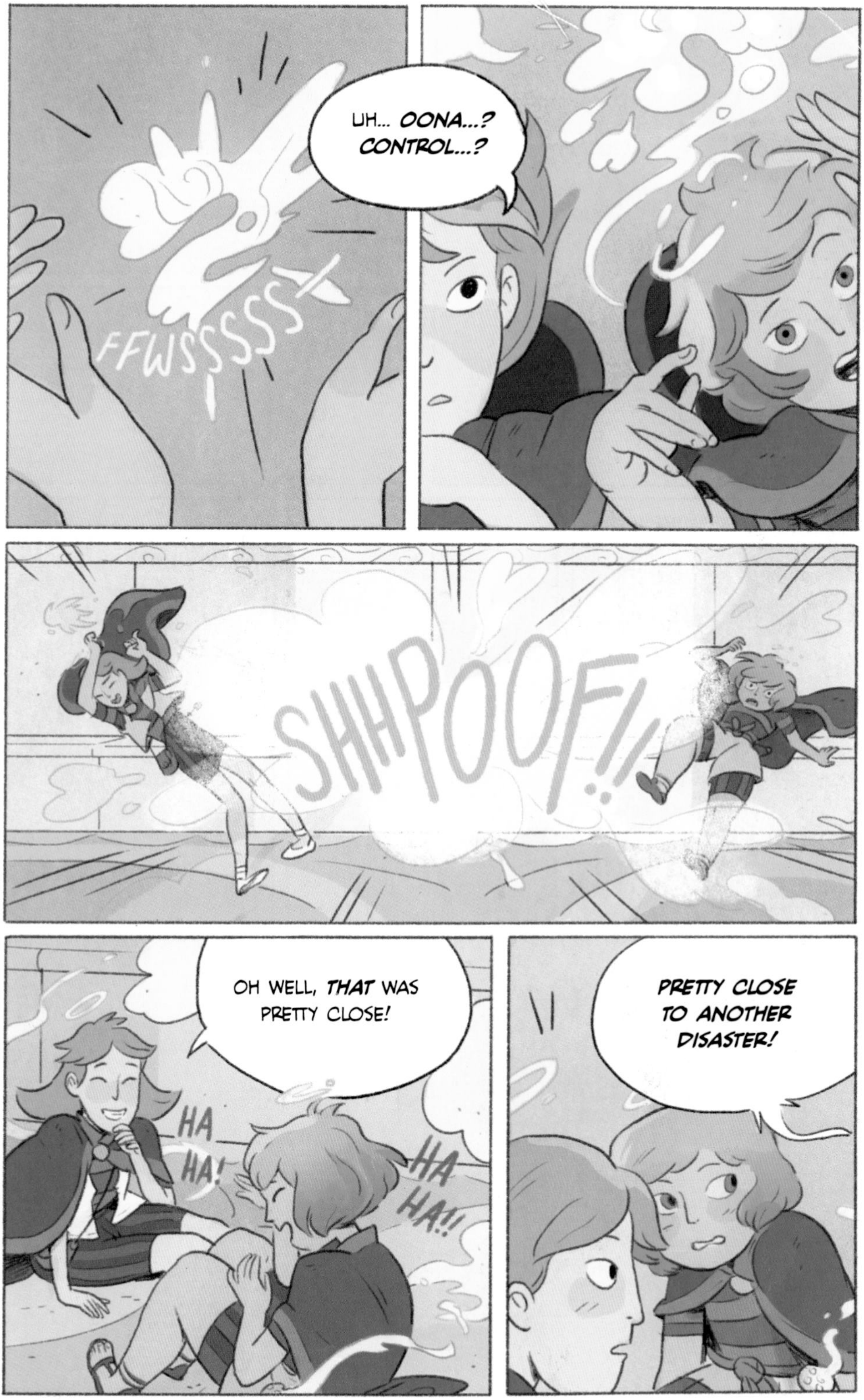
FFWSSSSS
UH... OONA...? CONTROL...?
SHHPOOF!!
OH WELL, THAT WAS PRETTY CLOSE!
HA HA!
HA HA!!
PRETTY CLOSE TO ANOTHER DISASTER!

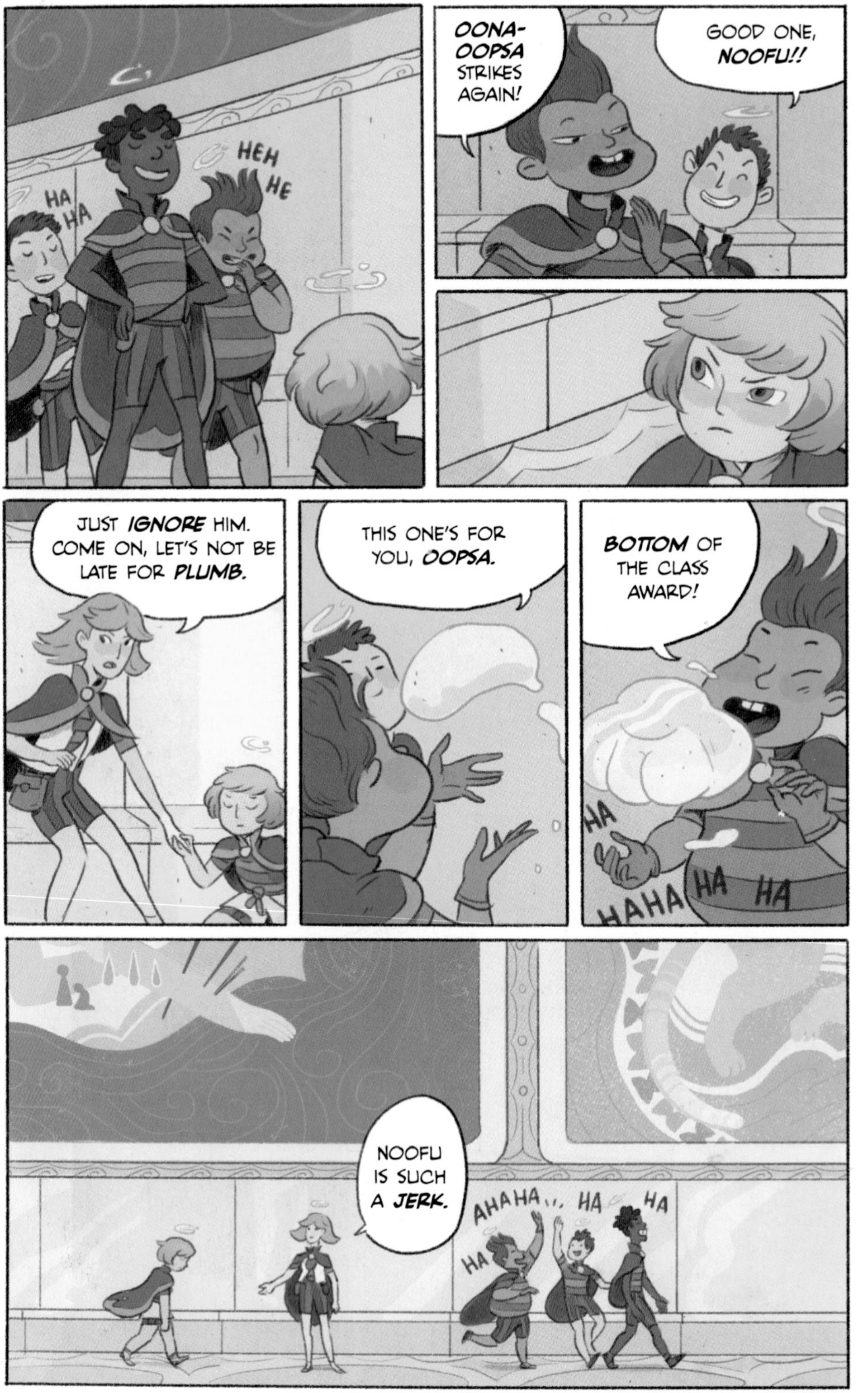
HA HA
HEH HE
OONA-OOPSA STRIKES AGAIN!
GOOD ONE, NOOFU!!
JUST IGNORE HIM. COME ON, LET'S NOT BE LATE FOR PLUMB.
THIS ONE'S FOR YOU, OOPSA.
BOTTOM OF THE CLASS AWARD!
HA
HAHA HA HA
NOOFU IS SUCH A JERK.
AHAHA HA HA
HA

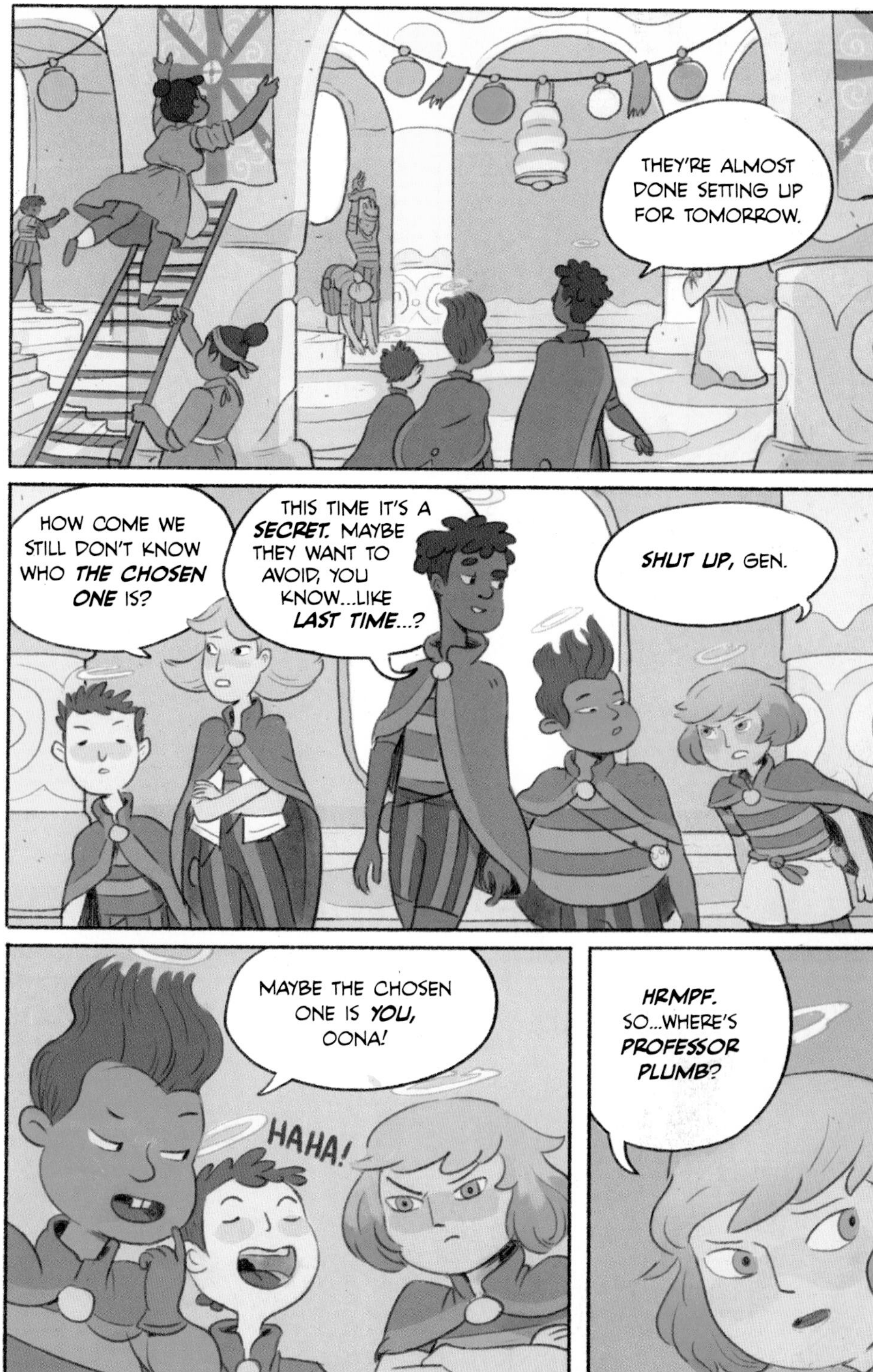
THEY'RE ALMOST DONE SETTING UP FOR TOMORROW.
HOW COME WE STILL DON'T KNOW WHO THE CHOSEN ONE IS?
THIS TIME IT'S A SECRET. MAYBE THEY WANT TO AVOID, YOU KNOW...LIKE LAST TIME...?
SHUT UP, GEN.
MAYBE THE CHOSEN ONE IS YOU, OONA!
HAHA!
HRMPF. SO...WHERE'S PROFESSOR PLUMB?

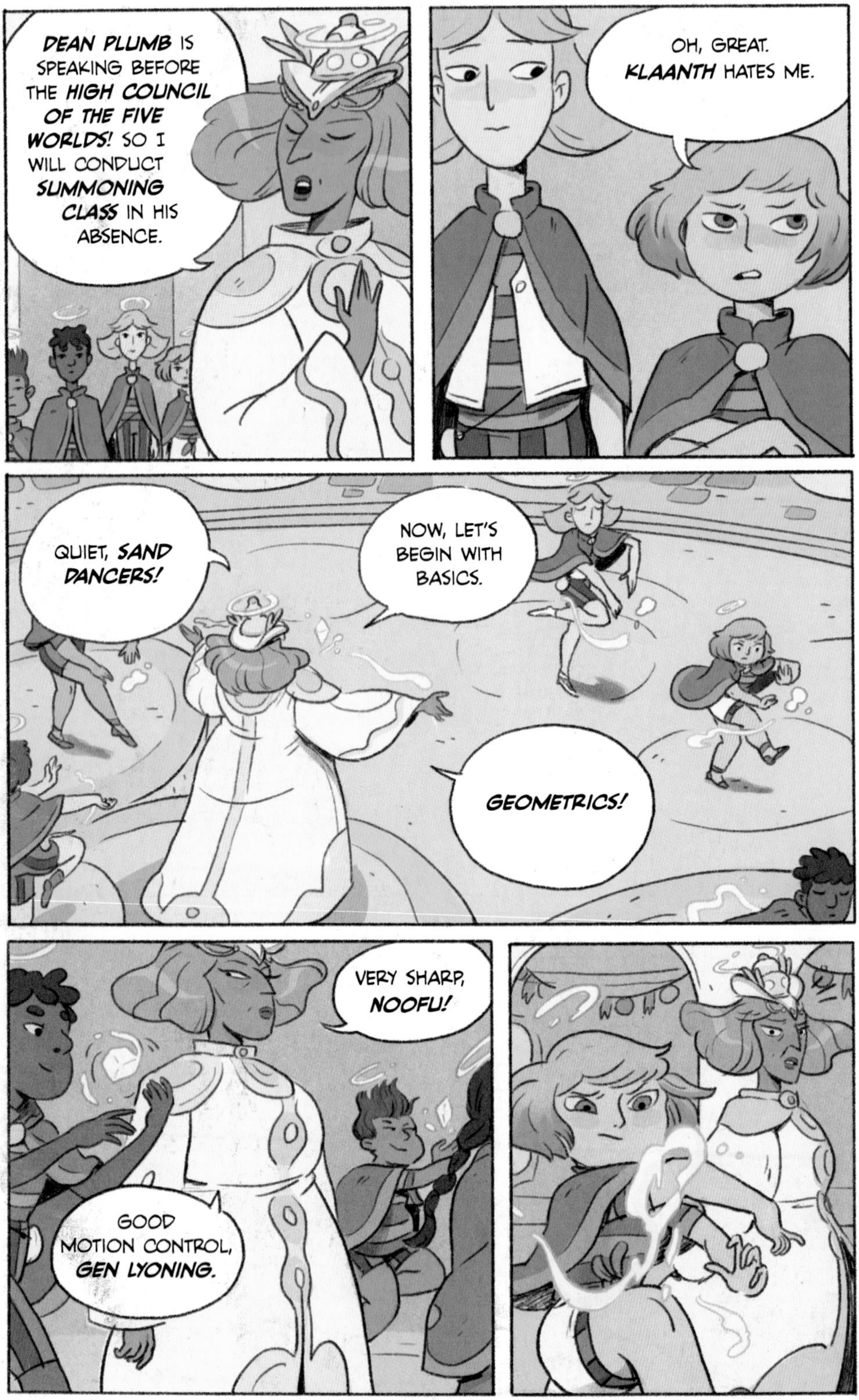
DEAN PLUMB IS SPEAKING BEFORE THE HIGH COUNCIL OF THE FIVE WORLDS! SO I WILL CONDUCT SUMMONING CLASS IN HIS ABSENCE.
OH, GREAT. KLAANTH HATES ME.
QUIET, SAND DANCERS!
NOW, LET'S BEGIN WITH BASICS.
GEOMETRICS!
VERY SHARP, NOOFU!
GOOD MOTION CONTROL, GEN LYONING.

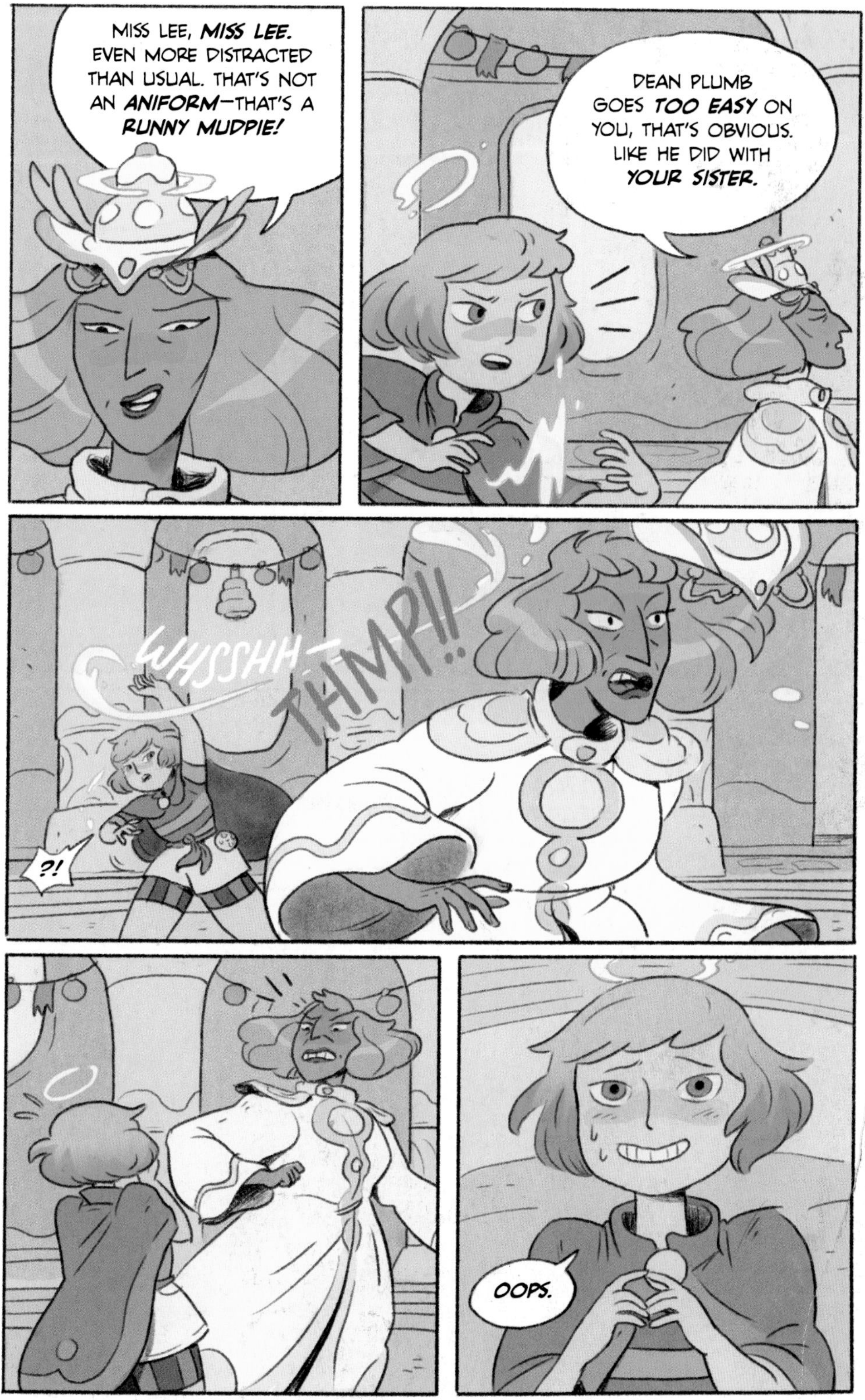
MISS LEE, MISS LEE. EVEN MORE DISTRACTED THAN USUAL. THAT'S NOT AN ANIFORM—THAT'S A RUNNY MUDPIE!
DEAN PLUMB GOES TOO EASY ON YOU, THAT'S OBVIOUS. LIKE HE DID WITH YOUR SISTER.
WHSSHH—
THMP!!
?!
OOPS.

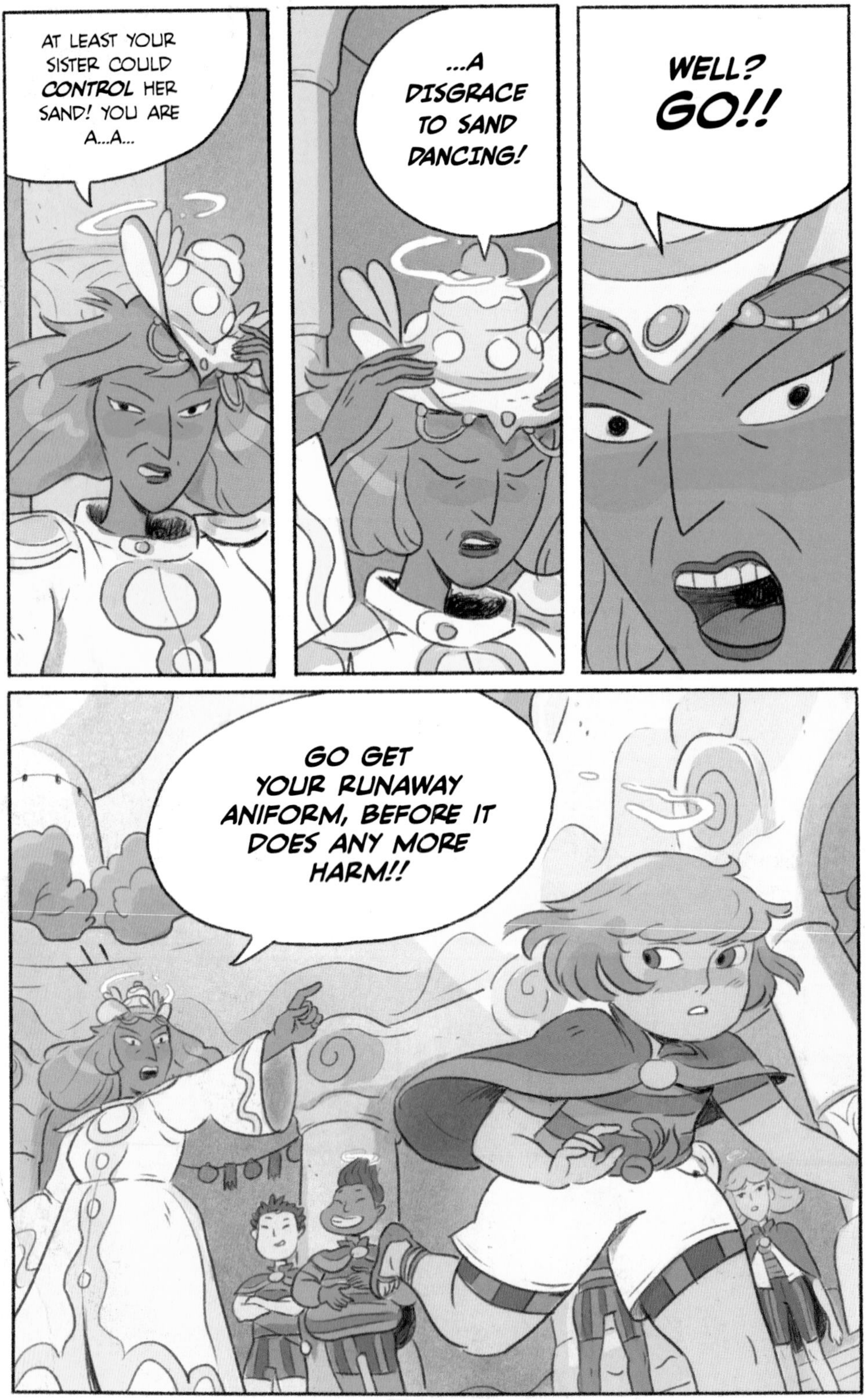
AT LEAST YOUR SISTER COULD CONTROL HER SAND! YOU ARE A...A...
...A DISGRACE TO SAND DANCING!
WELL? GO!!
GO GET YOUR RUNAWAY ANIFORM, BEFORE IT DOES ANY MORE HARM!!

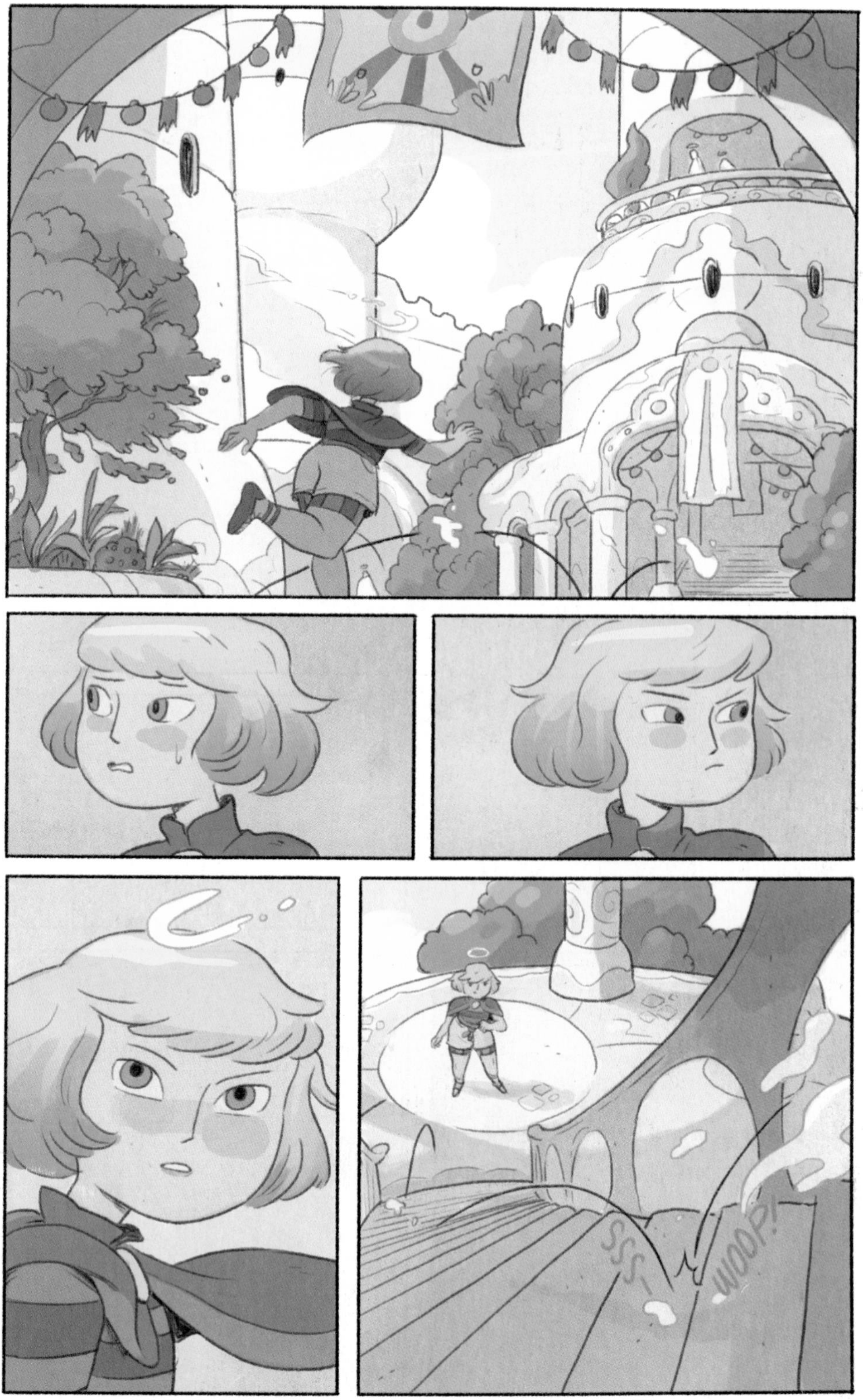
SSS—
WOOP!

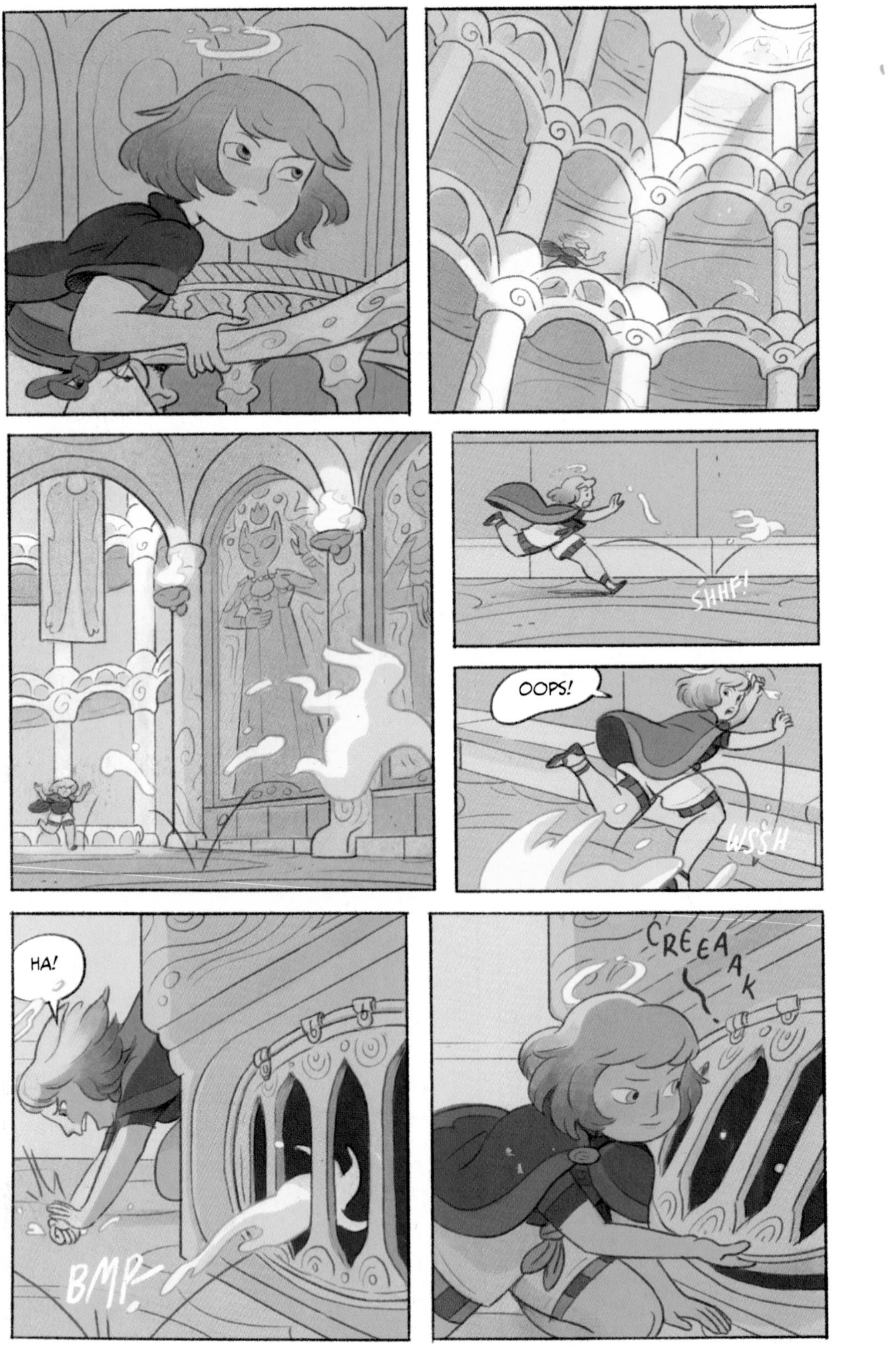
SHHF!
OOPS!
WSSH
HA!
BMP
CREEAAK

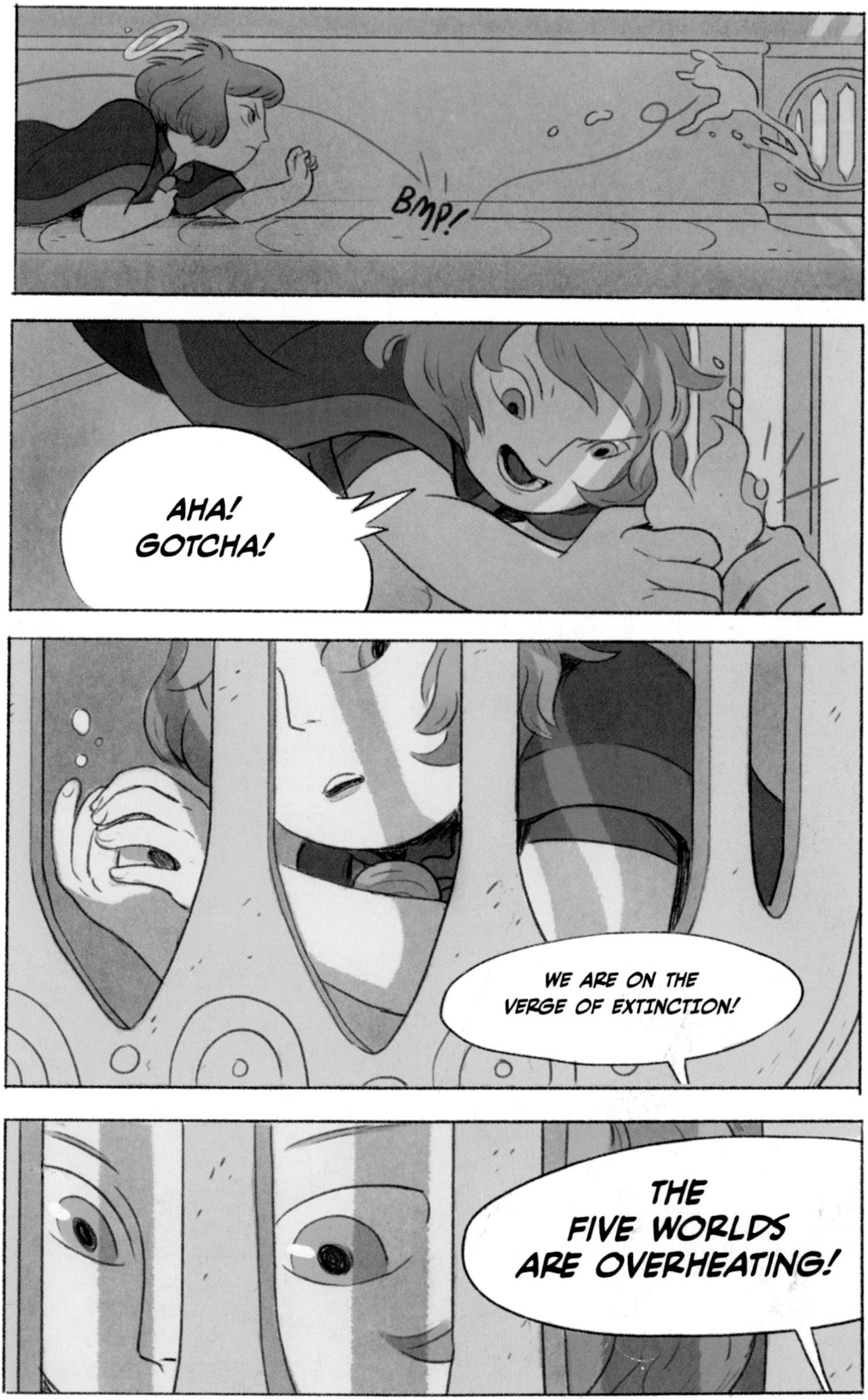
BMP!
AHA! GOTCHA!
WE ARE ON THE VERGE OF EXTINCTION!
THE FIVE WORLDS ARE OVERHEATING!

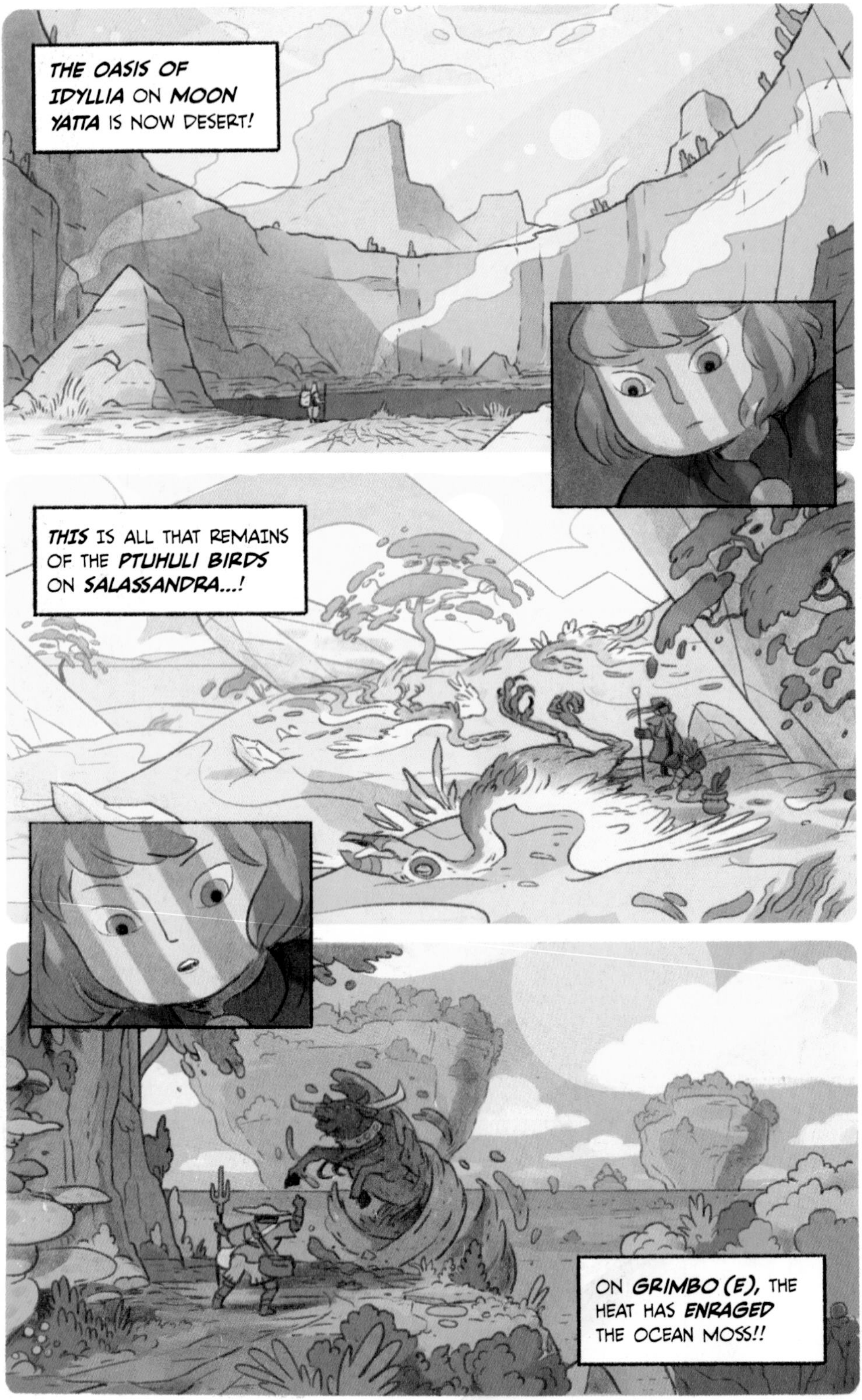
THE OASIS OF IDYLLIA ON MOON YATTA IS NOW DESERT!
THIS IS ALL THAT REMAINS OF THE PTUHULI BIRDS ON SALASSANDRA...!
ON GRIMBO (E), THE HEAT HAS ENRAGED THE OCEAN MOSS!!

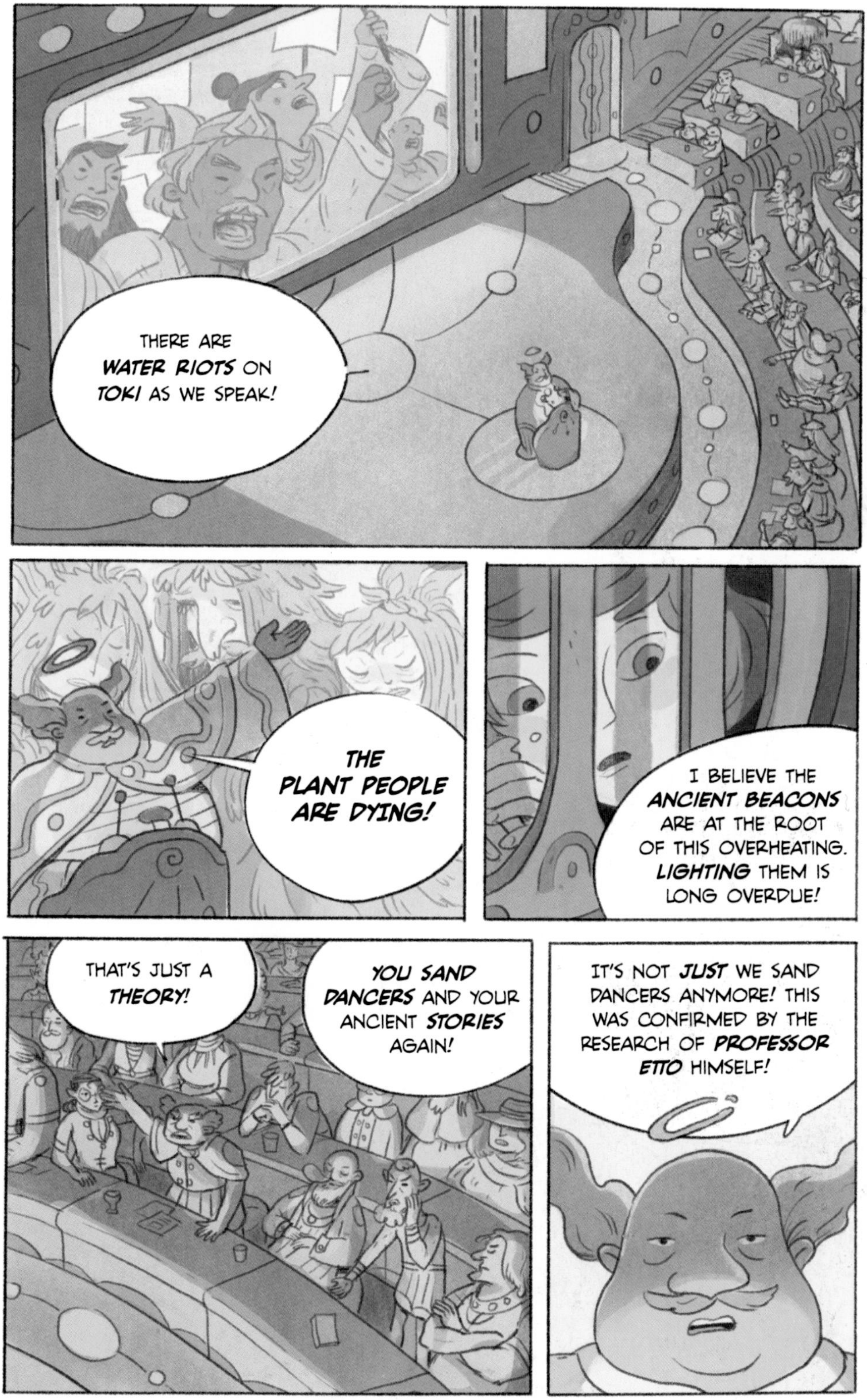
THERE ARE WATER RIOTS ON TOKI AS WE SPEAK!
THE PLANT PEOPLE ARE DYING!
I BELIEVE THE ANCIENT BEACONS ARE AT THE ROOT OF THIS OVERHEATING. LIGHTING THEM IS LONG OVERDUE!
THAT'S JUST A THEORY!
YOU SAND DANCERS AND YOUR ANCIENT STORIES AGAIN!
IT'S NOT JUST WE SAND DANCERS ANYMORE! THIS WAS CONFIRMED BY THE RESEARCH OF PROFESSOR ETTO HIMSELF!

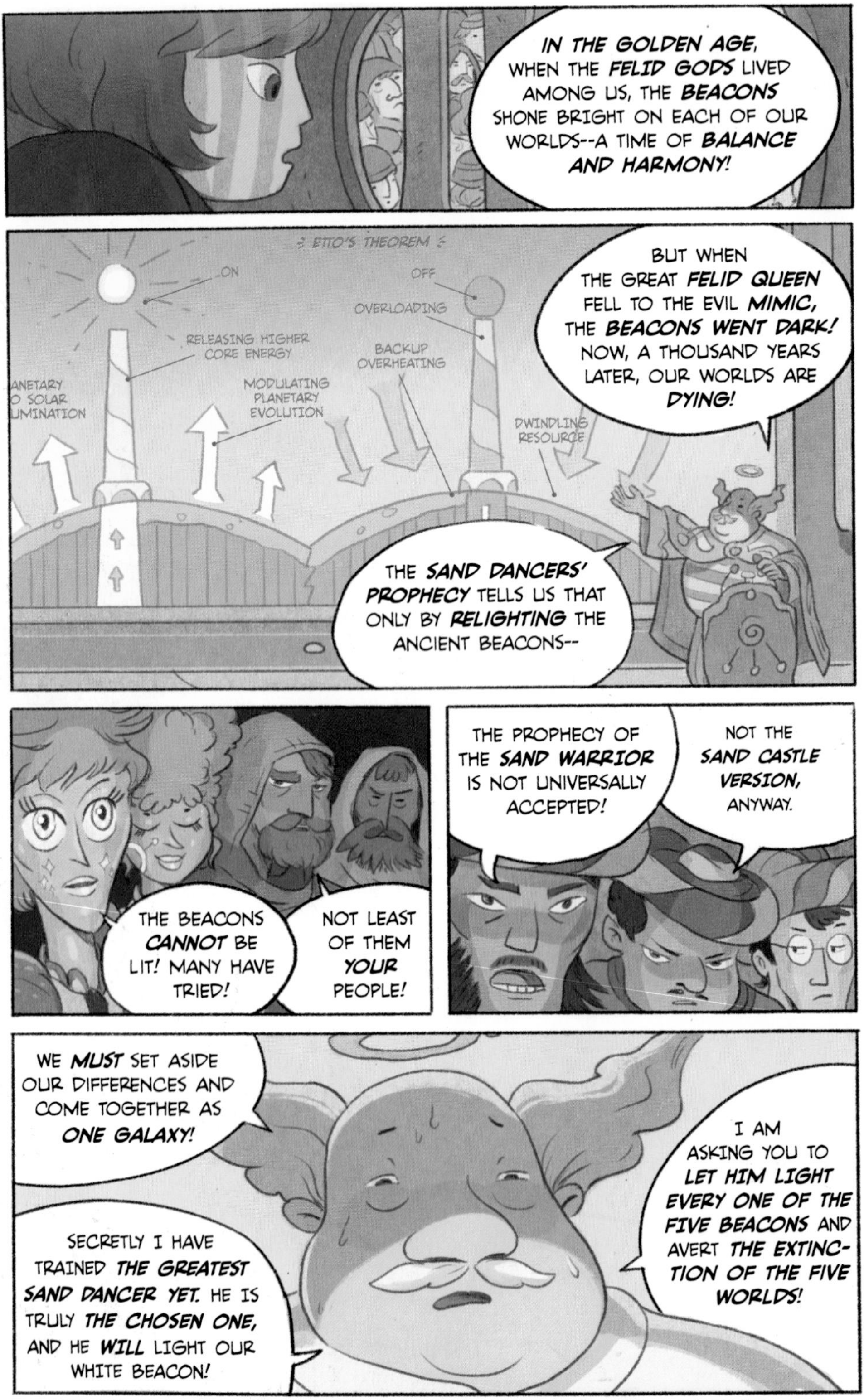
IN THE GOLDEN AGE, WHEN THE FELID GODS LIVED AMONG US, THE BEACONS SHONE BRIGHT ON EACH OF OUR WORLDS--A TIME OF BALANCE AND HARMONY!
ETTO'S THEOREM
ON
OFF
OVERLOADING
RELEASING HIGHER CORE ENERGY
BACKUP OVERHEATING
MODULATING PLANETARY EVOLUTION
DWINDLING RESOURCE
BUT WHEN THE GREAT FELID QUEEN FELL TO THE EVIL MIMIC, THE BEACONS WENT DARK! NOW, A THOUSAND YEARS LATER, OUR WORLDS ARE DYING!
THE SAND DANCERS' PROPHECY TELLS US THAT ONLY BY RELIGHTING THE ANCIENT BEACONS--
THE BEACONS CANNOT BE LIT! MANY HAVE TRIED!
NOT LEAST OF THEM YOUR PEOPLE!
THE PROPHECY OF THE SAND WARRIOR IS NOT UNIVERSALLY ACCEPTED!
NOT THE SAND CASTLE VERSION, ANYWAY.
WE MUST SET ASIDE OUR DIFFERENCES AND COME TOGETHER AS ONE GALAXY!
SECRETLY I HAVE TRAINED THE GREATEST SAND DANCER YET. HE IS TRULY THE CHOSEN ONE, AND HE WILL LIGHT OUR WHITE BEACON!
I AM ASKING YOU TO LET HIM LIGHT EVERY ONE OF THE FIVE BEACONS AND AVERT THE EXTINCTION OF THE FIVE WORLDS!

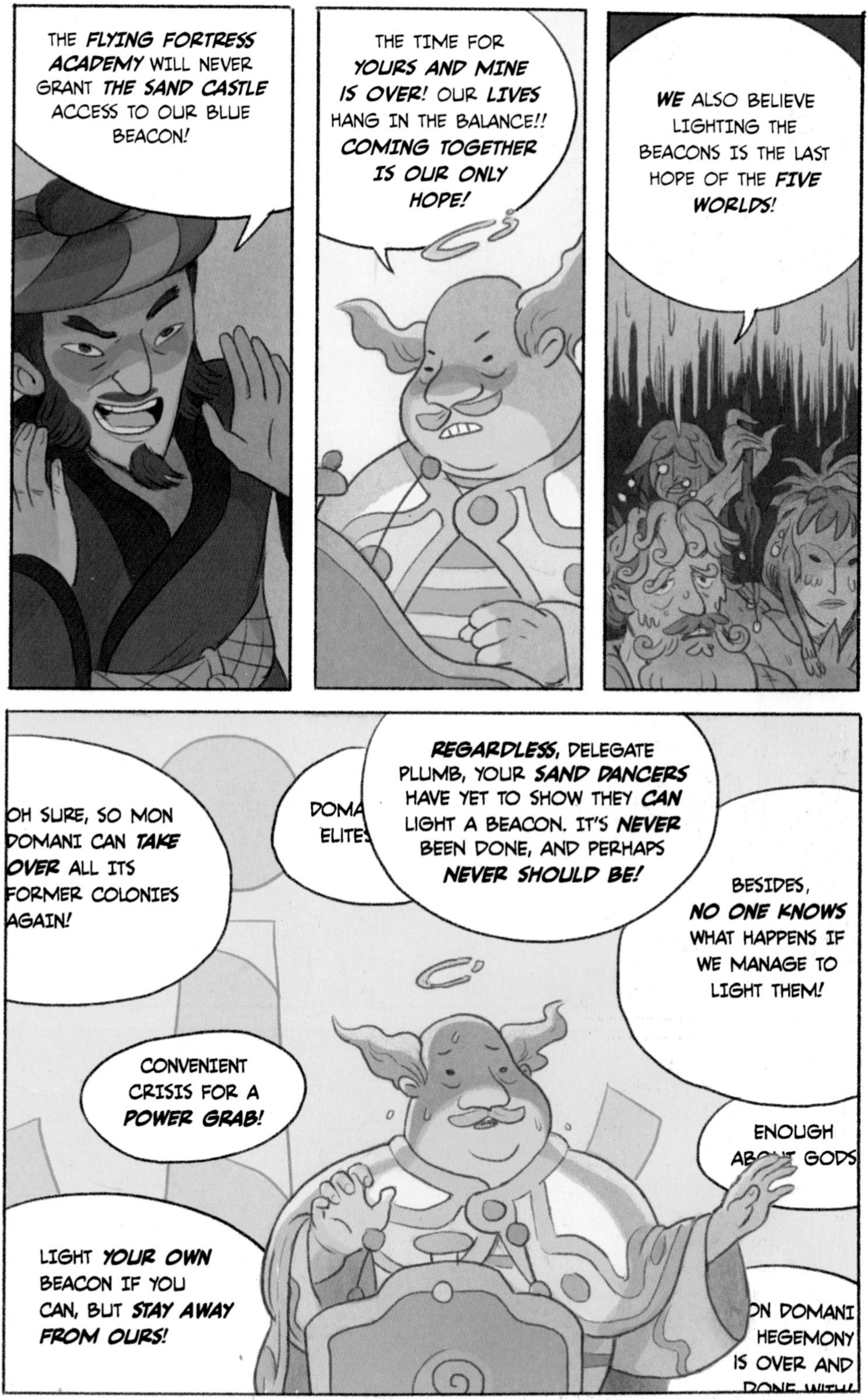
THE FLYING FORTRESS ACADEMY WILL NEVER GRANT THE SAND CASTLE ACCESS TO OUR BLUE BEACON!
THE TIME FOR YOURS AND MINE IS OVER! OUR LIVES HANG IN THE BALANCE!! COMING TOGETHER IS OUR ONLY HOPE!
WE ALSO BELIEVE LIGHTING THE BEACONS IS THE LAST HOPE OF THE FIVE WORLDS!
REGARDLESS, DELEGATE PLUMB, YOUR SAND DANCERS HAVE YET TO SHOW THEY CAN LIGHT A BEACON. IT'S NEVER BEEN DONE, AND PERHAPS NEVER SHOULD BE!
SURE, SO MON DOMANI CAN TAKE ALL ITS FORMER COLONIES
BESIDES, NO ONE KNOWS WHAT HAPPENS IF WE MANAGE TO LIGHT THEM!
CONVENIENT CRISIS FOR A POWER GRAB!
ENOUGH
LIGHT YOUR OWN BEACON IF YOU CAN, BUT STAY AWAY FROM OURS!
DOMANI HEGEMONY IS OVER AND

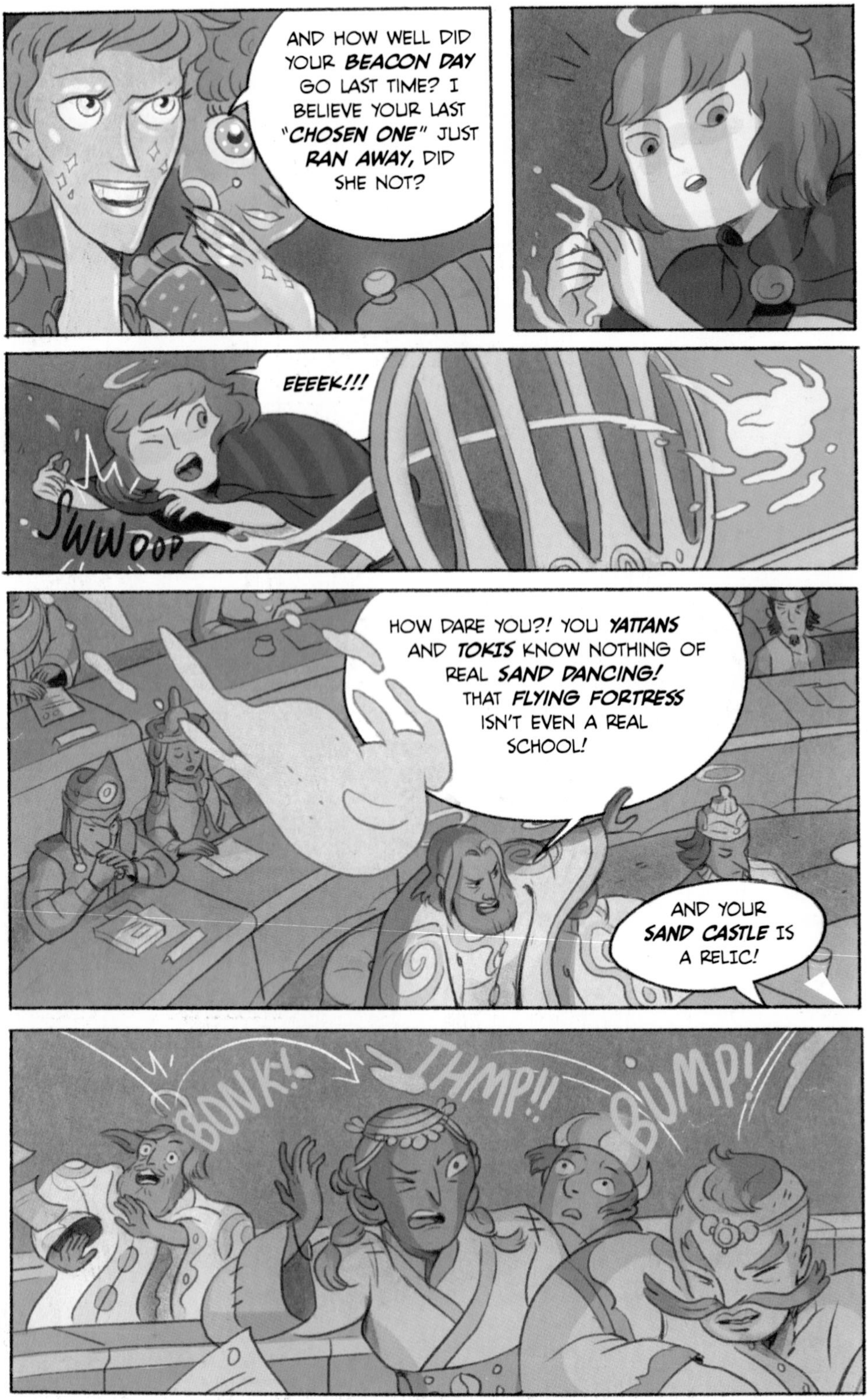
AND HOW WELL DID YOUR BEACON DAY GO LAST TIME? I BELIEVE YOUR LAST "CHOSEN ONE" JUST RAN AWAY, DID SHE NOT?
EEEEK!!!
SWWOOP
HOW DARE YOU?! YOU YATTANS AND TOKIS KNOW NOTHING OF REAL SAND DANCING! THAT FLYING FORTRESS ISN'T EVEN A REAL SCHOOL!
AND YOUR SAND CASTLE IS A RELIC!
BONK!
THMP!!
BUMP!

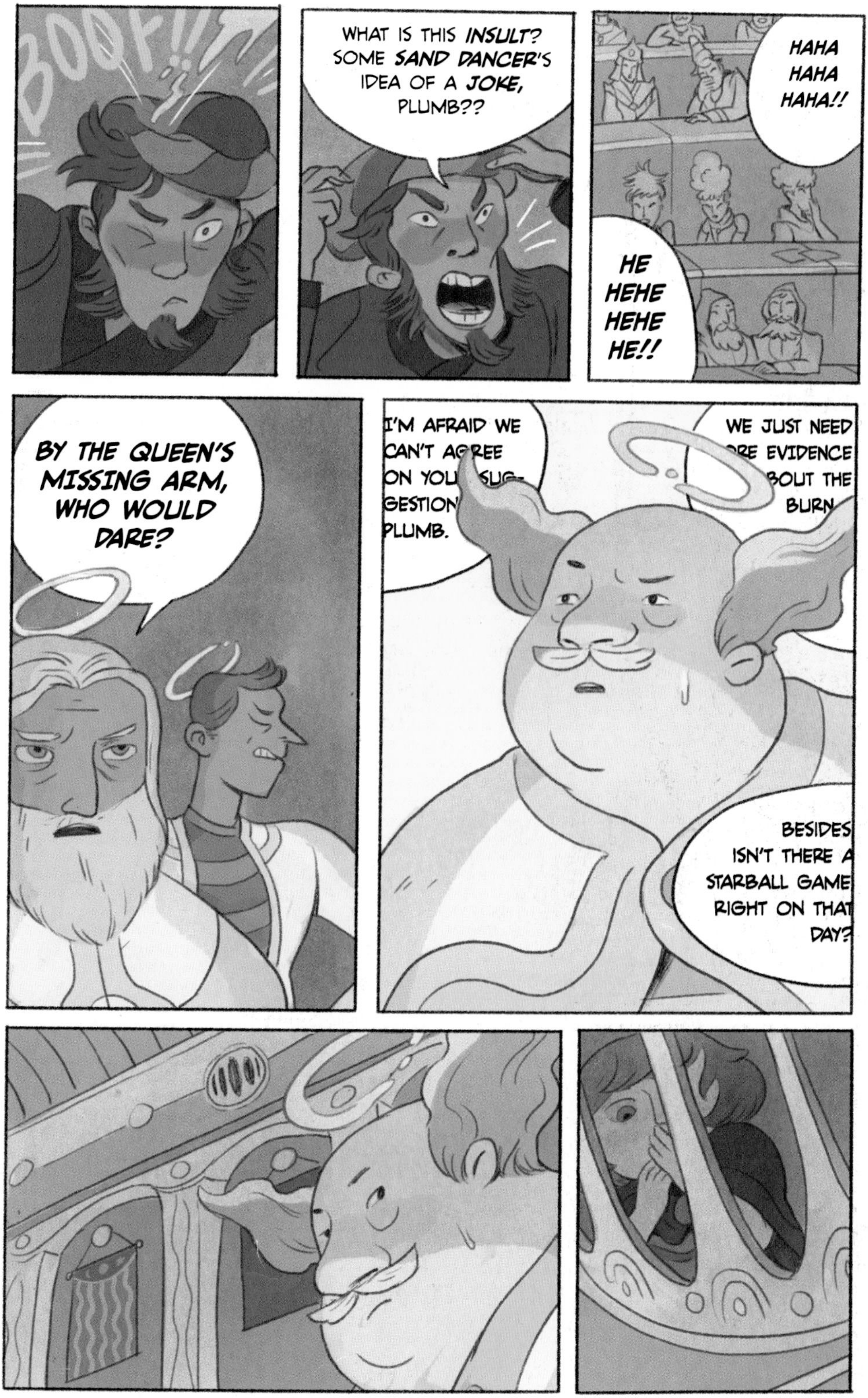
BOOF!!
WHAT IS THIS INSULT? SOME SAND DANCER'S IDEA OF A JOKE, PLUMB??
HAHA HAHA HAHA!!
HE HEHE HEHE HE!!
BY THE QUEEN'S MISSING ARM, WHO WOULD DARE?
I'M AFRAID WE CAN'T AGREE ON YOUR SUGGESTION, PLUMB.
WE JUST NEED MORE EVIDENCE ABOUT THE BURN.
BESIDES, ISN'T THERE A STARBALL GAME RIGHT ON THAT DAY?

Chapter 2

THE BOY IN THE MASK

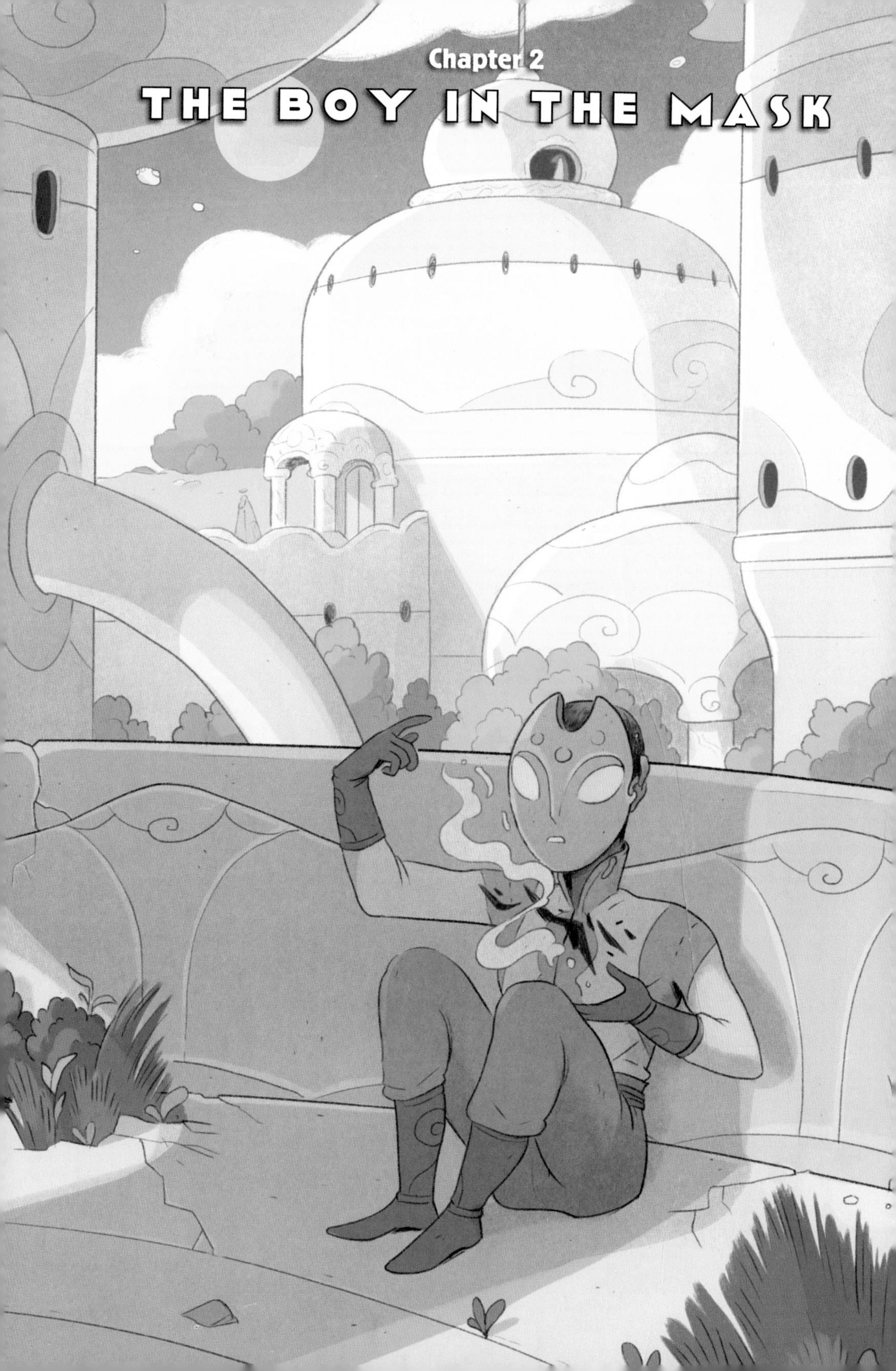

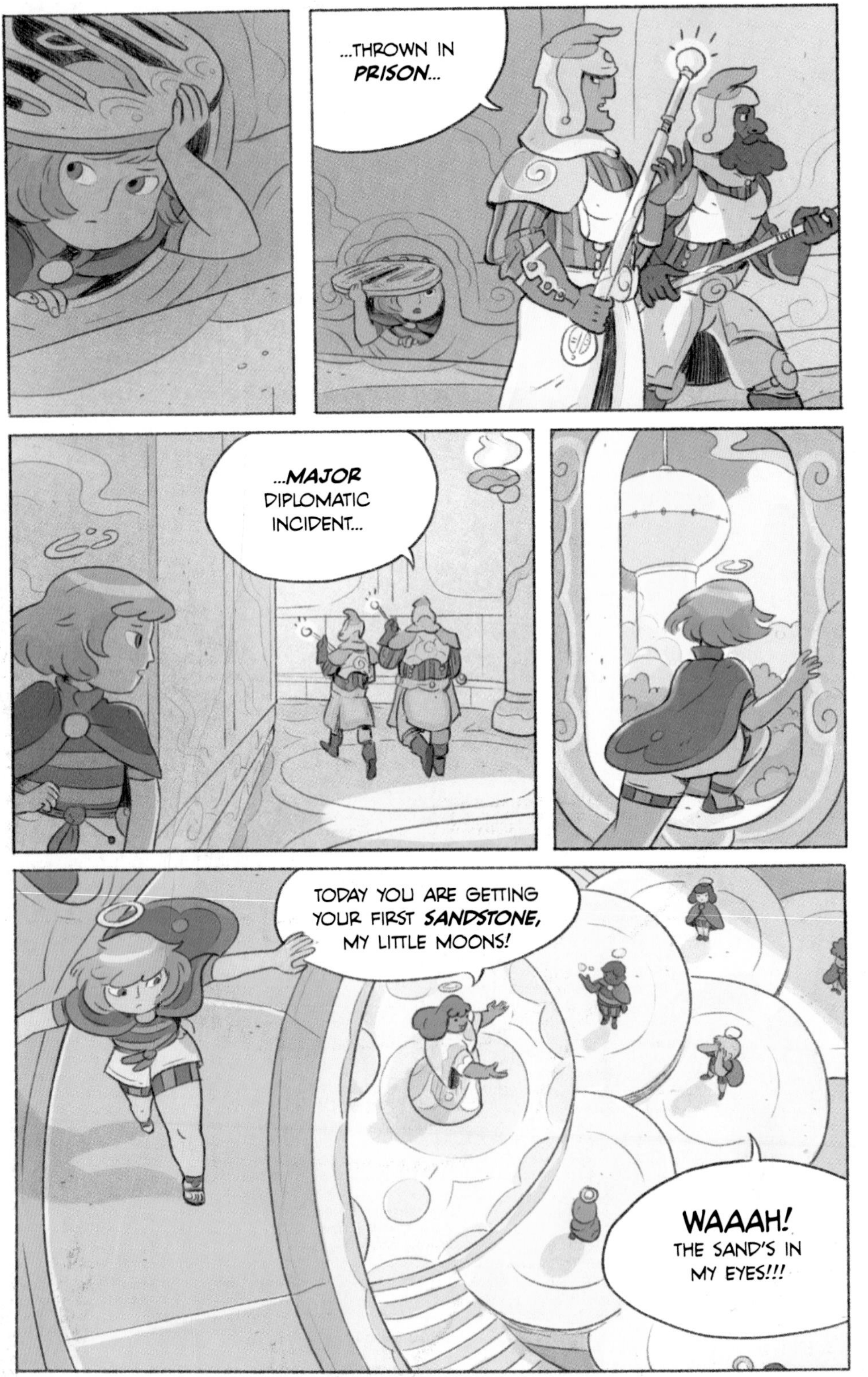

...THROWN IN PRISON...
...MAJOR DIPLOMATIC INCIDENT...
TODAY YOU ARE GETTING YOUR FIRST SANDSTONE, MY LITTLE MOONS!
WAAAH! THE SAND'S IN MY EYES!!!

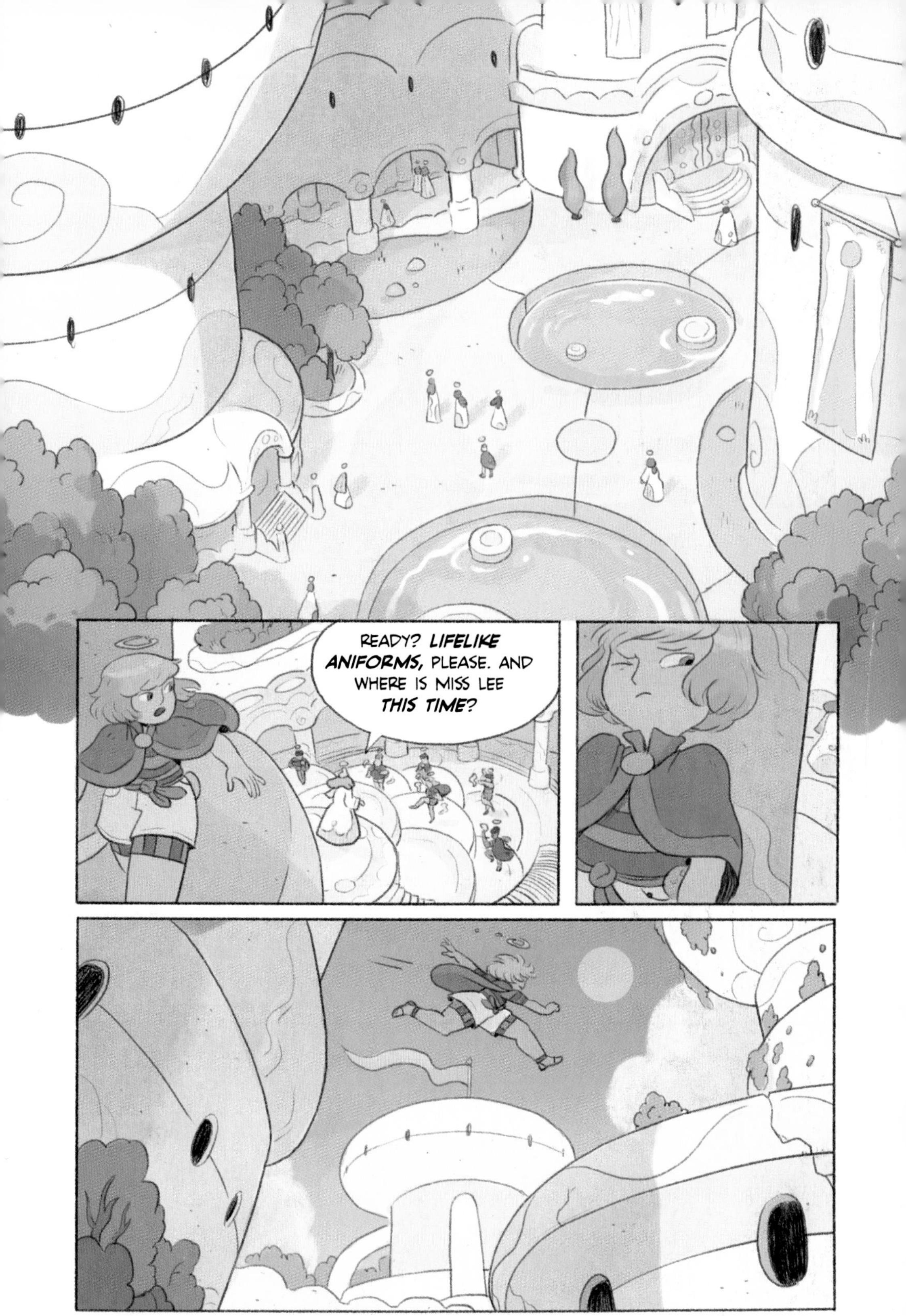
READY? ***LIFELIKE ANIFORMS,*** PLEASE. AND WHERE IS MISS LEE ***THIS TIME?***

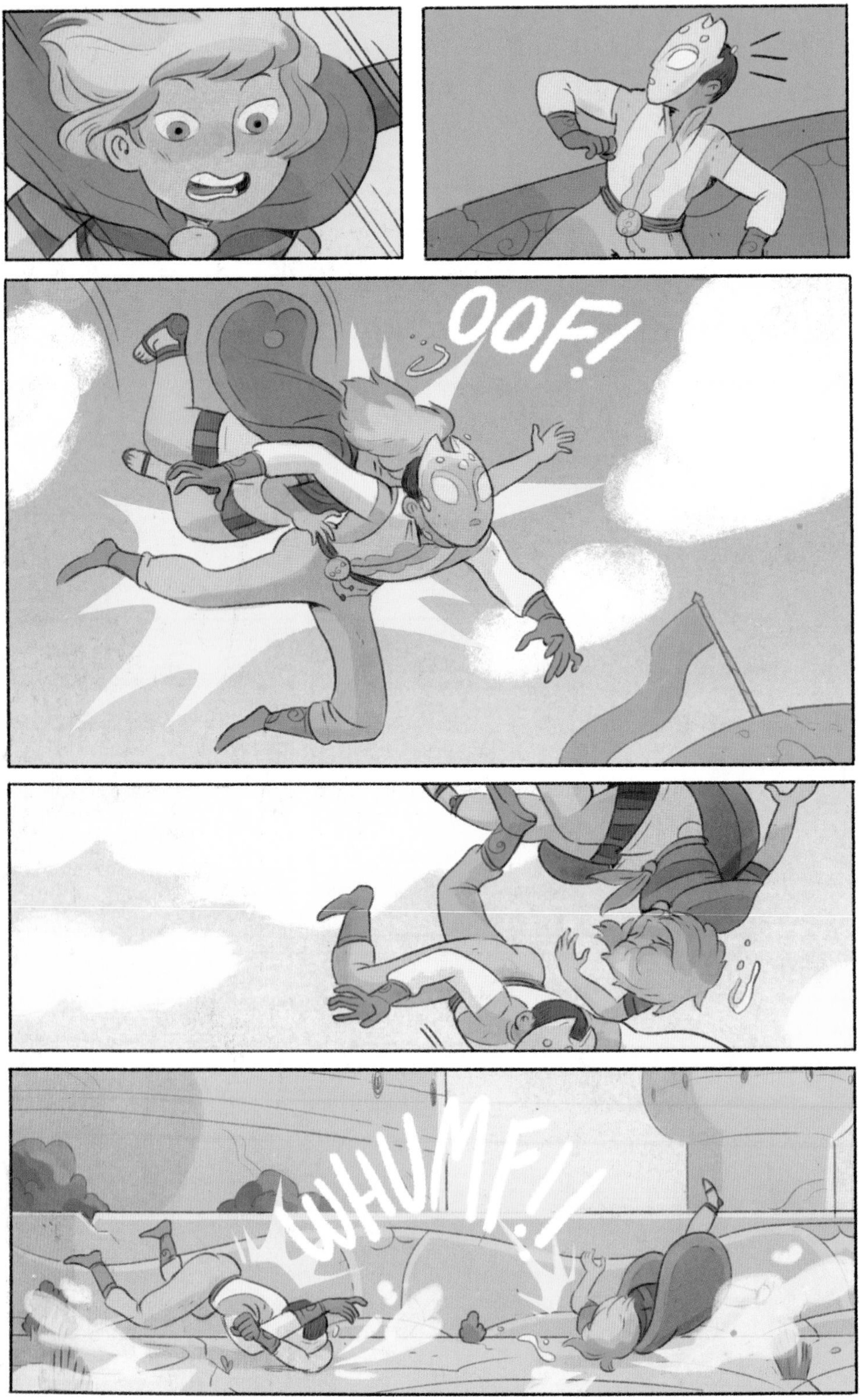
OOF!
WHUMF!!

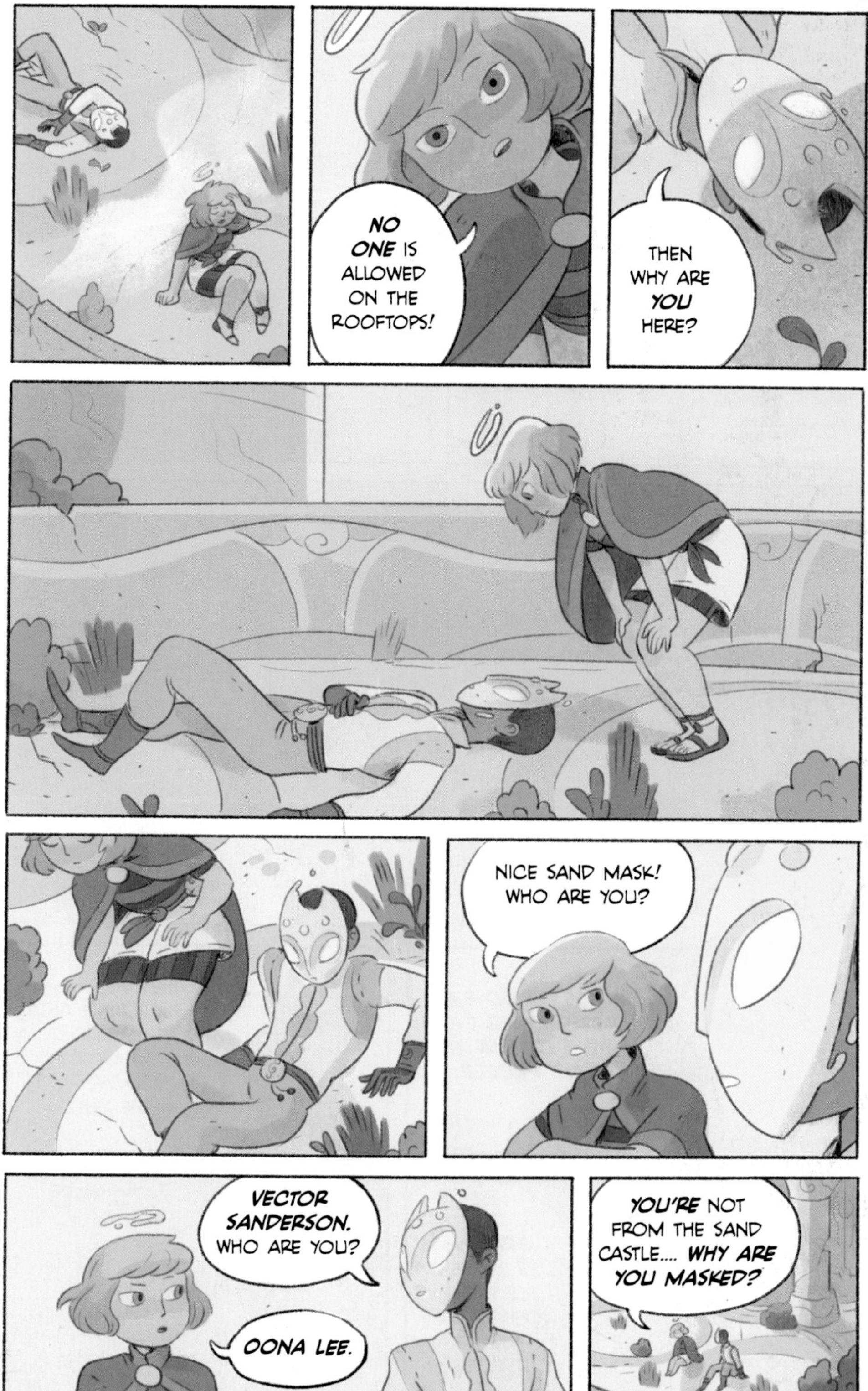
NO ONE IS ALLOWED ON THE ROOFTOPS!
THEN WHY ARE YOU HERE?
NICE SAND MASK! WHO ARE YOU?
VECTOR SANDERSON. WHO ARE YOU?
OONA LEE.
YOU'RE NOT FROM THE SAND CASTLE.... WHY ARE YOU MASKED?

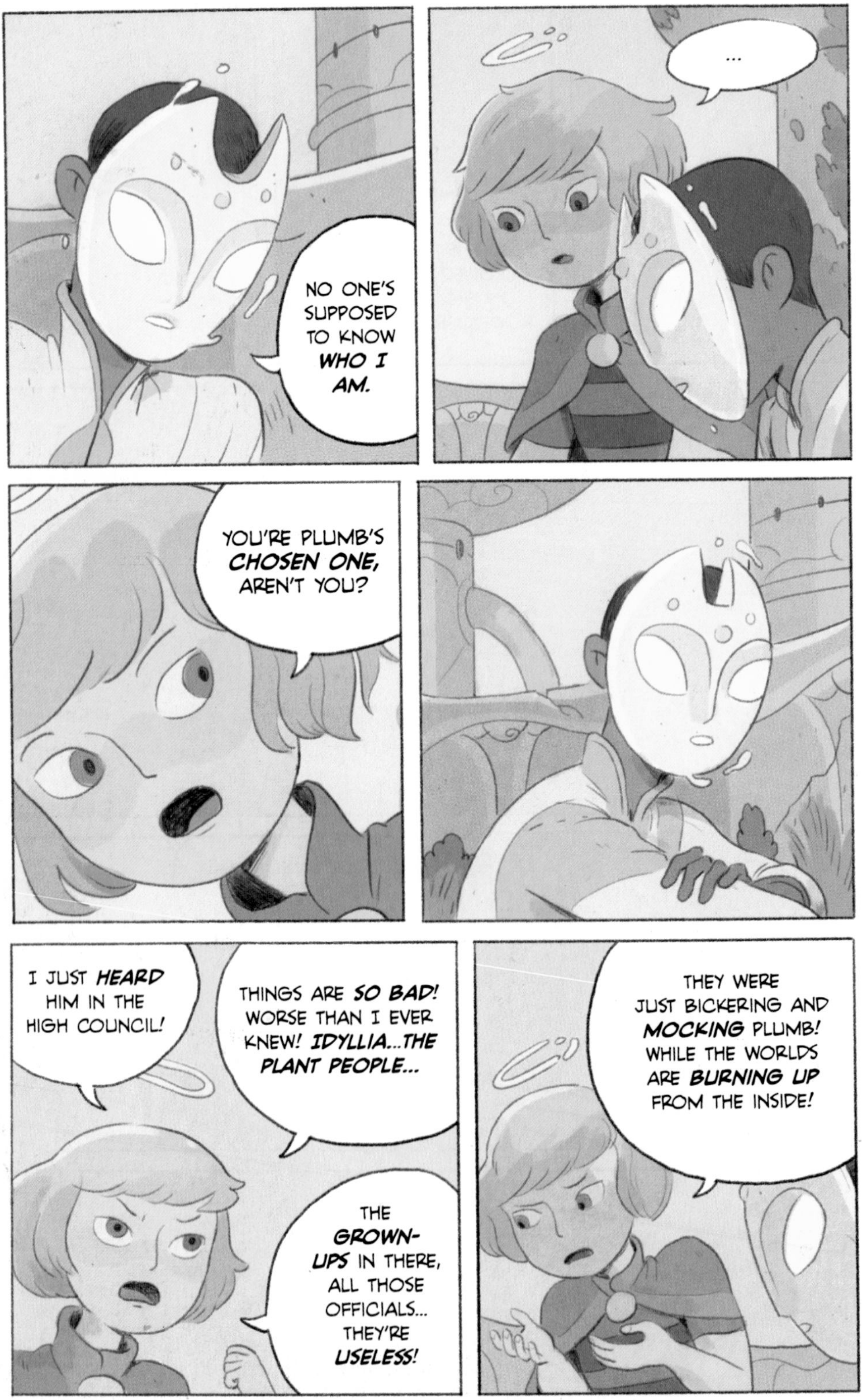
NO ONE'S SUPPOSED TO KNOW WHO I AM.
...
YOU'RE PLUMB'S CHOSEN ONE, AREN'T YOU?
I JUST HEARD HIM IN THE HIGH COUNCIL!
THINGS ARE SO BAD! WORSE THAN I EVER KNEW! IDYLLIA...THE PLANT PEOPLE...
THE GROWN-UPS IN THERE, ALL THOSE OFFICIALS... THEY'RE USELESS!
THEY WERE JUST BICKERING AND MOCKING PLUMB! WHILE THE WORLDS ARE BURNING UP FROM THE INSIDE!

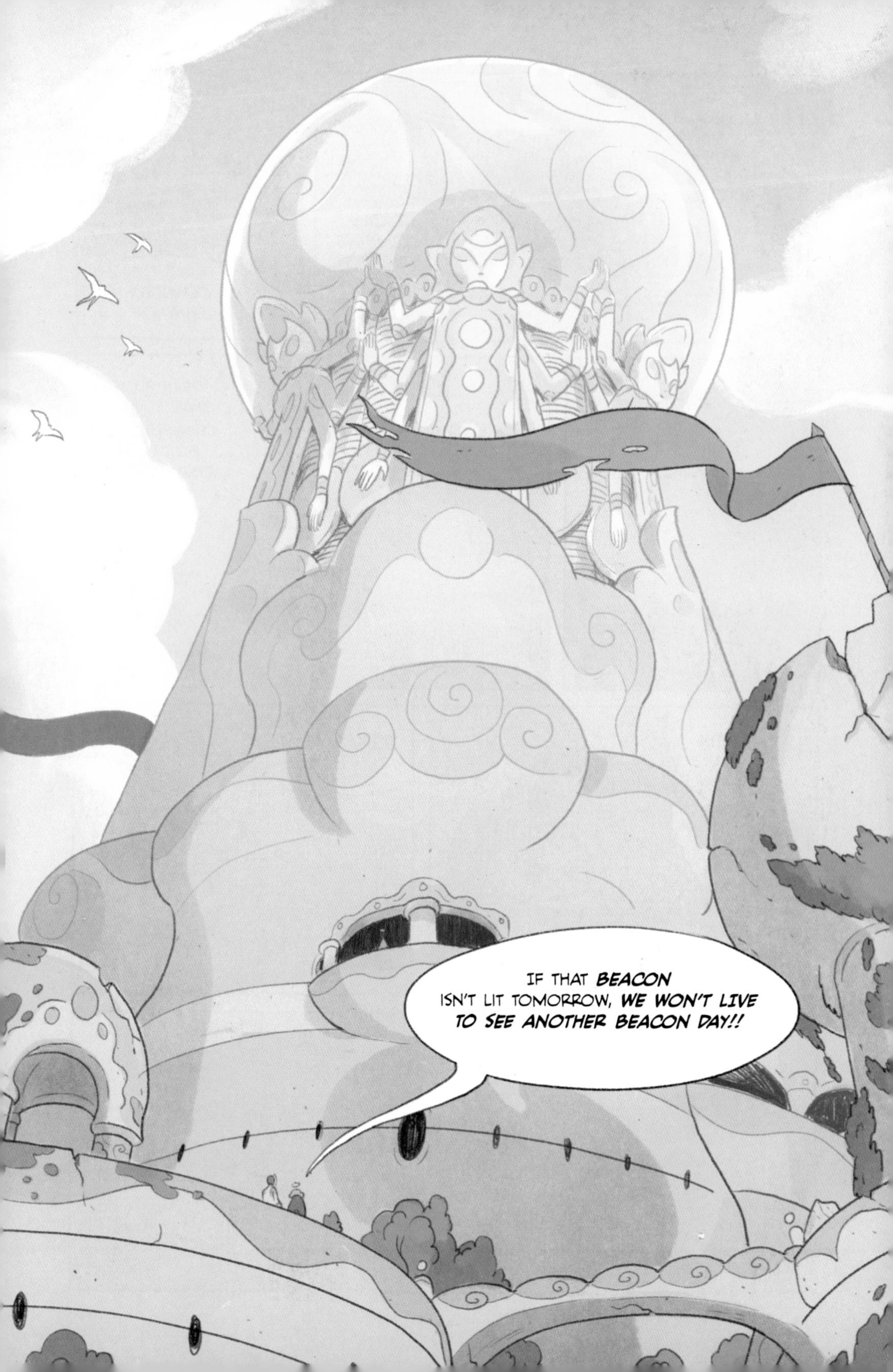
IF THAT BEACON ISN'T LIT TOMORROW, WE WON'T LIVE TO SEE ANOTHER BEACON DAY!!

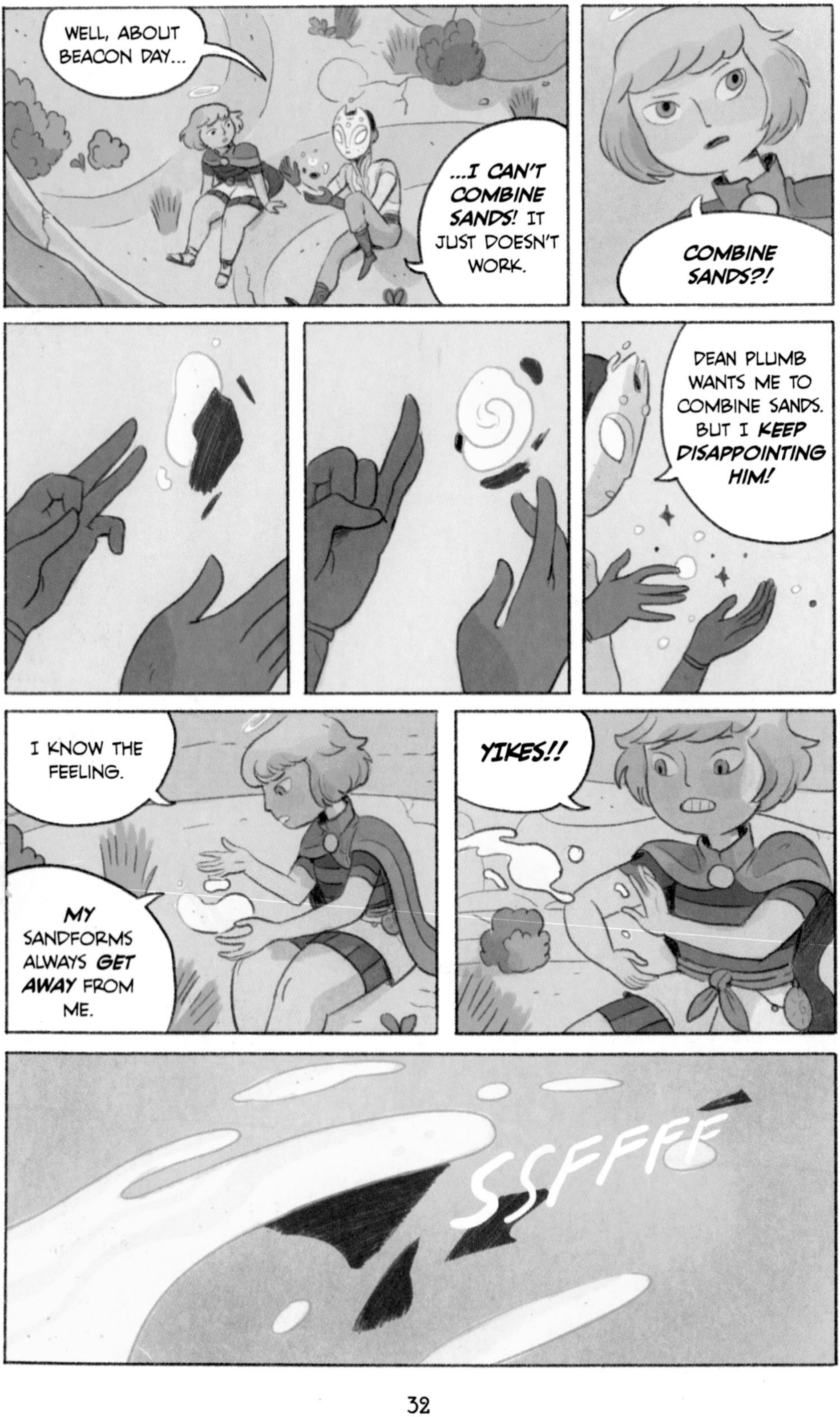
WELL, ABOUT BEACON DAY...
...I CAN'T COMBINE SANDS! IT JUST DOESN'T WORK.
COMBINE SANDS?!
DEAN PLUMB WANTS ME TO COMBINE SANDS. BUT I KEEP DISAPPOINTING HIM!
I KNOW THE FEELING.
MY SANDFORMS ALWAYS GET AWAY FROM ME.
YIKES!!
SSFFFF

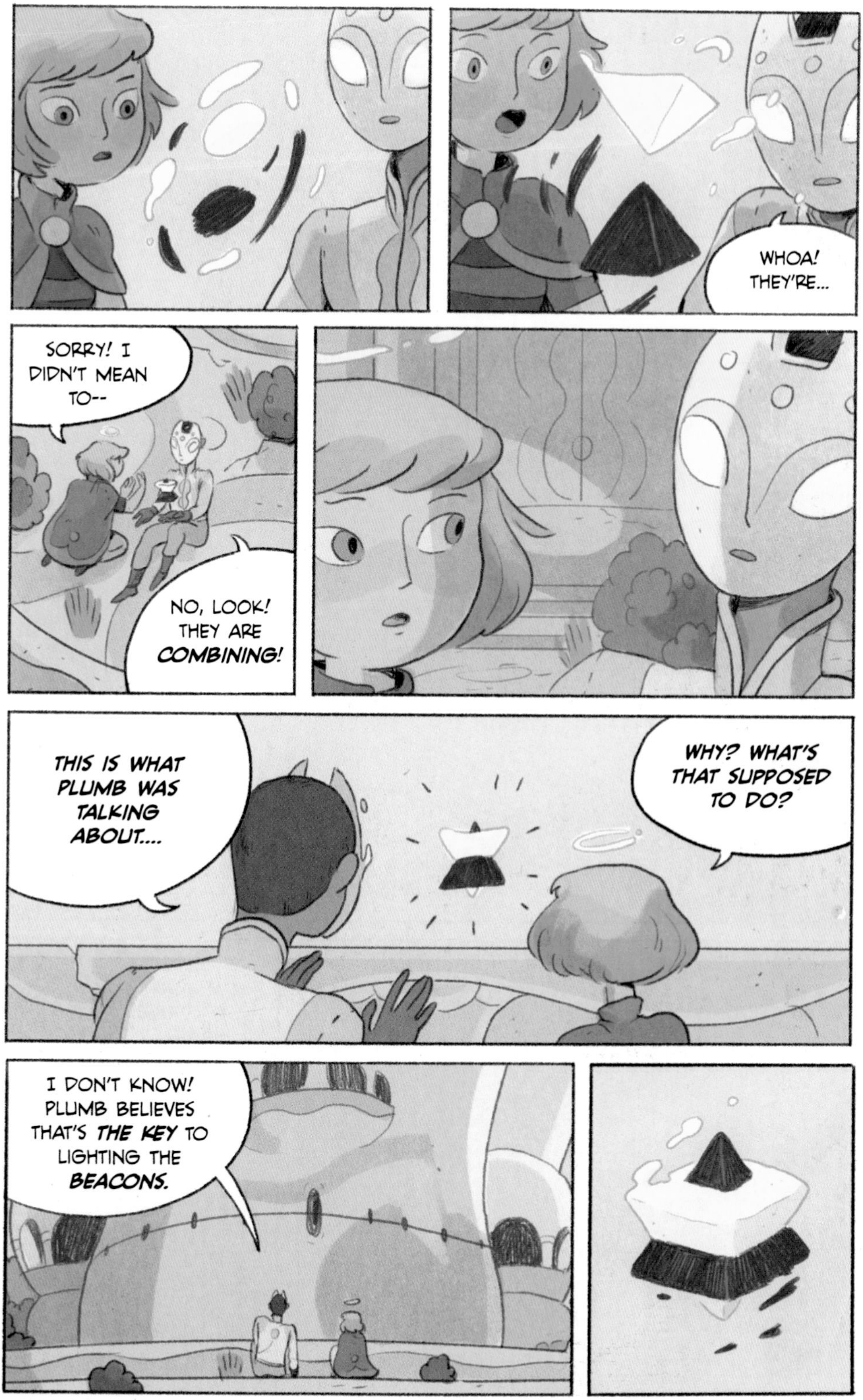
WHOA! THEY'RE...
SORRY! I DIDN'T MEAN TO--
NO, LOOK! THEY ARE COMBINING!
THIS IS WHAT PLUMB WAS TALKING ABOUT....
WHY? WHAT'S THAT SUPPOSED TO DO?
I DON'T KNOW! PLUMB BELIEVES THAT'S THE KEY TO LIGHTING THE BEACONS.

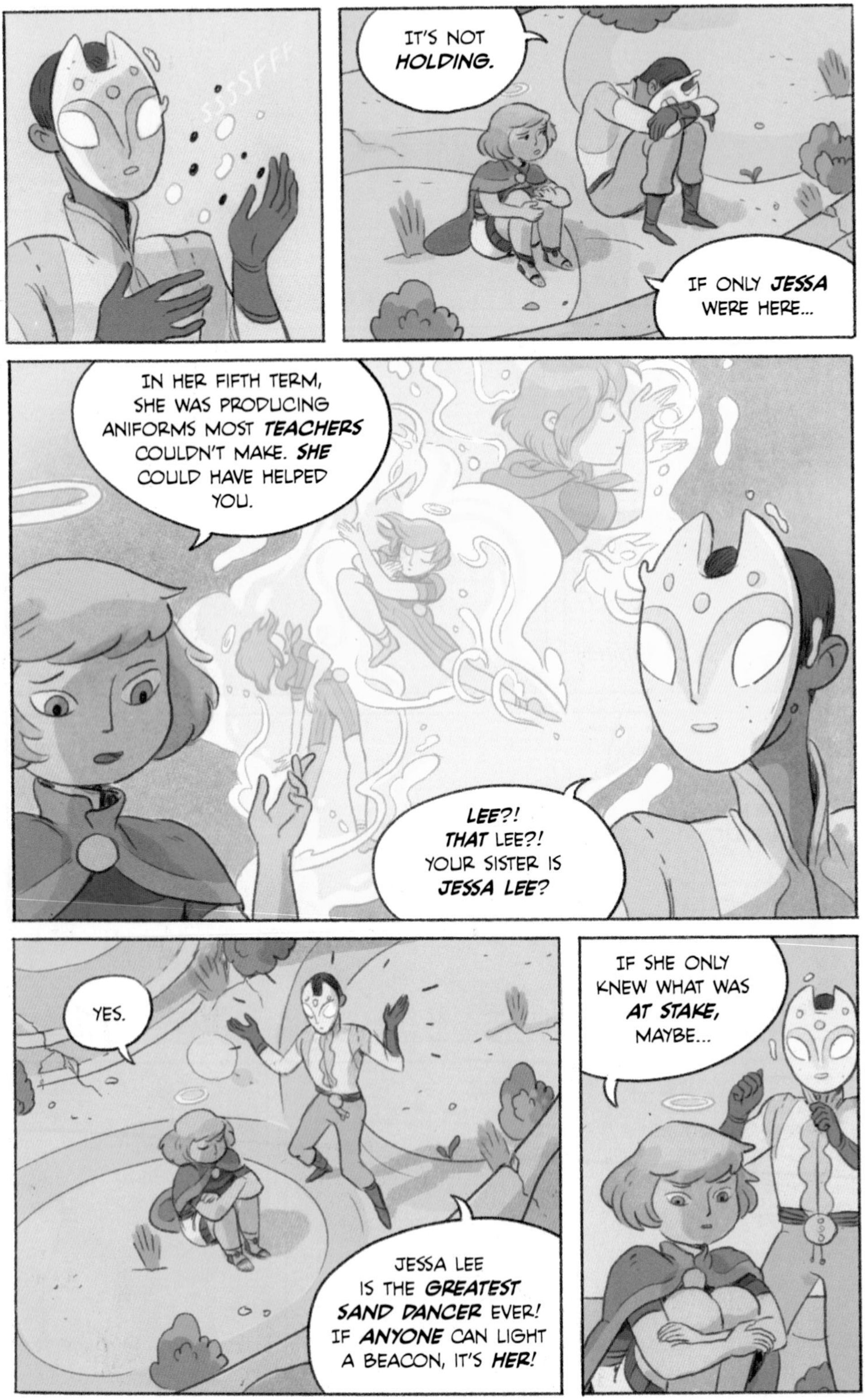
SSSSFFF
IT'S NOT **HOLDING.**
IF ONLY **JESSA** WERE HERE...
IN HER FIFTH TERM, SHE WAS PRODUCING ANIFORMS MOST **TEACHERS** COULDN'T MAKE. **SHE** COULD HAVE HELPED YOU.
LEE?! **THAT** LEE?! YOUR SISTER IS **JESSA LEE?**
YES.
JESSA LEE IS THE **GREATEST SAND DANCER** EVER! IF **ANYONE** CAN LIGHT A BEACON, IT'S **HER!**
IF SHE ONLY KNEW WHAT WAS **AT STAKE,** MAYBE...

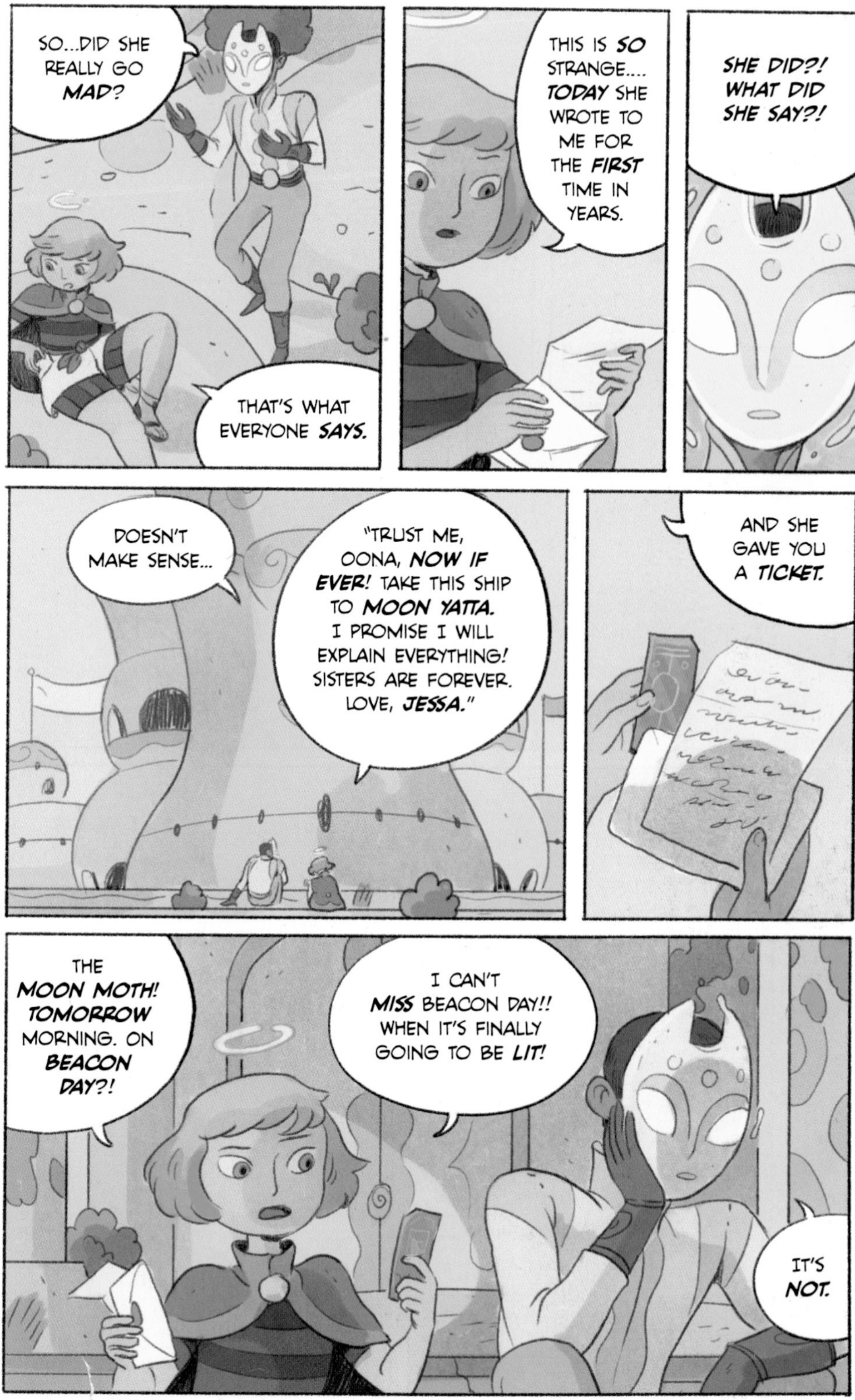
SO...DID SHE REALLY GO MAD?
THAT'S WHAT EVERYONE SAYS.
THIS IS SO STRANGE.... TODAY SHE WROTE TO ME FOR THE FIRST TIME IN YEARS.
SHE DID?! WHAT DID SHE SAY?!
DOESN'T MAKE SENSE...
"TRUST ME, OONA, NOW IF EVER! TAKE THIS SHIP TO MOON YATTA. I PROMISE I WILL EXPLAIN EVERYTHING! SISTERS ARE FOREVER. LOVE, JESSA."
AND SHE GAVE YOU A TICKET.
THE MOON MOTH! TOMORROW MORNING. ON BEACON DAY?!
I CAN'T MISS BEACON DAY!! WHEN IT'S FINALLY GOING TO BE LIT!
IT'S NOT.

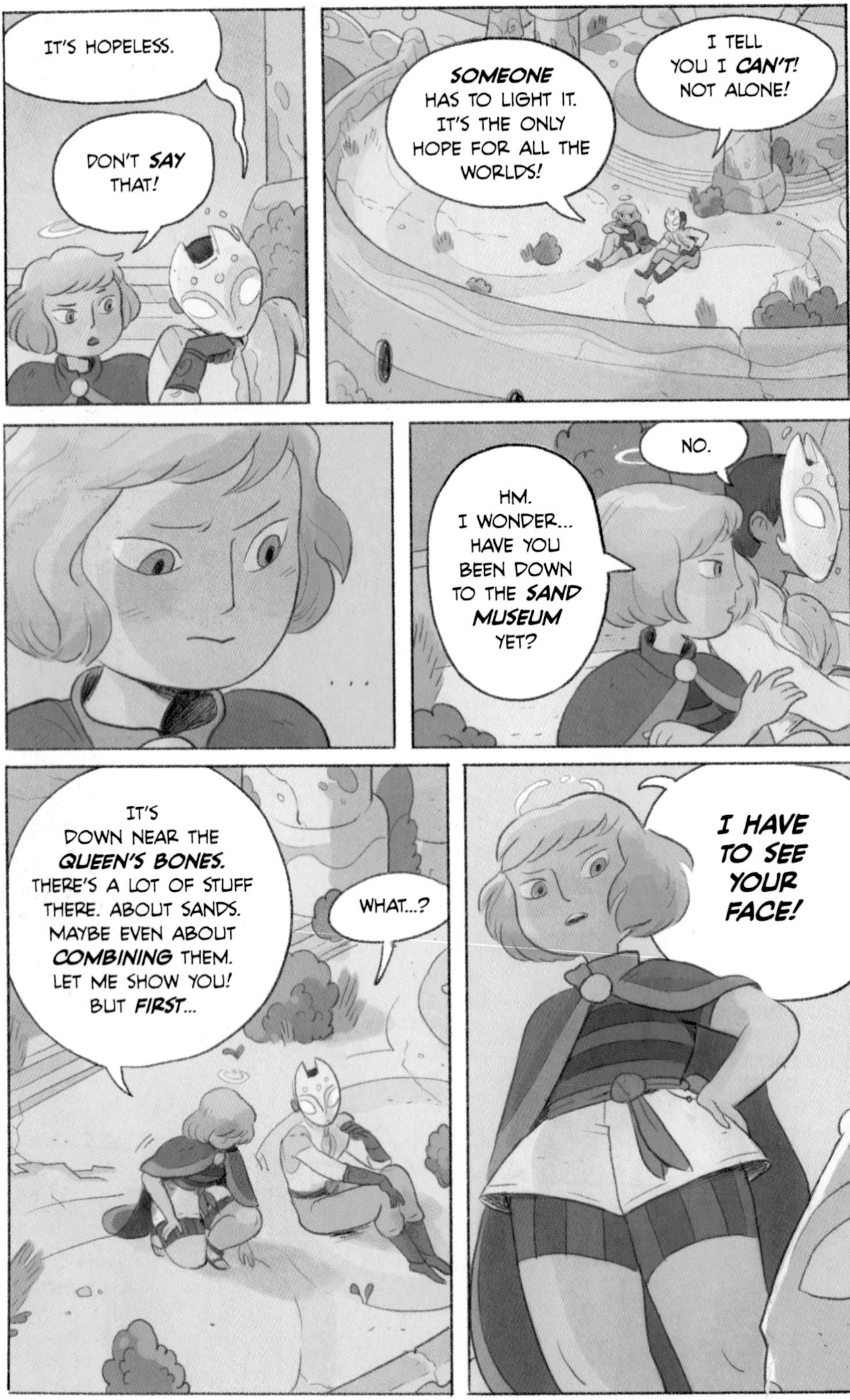
IT'S HOPELESS.
DON'T SAY THAT!
SOMEONE HAS TO LIGHT IT. IT'S THE ONLY HOPE FOR ALL THE WORLDS!
I TELL YOU I CAN'T! NOT ALONE!
...
NO.
HM. I WONDER... HAVE YOU BEEN DOWN TO THE SAND MUSEUM YET?
IT'S DOWN NEAR THE QUEEN'S BONES. THERE'S A LOT OF STUFF THERE. ABOUT SANDS. MAYBE EVEN ABOUT COMBINING THEM. LET ME SHOW YOU! BUT FIRST...
WHAT...?
I HAVE TO SEE YOUR FACE!

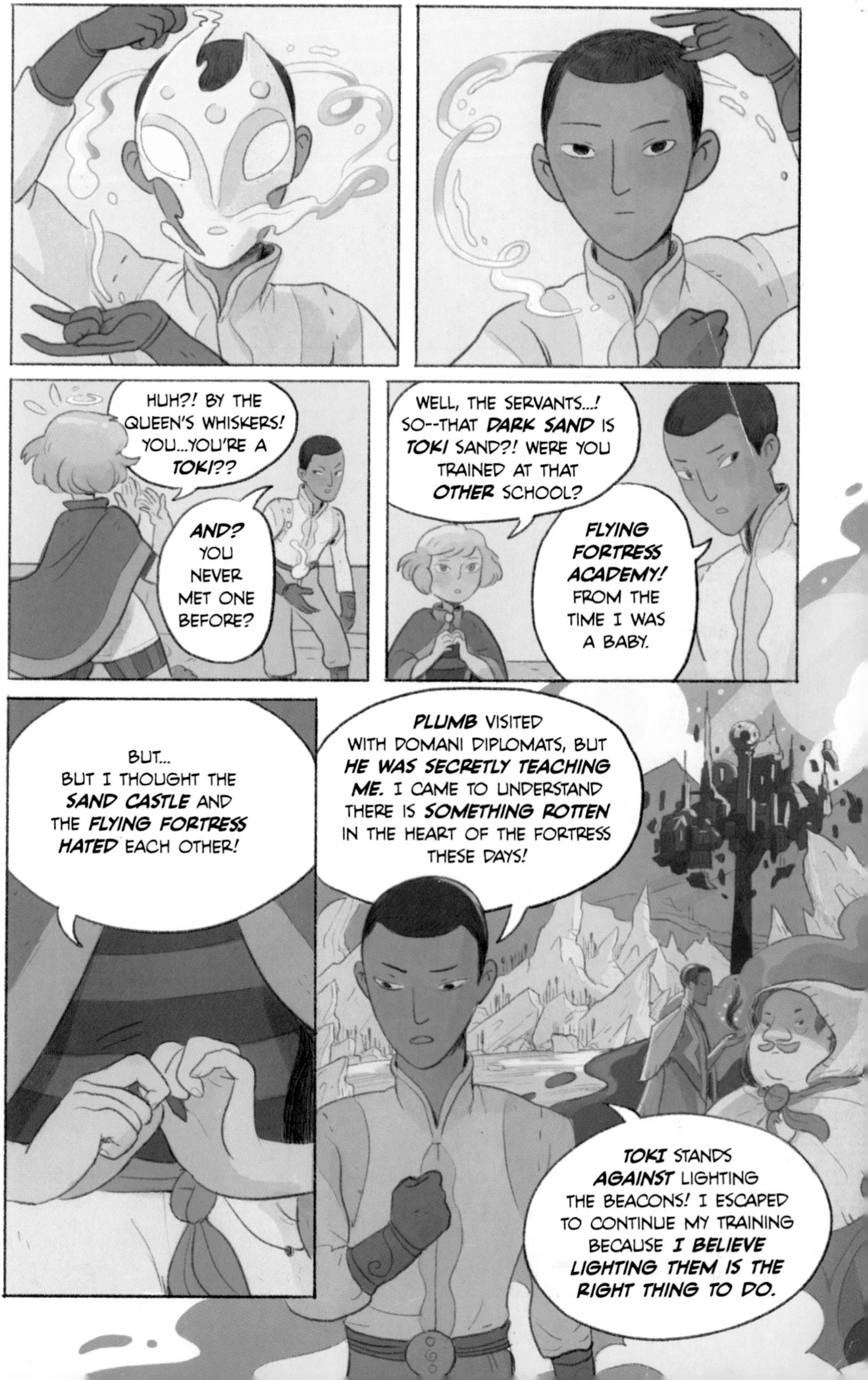
HUH?! BY THE QUEEN'S WHISKERS! YOU...YOU'RE A *TOKI*??
AND? YOU NEVER MET ONE BEFORE?
WELL, THE SERVANTS...! SO--THAT *DARK SAND* IS *TOKI* SAND?! WERE YOU TRAINED AT THAT *OTHER* SCHOOL?
FLYING FORTRESS ACADEMY! FROM THE TIME I WAS A BABY.
BUT... BUT I THOUGHT THE *SAND CASTLE* AND THE *FLYING FORTRESS HATED* EACH OTHER!
PLUMB VISITED WITH DOMANI DIPLOMATS, BUT *HE WAS SECRETLY TEACHING ME.* I CAME TO UNDERSTAND THERE IS *SOMETHING ROTTEN* IN THE HEART OF THE FORTRESS THESE DAYS!
TOKI STANDS *AGAINST* LIGHTING THE BEACONS! I ESCAPED TO CONTINUE MY TRAINING BECAUSE *I BELIEVE LIGHTING THEM IS THE RIGHT THING TO DO.*

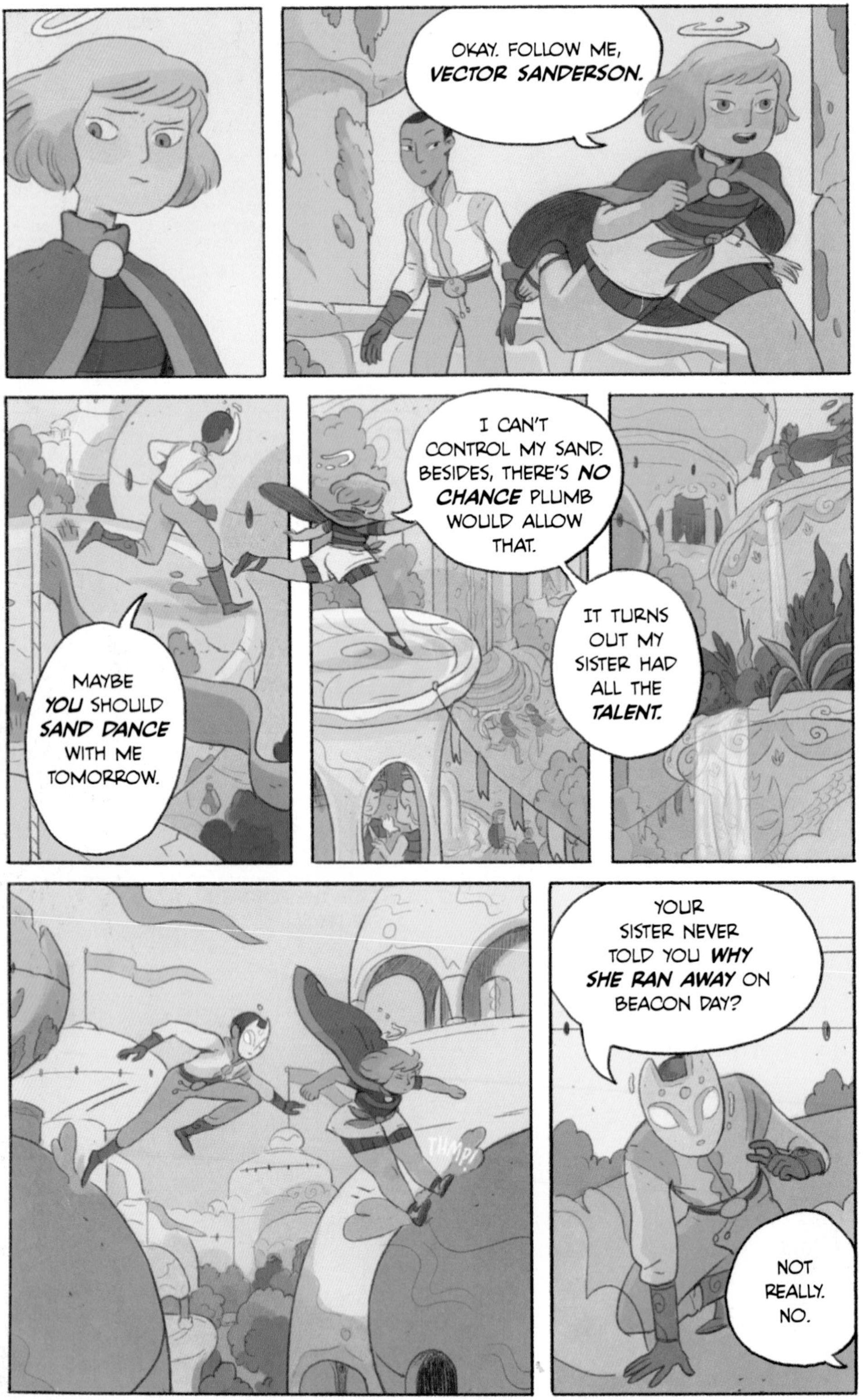
OKAY. FOLLOW ME, **VECTOR SANDERSON.**
I CAN'T CONTROL MY SAND. BESIDES, THERE'S **NO CHANCE** PLUMB WOULD ALLOW THAT.
IT TURNS OUT MY SISTER HAD ALL THE **TALENT.**
MAYBE **YOU** SHOULD **SAND DANCE** WITH ME TOMORROW.
THMP!
YOUR SISTER NEVER TOLD YOU **WHY SHE RAN AWAY** ON BEACON DAY?
NOT REALLY. NO.

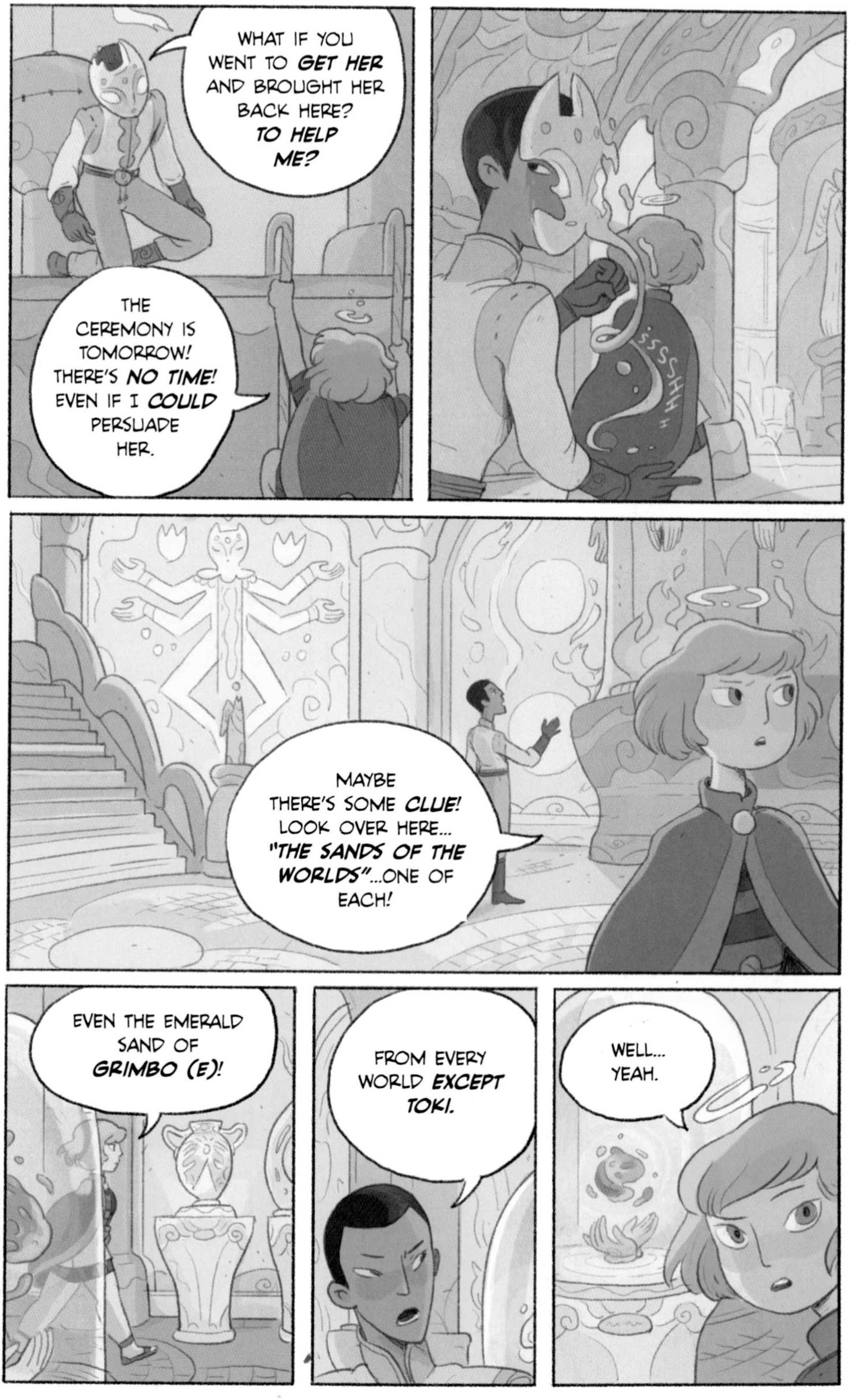
WHAT IF YOU WENT TO GET HER AND BROUGHT HER BACK HERE? TO HELP ME?
THE CEREMONY IS TOMORROW! THERE'S NO TIME! EVEN IF I COULD PERSUADE HER.
SSSSHHH
MAYBE THERE'S SOME CLUE! LOOK OVER HERE... "THE SANDS OF THE WORLDS"...ONE OF EACH!
EVEN THE EMERALD SAND OF GRIMBO (E)!
FROM EVERY WORLD EXCEPT TOKI.
WELL... YEAH.

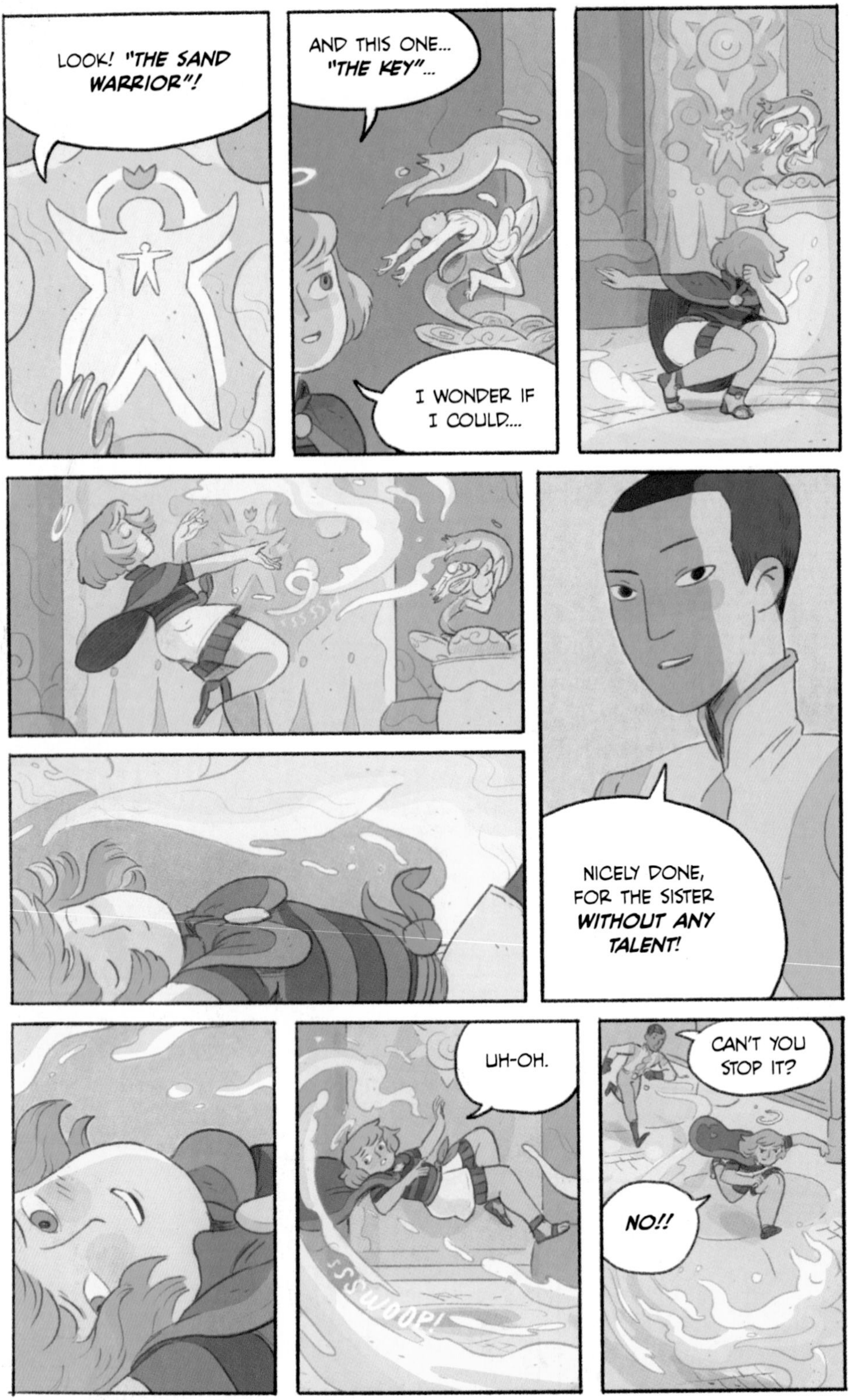
LOOK! "THE SAND WARRIOR"!
AND THIS ONE... "THE KEY"...
I WONDER IF I COULD...
SSSSSH
NICELY DONE, FOR THE SISTER WITHOUT ANY TALENT!
UH-OH.
SSSWOOP!
CAN'T YOU STOP IT?
NO!!

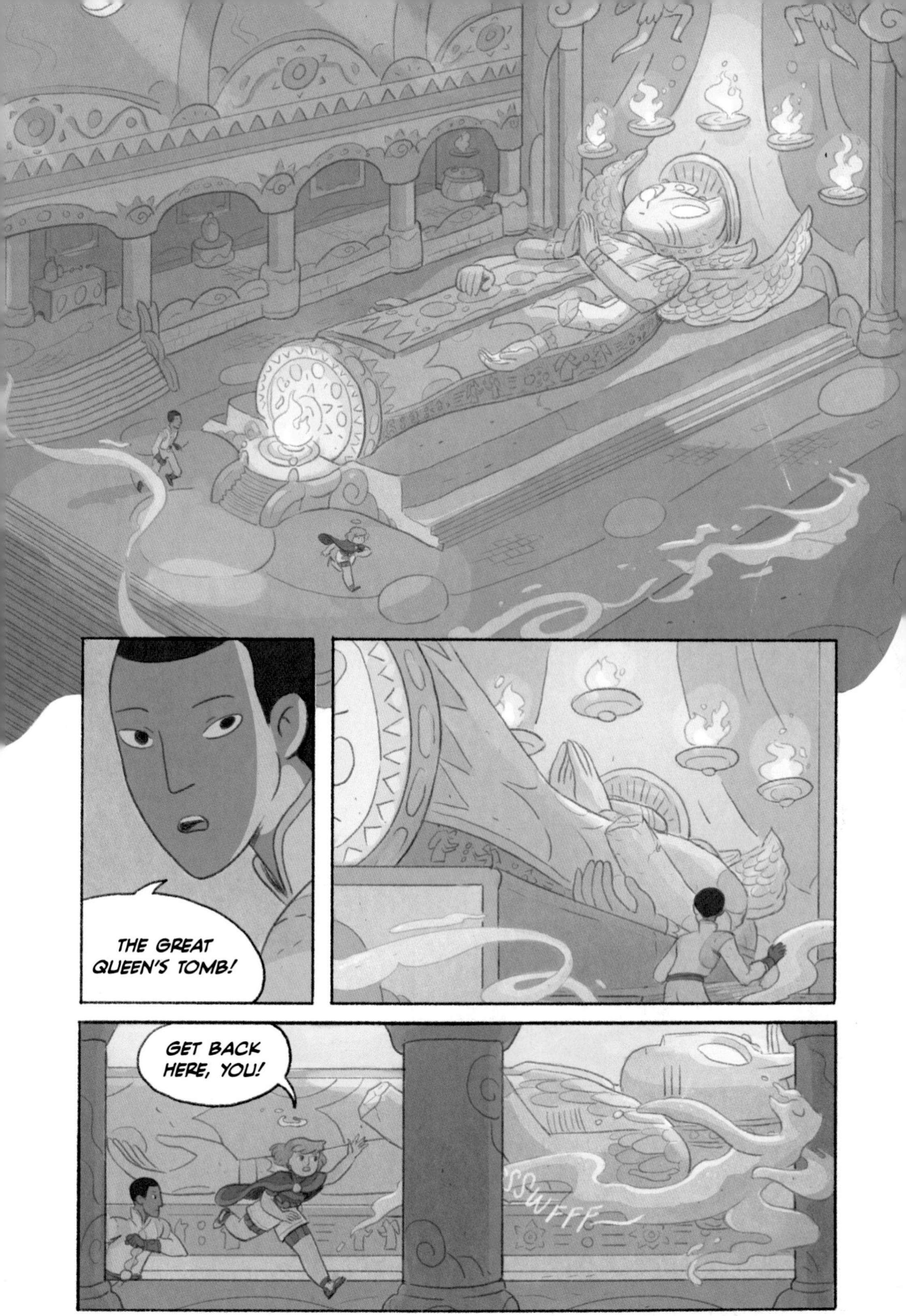
THE GREAT QUEEN'S TOMB!
GET BACK HERE, YOU!
SSWFFF

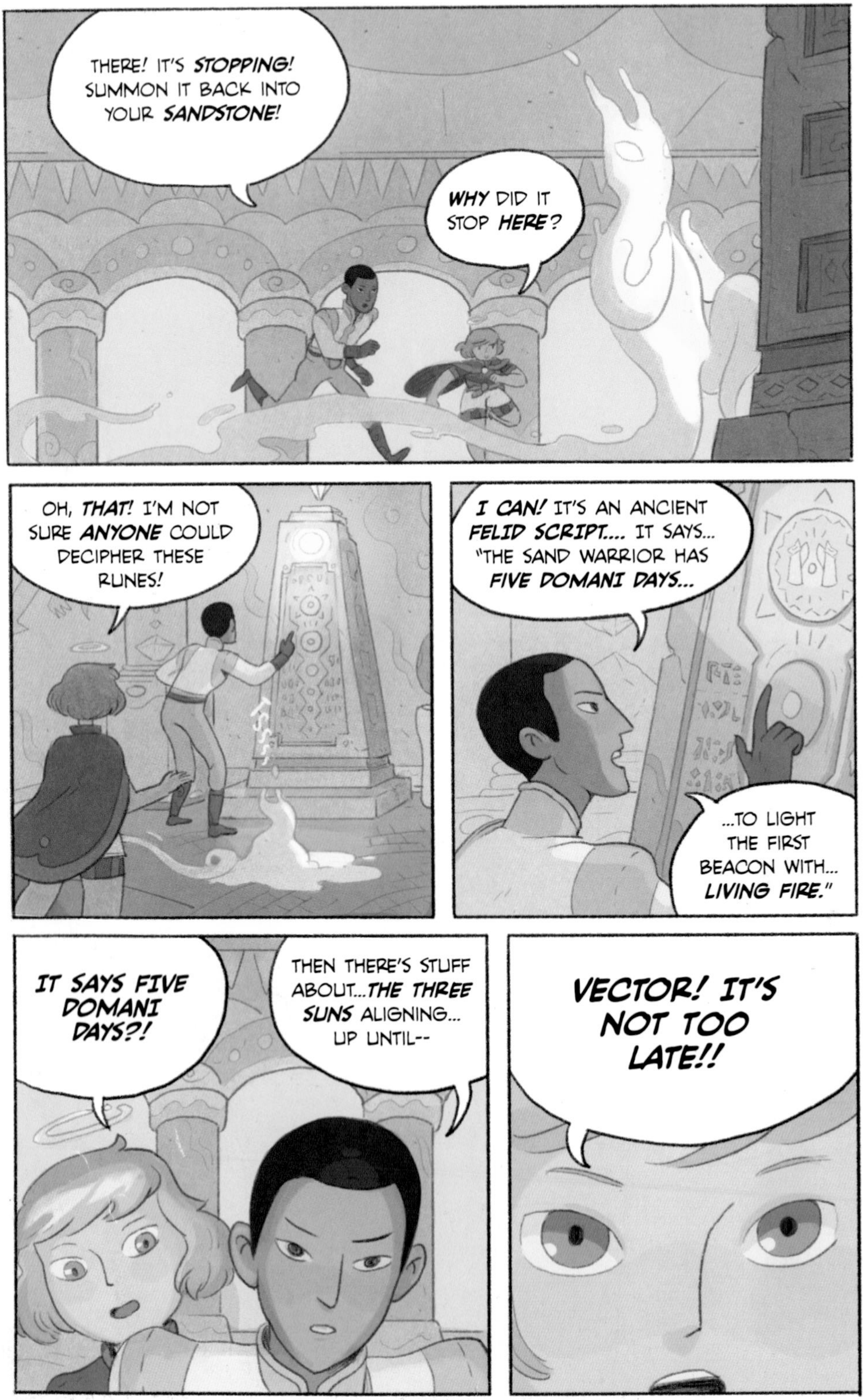
THERE! IT'S STOPPING! SUMMON IT BACK INTO YOUR SANDSTONE!
WHY DID IT STOP HERE?
OH, THAT! I'M NOT SURE ANYONE COULD DECIPHER THESE RUNES!
I CAN! IT'S AN ANCIENT FELID SCRIPT.... IT SAYS... "THE SAND WARRIOR HAS FIVE DOMANI DAYS...
...TO LIGHT THE FIRST BEACON WITH... LIVING FIRE."
IT SAYS FIVE DOMANI DAYS?!
THEN THERE'S STUFF ABOUT...THE THREE SUNS ALIGNING... UP UNTIL--
VECTOR! IT'S NOT TOO LATE!!

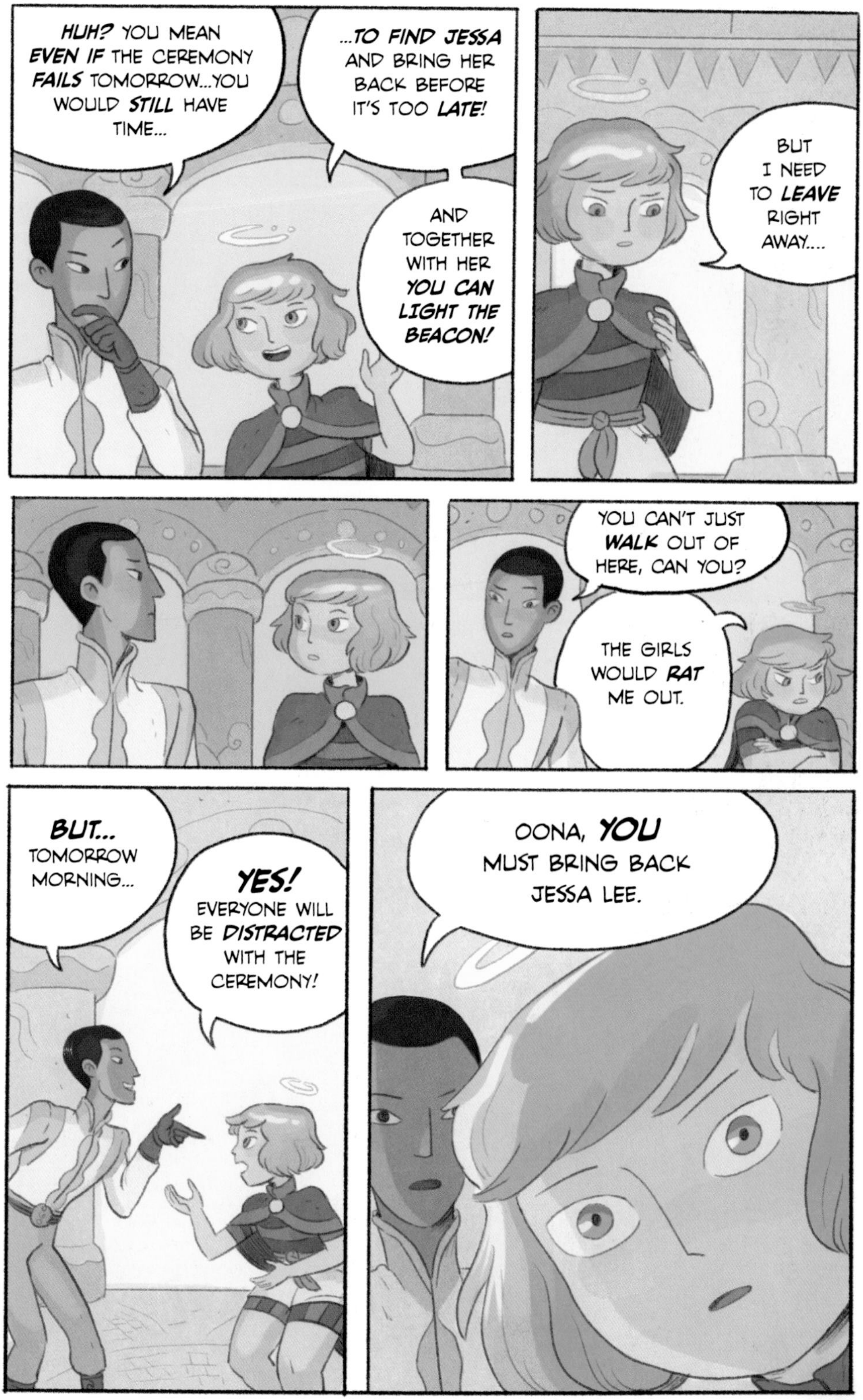
HUH? YOU MEAN EVEN IF THE CEREMONY FAILS TOMORROW...YOU WOULD STILL HAVE TIME...
...TO FIND JESSA AND BRING HER BACK BEFORE IT'S TOO LATE!
AND TOGETHER WITH HER YOU CAN LIGHT THE BEACON!
BUT I NEED TO LEAVE RIGHT AWAY....
YOU CAN'T JUST WALK OUT OF HERE, CAN YOU?
THE GIRLS WOULD RAT ME OUT.
BUT... TOMORROW MORNING...
YES! EVERYONE WILL BE DISTRACTED WITH THE CEREMONY!
OONA, YOU MUST BRING BACK JESSA LEE.

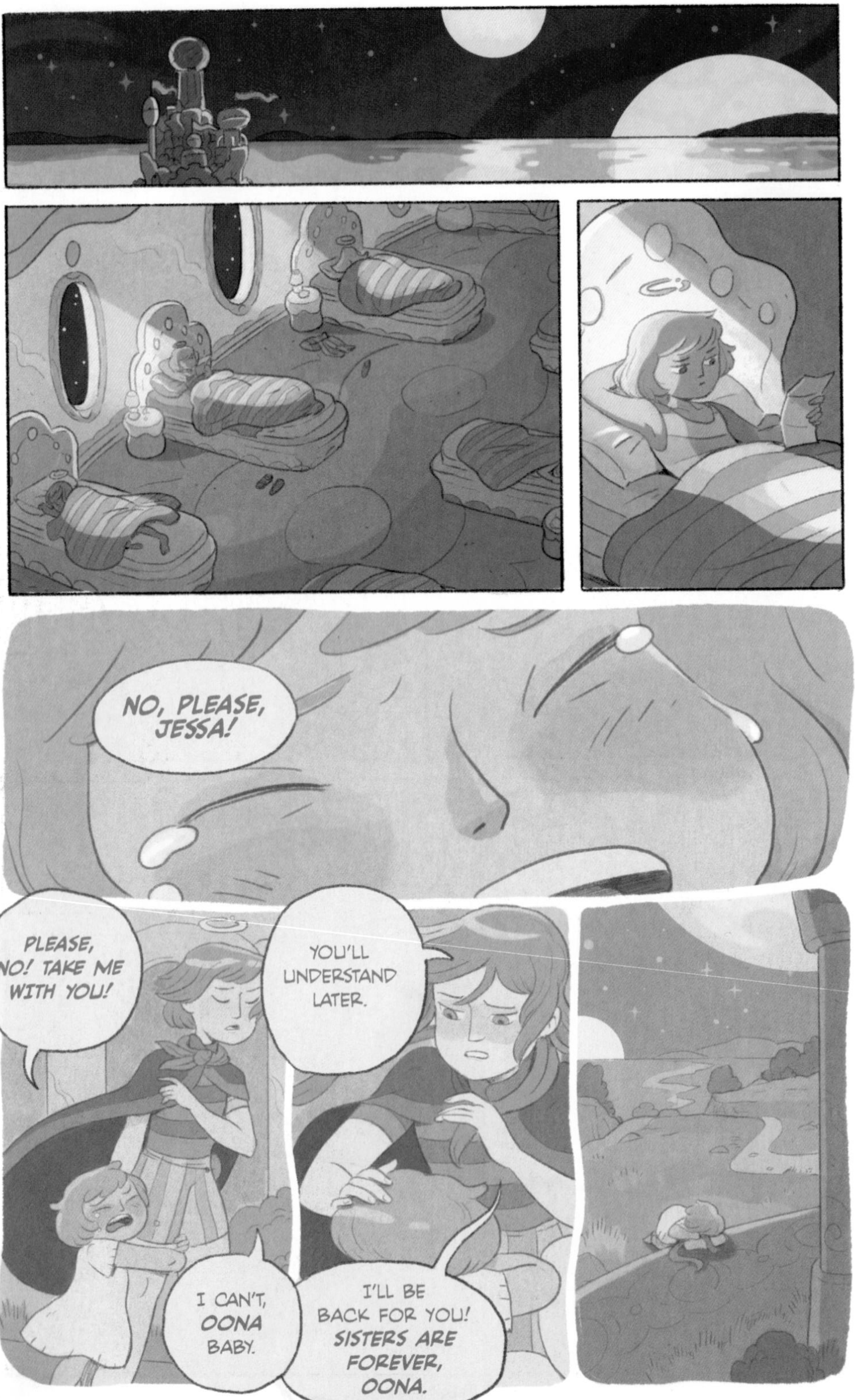
NO, PLEASE, JESSA!
PLEASE, NO! TAKE ME WITH YOU!
YOU'LL UNDERSTAND LATER.
I CAN'T, OONA BABY.
I'LL BE BACK FOR YOU! SISTERS ARE FOREVER, OONA.

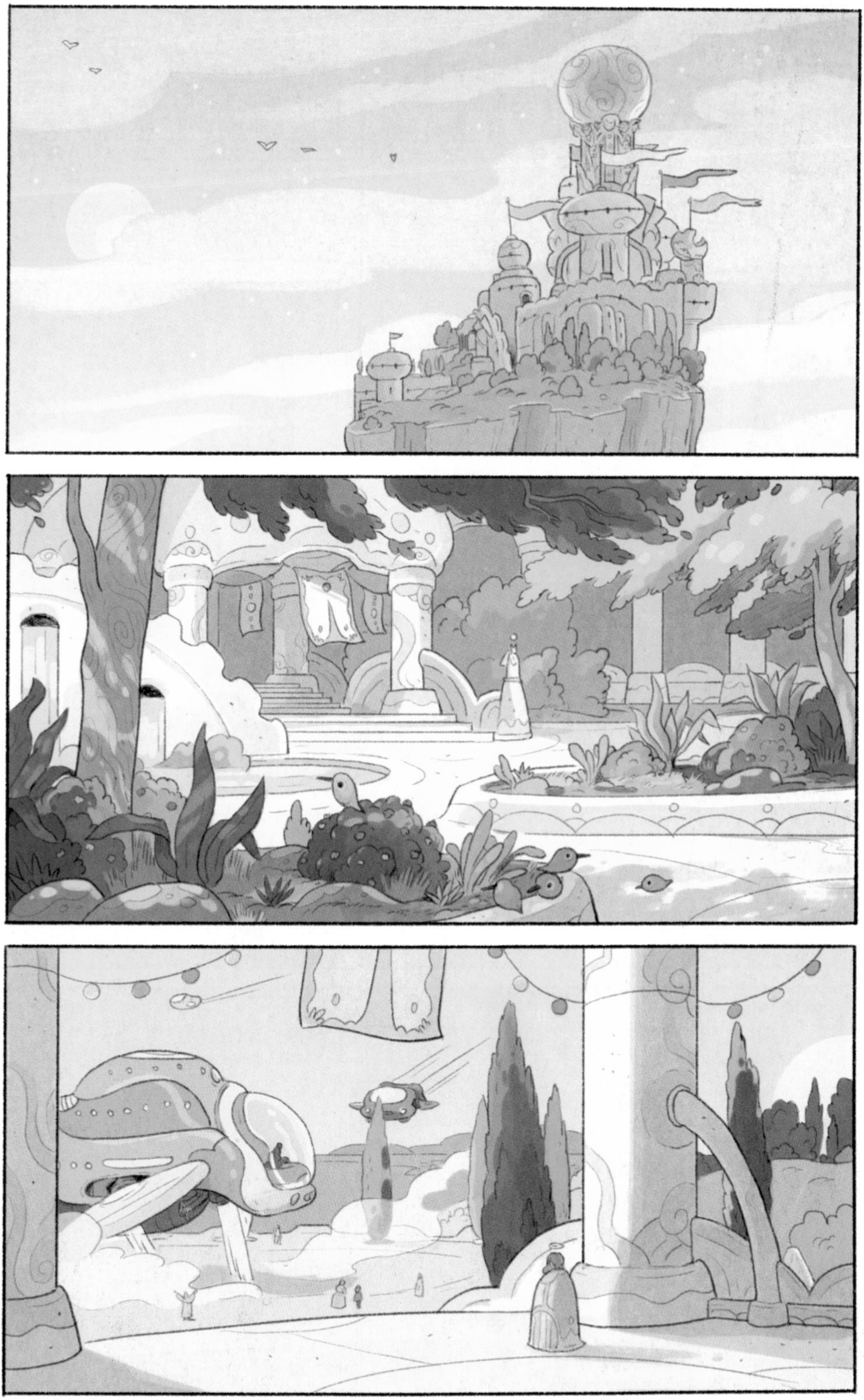

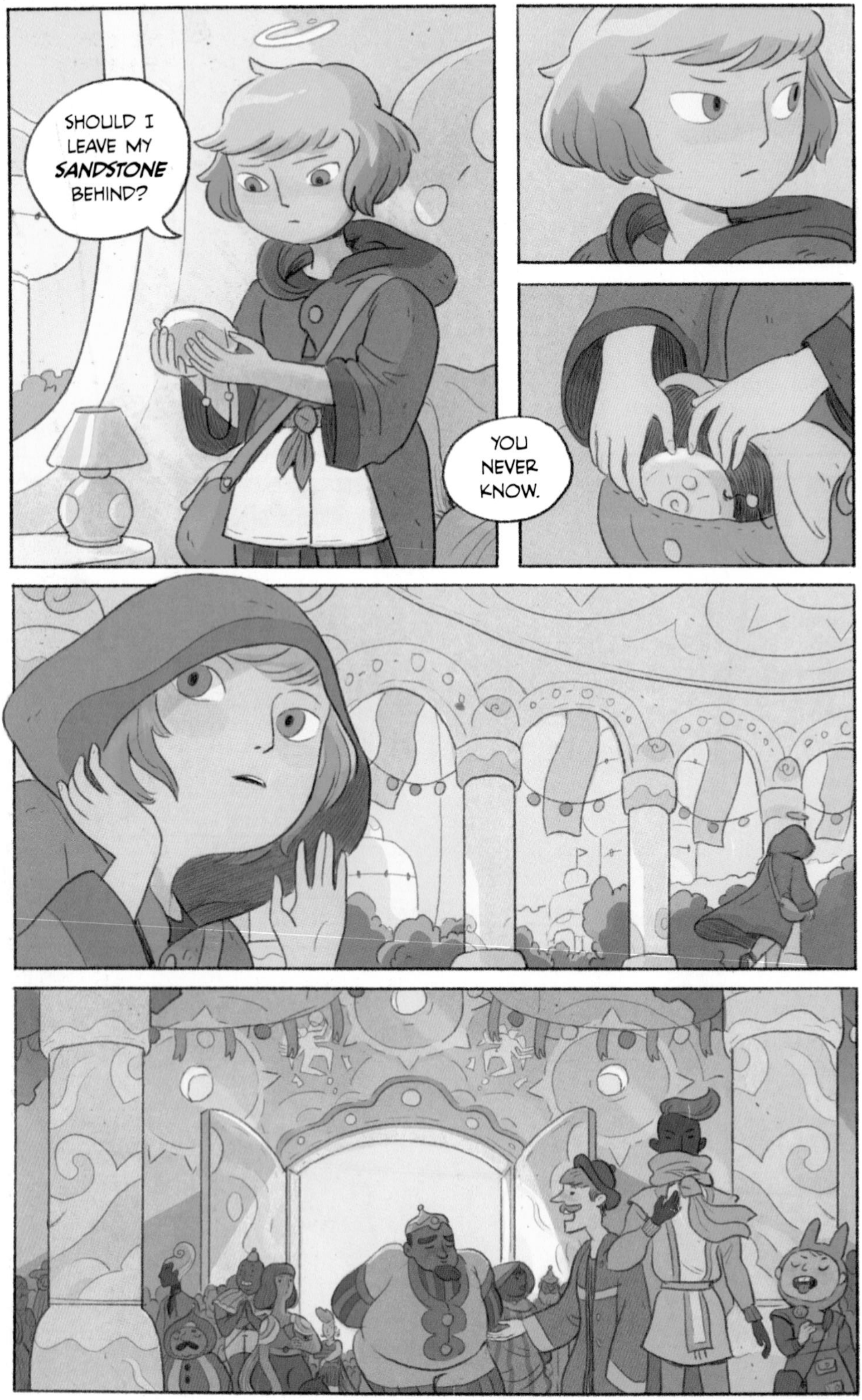
SHOULD I LEAVE MY SANDSTONE BEHIND?
YOU NEVER KNOW.

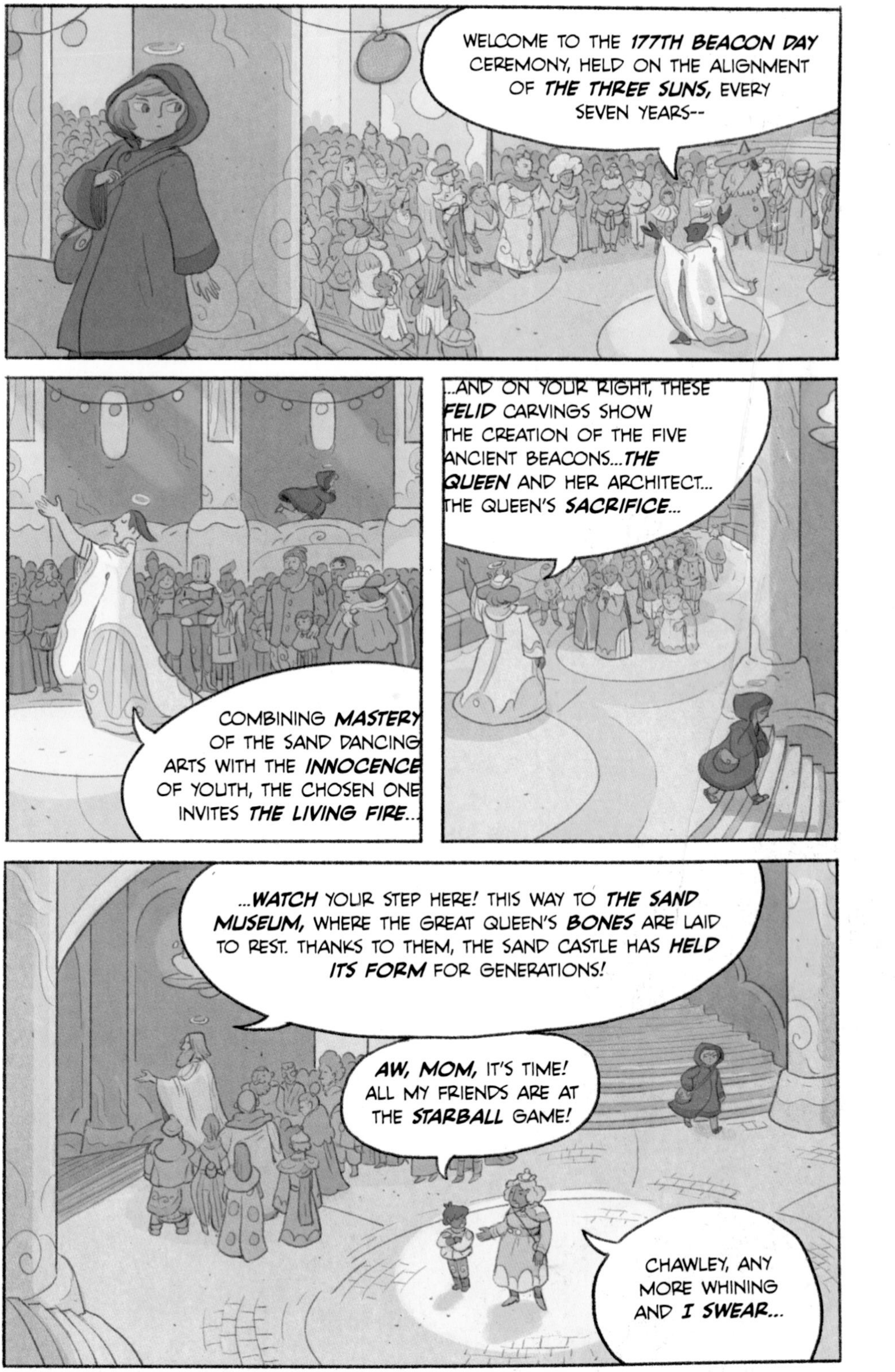
WELCOME TO THE 177TH BEACON DAY CEREMONY, HELD ON THE ALIGNMENT OF THE THREE SUNS, EVERY SEVEN YEARS--
COMBINING MASTERY OF THE SAND DANCING ARTS WITH THE INNOCENCE OF YOUTH, THE CHOSEN ONE INVITES THE LIVING FIRE...
...AND ON YOUR RIGHT, THESE FELID CARVINGS SHOW THE CREATION OF THE FIVE ANCIENT BEACONS...THE QUEEN AND HER ARCHITECT... THE QUEEN'S SACRIFICE...
...WATCH YOUR STEP HERE! THIS WAY TO THE SAND MUSEUM, WHERE THE GREAT QUEEN'S BONES ARE LAID TO REST. THANKS TO THEM, THE SAND CASTLE HAS HELD ITS FORM FOR GENERATIONS!
AW, MOM, IT'S TIME! ALL MY FRIENDS ARE AT THE STARBALL GAME!
CHAWLEY, ANY MORE WHINING AND I SWEAR...

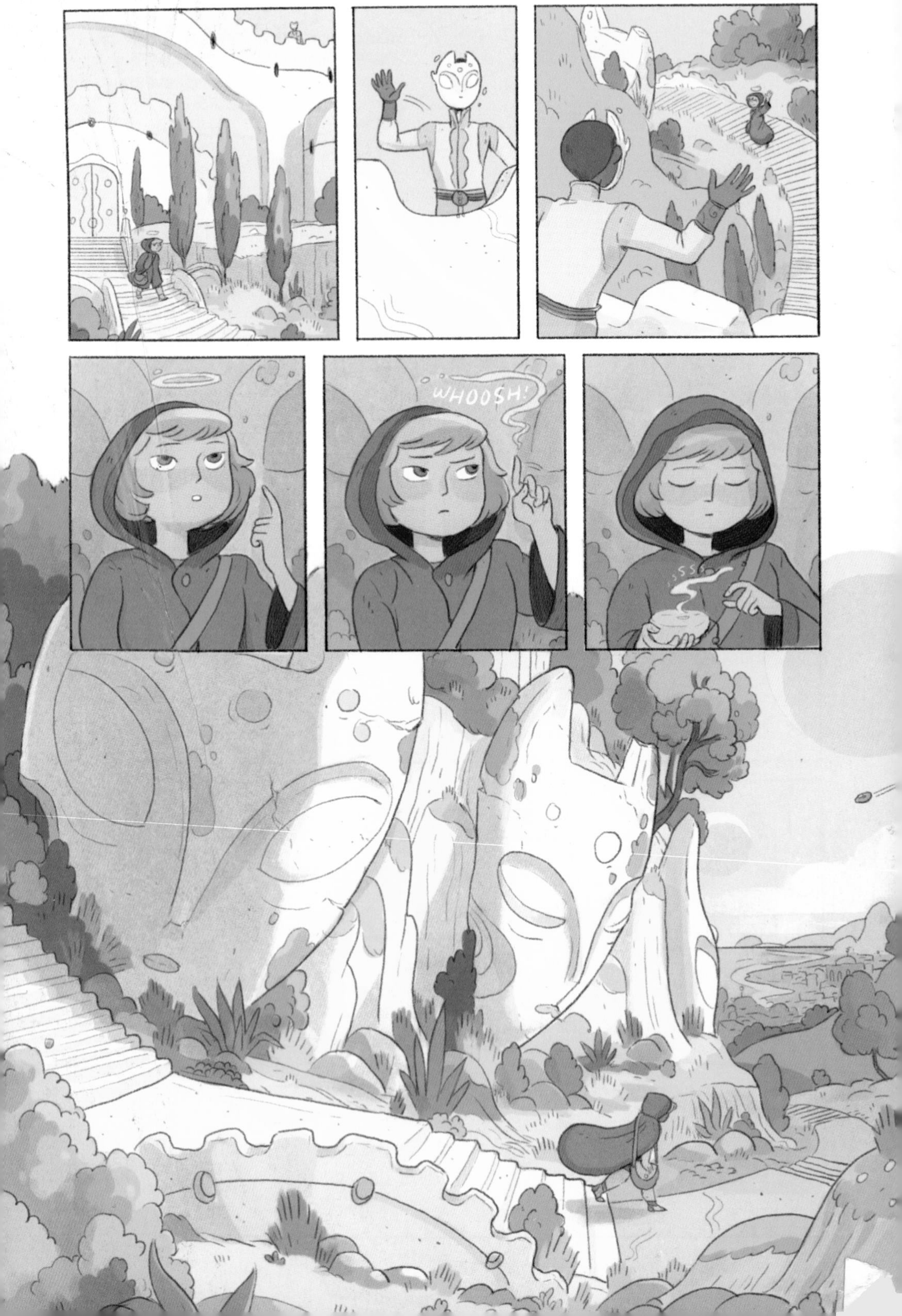
WHOOSH!

Chapter 3

COLLISION AT STARBALL STADIUM

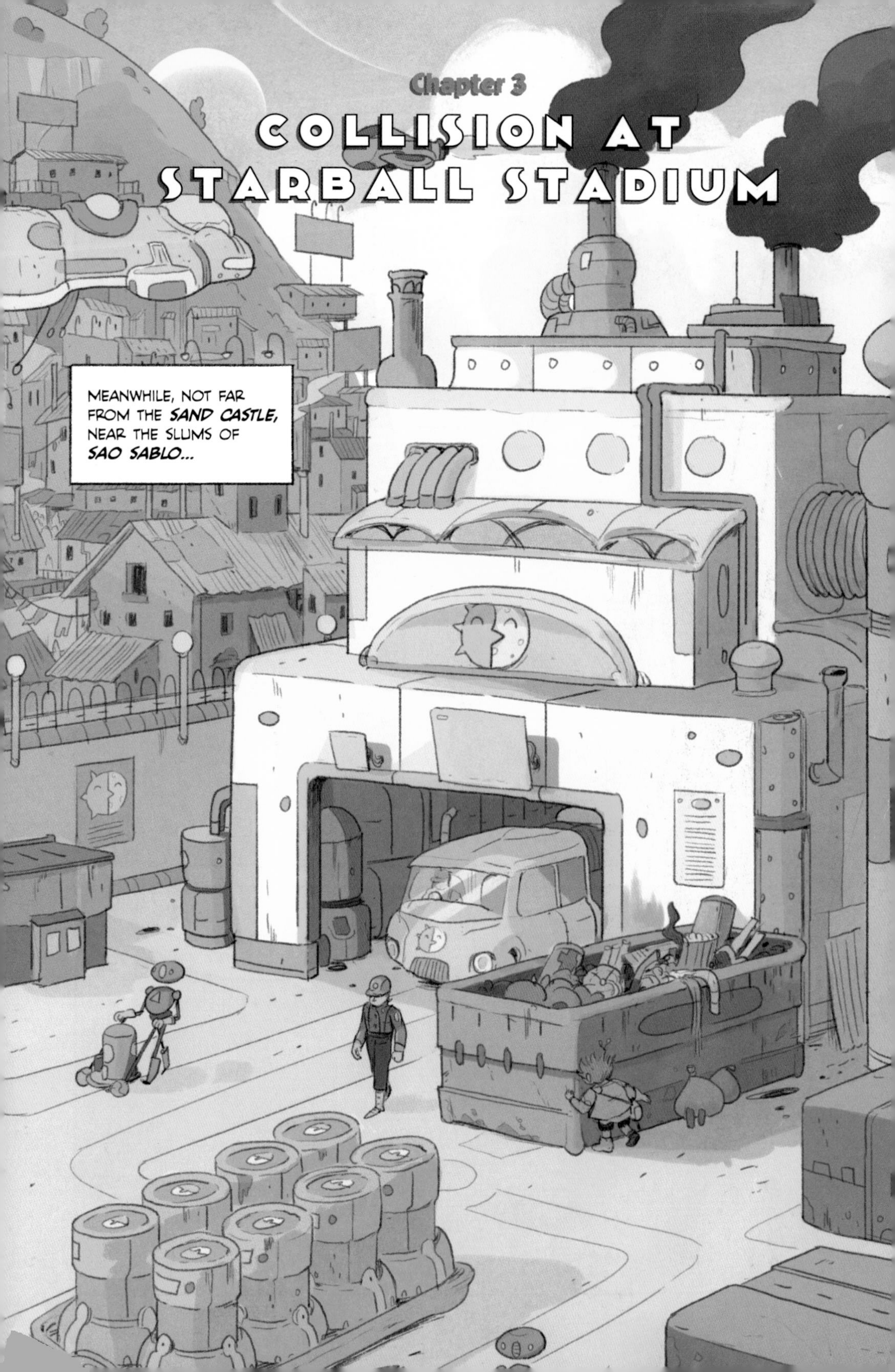
MEANWHILE, NOT FAR FROM THE *SAND CASTLE,* NEAR THE SLUMS OF *SAO SABLO...*

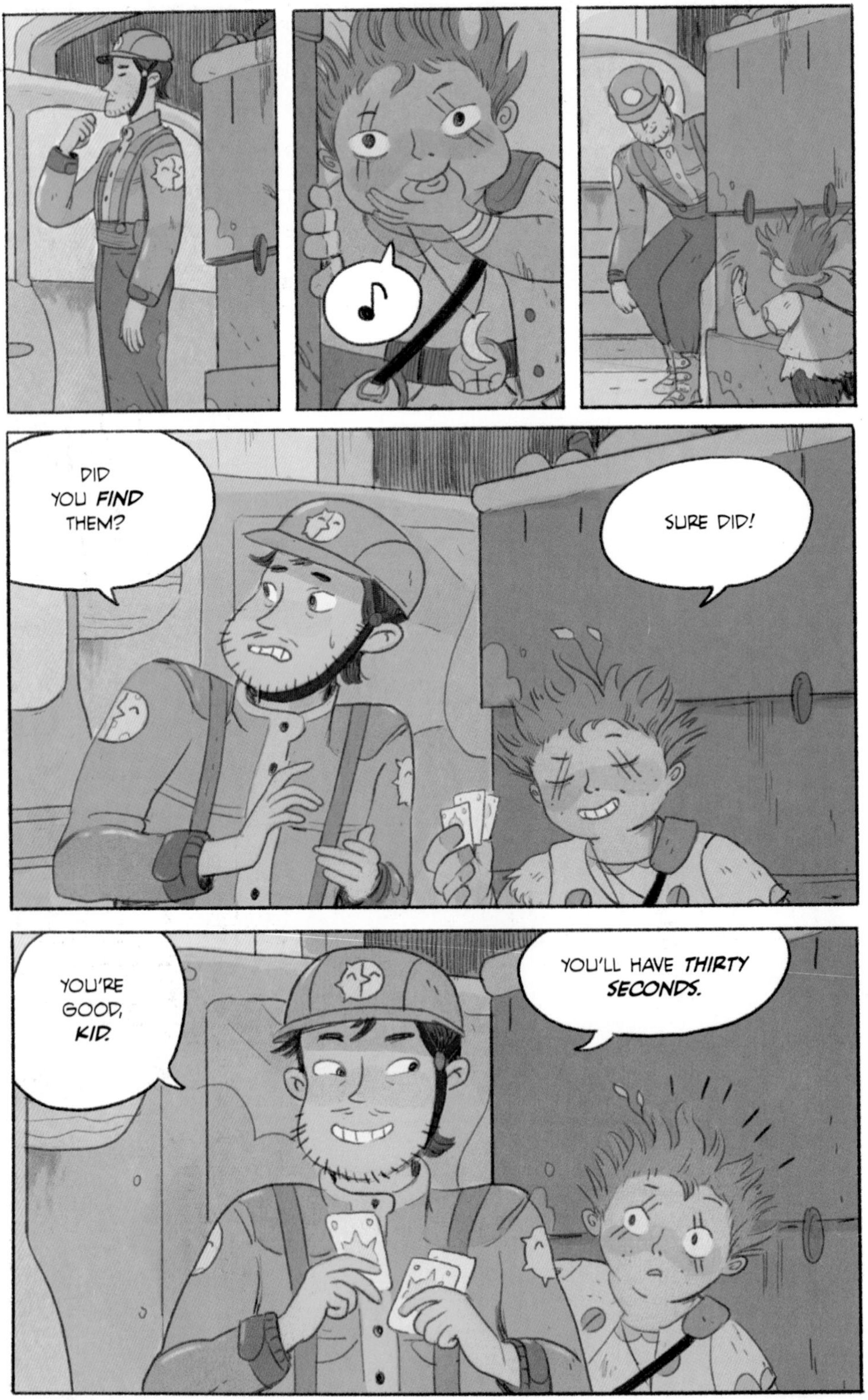
♪
DID YOU FIND THEM?
SURE DID!
YOU'RE GOOD, KID.
YOU'LL HAVE THIRTY SECONDS.

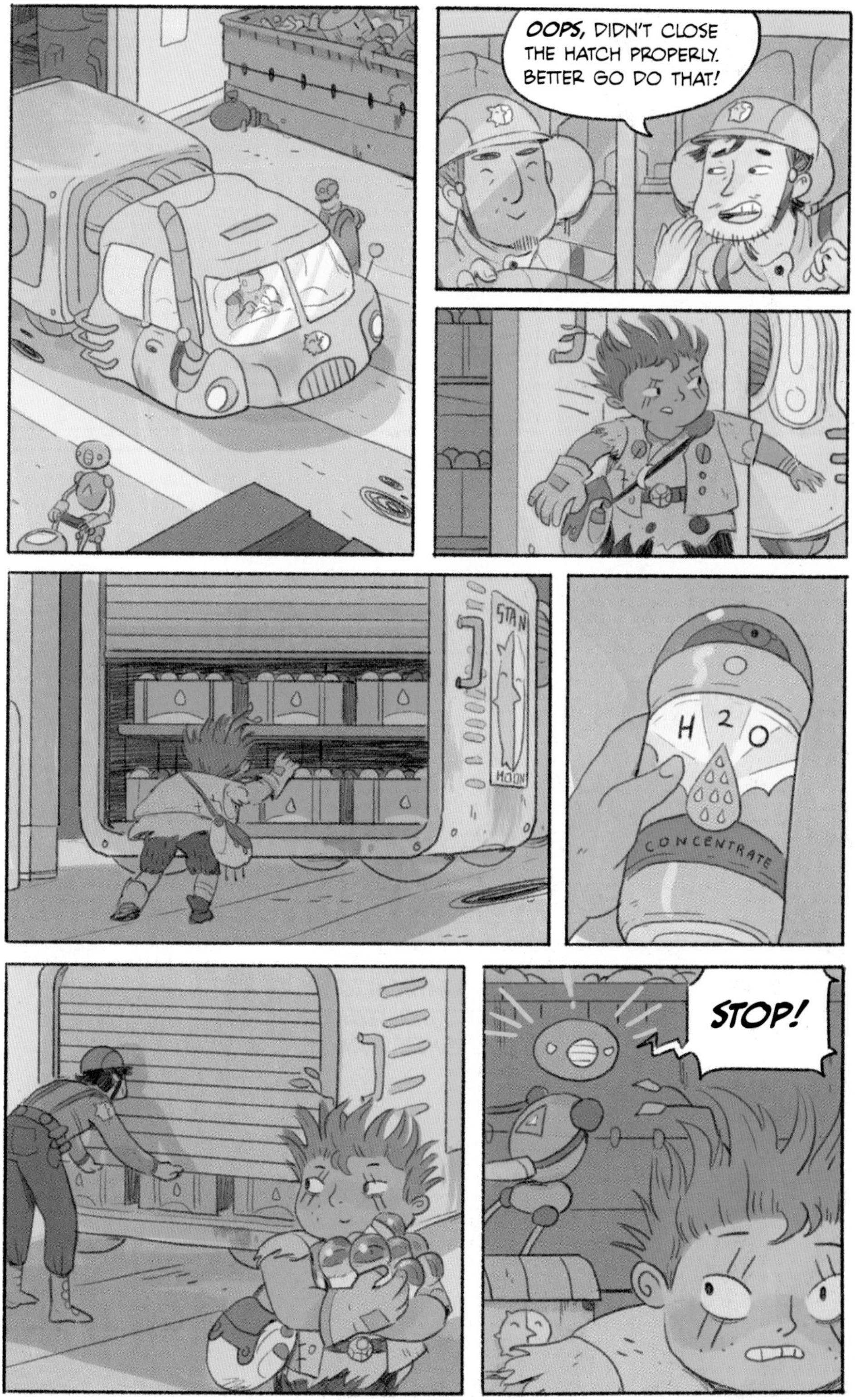
OOPS, DIDN'T CLOSE THE HATCH PROPERLY. BETTER GO DO THAT!
STAN
MOON
H 2 O
CONCENTRATE
STOP!

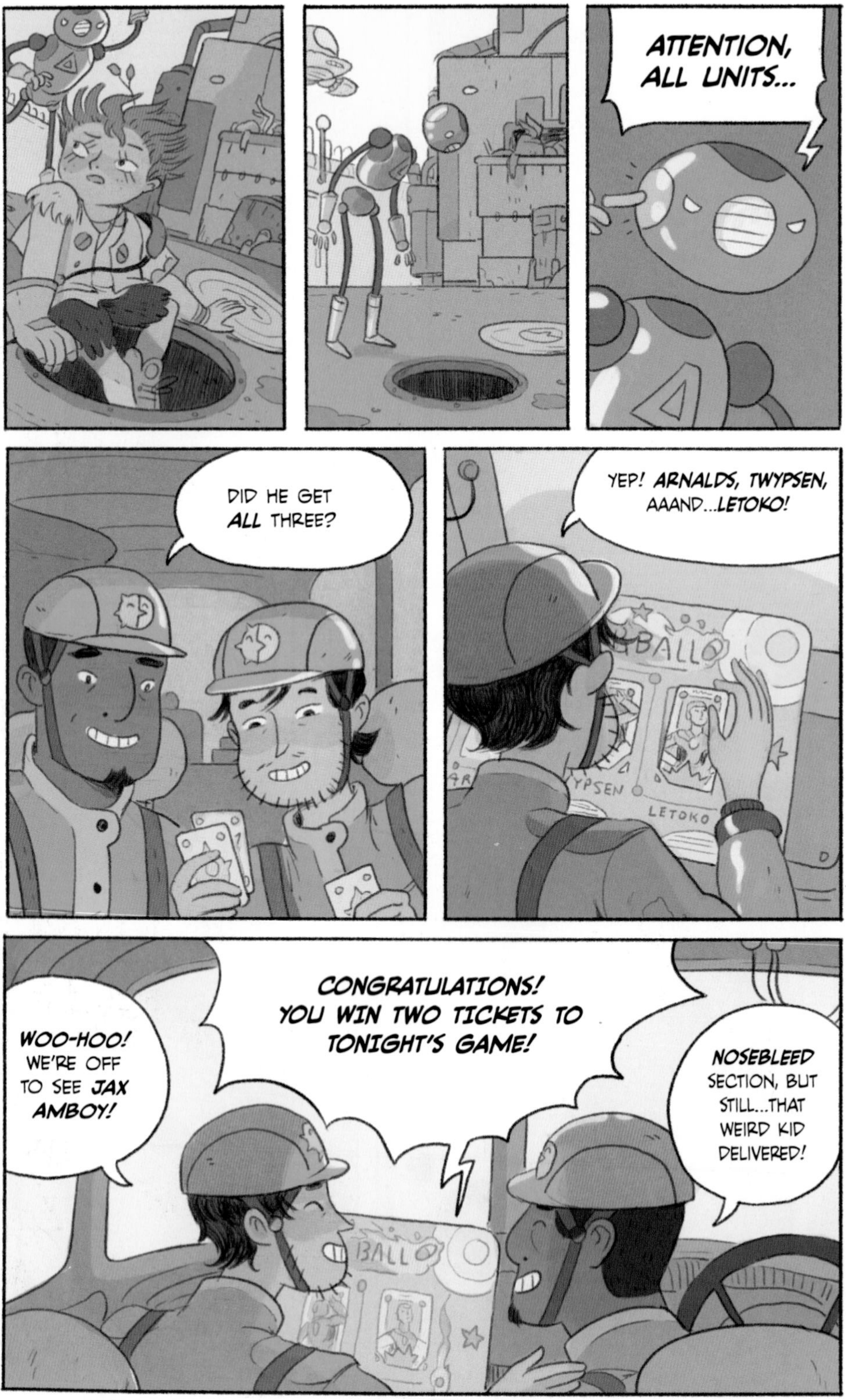
ATTENTION, ALL UNITS...
DID HE GET ALL THREE?
YEP! ARNALDS, TWYPSEN, AAAND...LETOKO!
WOO-HOO! WE'RE OFF TO SEE JAX AMBOY!
CONGRATULATIONS! YOU WIN TWO TICKETS TO TONIGHT'S GAME!
NOSEBLEED SECTION, BUT STILL...THAT WEIRD KID DELIVERED!

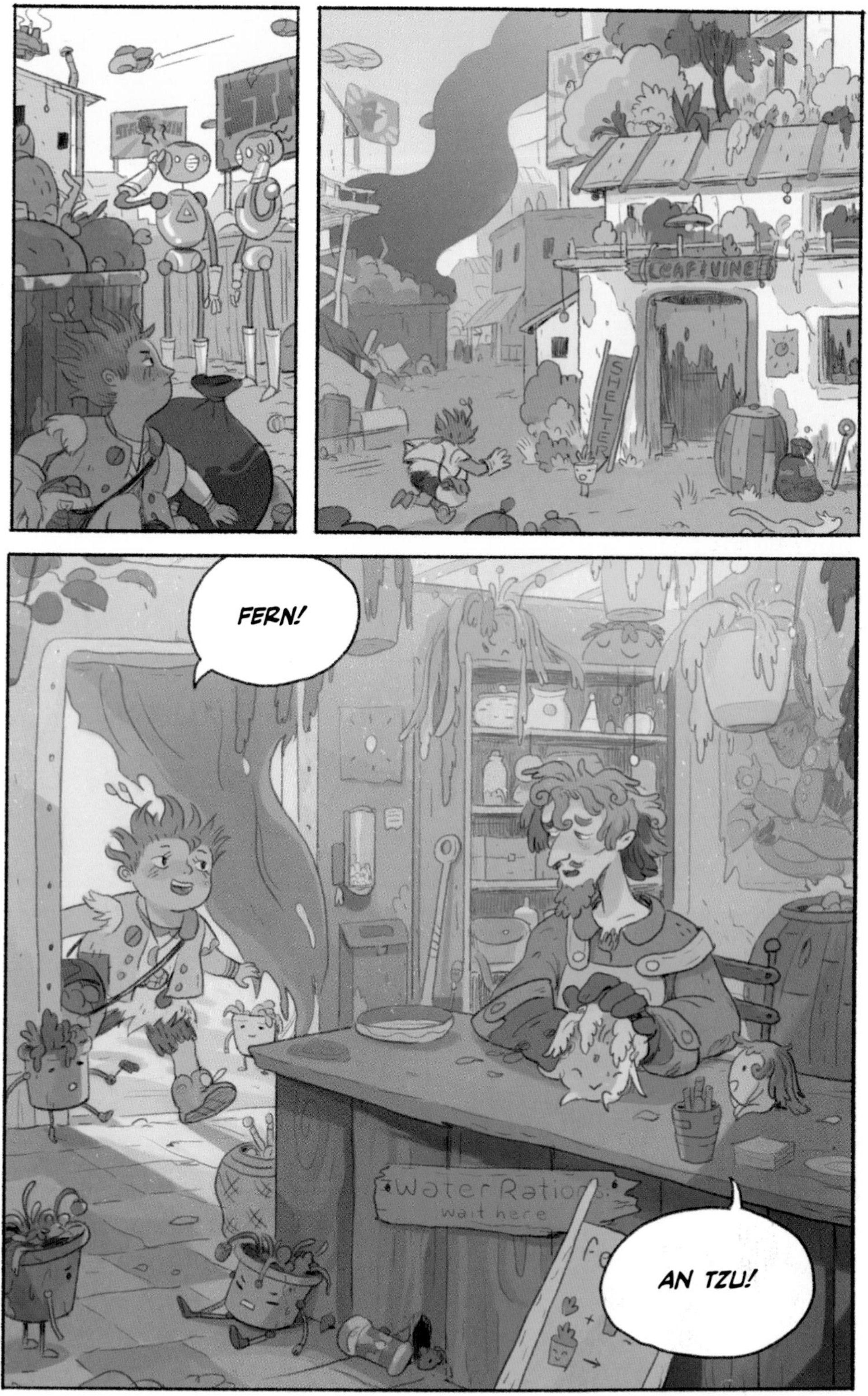
LEAF & VINE
SHELTER
FERN!
Water Rations:
wait here
AN TZU!

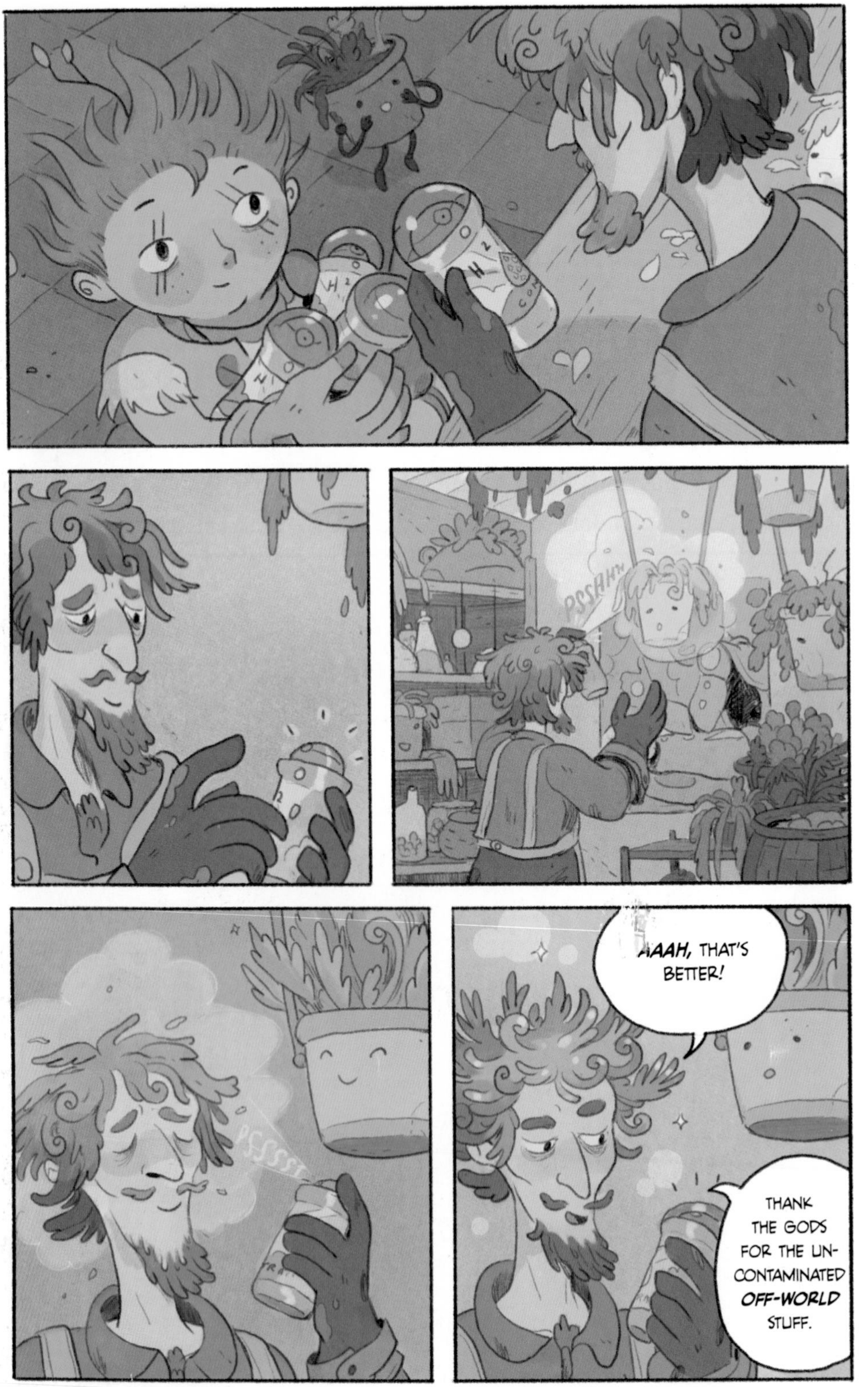
AAAH, THAT'S BETTER!
THANK THE GODS FOR THE UN-CONTAMINATED ***OFF-WORLD*** STUFF.

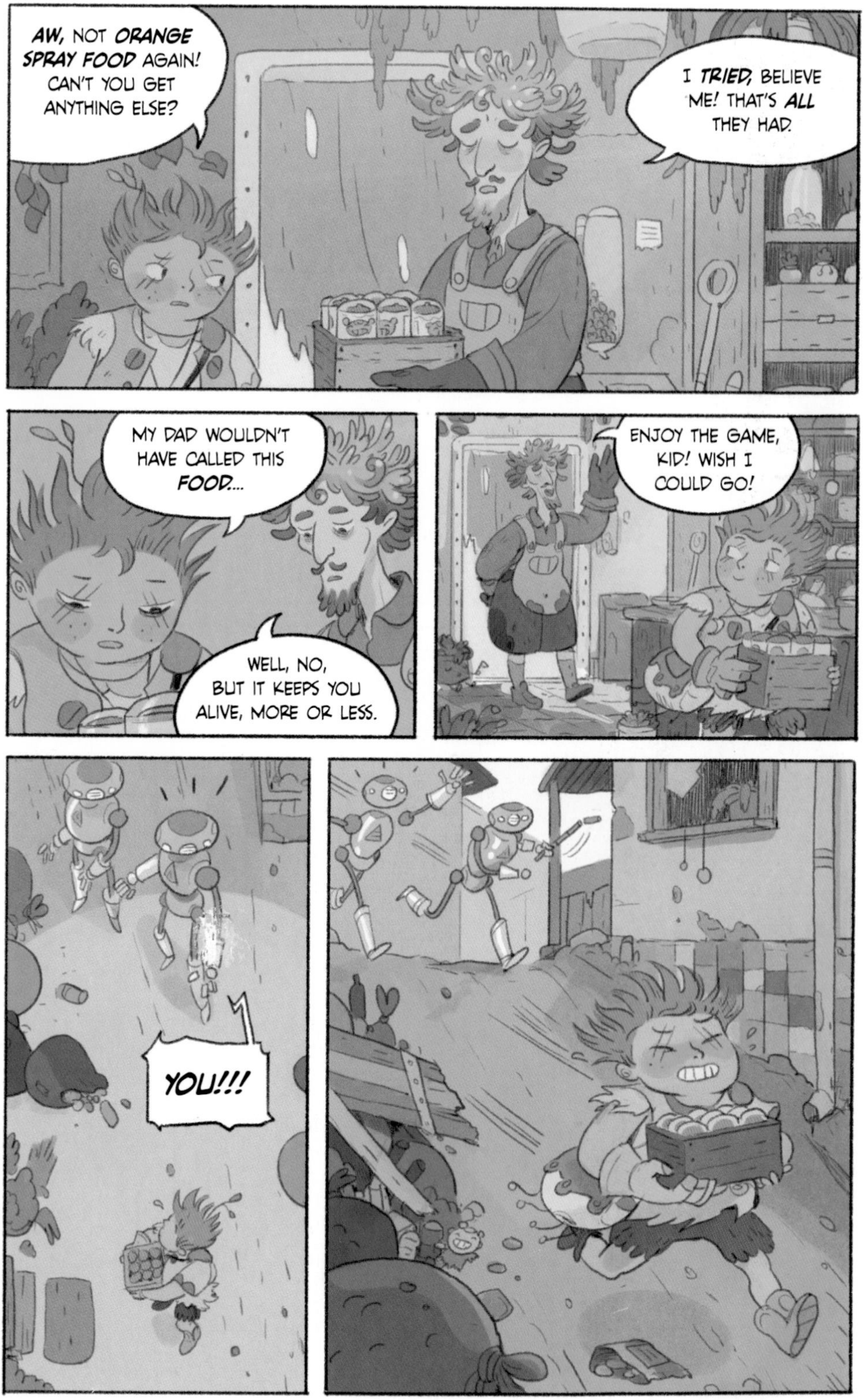
AW, NOT ORANGE SPRAY FOOD AGAIN! CAN'T YOU GET ANYTHING ELSE?
I TRIED, BELIEVE ME! THAT'S ALL THEY HAD.
MY DAD WOULDN'T HAVE CALLED THIS FOOD...
WELL, NO, BUT IT KEEPS YOU ALIVE, MORE OR LESS.
ENJOY THE GAME, KID! WISH I COULD GO!
YOU!!!

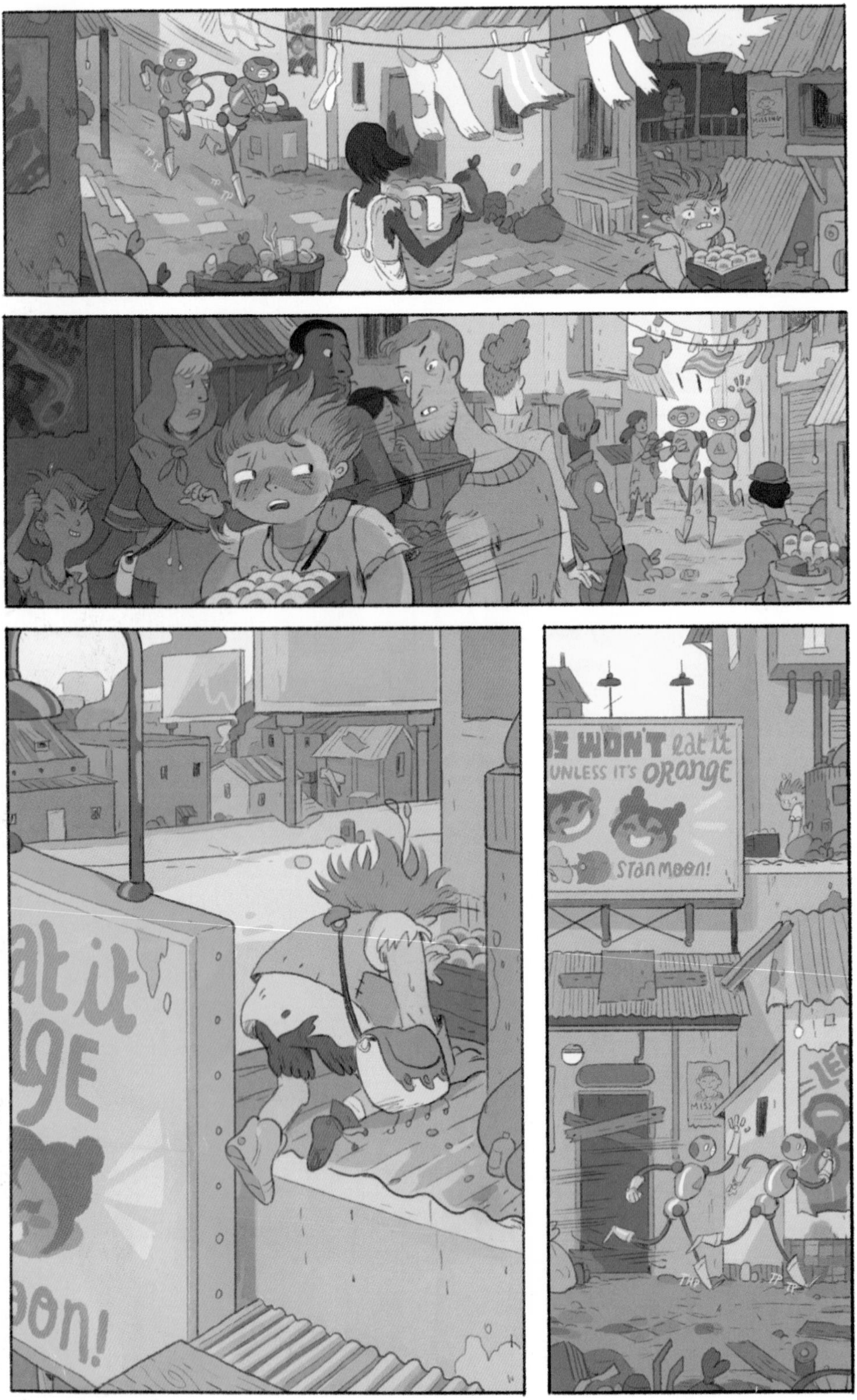
MISSING
UNLESS IT'S ORANGE
Stan Moon!

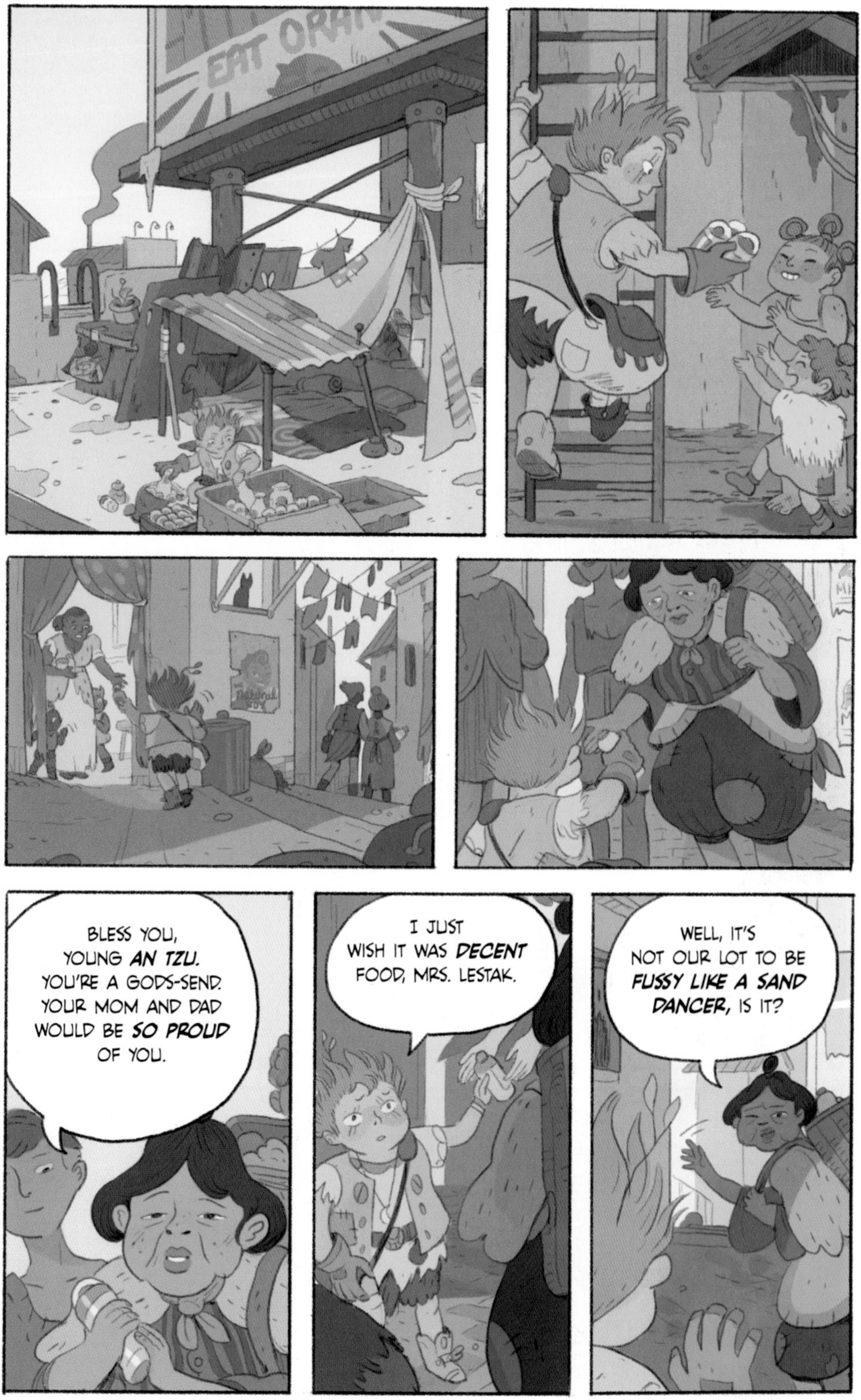
BLESS YOU, YOUNG **AN TZU.** YOU'RE A GODS-SEND. YOUR MOM AND DAD WOULD BE **SO PROUD** OF YOU.
I JUST WISH IT WAS **DECENT** FOOD, MRS. LESTAK.
WELL, IT'S NOT OUR LOT TO BE **FUSSY LIKE A SAND DANCER,** IS IT?

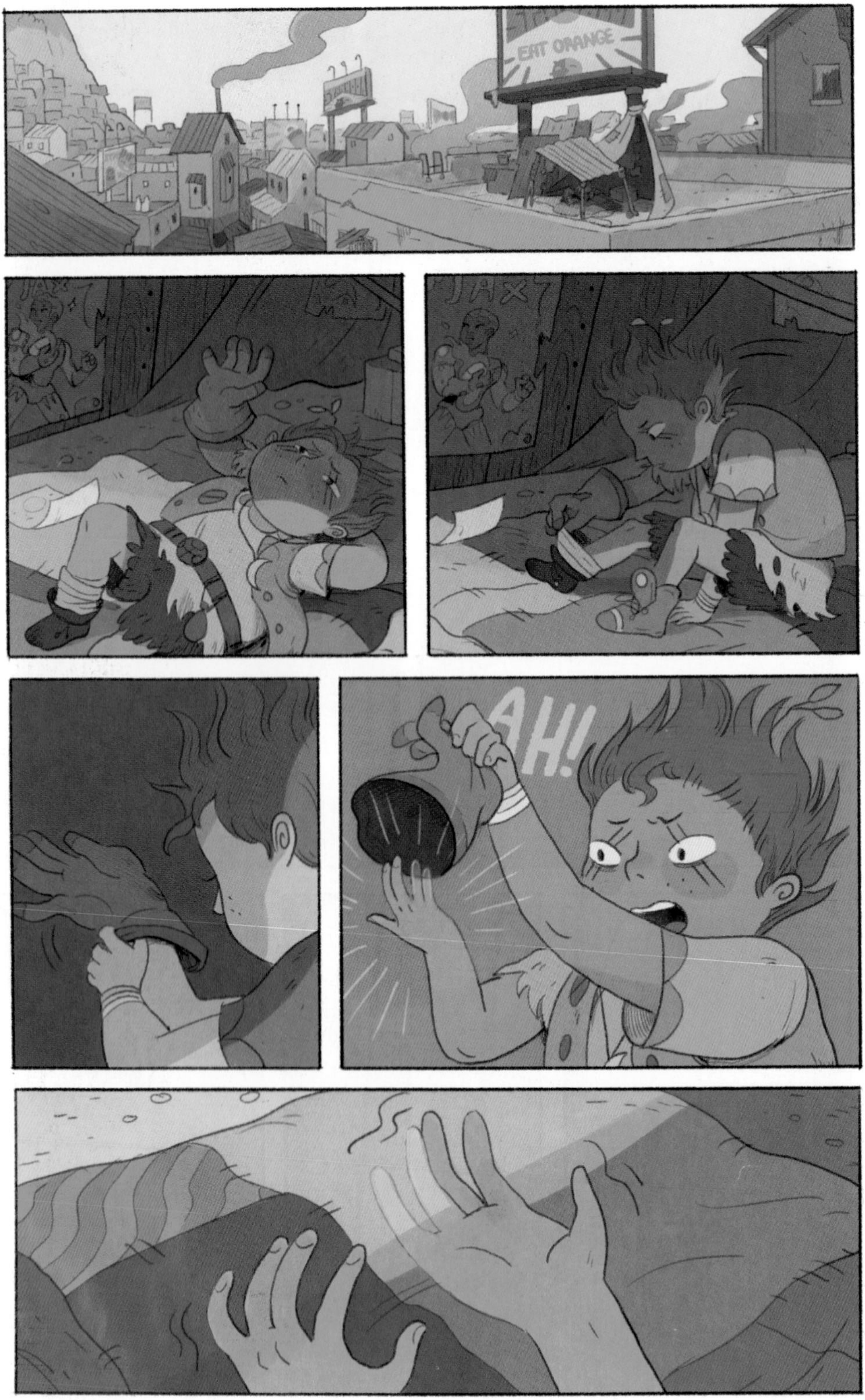
EAT ORANGE
JAX7
AH!

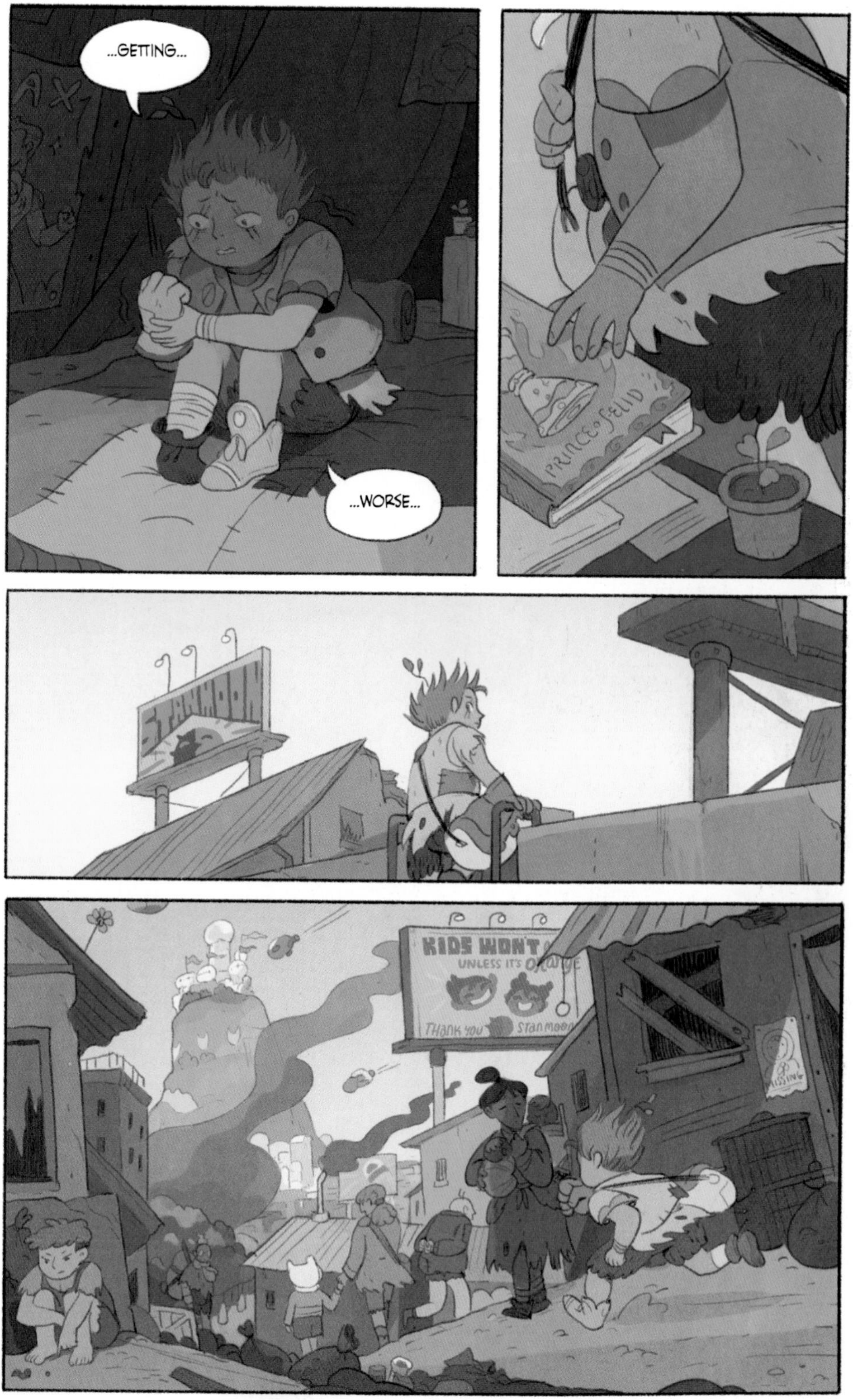
...GETTING...
...WORSE...
PRINCE FELID
STANMOON
KIDS WON'T
UNLESS IT'S
THANK YOU STANMOON
MISSING

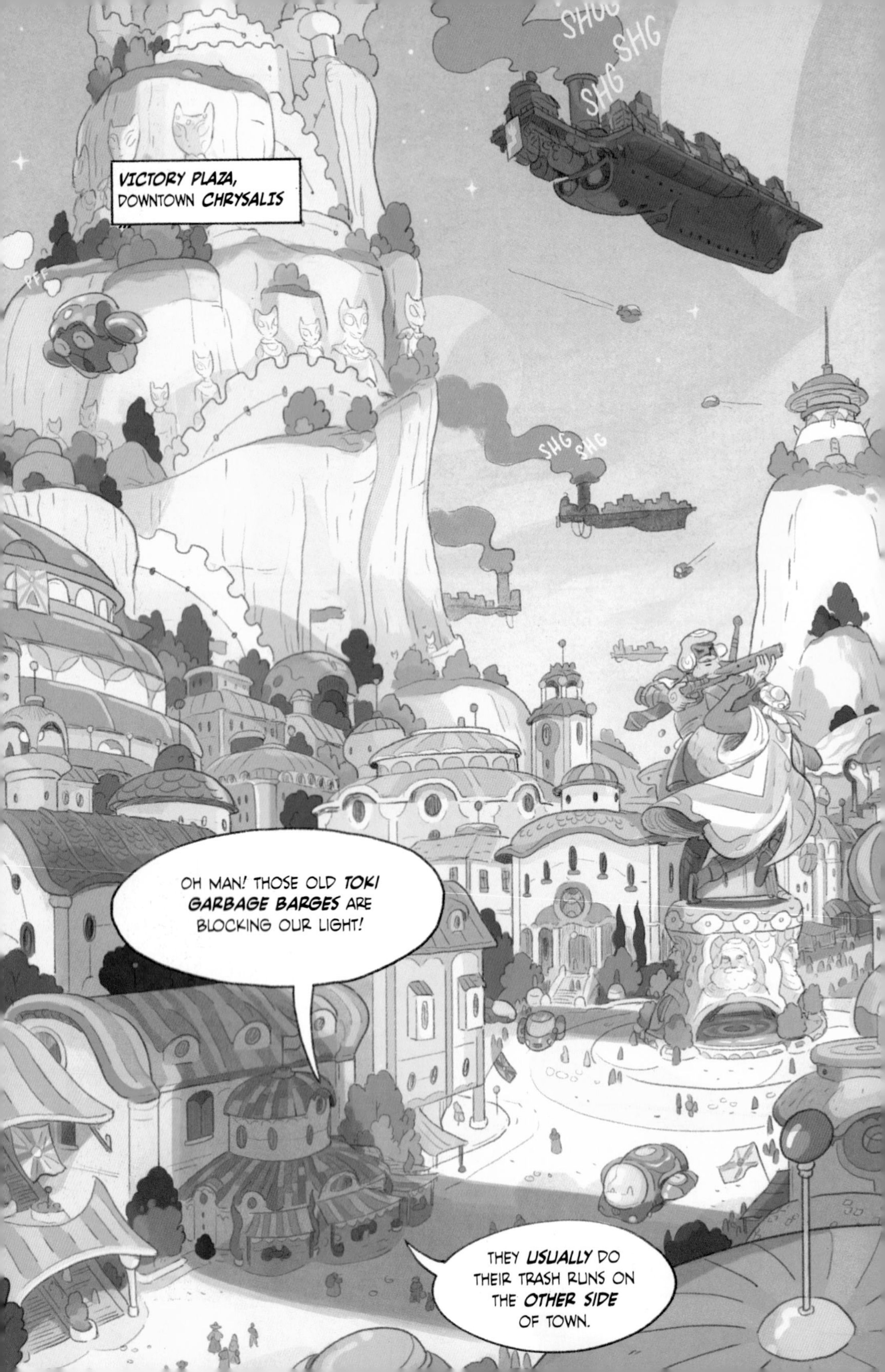
VICTORY PLAZA, DOWNTOWN CHRYSALIS
SHUG SHG SHG
SHG SHG
OH MAN! THOSE OLD TOKI GARBAGE BARGES ARE BLOCKING OUR LIGHT!
THEY USUALLY DO THEIR TRASH RUNS ON THE OTHER SIDE OF TOWN.

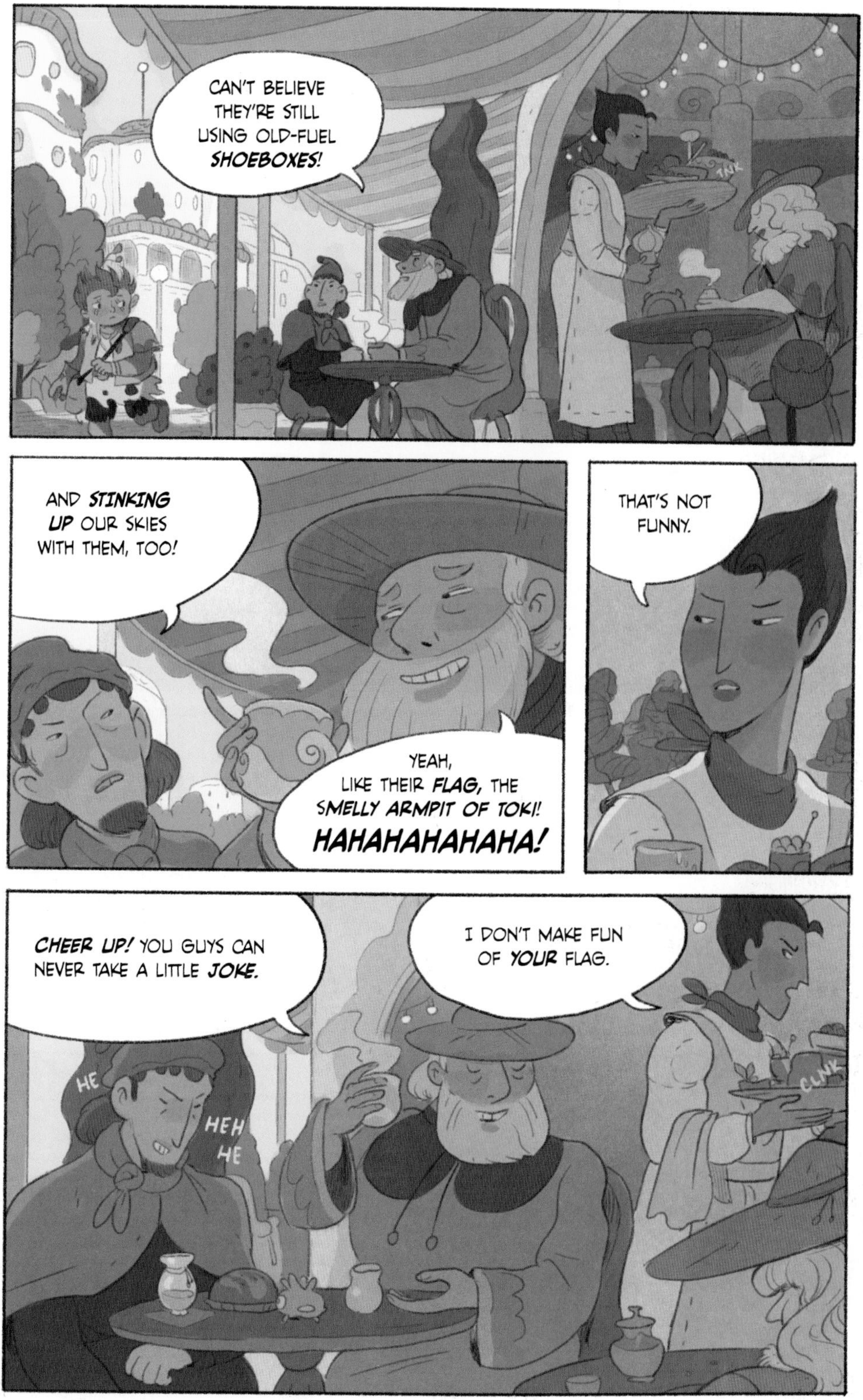
CAN'T BELIEVE THEY'RE STILL USING OLD-FUEL SHOEBOXES!
TNK
AND STINKING UP OUR SKIES WITH THEM, TOO!
YEAH, LIKE THEIR FLAG, THE SMELLY ARMPIT OF TOKI! HAHAHAHAHAHA!
THAT'S NOT FUNNY.
CHEER UP! YOU GUYS CAN NEVER TAKE A LITTLE JOKE.
HE
HEH
HE
I DON'T MAKE FUN OF YOUR FLAG.
CLNK

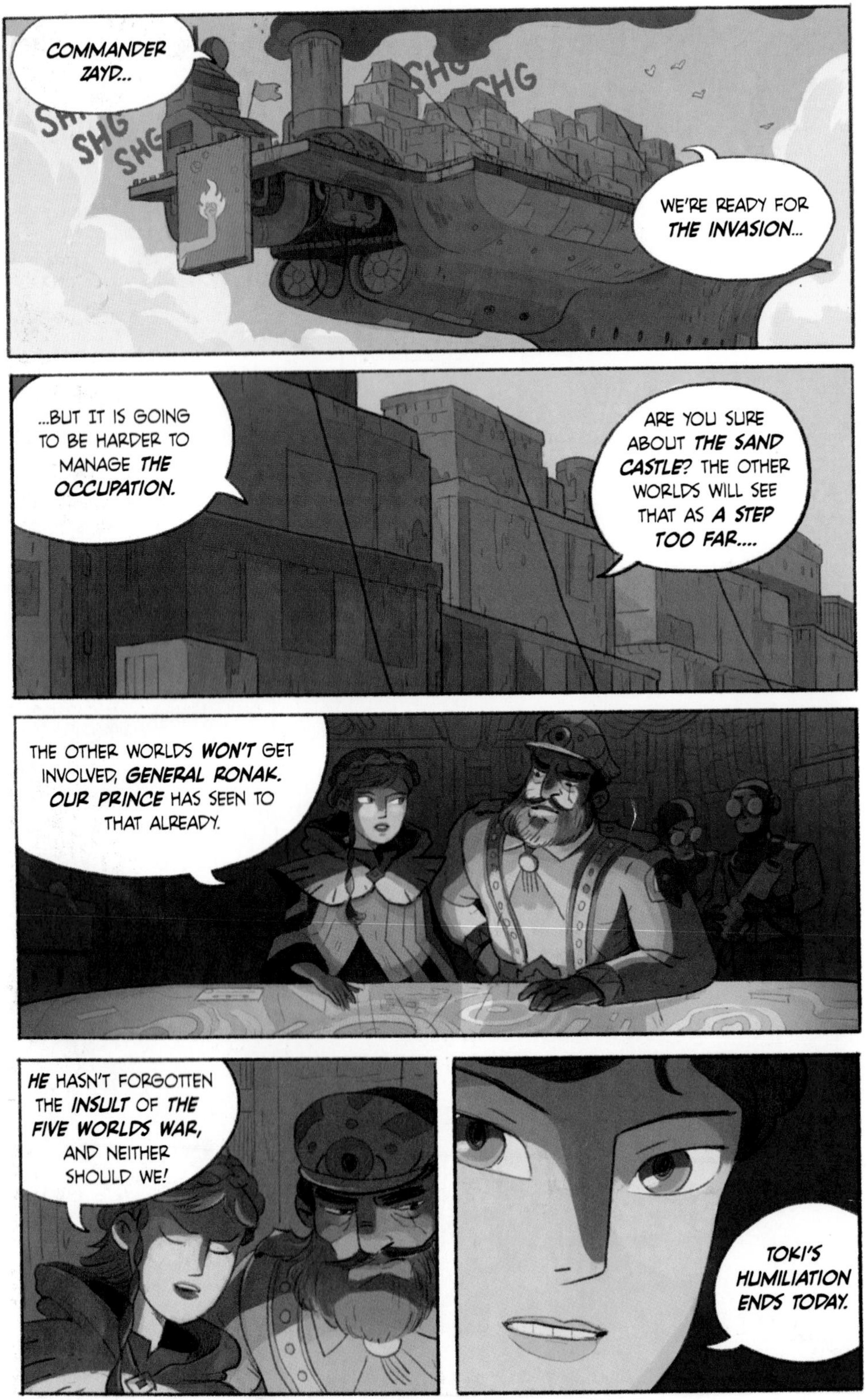
COMMANDER ZAYD...
SHG SHG SHG SHG SHG
WE'RE READY FOR THE INVASION...
...BUT IT IS GOING TO BE HARDER TO MANAGE THE OCCUPATION.
ARE YOU SURE ABOUT THE SAND CASTLE? THE OTHER WORLDS WILL SEE THAT AS A STEP TOO FAR....
THE OTHER WORLDS WON'T GET INVOLVED, GENERAL RONAK. OUR PRINCE HAS SEEN TO THAT ALREADY.
HE HASN'T FORGOTTEN THE INSULT OF THE FIVE WORLDS WAR, AND NEITHER SHOULD WE!
TOKI'S HUMILIATION ENDS TODAY.

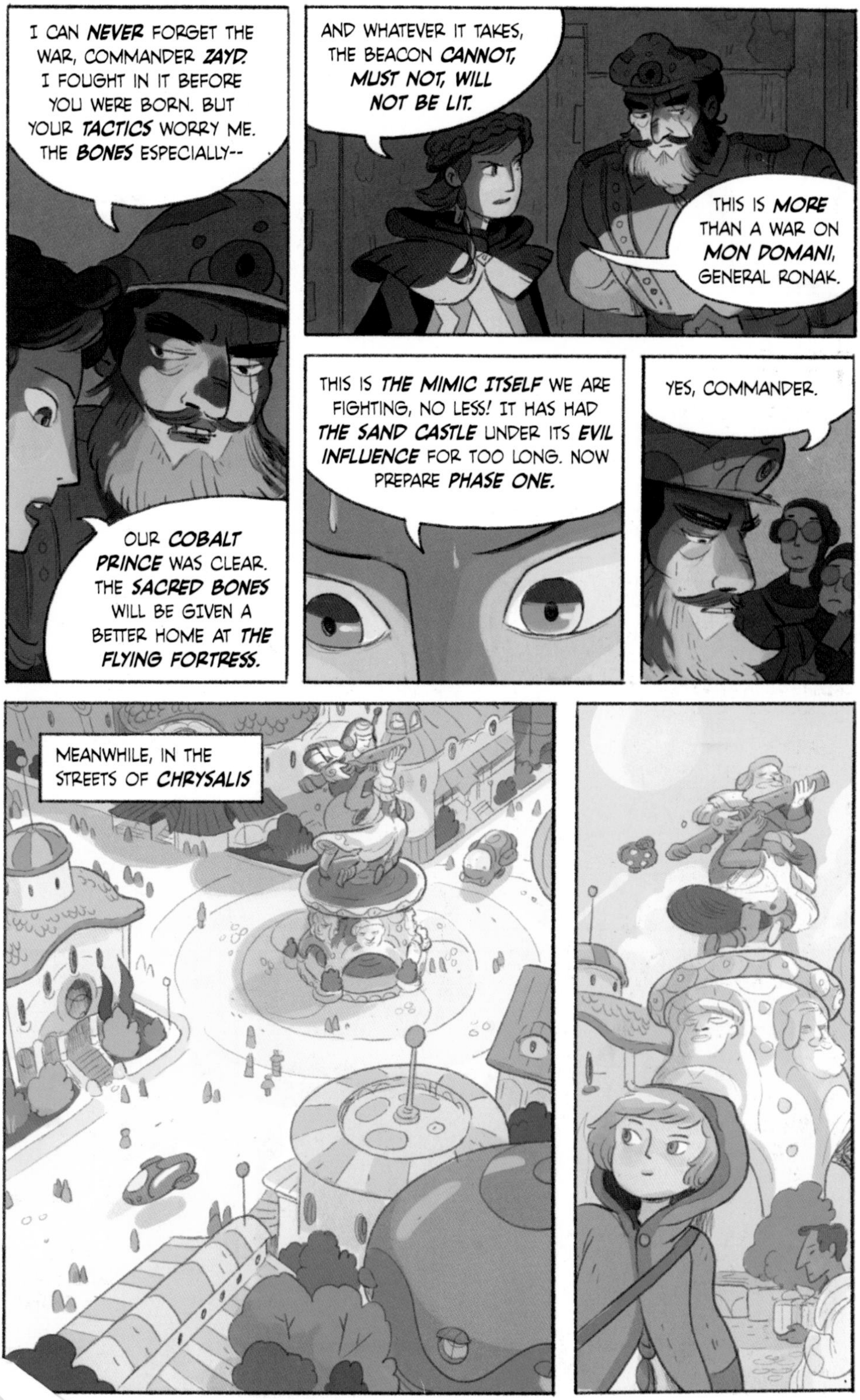
I CAN NEVER FORGET THE WAR, COMMANDER ZAYD. I FOUGHT IN IT BEFORE YOU WERE BORN. BUT YOUR TACTICS WORRY ME. THE BONES ESPECIALLY--
OUR COBALT PRINCE WAS CLEAR. THE SACRED BONES WILL BE GIVEN A BETTER HOME AT THE FLYING FORTRESS.
AND WHATEVER IT TAKES, THE BEACON CANNOT, MUST NOT, WILL NOT BE LIT.
THIS IS MORE THAN A WAR ON MON DOMANI, GENERAL RONAK.
THIS IS THE MIMIC ITSELF WE ARE FIGHTING, NO LESS! IT HAS HAD THE SAND CASTLE UNDER ITS EVIL INFLUENCE FOR TOO LONG. NOW PREPARE PHASE ONE.
YES, COMMANDER.
MEANWHILE, IN THE STREETS OF CHRYSALIS

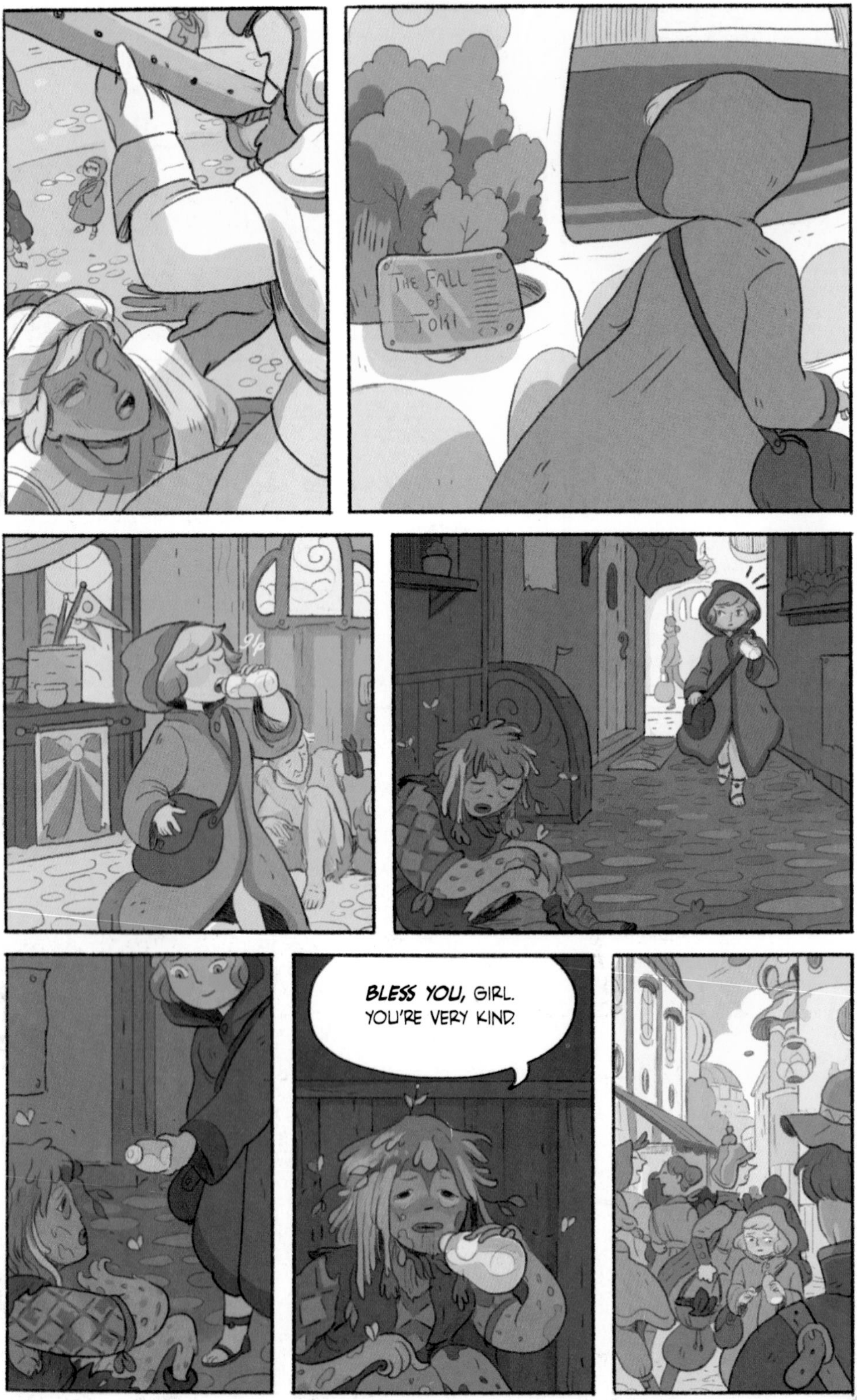
THE FALL of TOKI
glp
BLESS YOU, GIRL. YOU'RE VERY KIND.

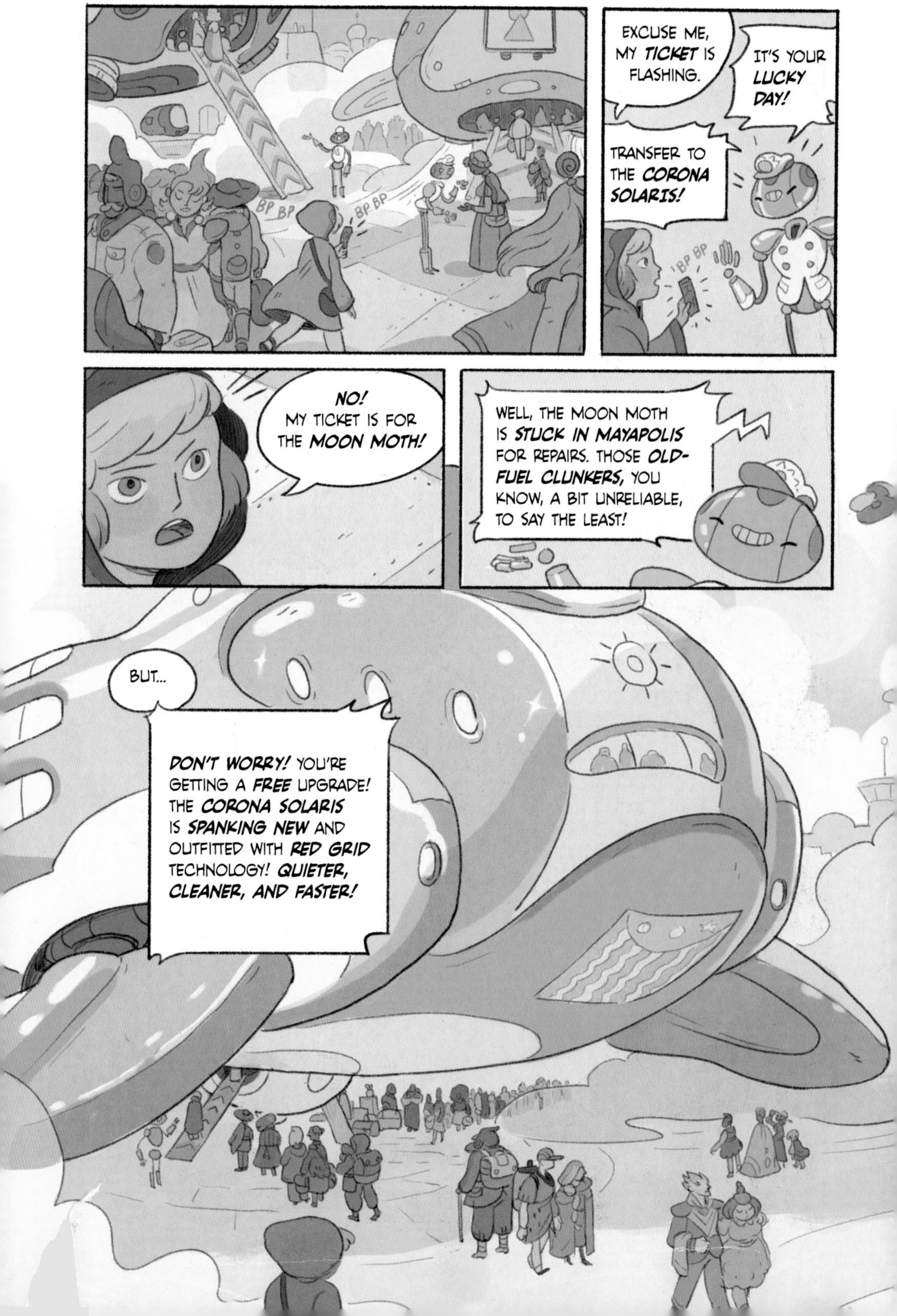

BP BP
BP BP
EXCUSE ME, MY TICKET IS FLASHING.
IT'S YOUR LUCKY DAY!
TRANSFER TO THE CORONA SOLARIS!
BP BP
NO! MY TICKET IS FOR THE MOON MOTH!
WELL, THE MOON MOTH IS STUCK IN MAYAPOLIS FOR REPAIRS. THOSE OLD-FUEL CLUNKERS, YOU KNOW, A BIT UNRELIABLE, TO SAY THE LEAST!
BUT...
DON'T WORRY! YOU'RE GETTING A FREE UPGRADE! THE CORONA SOLARIS IS SPANKING NEW AND OUTFITTED WITH RED GRID TECHNOLOGY! QUIETER, CLEANER, AND FASTER!

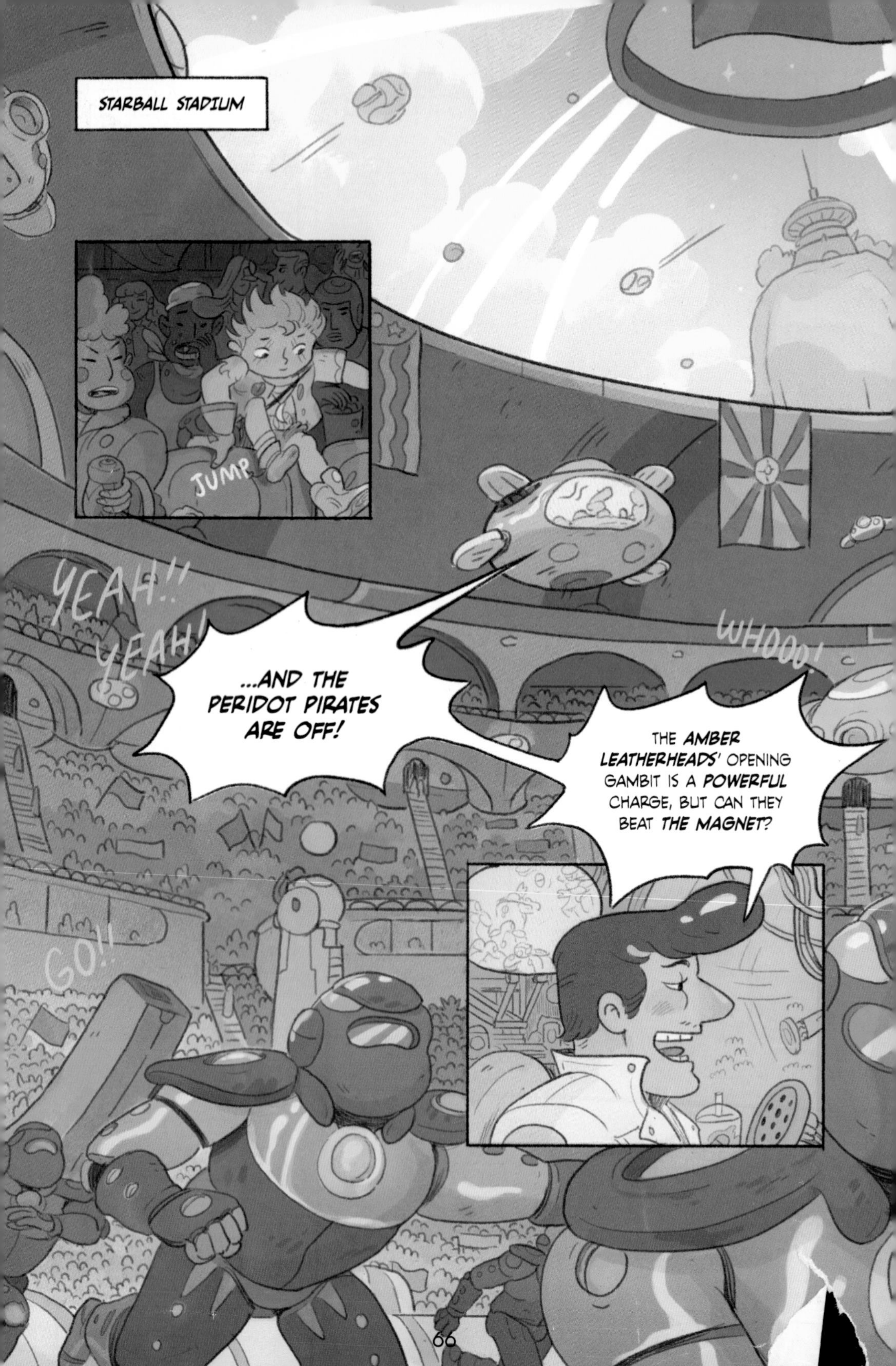
STARBALL STADIUM
JUMP
YEAH!! YEAH!
WHOOO!
...AND THE PERIDOT PIRATES ARE OFF!
THE AMBER LEATHERHEADS' OPENING GAMBIT IS A POWERFUL CHARGE, BUT CAN THEY BEAT THE MAGNET?
GO!!

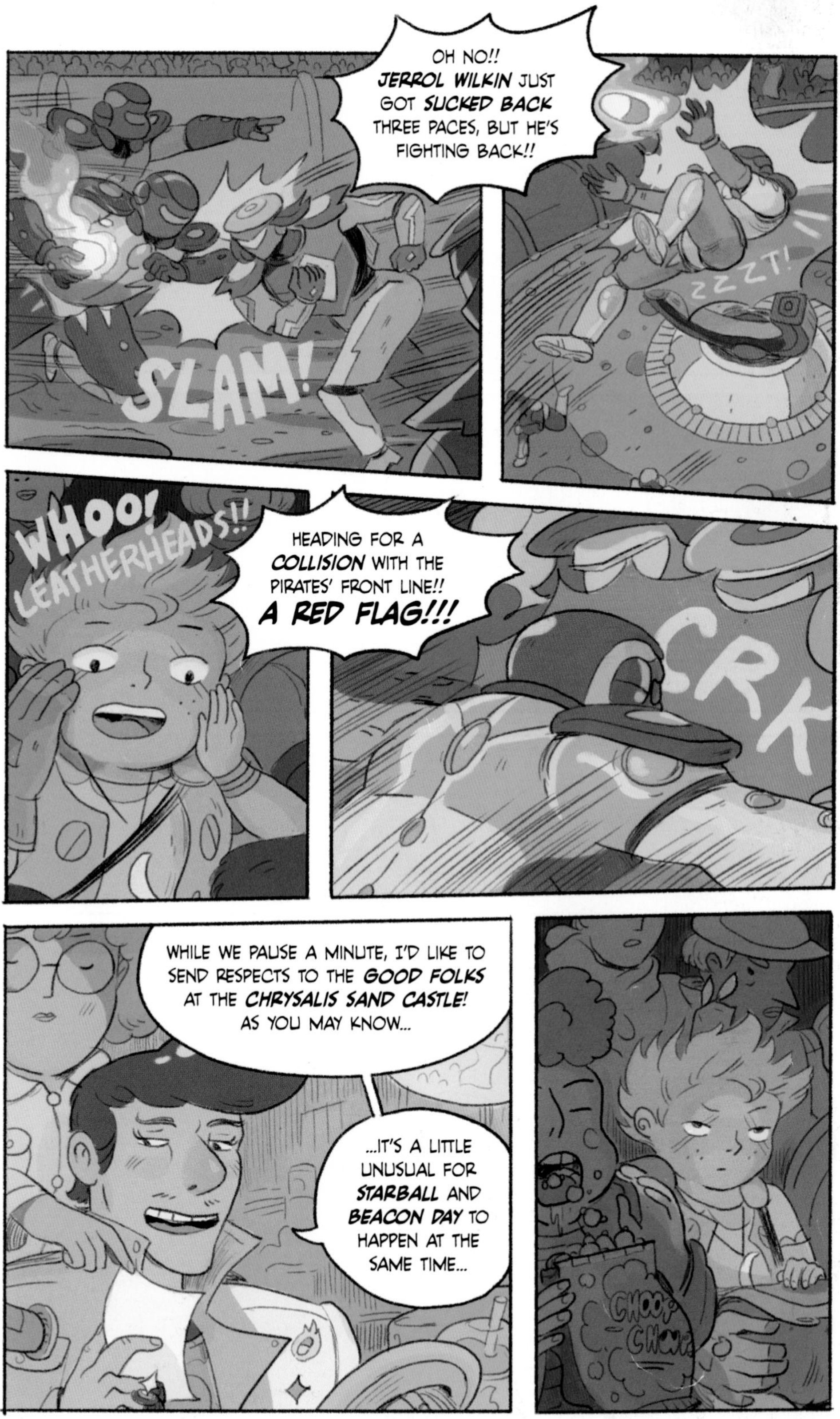
OH NO!! JERROL WILKIN JUST GOT SUCKED BACK THREE PACES, BUT HE'S FIGHTING BACK!!
SLAM!
ZZZT!
WHOO! LEATHERHEADS!!
HEADING FOR A COLLISION WITH THE PIRATES' FRONT LINE!! A RED FLAG!!!
CRK
WHILE WE PAUSE A MINUTE, I'D LIKE TO SEND RESPECTS TO THE GOOD FOLKS AT THE CHRYSALIS SAND CASTLE! AS YOU MAY KNOW...
...IT'S A LITTLE UNUSUAL FOR STARBALL AND BEACON DAY TO HAPPEN AT THE SAME TIME...

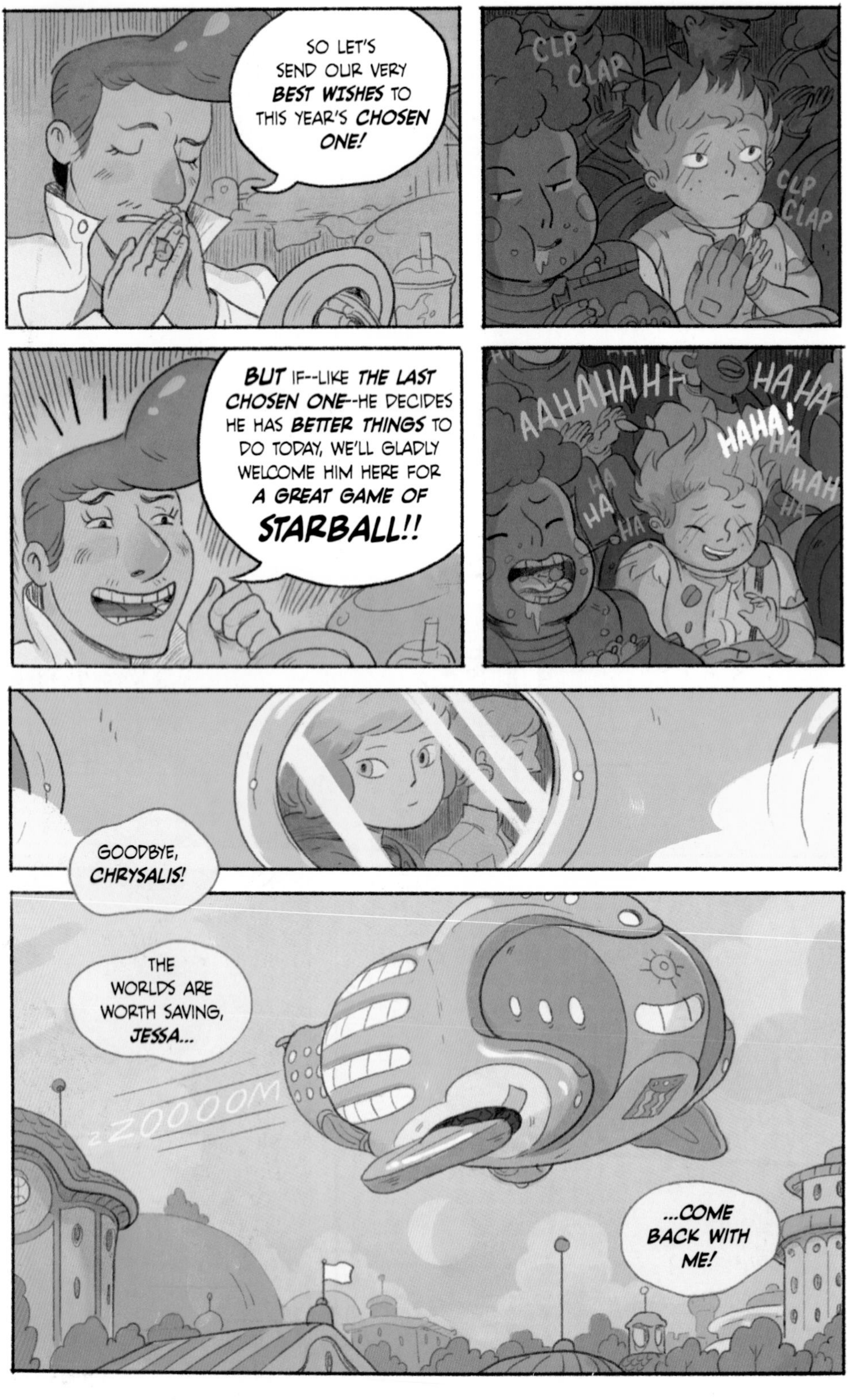
SO LET'S SEND OUR VERY **BEST WISHES** TO THIS YEAR'S **CHOSEN ONE!**
CLP CLAP
CLP CLAP
BUT IF--LIKE **THE LAST CHOSEN ONE**--HE DECIDES HE HAS **BETTER THINGS** TO DO TODAY, WE'LL GLADLY WELCOME HIM HERE FOR **A GREAT GAME OF STARBALL!!**
AAHAHAHH
HA HA
HAHA!
HA
HAH
HA HA
HA
GOODBYE, **CHRYSALIS!**
THE WORLDS ARE WORTH SAVING, **JESSA...**
zZOOOOM
...COME BACK WITH ME!

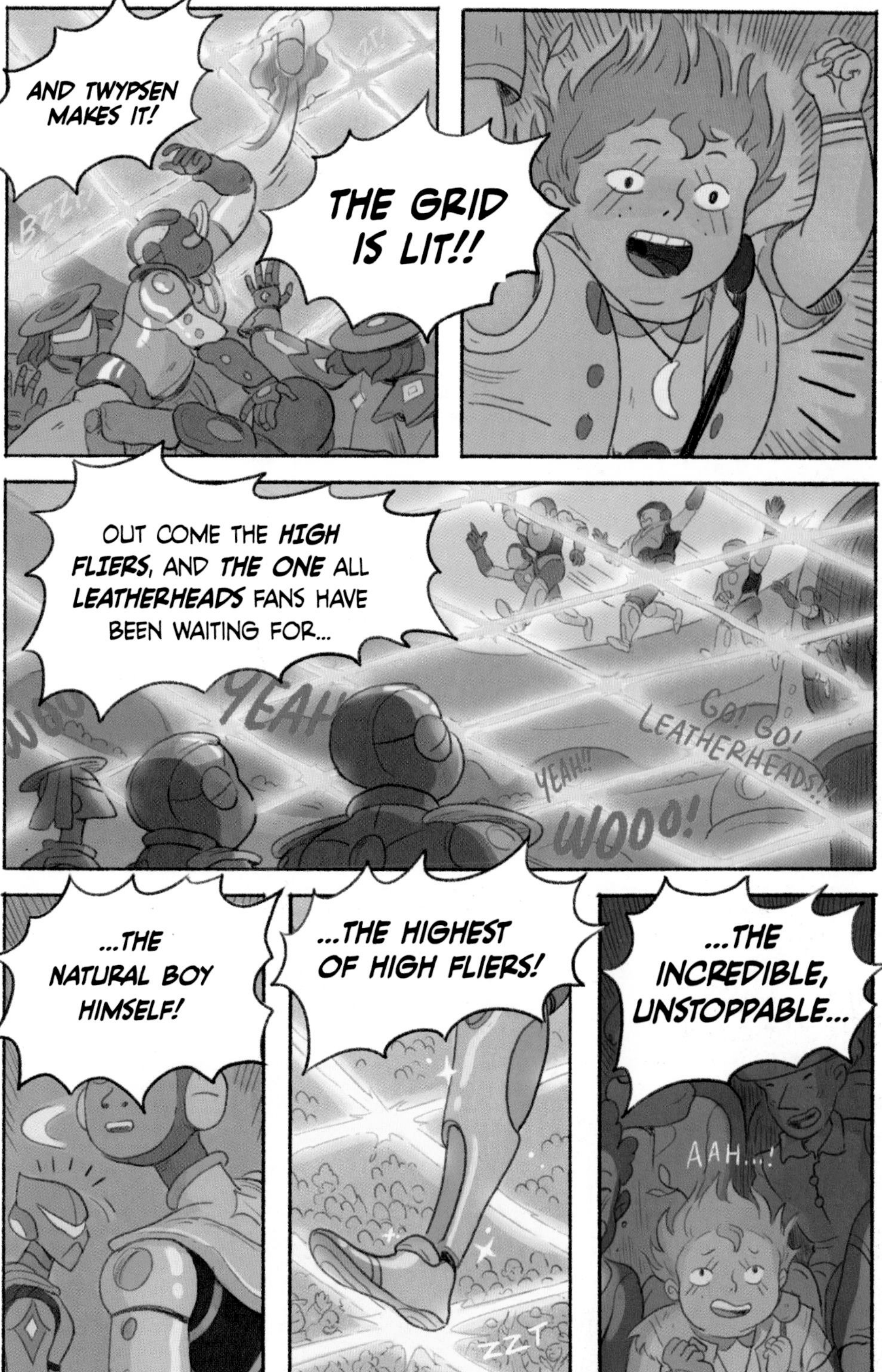
AND TWYPSEN MAKES IT!
THE GRID IS LIT!!
OUT COME THE HIGH FLIERS, AND THE ONE ALL LEATHERHEADS FANS HAVE BEEN WAITING FOR...
YEAH
GO! GO! LEATHERHEADS!!
YEAH!!
WOOO!
...THE NATURAL BOY HIMSELF!
...THE HIGHEST OF HIGH FLIERS!
ZZT
...THE INCREDIBLE, UNSTOPPABLE...
AAH...!

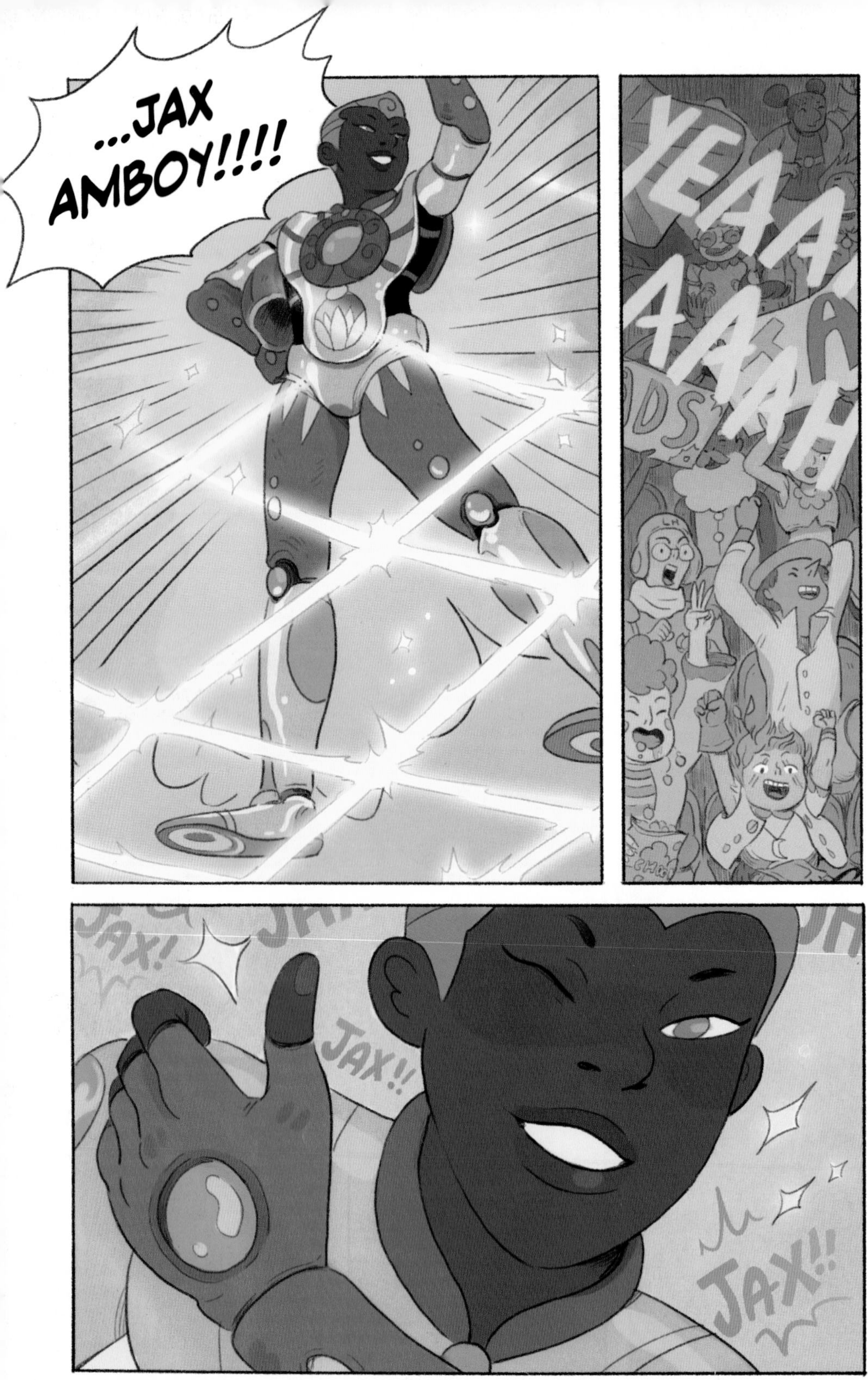

...JAX AMBOY!!!!
YEAAAAAAH
JAX!
JAX!!
JAX!!

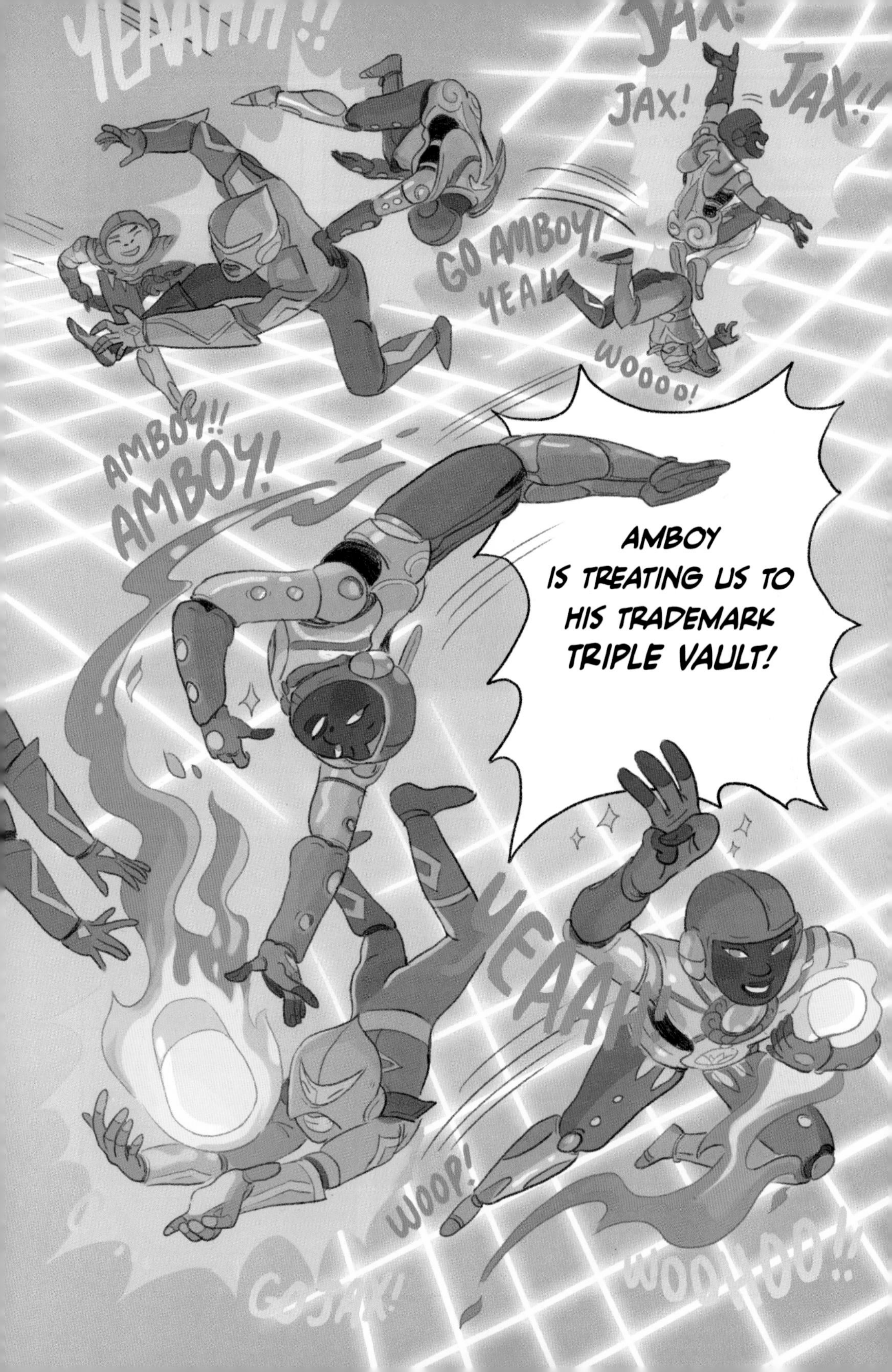
YEAAHH!!
JAX!
JAX!
JAX!!
GO AMBOY!
YEAH
WOOOO!
AMBOY!!
AMBOY!
AMBOY IS TREATING US TO HIS TRADEMARK TRIPLE VAULT!
YEAAH
WOOP!
GO JAX!
WOOHOO!!

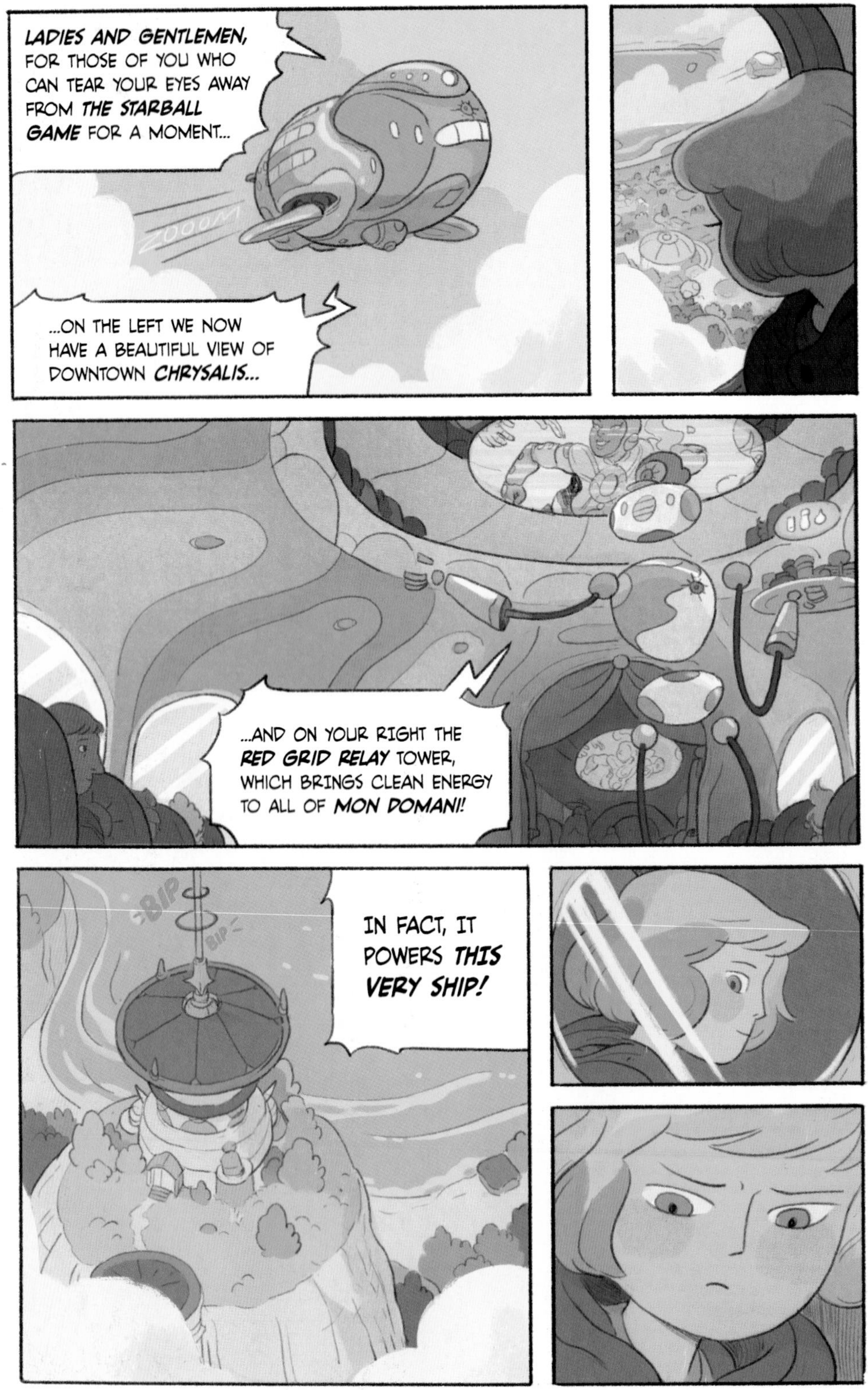
LADIES AND GENTLEMEN, FOR THOSE OF YOU WHO CAN TEAR YOUR EYES AWAY FROM THE STARBALL GAME FOR A MOMENT...
ZOOOM
...ON THE LEFT WE NOW HAVE A BEAUTIFUL VIEW OF DOWNTOWN CHRYSALIS...
...AND ON YOUR RIGHT THE RED GRID RELAY TOWER, WHICH BRINGS CLEAN ENERGY TO ALL OF MON DOMANI!
BIP
BIP
IN FACT, IT POWERS THIS VERY SHIP!

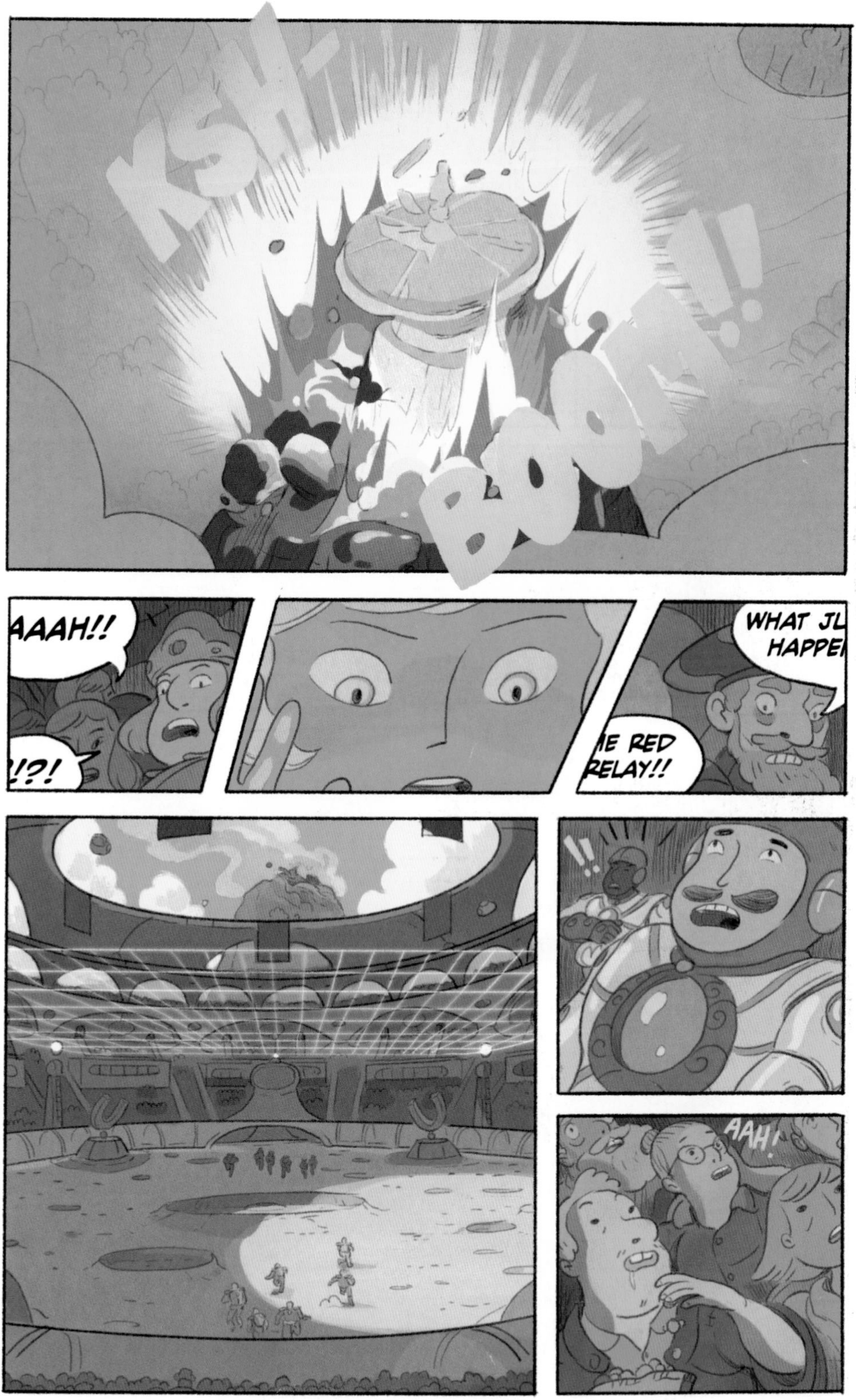
KSH-
BOOM!!
AAAH!!
!?!
WHAT JU
HAPPEN
HE RED
RELAY!!
!!
AAH!

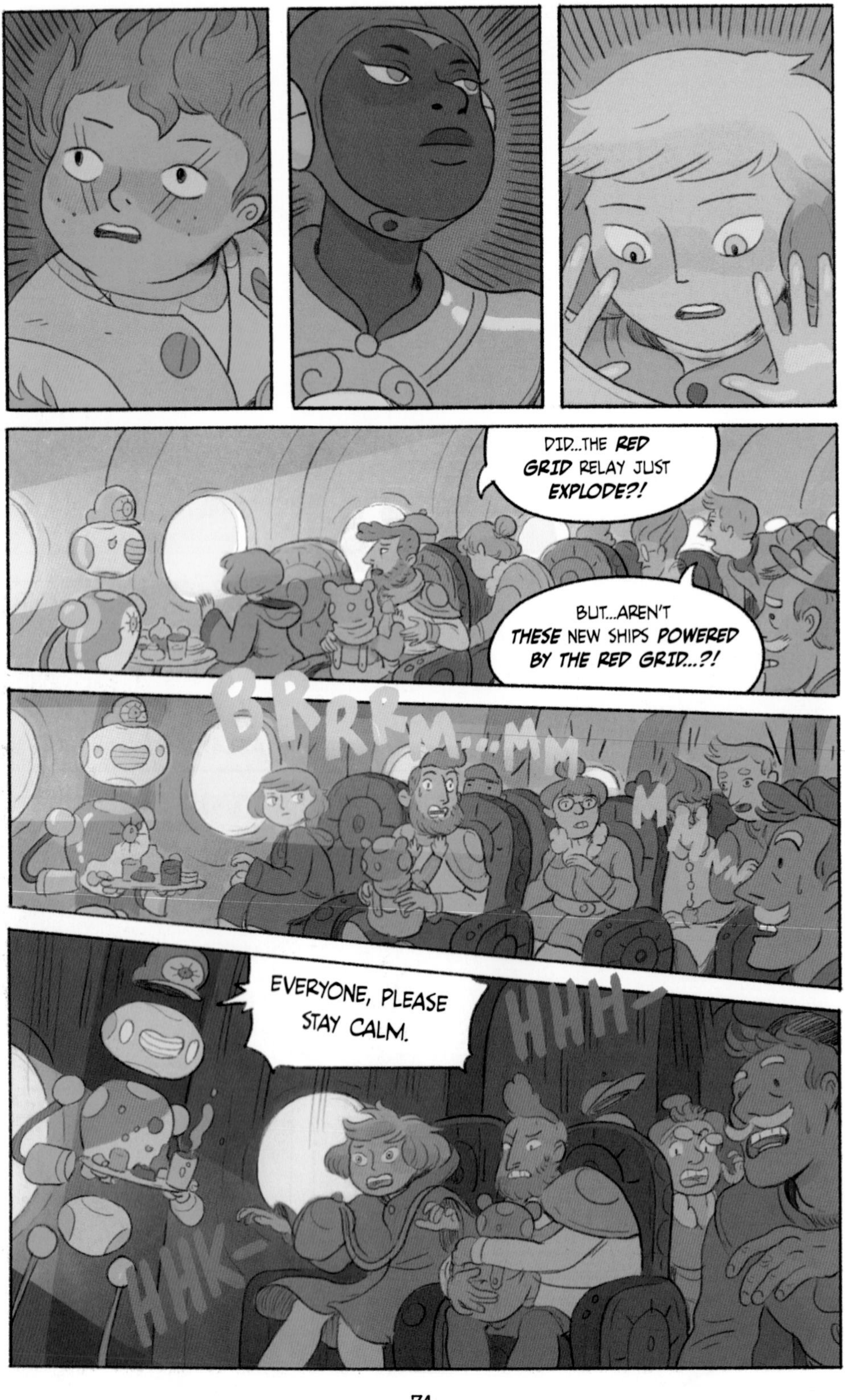
DID...THE RED GRID RELAY JUST EXPLODE?!
BUT...AREN'T THESE NEW SHIPS POWERED BY THE RED GRID...?!
BRRRM...MM
EVERYONE, PLEASE STAY CALM.
HHH-
HHK-

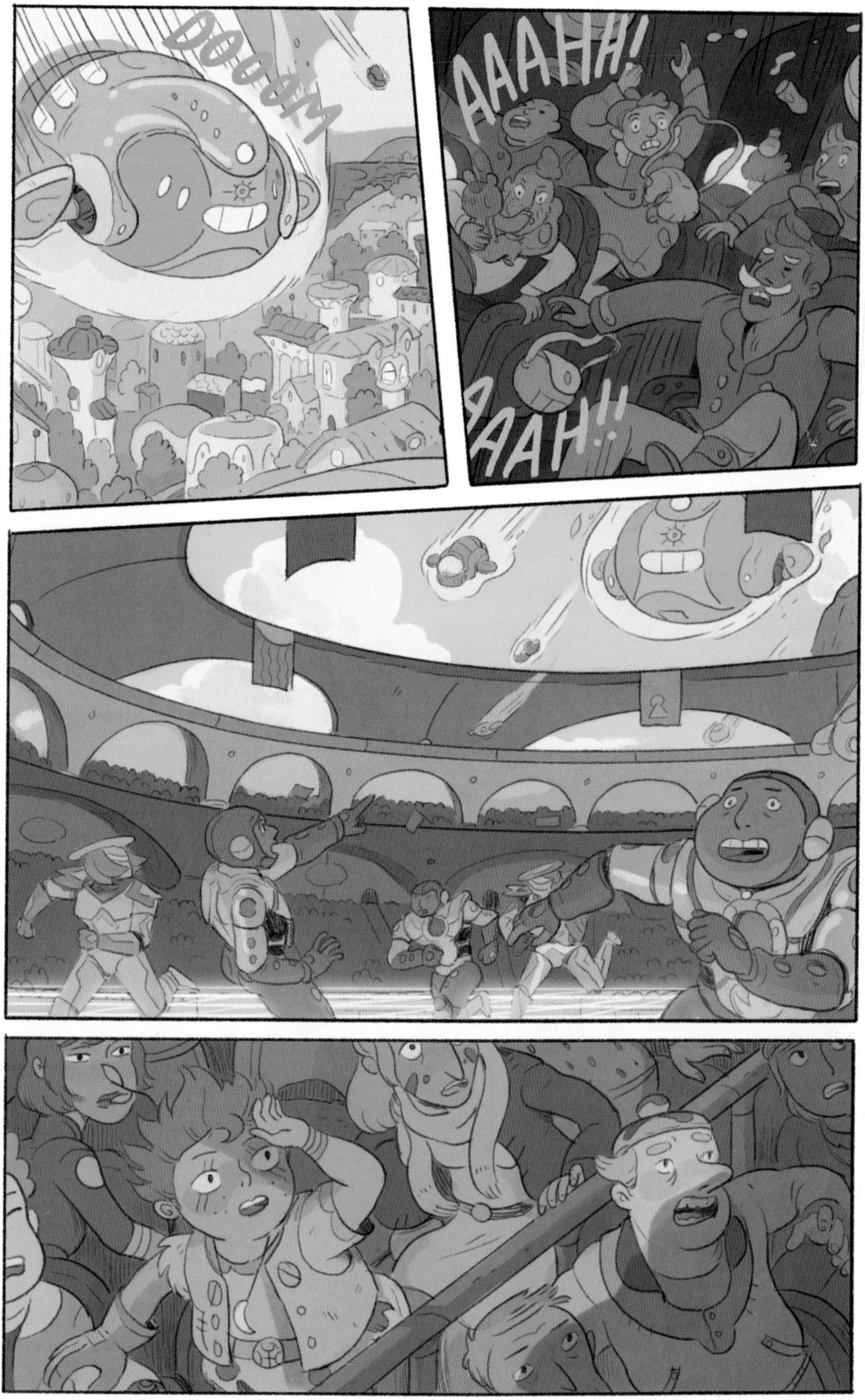
DOOOOM
AAAHH!
AAAH!!

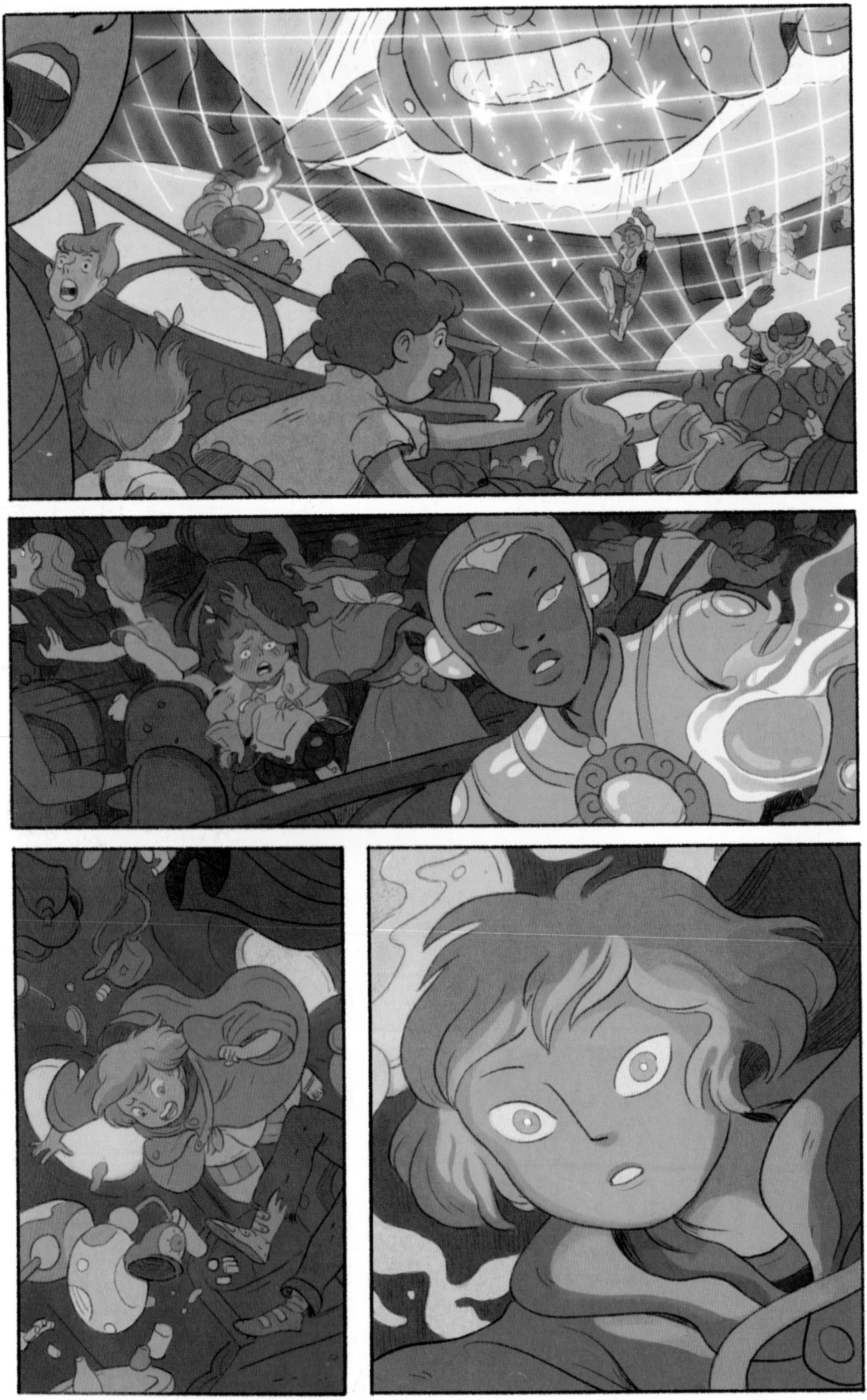

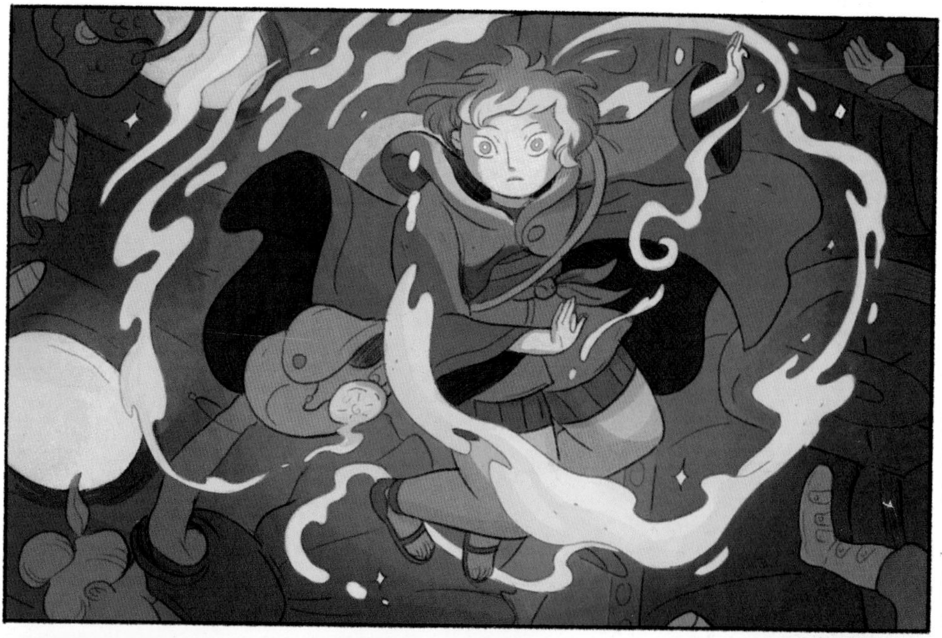

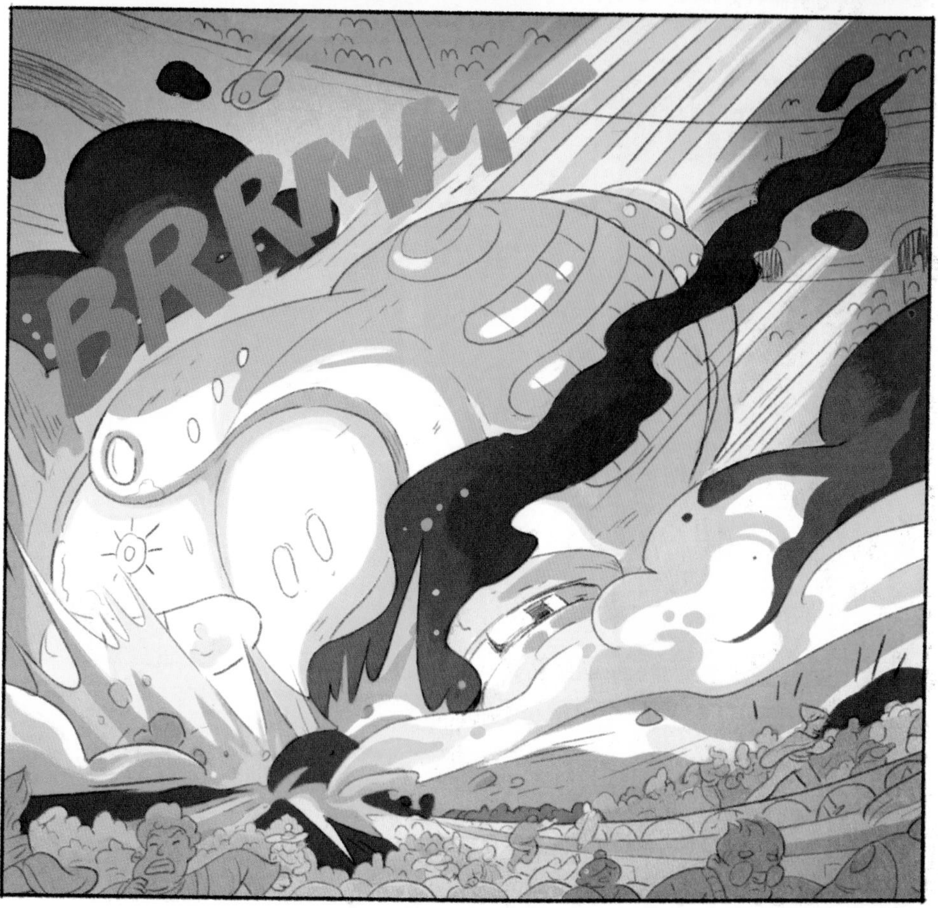
BRRMM–

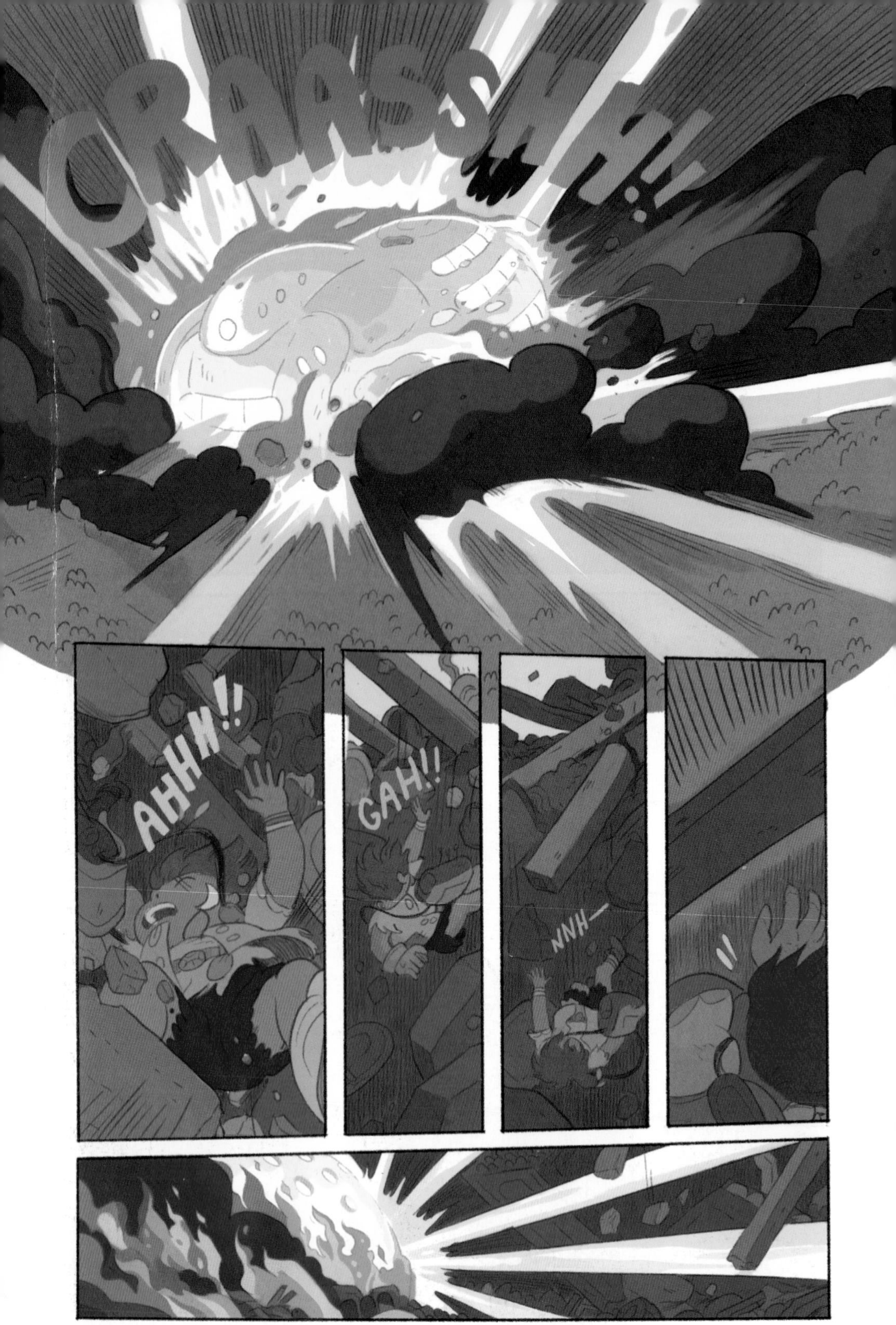
CRAASHH!!
AHHH!!
GAH!!
NNH—
!!

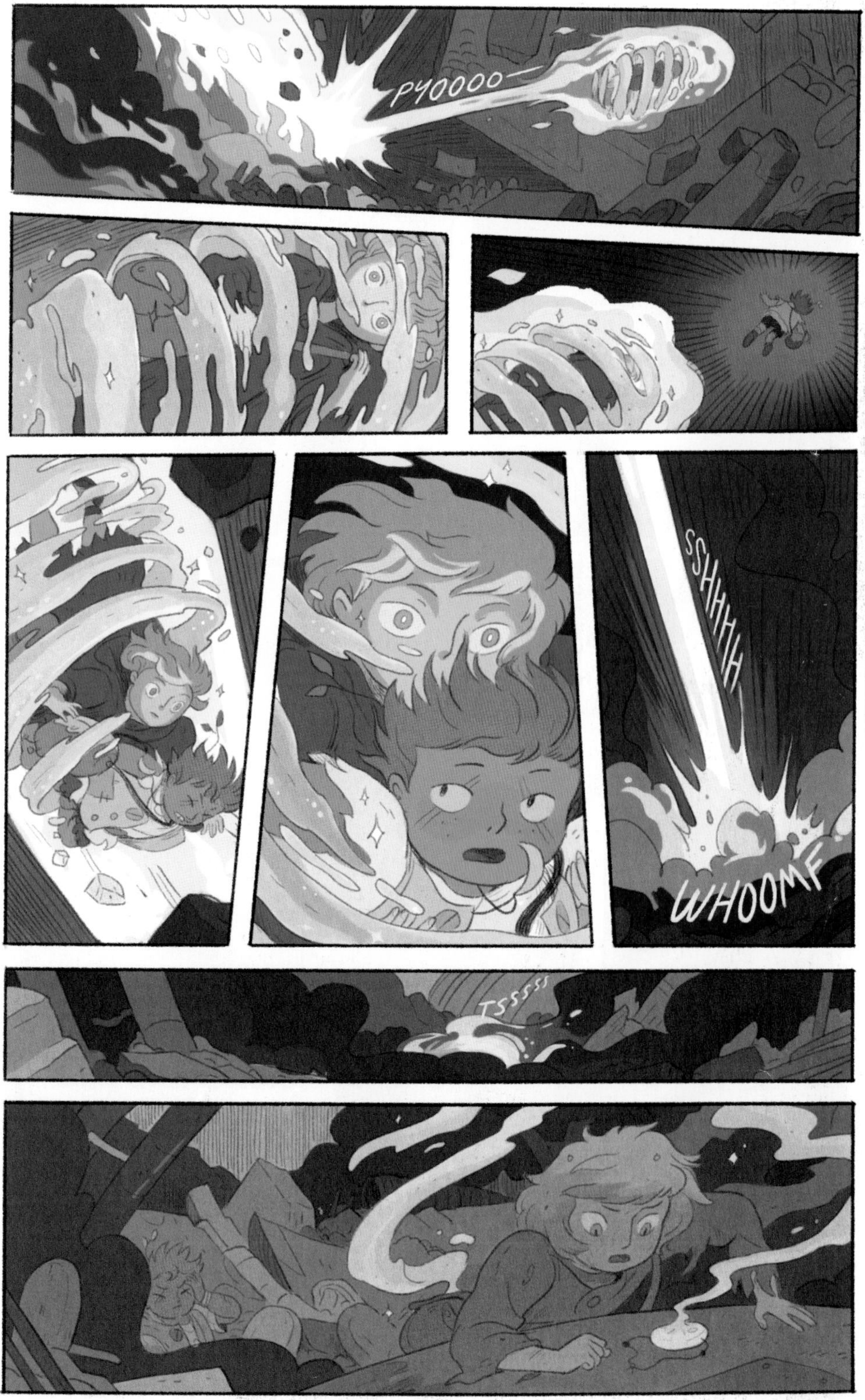
PYOOOO—
SSHHHHH
WHOOMF
TSSSSS

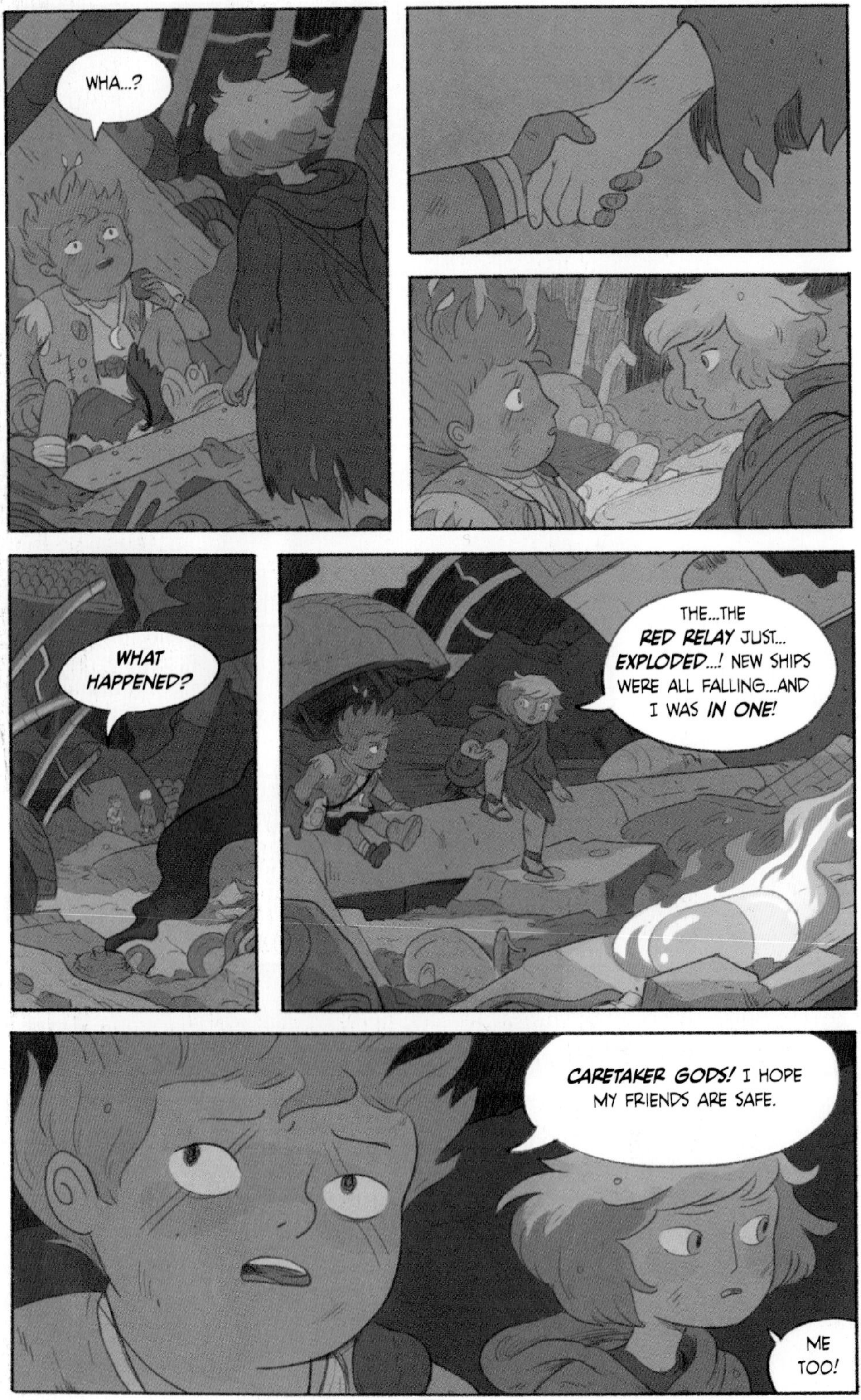
WHA...?
WHAT HAPPENED?
THE...THE RED RELAY JUST... EXPLODED...! NEW SHIPS WERE ALL FALLING...AND I WAS IN ONE!
CARETAKER GODS! I HOPE MY FRIENDS ARE SAFE.
ME TOO!

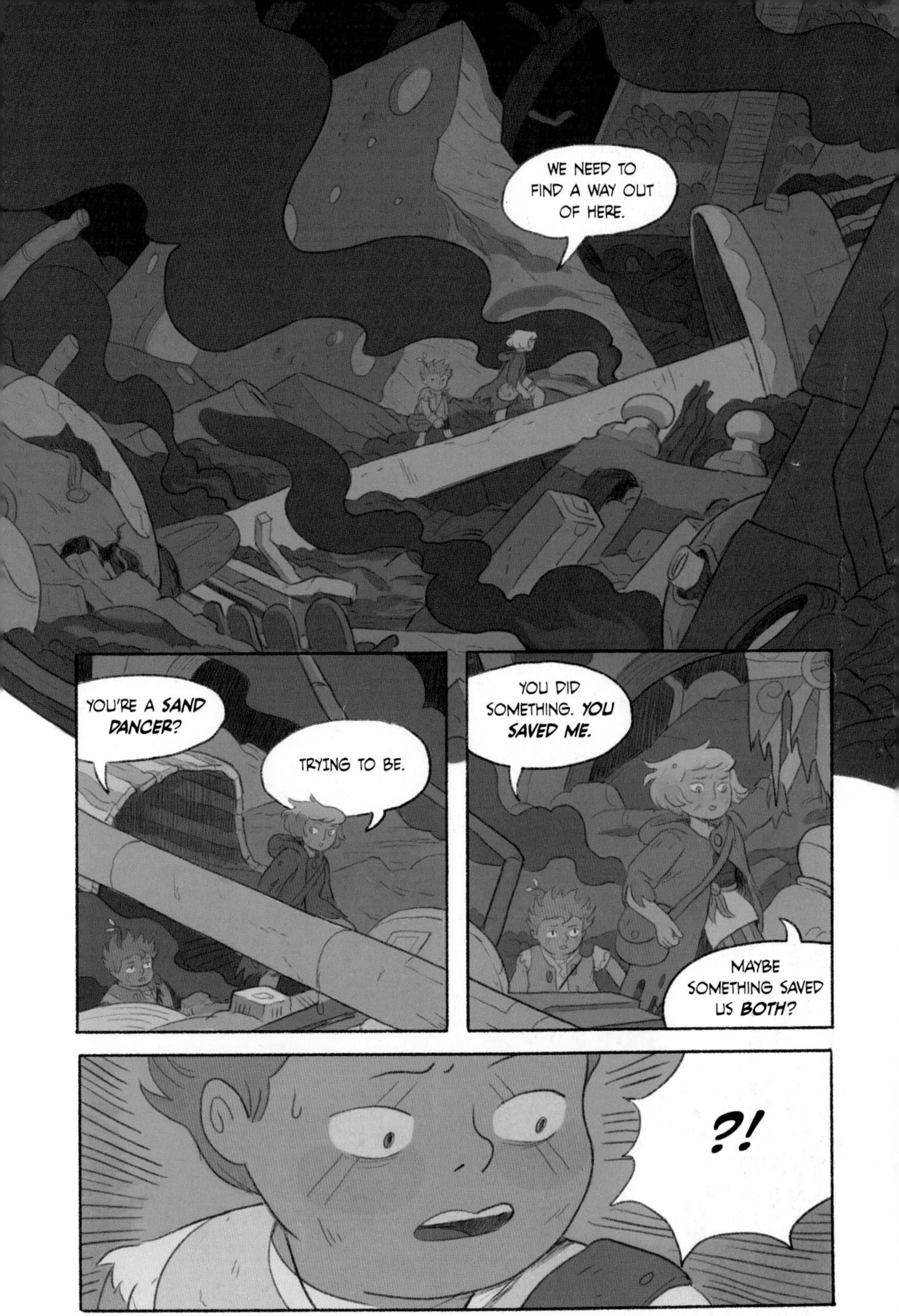
WE NEED TO FIND A WAY OUT OF HERE.
YOU'RE A SAND DANCER?
TRYING TO BE.
YOU DID SOMETHING. YOU SAVED ME.
MAYBE SOMETHING SAVED US BOTH?
?!

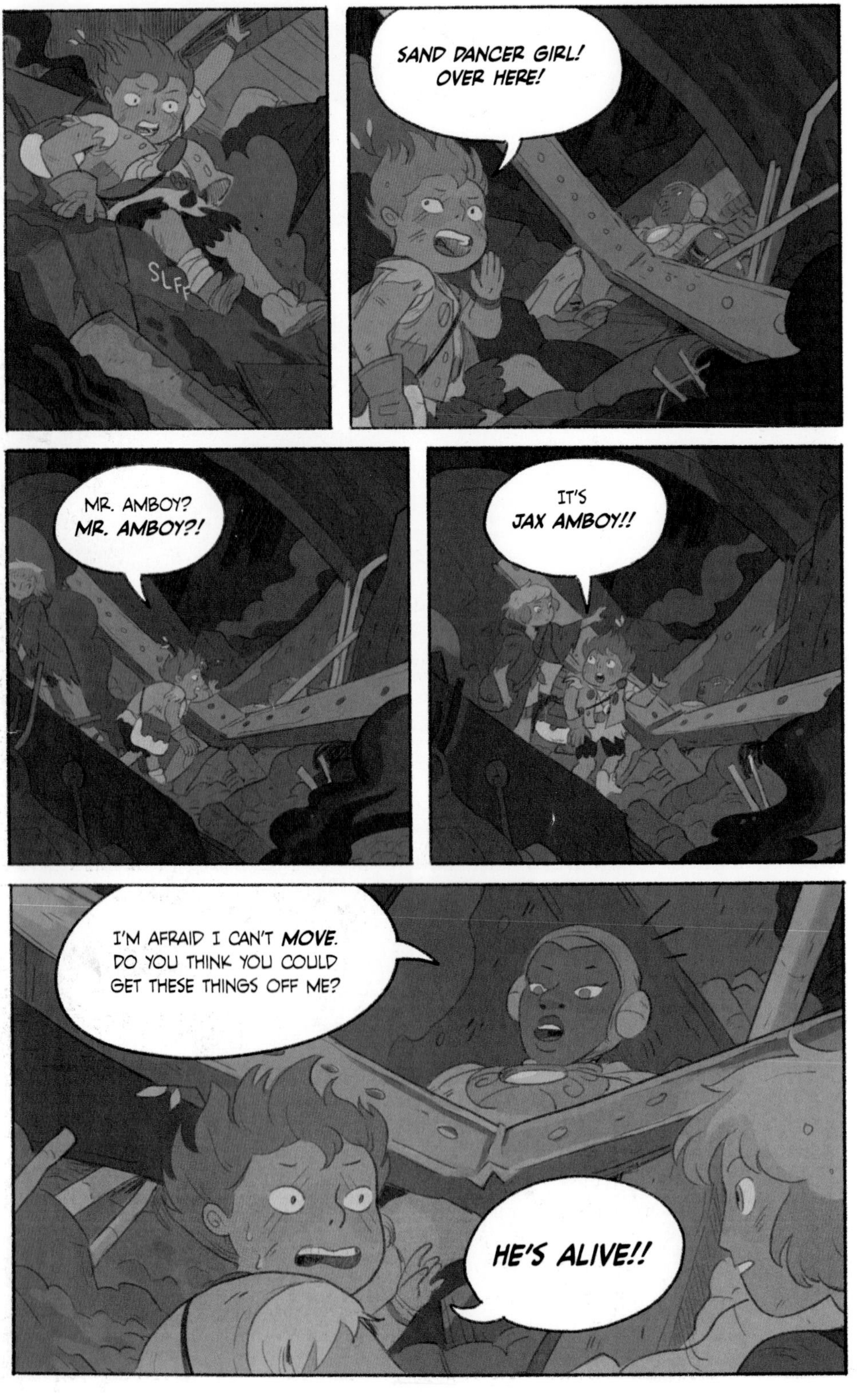
SLFF
SAND DANCER GIRL! OVER HERE!
MR. AMBOY? MR. AMBOY?!
IT'S JAX AMBOY!!
I'M AFRAID I CAN'T MOVE. DO YOU THINK YOU COULD GET THESE THINGS OFF ME?
HE'S ALIVE!!

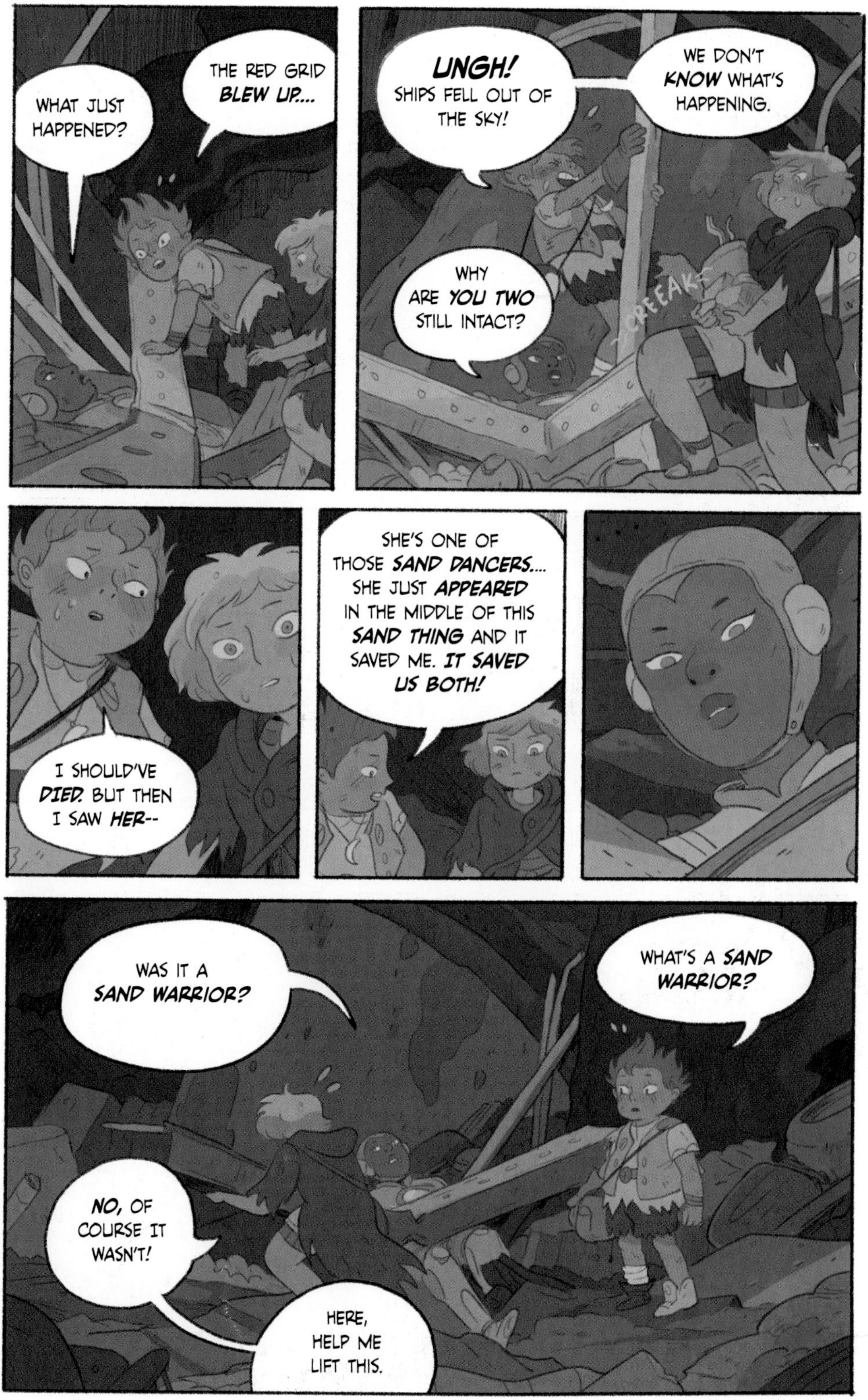
WHAT JUST HAPPENED?
THE RED GRID BLEW UP....
UNGH! SHIPS FELL OUT OF THE SKY!
WE DON'T KNOW WHAT'S HAPPENING.
CREEAK
WHY ARE YOU TWO STILL INTACT?
I SHOULD'VE DIED. BUT THEN I SAW HER--
SHE'S ONE OF THOSE SAND DANCERS.... SHE JUST APPEARED IN THE MIDDLE OF THIS SAND THING AND IT SAVED ME. IT SAVED US BOTH!
WAS IT A SAND WARRIOR?
WHAT'S A SAND WARRIOR?
NO, OF COURSE IT WASN'T!
HERE, HELP ME LIFT THIS.

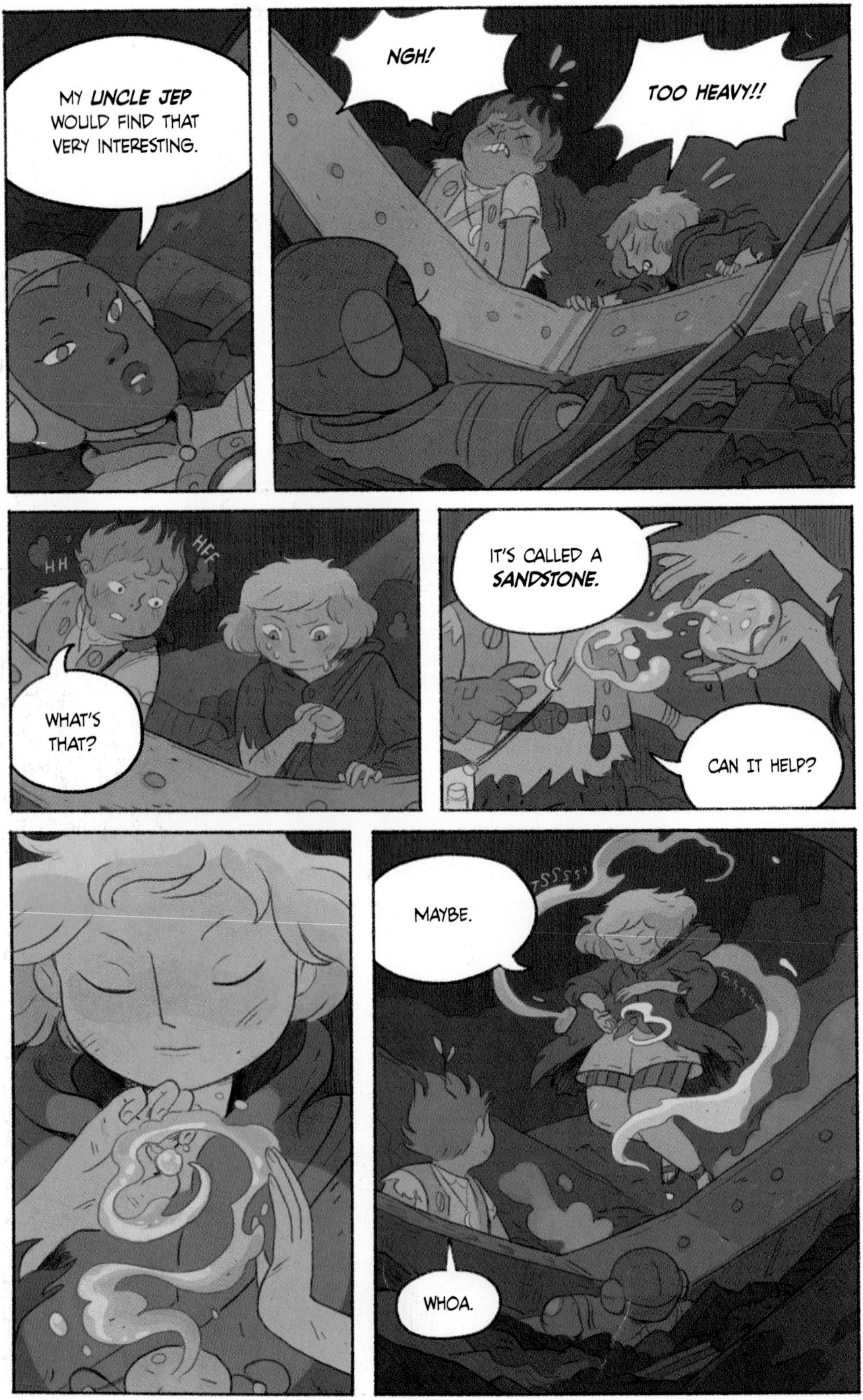
MY UNCLE JEP WOULD FIND THAT VERY INTERESTING.
NGH!
TOO HEAVY!!
HH
HFF
WHAT'S THAT?
IT'S CALLED A SANDSTONE.
CAN IT HELP?
MAYBE.
WHOA.

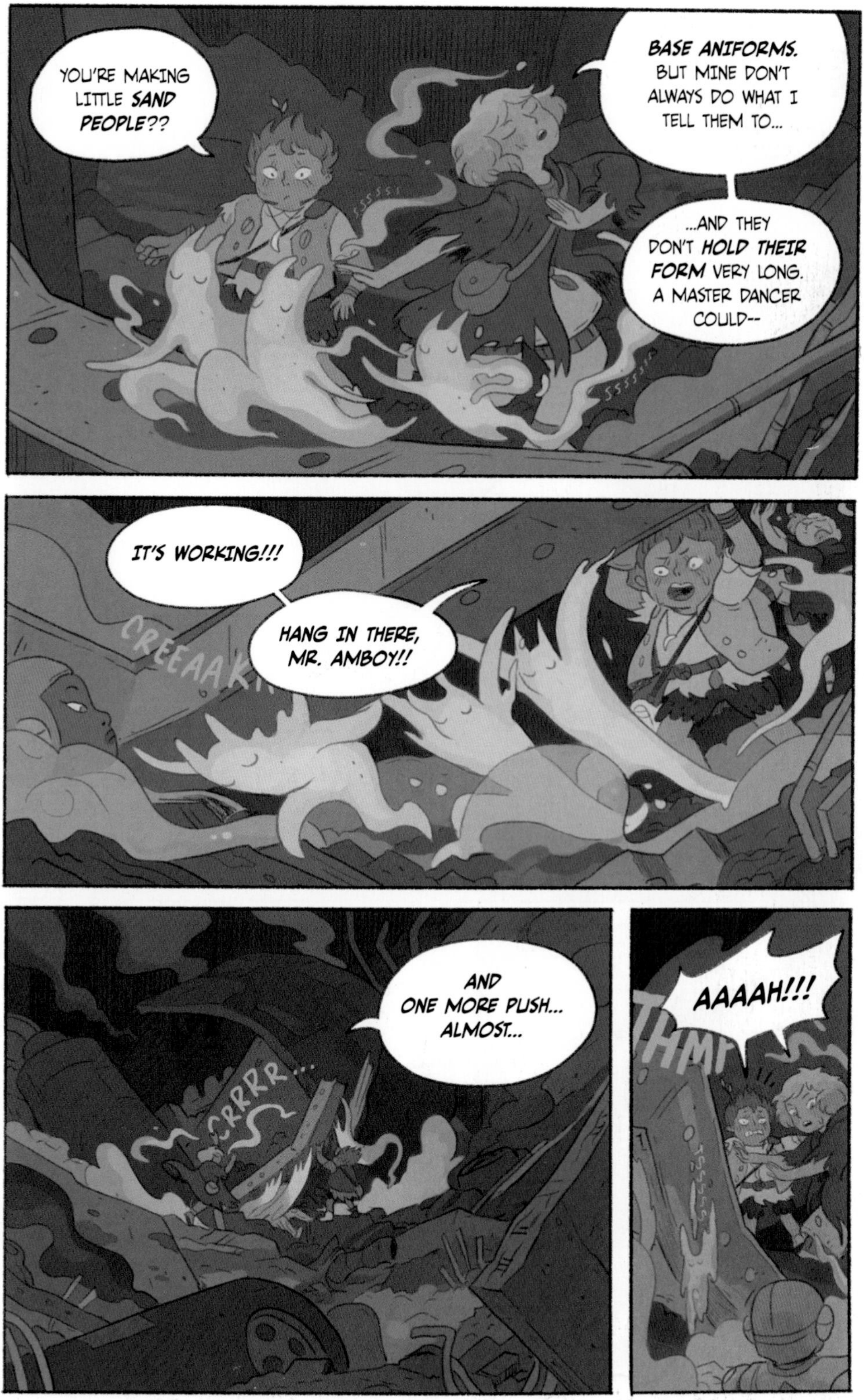
YOU'RE MAKING LITTLE SAND PEOPLE??
BASE ANIFORMS. BUT MINE DON'T ALWAYS DO WHAT I TELL THEM TO...
...AND THEY DON'T HOLD THEIR FORM VERY LONG. A MASTER DANCER COULD--
IT'S WORKING!!!
HANG IN THERE, MR. AMBOY!!
CREEAAK
AND ONE MORE PUSH... ALMOST...
CRRRR...
AAAAH!!!
THMP

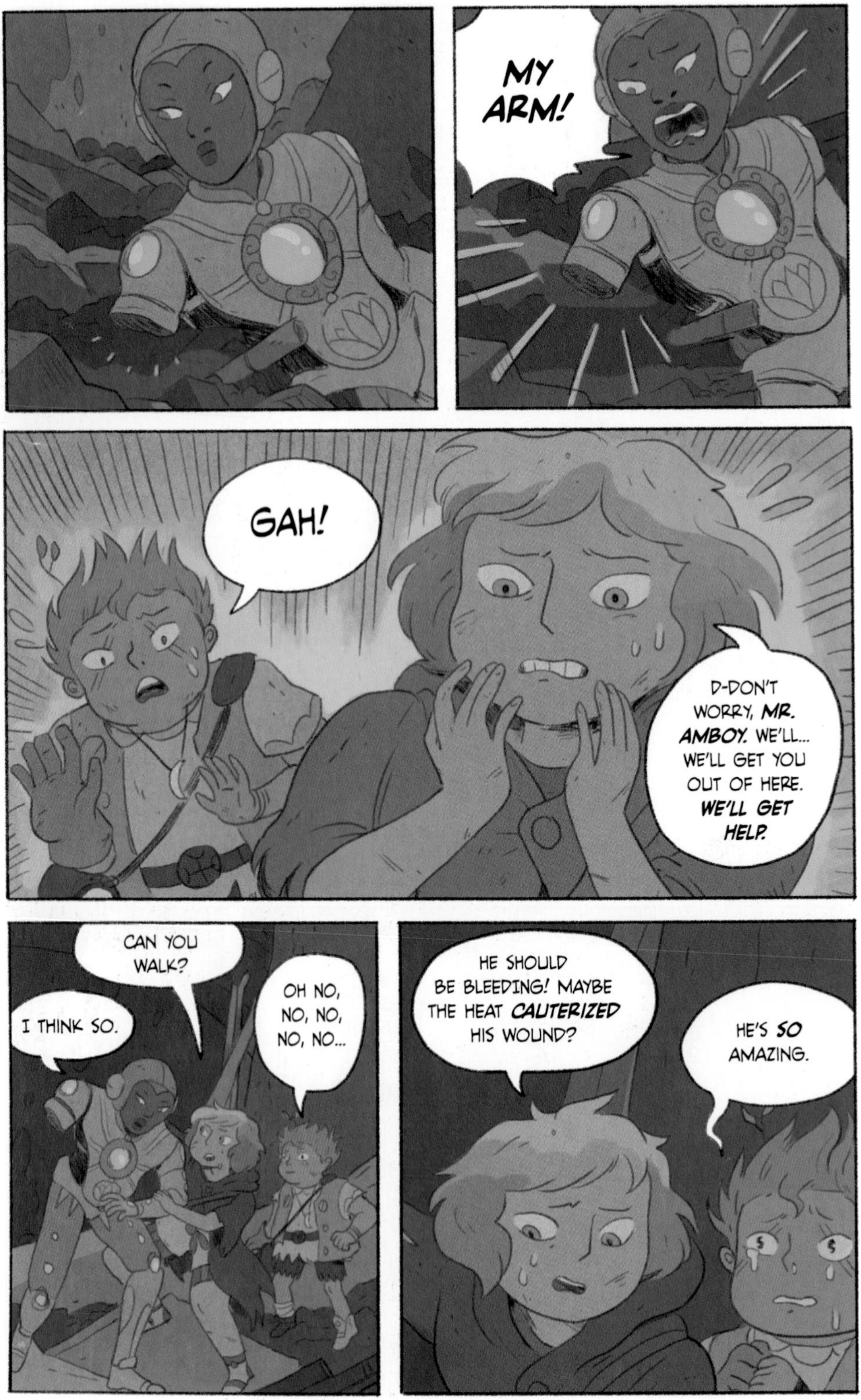
MY ARM!
GAH!
D-DON'T WORRY, MR. AMBOY. WE'LL... WE'LL GET YOU OUT OF HERE. WE'LL GET HELP.
CAN YOU WALK?
I THINK SO.
OH NO, NO, NO, NO, NO...
HE SHOULD BE BLEEDING! MAYBE THE HEAT CAUTERIZED HIS WOUND?
HE'S SO AMAZING.

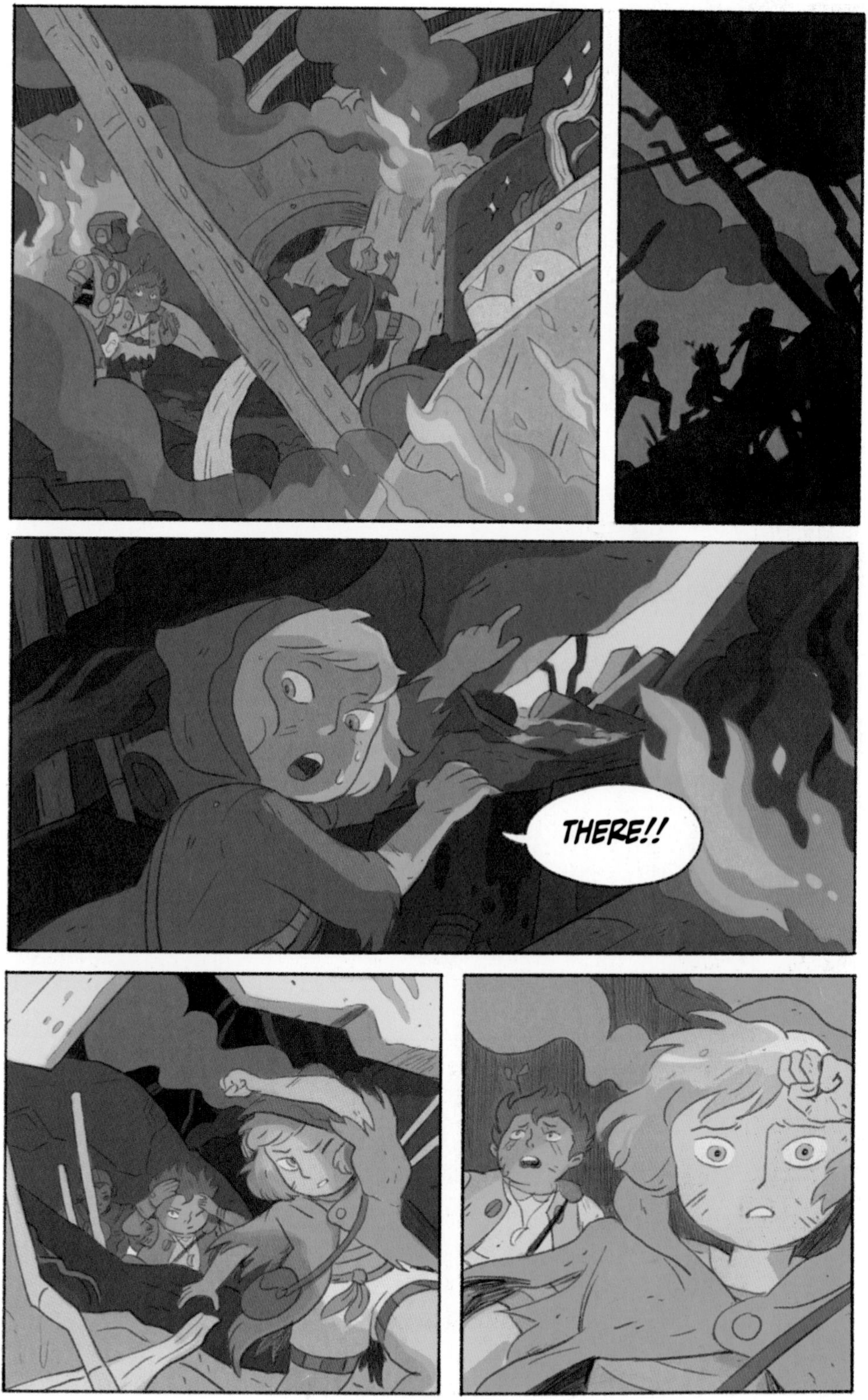
THERE!!

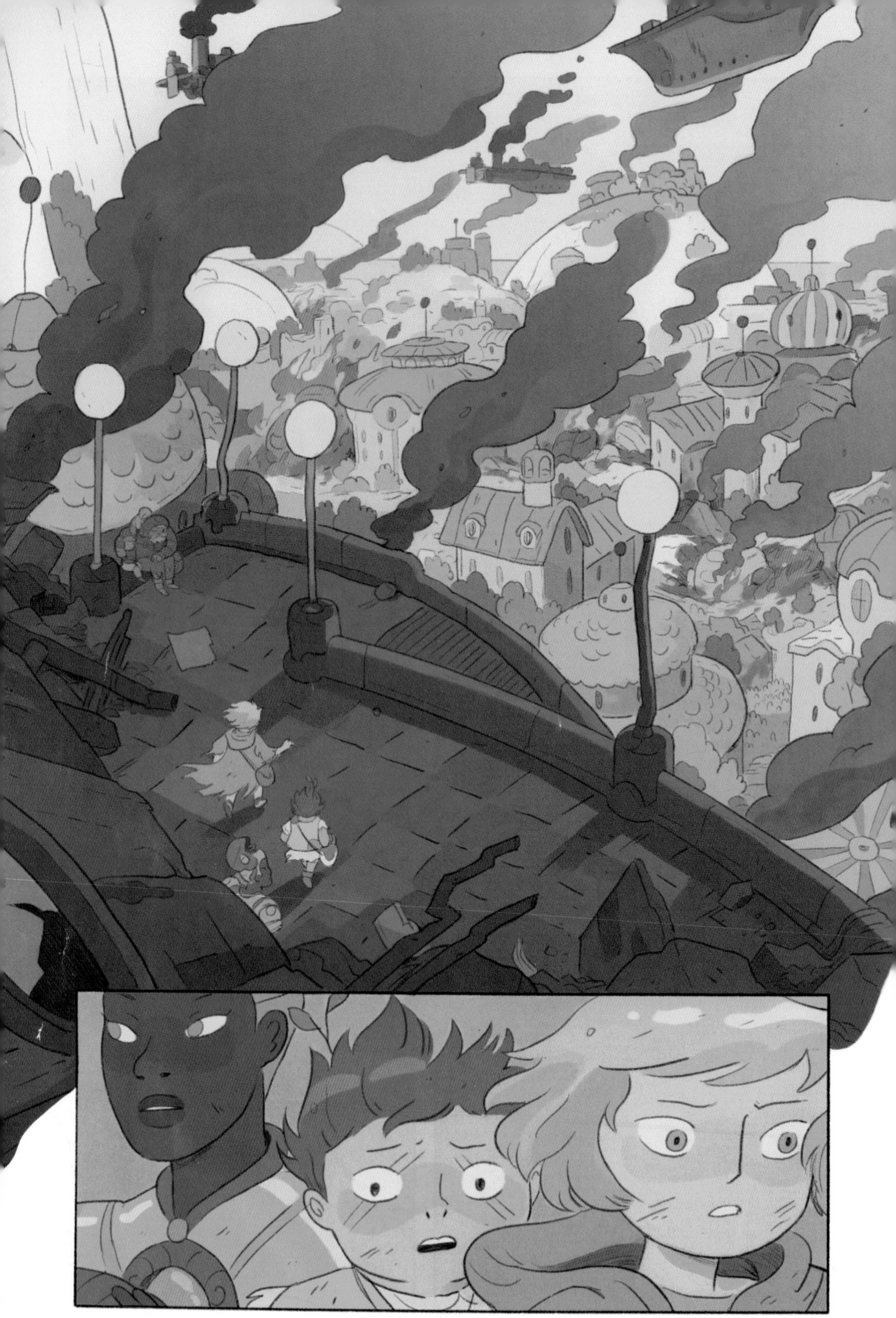

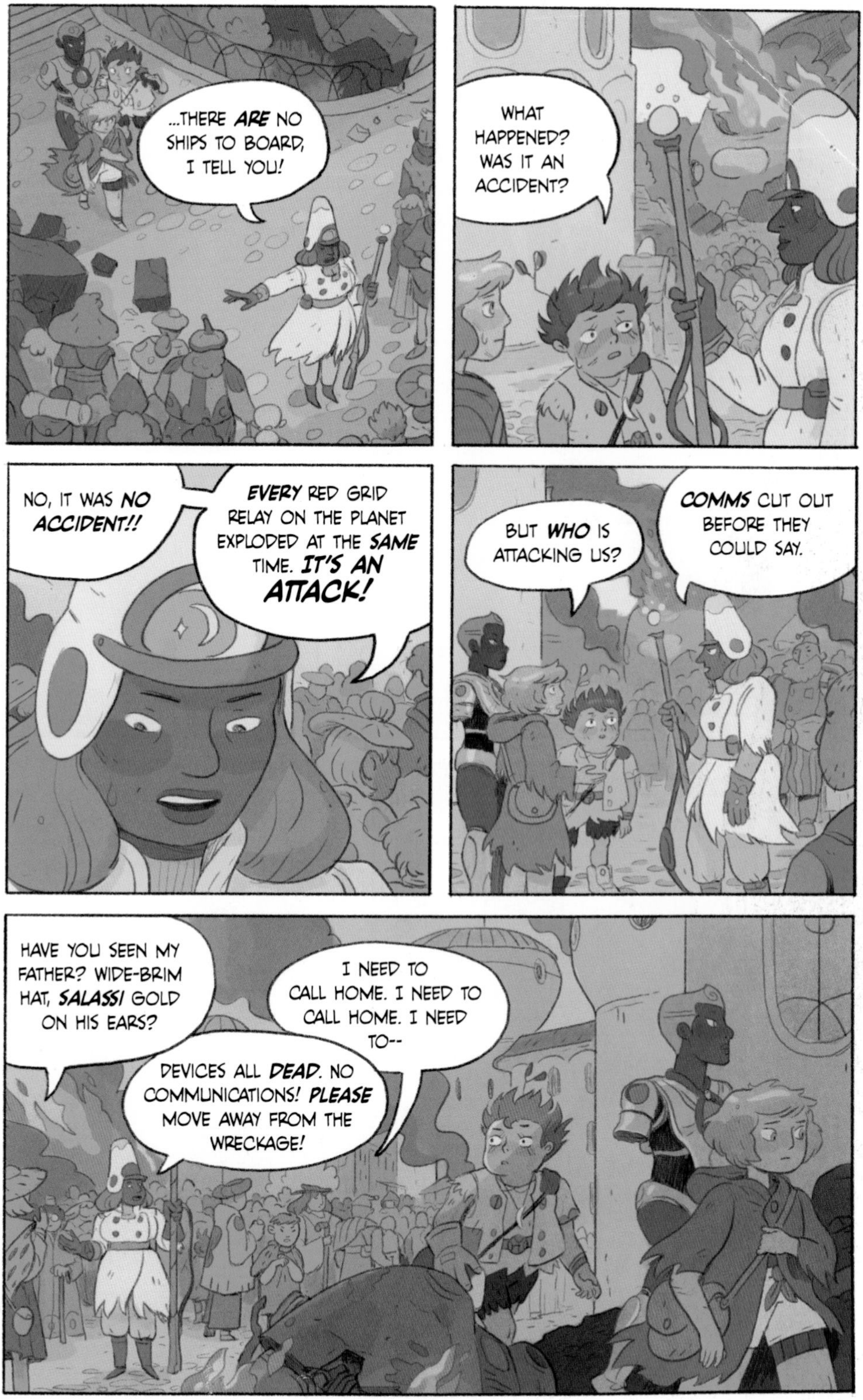
...THERE ARE NO SHIPS TO BOARD, I TELL YOU!
WHAT HAPPENED? WAS IT AN ACCIDENT?
NO, IT WAS NO ACCIDENT!!
EVERY RED GRID RELAY ON THE PLANET EXPLODED AT THE SAME TIME. IT'S AN ATTACK!
BUT WHO IS ATTACKING US?
COMMS CUT OUT BEFORE THEY COULD SAY.
HAVE YOU SEEN MY FATHER? WIDE-BRIM HAT, SALASSI GOLD ON HIS EARS?
I NEED TO CALL HOME. I NEED TO CALL HOME. I NEED TO--
DEVICES ALL DEAD. NO COMMUNICATIONS! PLEASE MOVE AWAY FROM THE WRECKAGE!

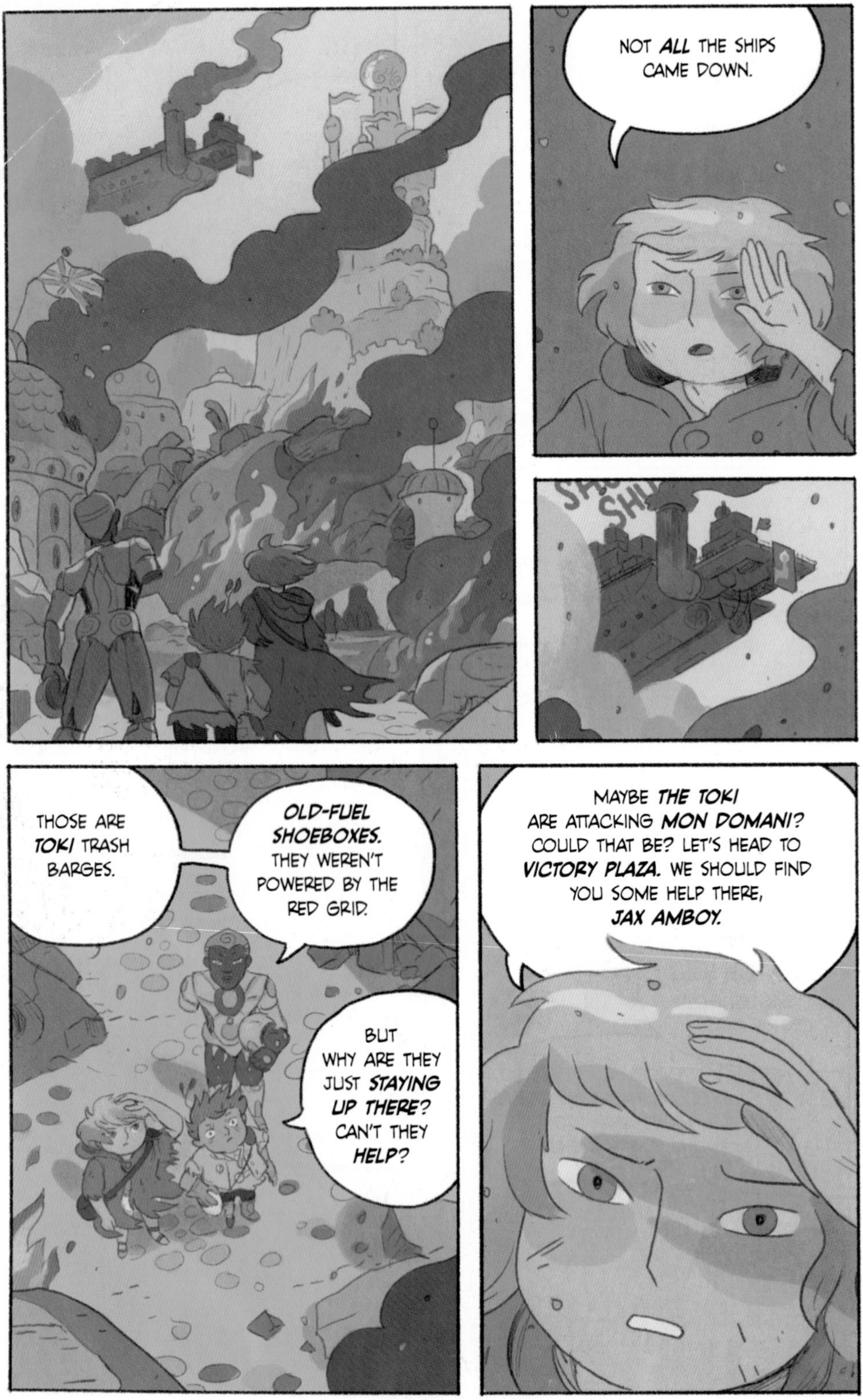
NOT ALL THE SHIPS CAME DOWN.
THOSE ARE TOKI TRASH BARGES.
OLD-FUEL SHOEBOXES. THEY WEREN'T POWERED BY THE RED GRID.
BUT WHY ARE THEY JUST STAYING UP THERE? CAN'T THEY HELP?
MAYBE THE TOKI ARE ATTACKING MON DOMANI? COULD THAT BE? LET'S HEAD TO VICTORY PLAZA. WE SHOULD FIND YOU SOME HELP THERE, JAX AMBOY.

Chapter 4

THE FALL OF THE SAND CASTLE

COMMANDER ZAYD, PHASE ONE IS COMPLETE.

WITHOUT THE RED GRID RELAY...

SHG SHG

SHG SH

...MON DOMANI HAS NO AIR FORCE OR MAJOR TRANSPORTS.

GOOD. INITIATE PHASE TWO. HEAD TO THE SAND CASTLE.

THEY'RE IN FOR A SURPRISE.

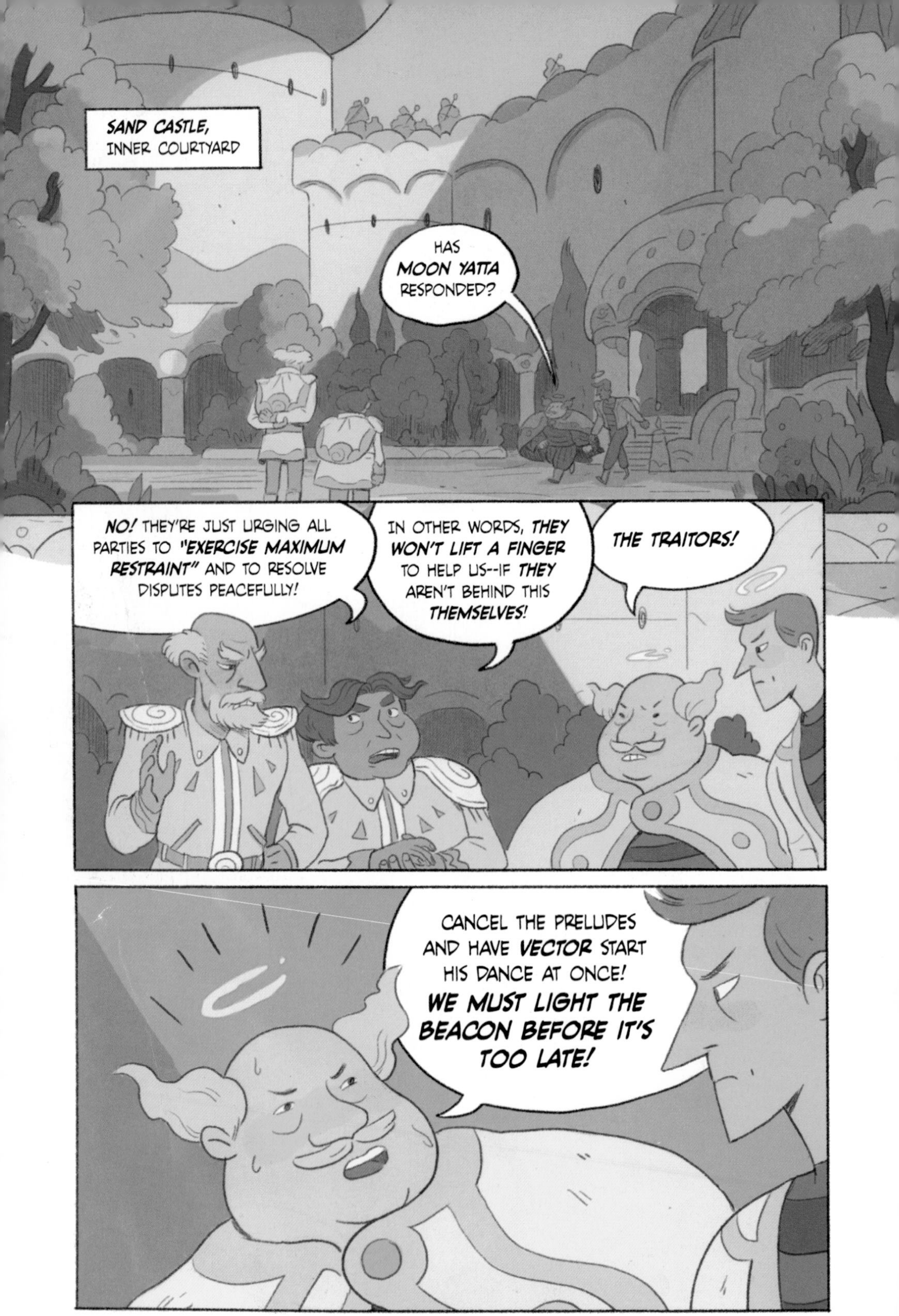
SAND CASTLE, INNER COURTYARD
HAS MOON YATTA RESPONDED?
NO! THEY'RE JUST URGING ALL PARTIES TO "EXERCISE MAXIMUM RESTRAINT" AND TO RESOLVE DISPUTES PEACEFULLY!
IN OTHER WORDS, THEY WON'T LIFT A FINGER TO HELP US--IF THEY AREN'T BEHIND THIS THEMSELVES!
THE TRAITORS!
CANCEL THE PRELUDES AND HAVE VECTOR START HIS DANCE AT ONCE! WE MUST LIGHT THE BEACON BEFORE IT'S TOO LATE!

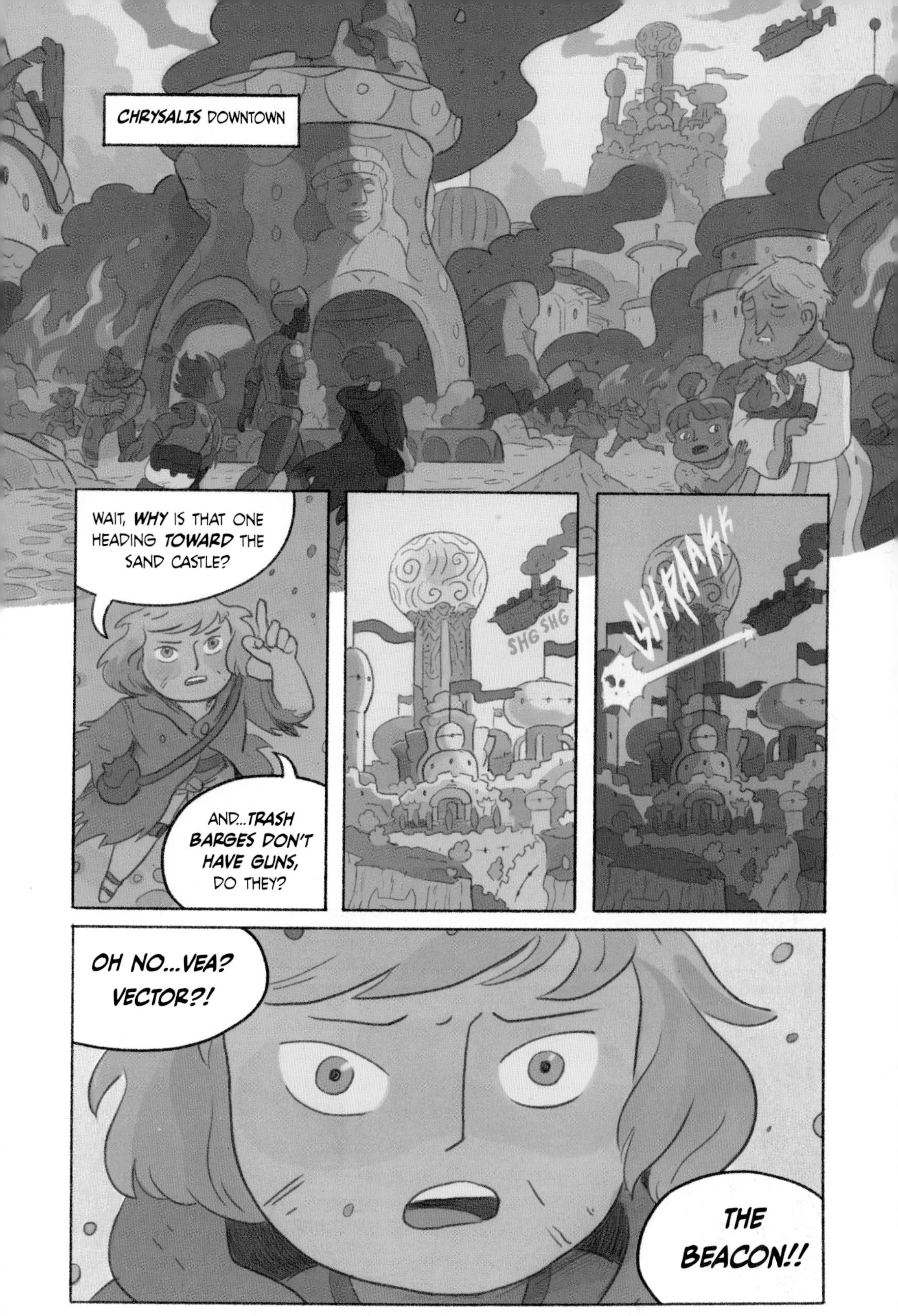
CHRYSALIS DOWNTOWN
WAIT, WHY IS THAT ONE HEADING TOWARD THE SAND CASTLE?
AND...TRASH BARGES DON'T HAVE GUNS, DO THEY?
SHG SHG
SHRAAKK
OH NO...VEA? VECTOR?!
THE BEACON!!

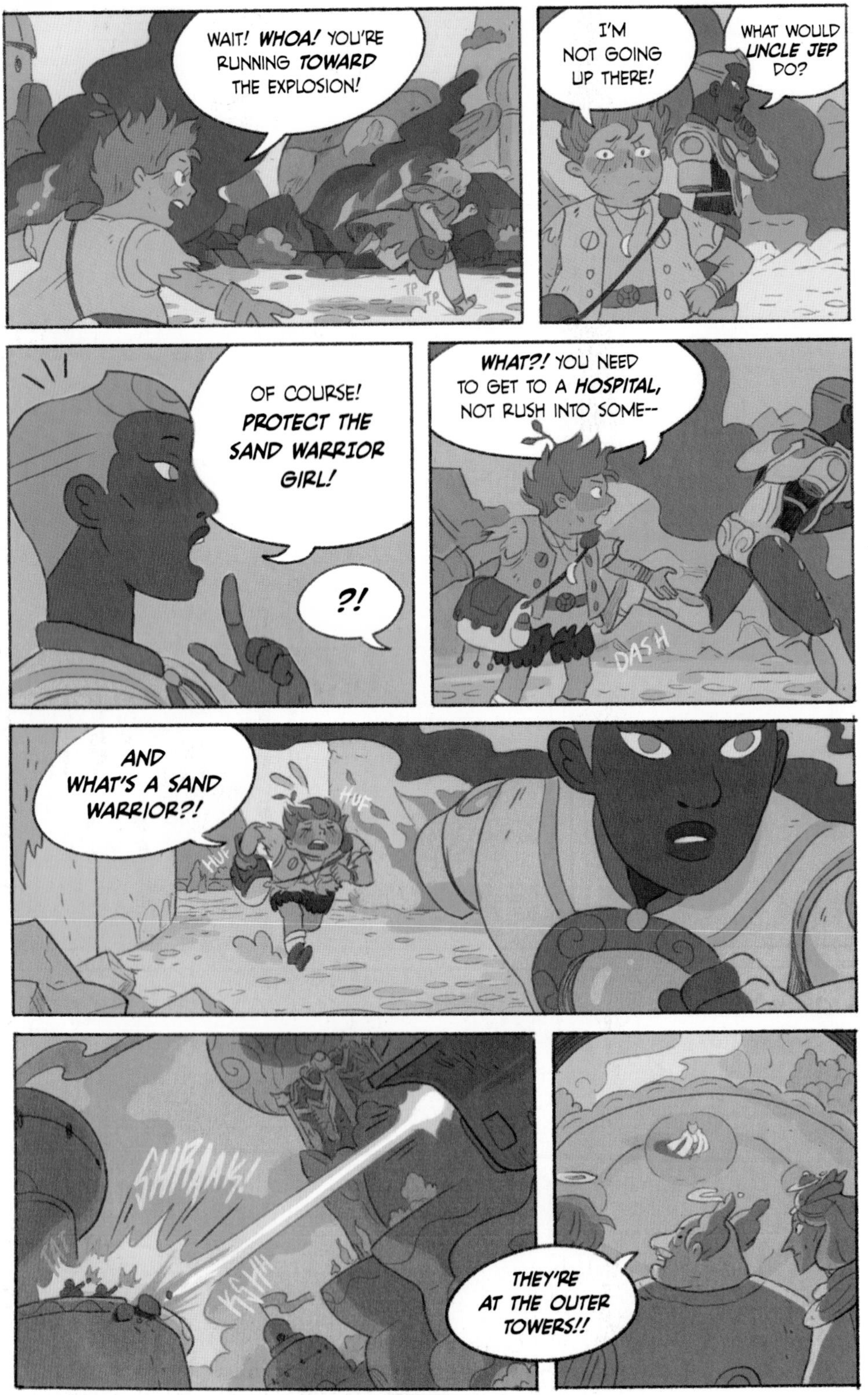
WAIT! WHOA! YOU'RE RUNNING TOWARD THE EXPLOSION!
TP TP
I'M NOT GOING UP THERE!
WHAT WOULD UNCLE JEP DO?
OF COURSE! PROTECT THE SAND WARRIOR GIRL!
?!
WHAT?! YOU NEED TO GET TO A HOSPITAL, NOT RUSH INTO SOME--
DASH
AND WHAT'S A SAND WARRIOR?!
HUF
HUF
SHRAAK!
KSHH
THEY'RE AT THE OUTER TOWERS!!

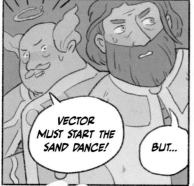

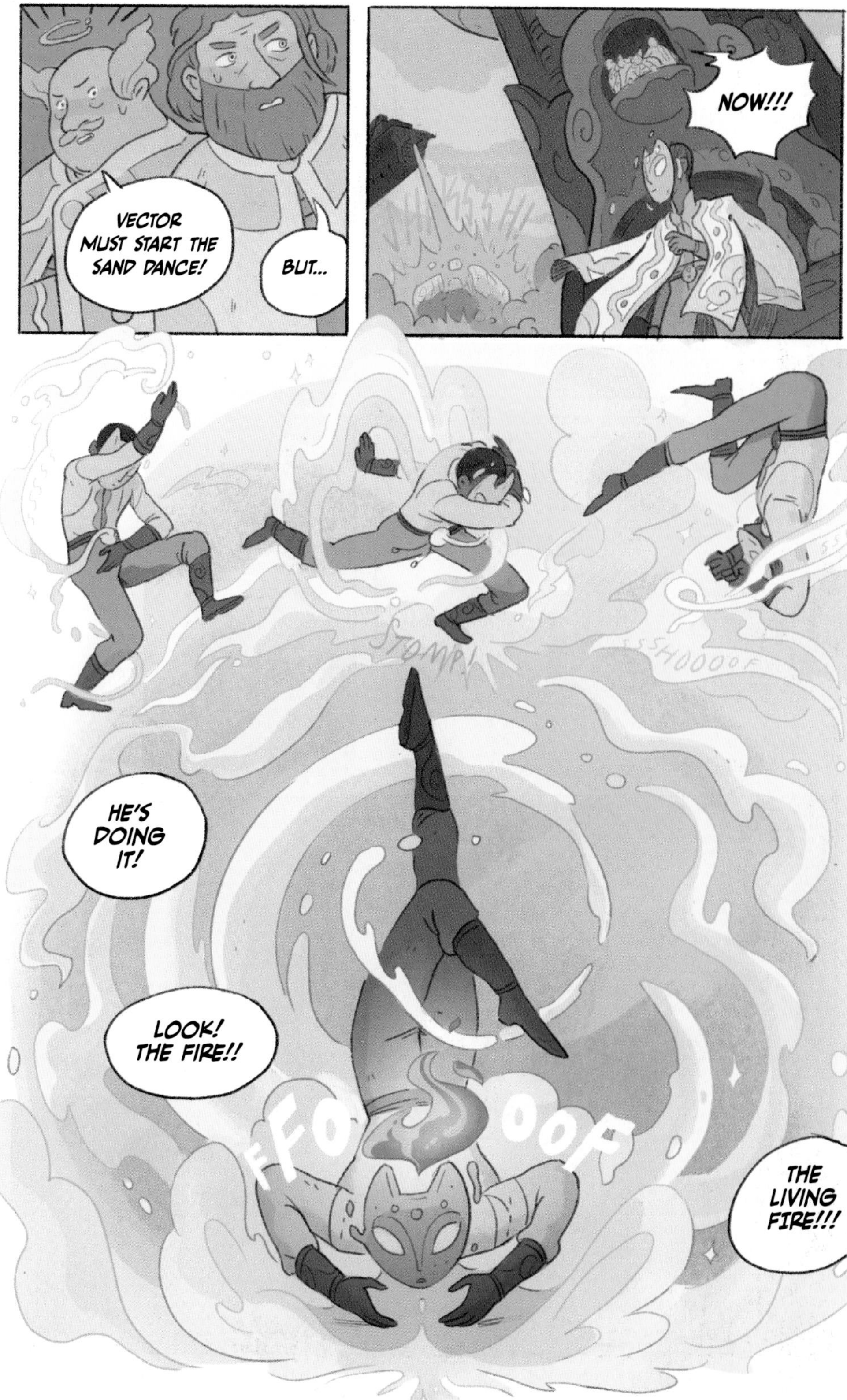
VECTOR MUST START THE SAND DANCE!
BUT...
NOW!!!
STOMP!
SSHOOOOF
HE'S DOING IT!
LOOK! THE FIRE!!
THE LIVING FIRE!!!

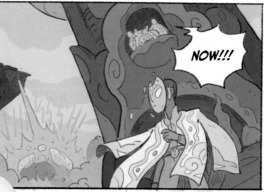

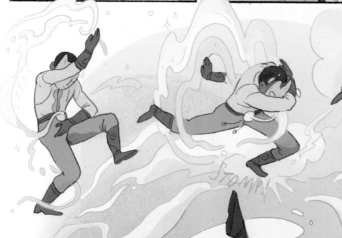

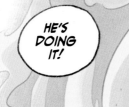

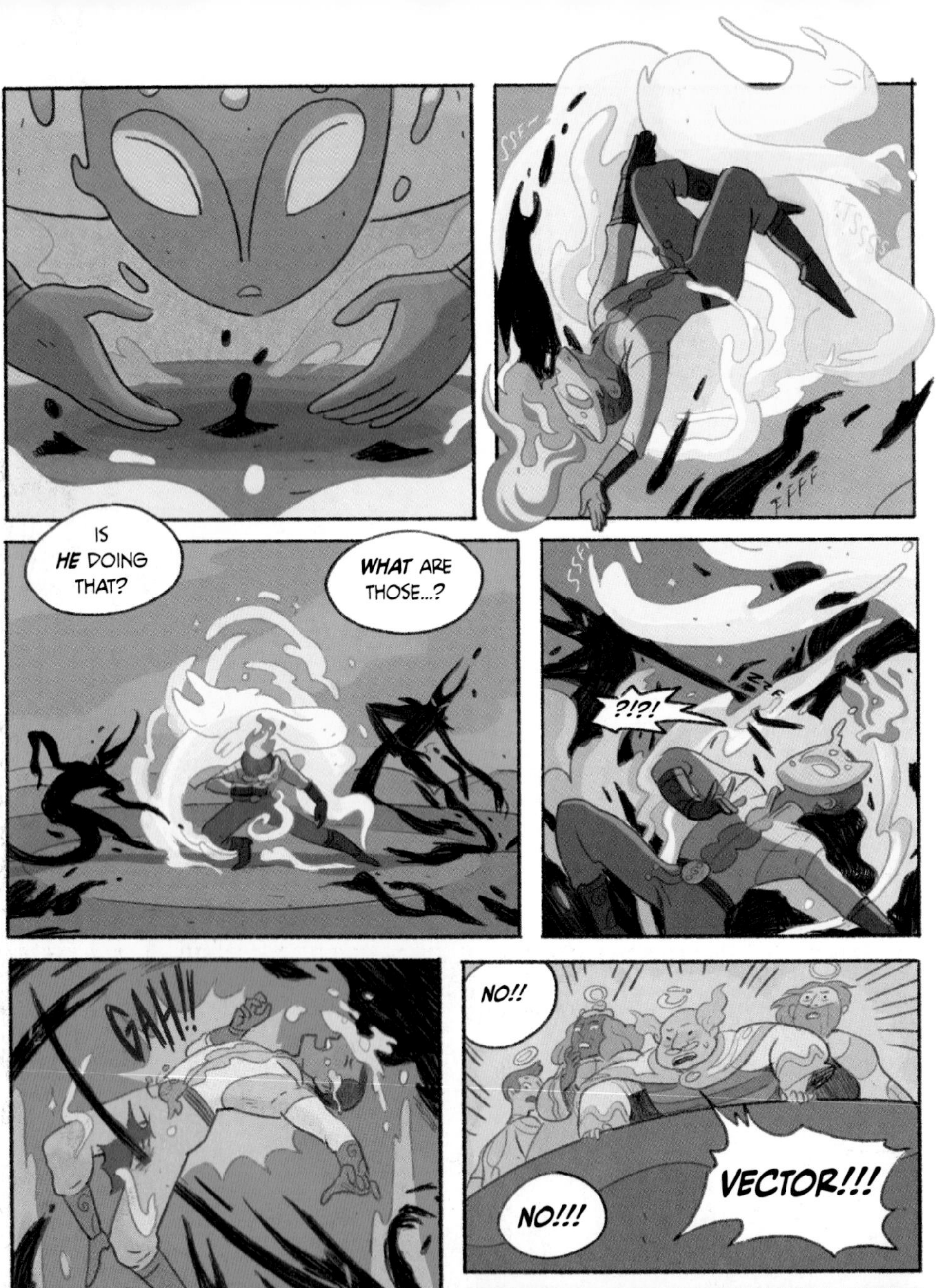
IS HE DOING THAT?
WHAT ARE THOSE...?
?!?!
GAH!!
NO!!
NO!!!
VECTOR!!!

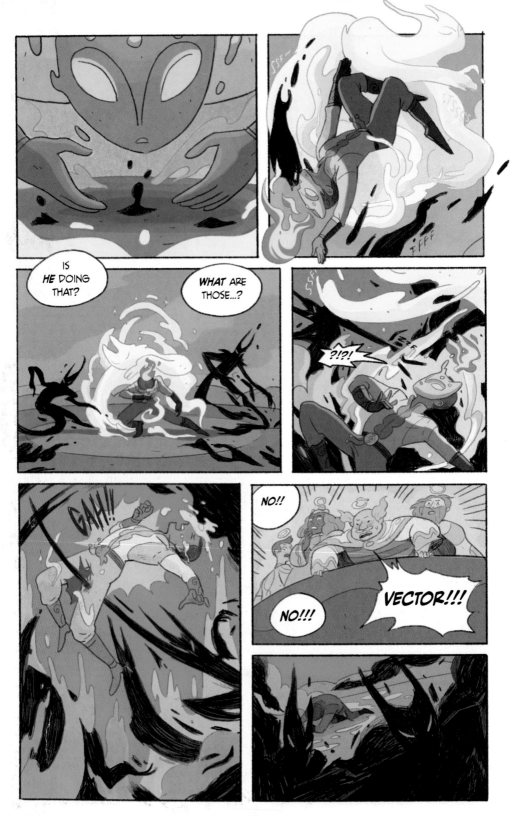

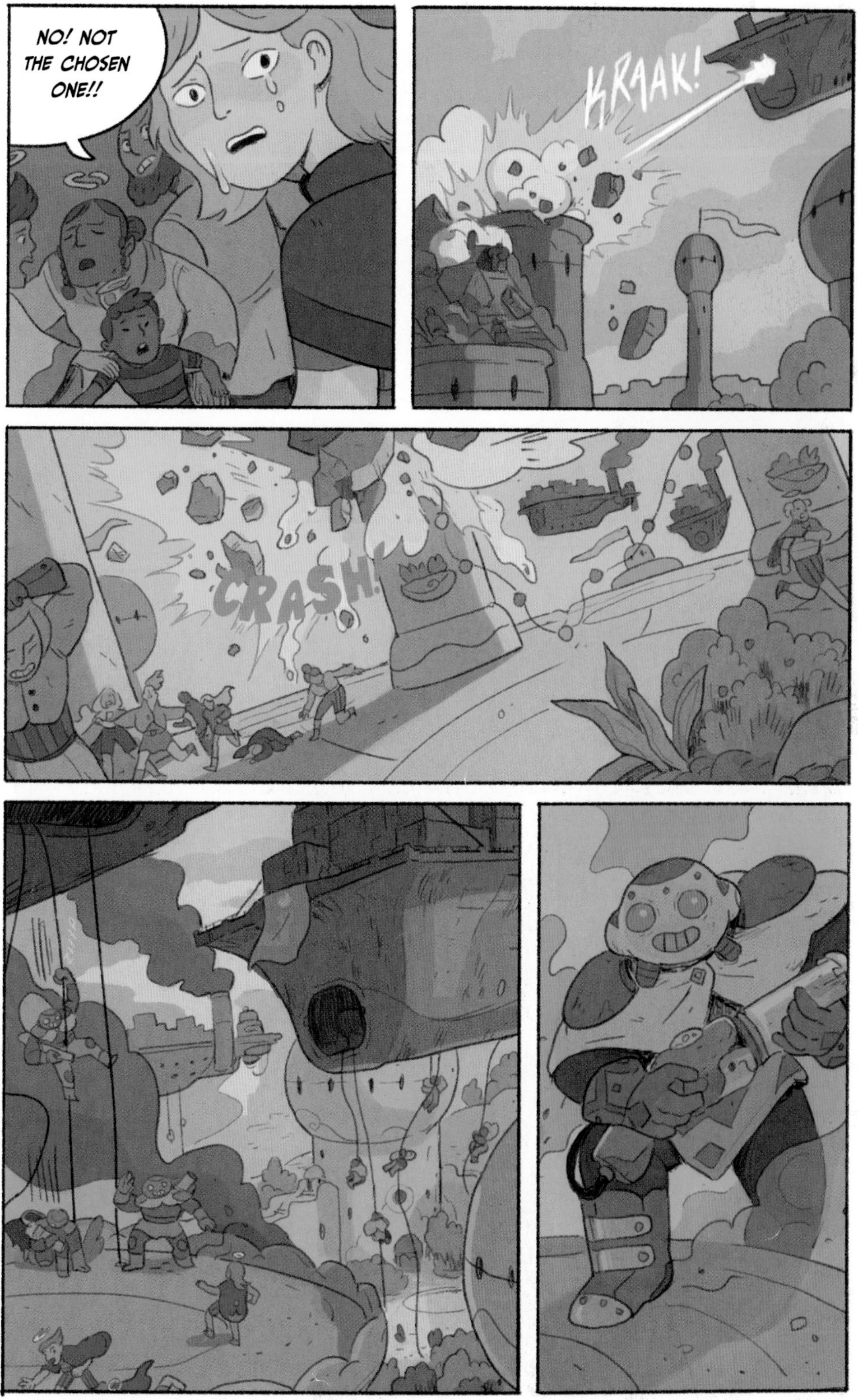
NO! NOT THE CHOSEN ONE!!
KRAAK!
CRASH!

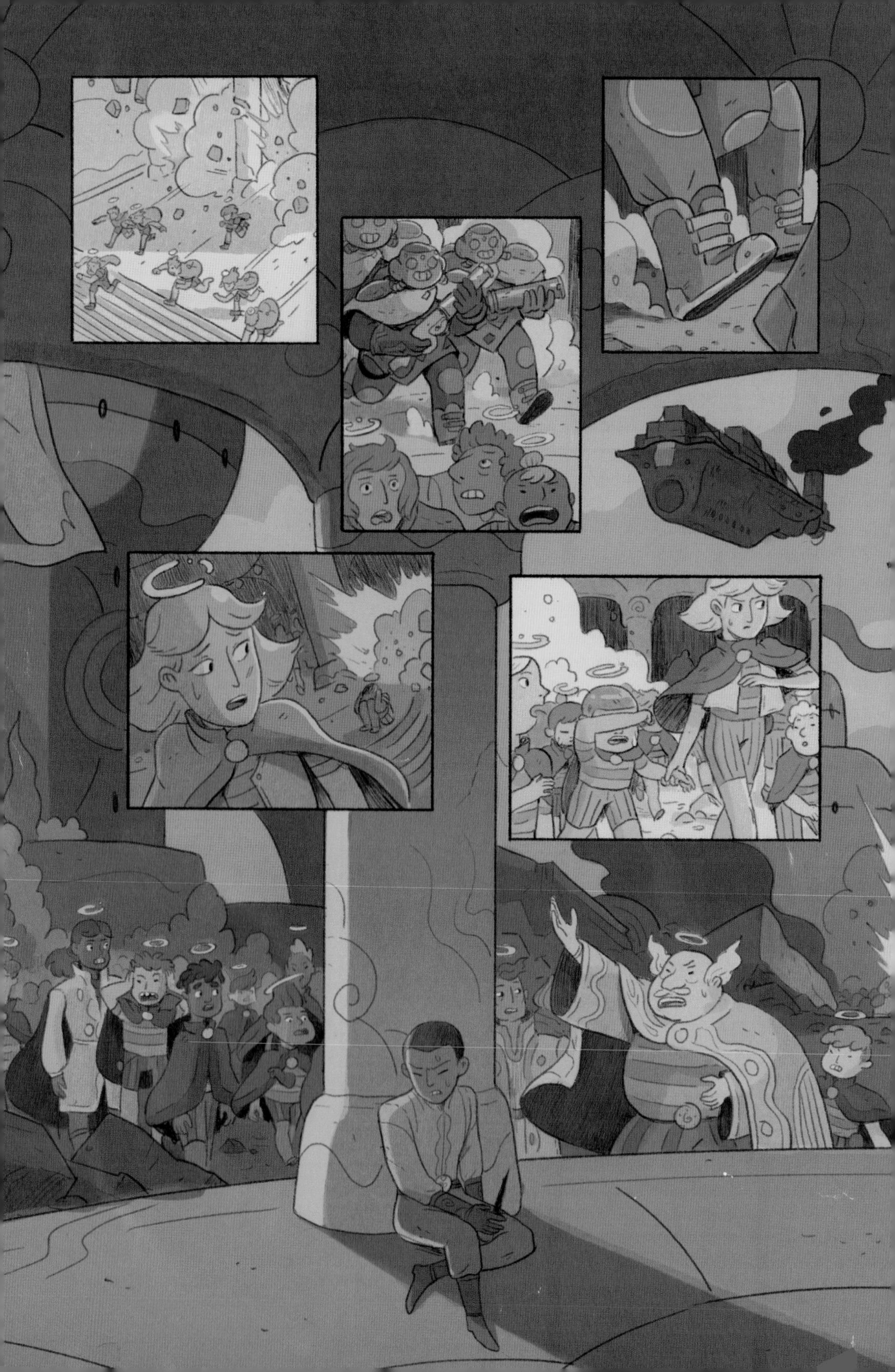

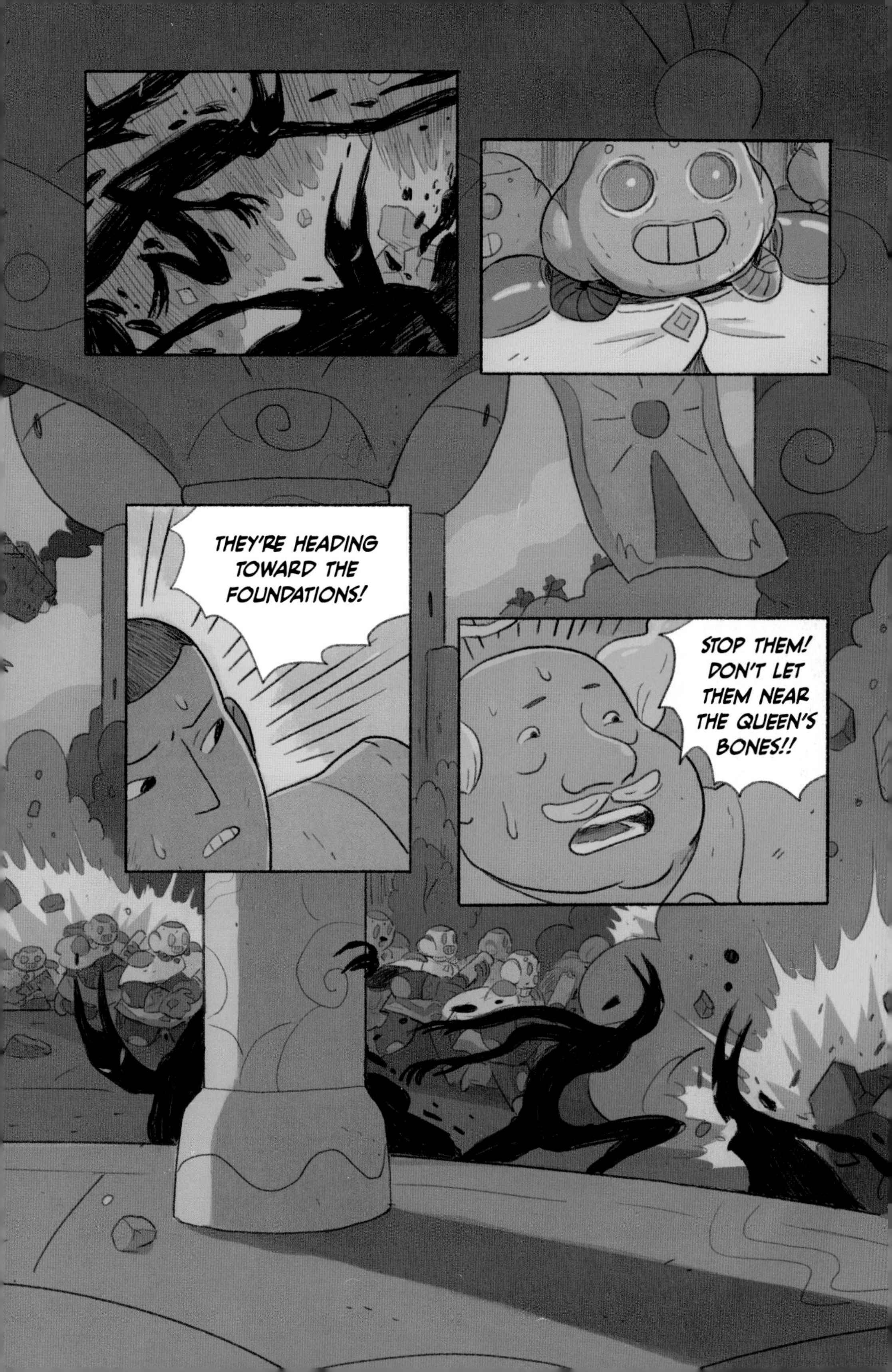
THEY'RE HEADING TOWARD THE FOUNDATIONS!
STOP THEM! DON'T LET THEM NEAR THE QUEEN'S BONES!!

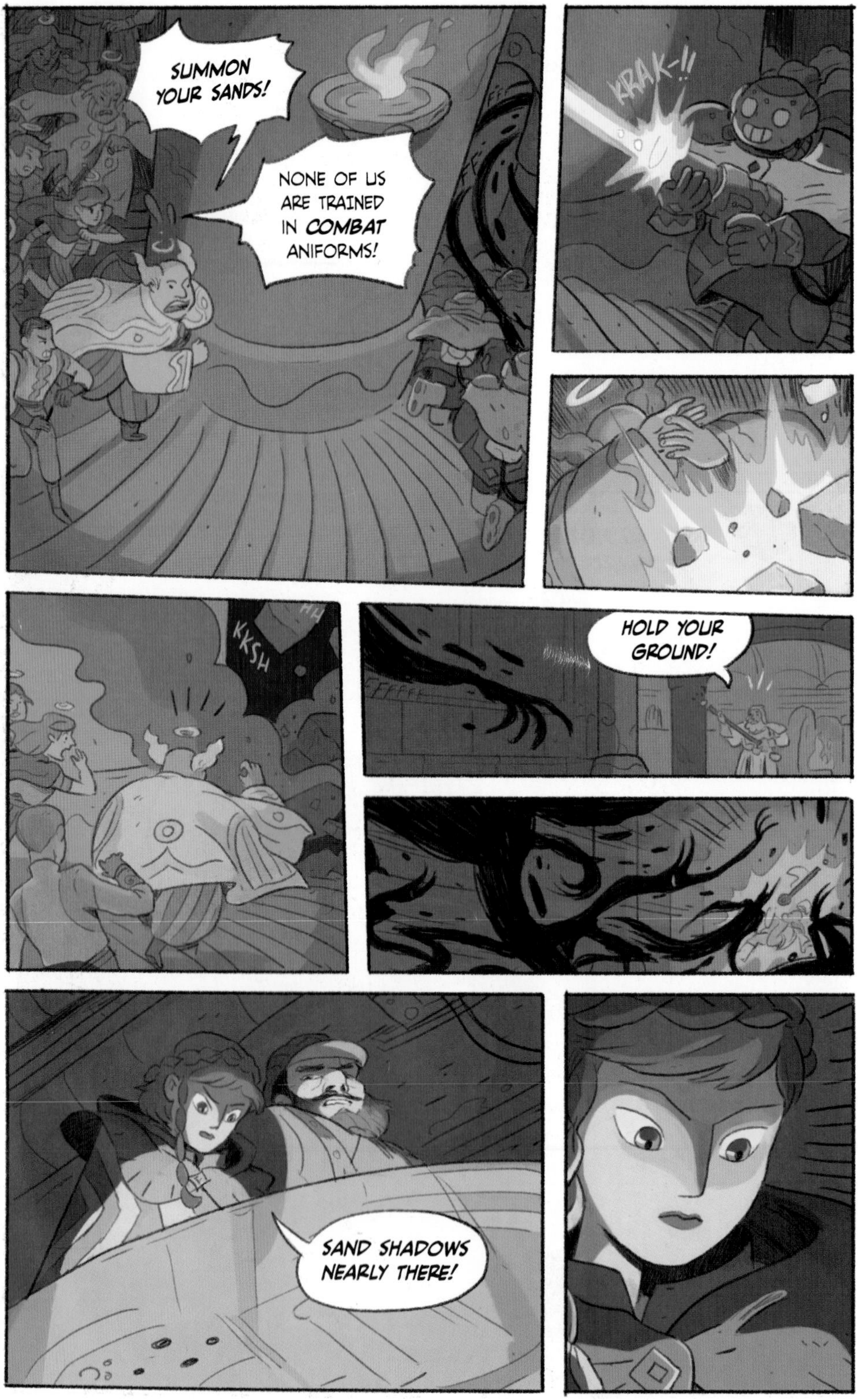
SUMMON YOUR SANDS!
NONE OF US ARE TRAINED IN COMBAT ANIFORMS!
KRAK-!!
KKSH
HOLD YOUR GROUND!
SAND SHADOWS NEARLY THERE!

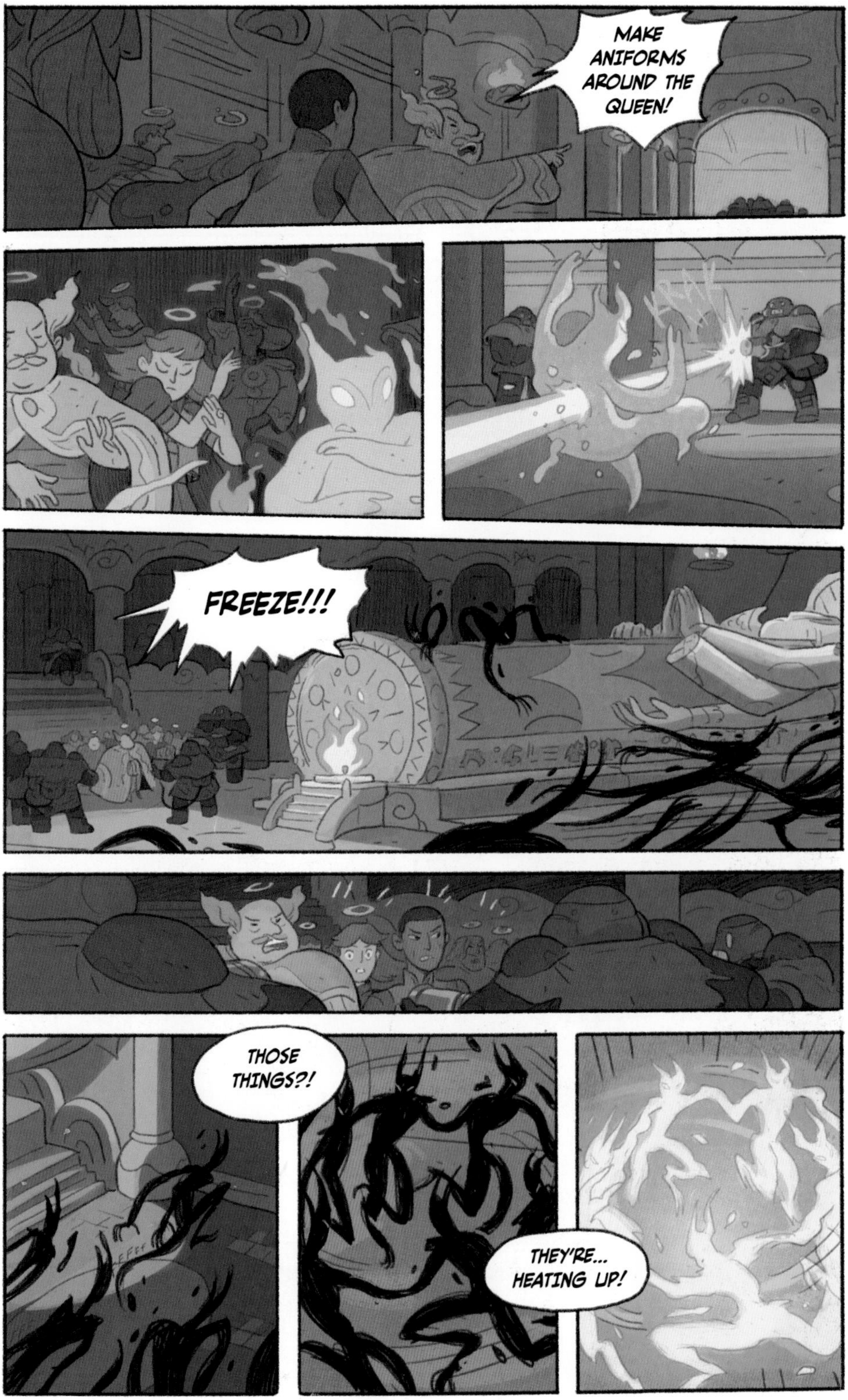
MAKE ANIFORMS AROUND THE QUEEN!
FREEZE!!!
THOSE THINGS?!
THEY'RE... HEATING UP!

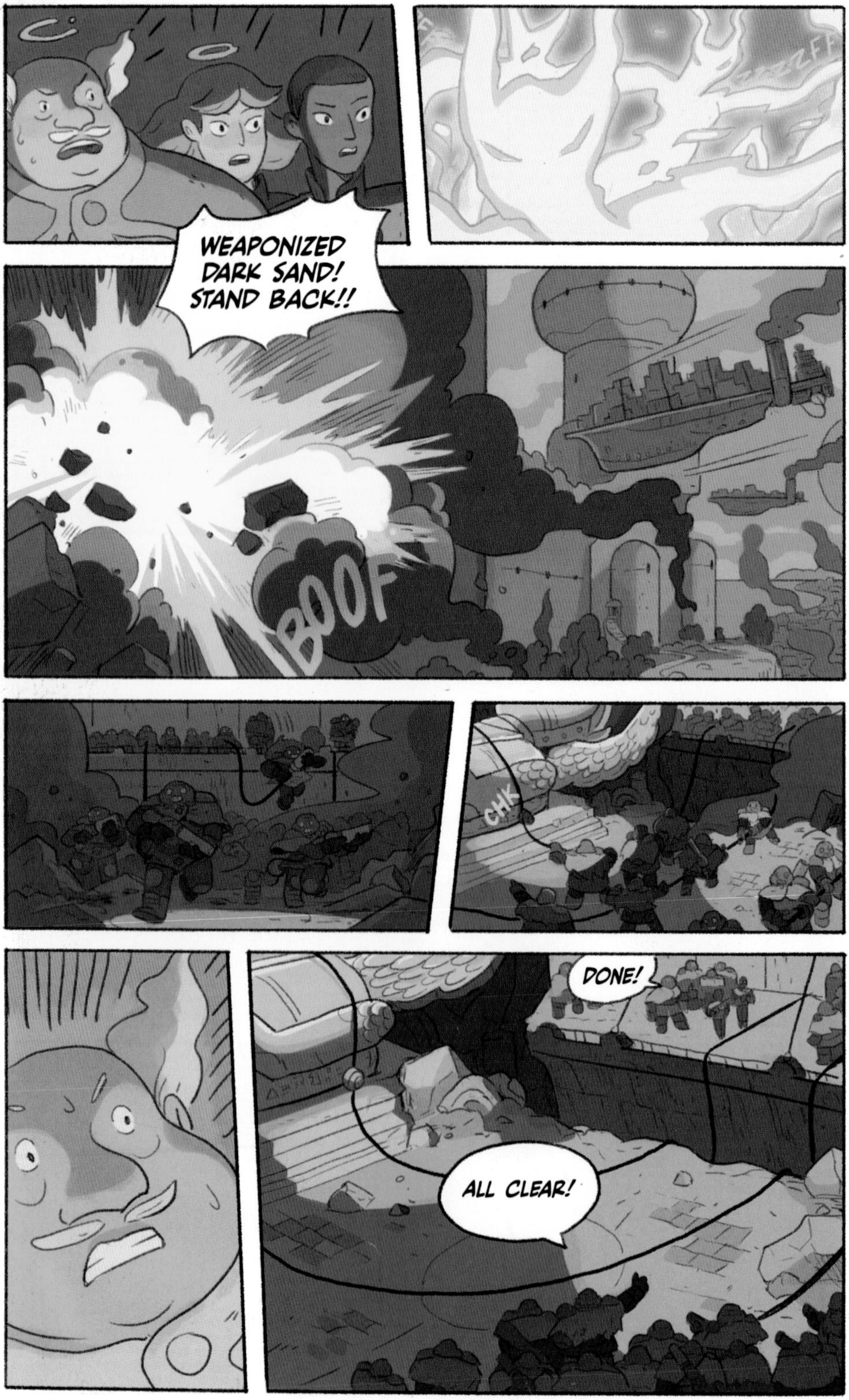
WEAPONIZED DARK SAND! STAND BACK!!
BOOF
CHK
DONE!
ALL CLEAR!

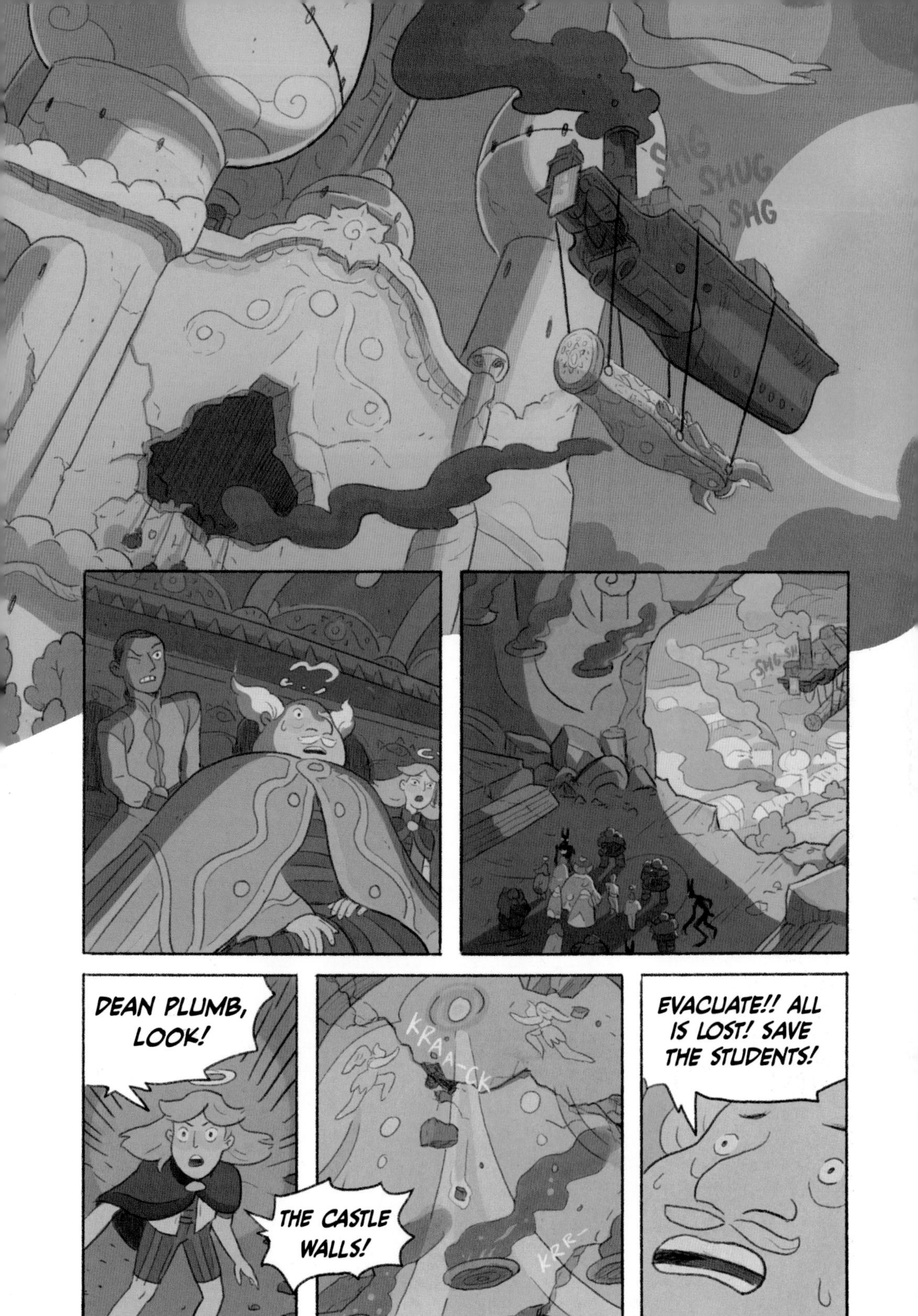
SHG
SHUG
SHG
SHG SH
DEAN PLUMB, LOOK!
THE CASTLE WALLS!
KRAA-CK
KRR-
EVACUATE!! ALL IS LOST! SAVE THE STUDENTS!

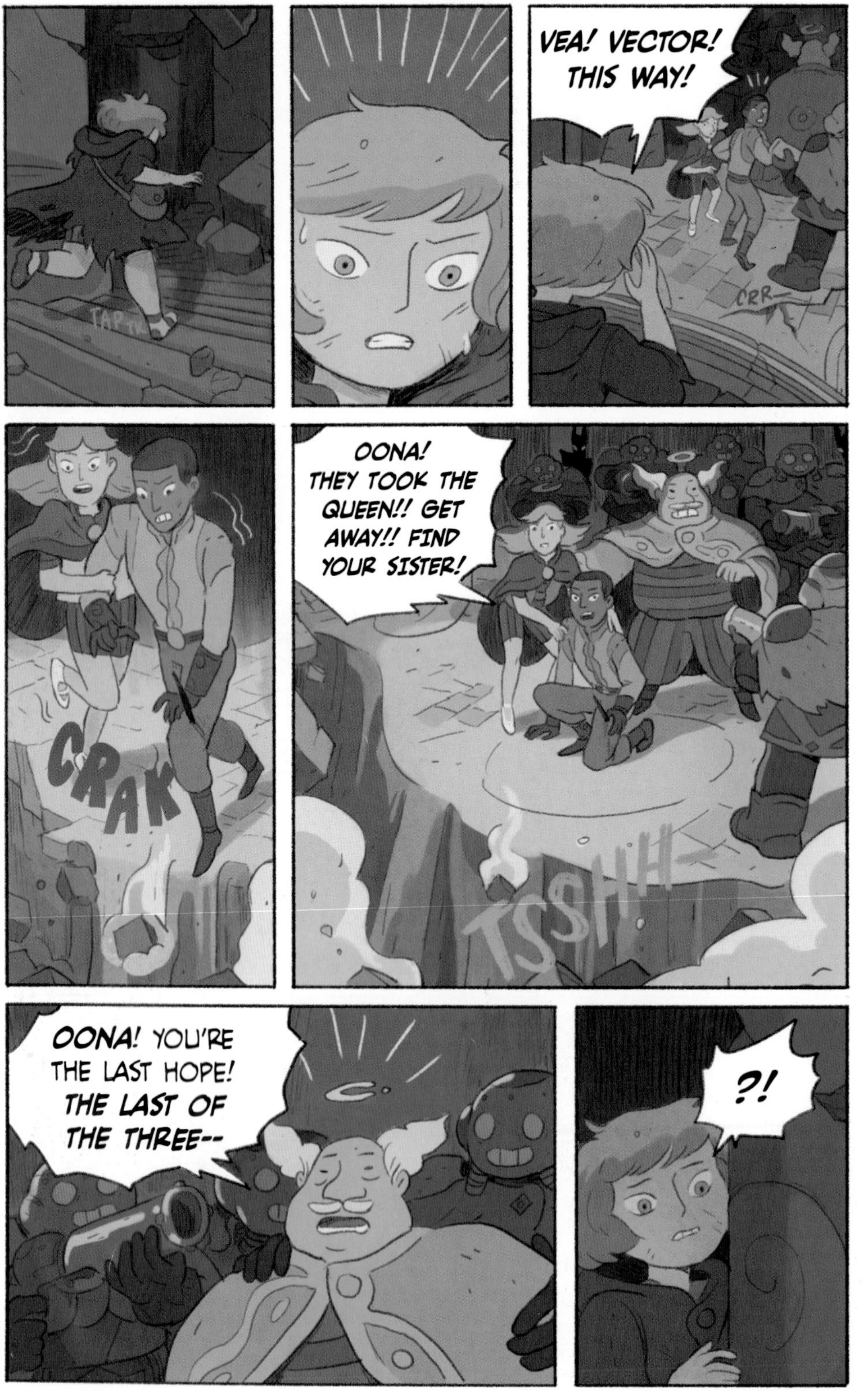
TAP TA
VEA! VECTOR! THIS WAY!
CRR
CRAK
OONA! THEY TOOK THE QUEEN!! GET AWAY!! FIND YOUR SISTER!
TSSHH
OONA! YOU'RE THE LAST HOPE! THE LAST OF THE THREE--
?!

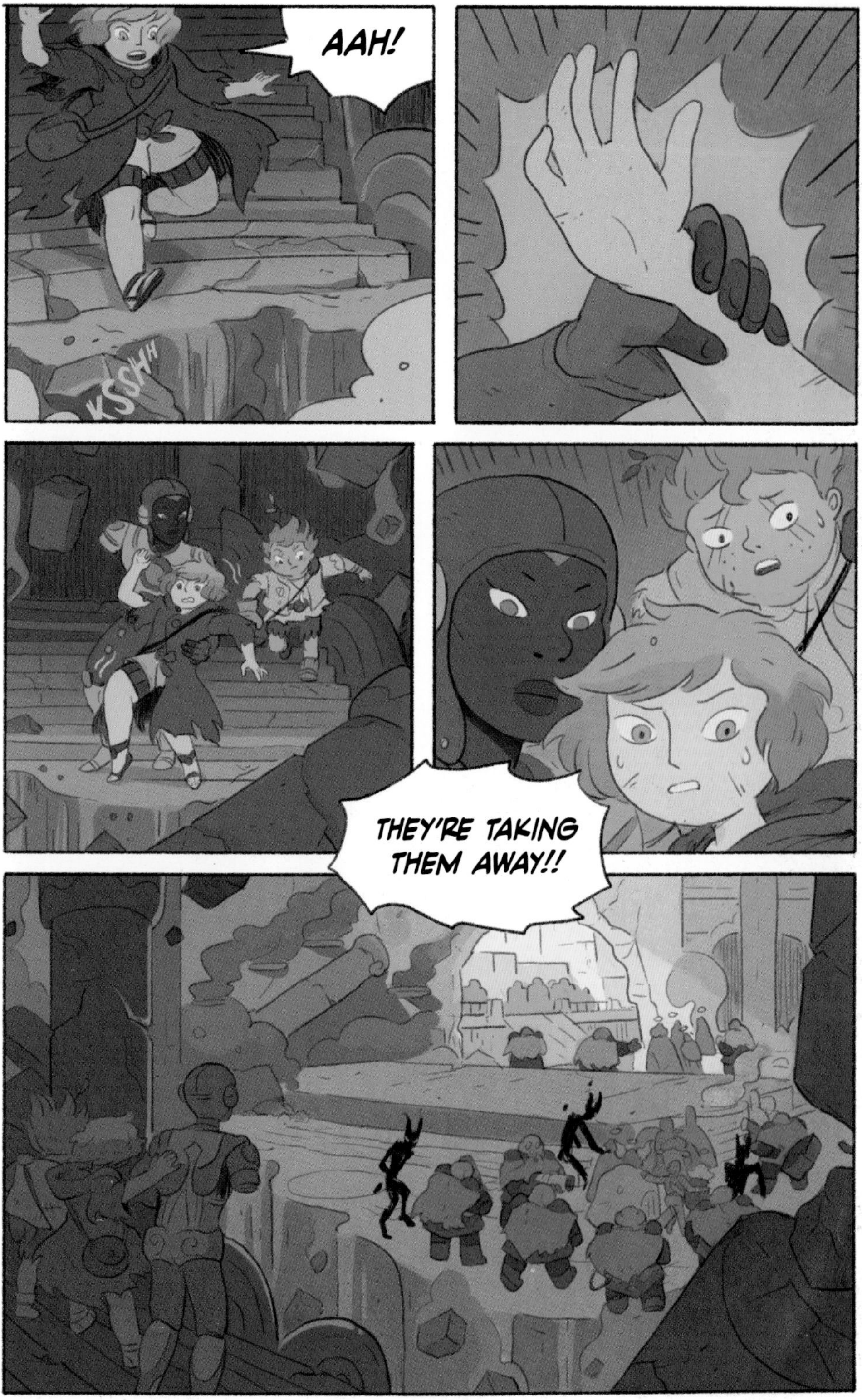
AAH!
KSSH
THEY'RE TAKING THEM AWAY!!

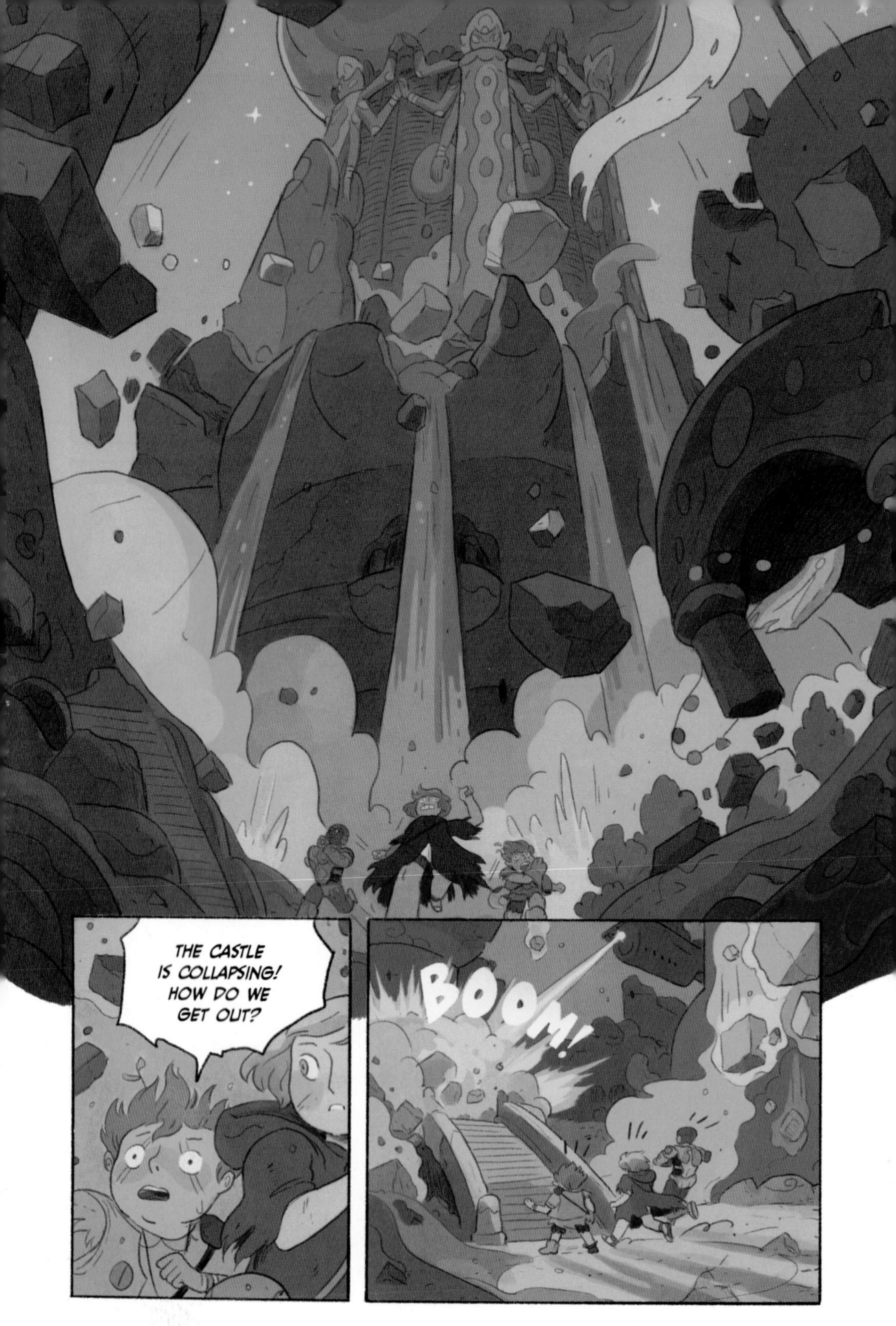
THE CASTLE IS COLLAPSING! HOW DO WE GET OUT?
BOOM!

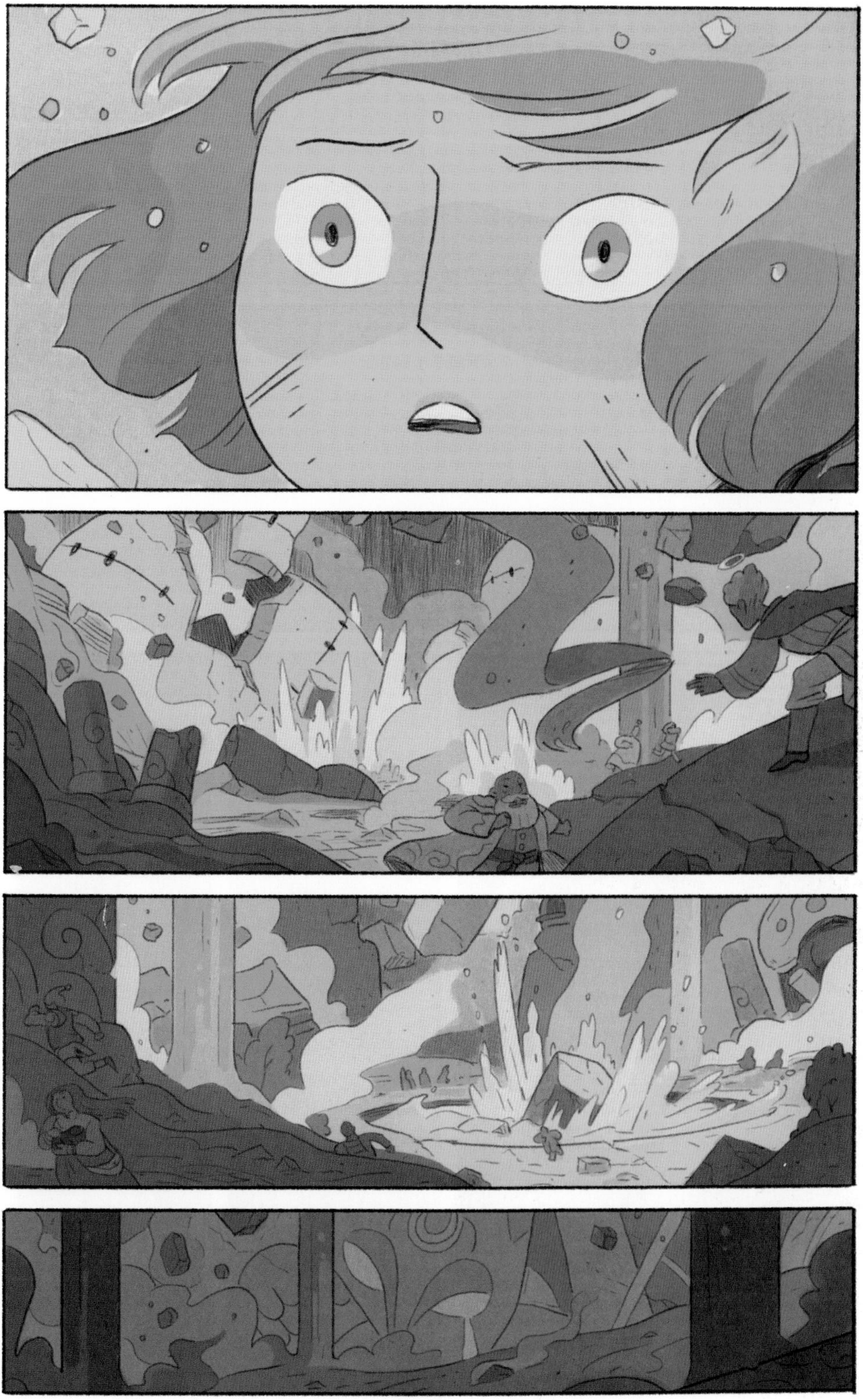

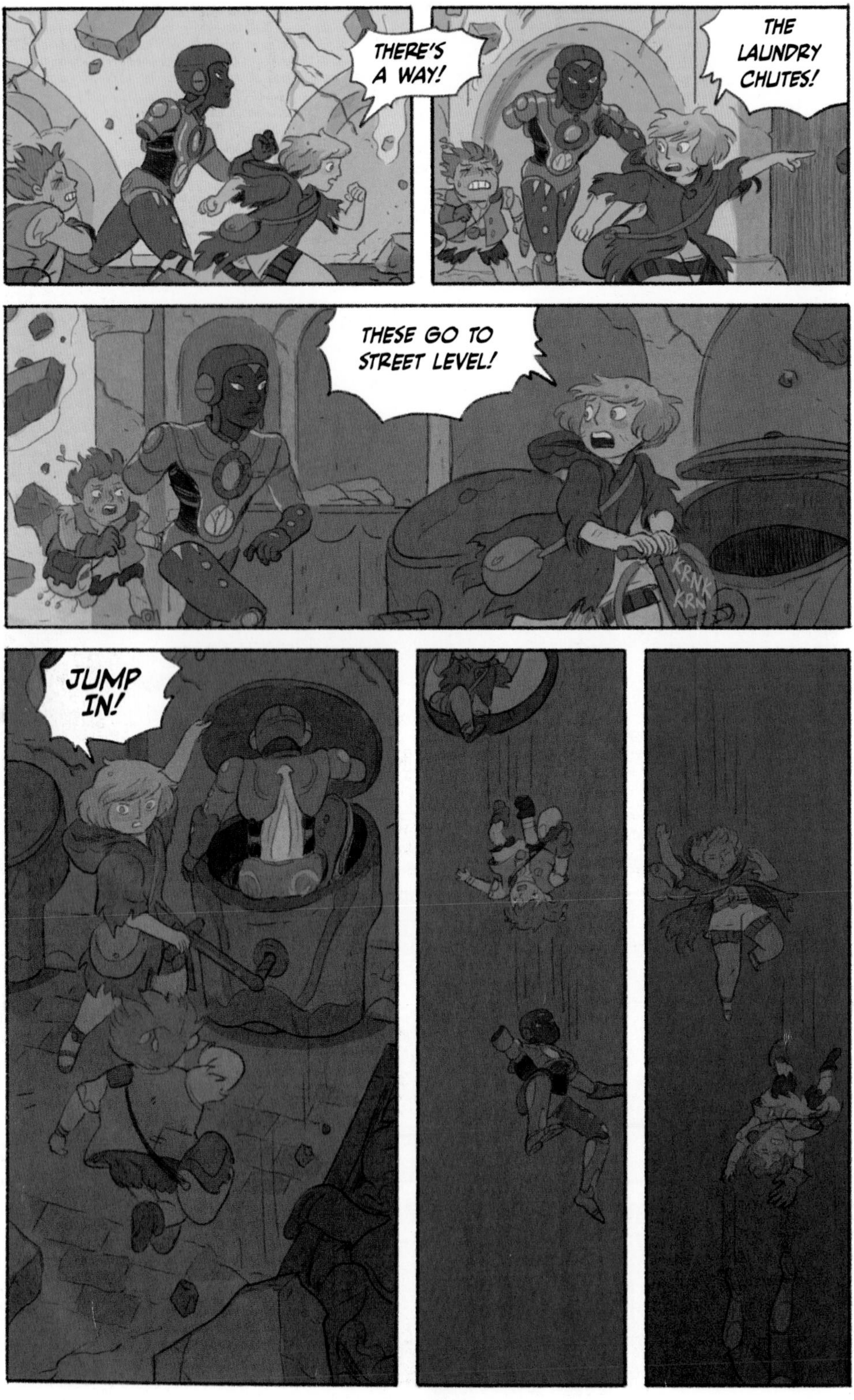
THERE'S A WAY!
THE LAUNDRY CHUTES!
THESE GO TO STREET LEVEL!
KRNK KRN
JUMP IN!

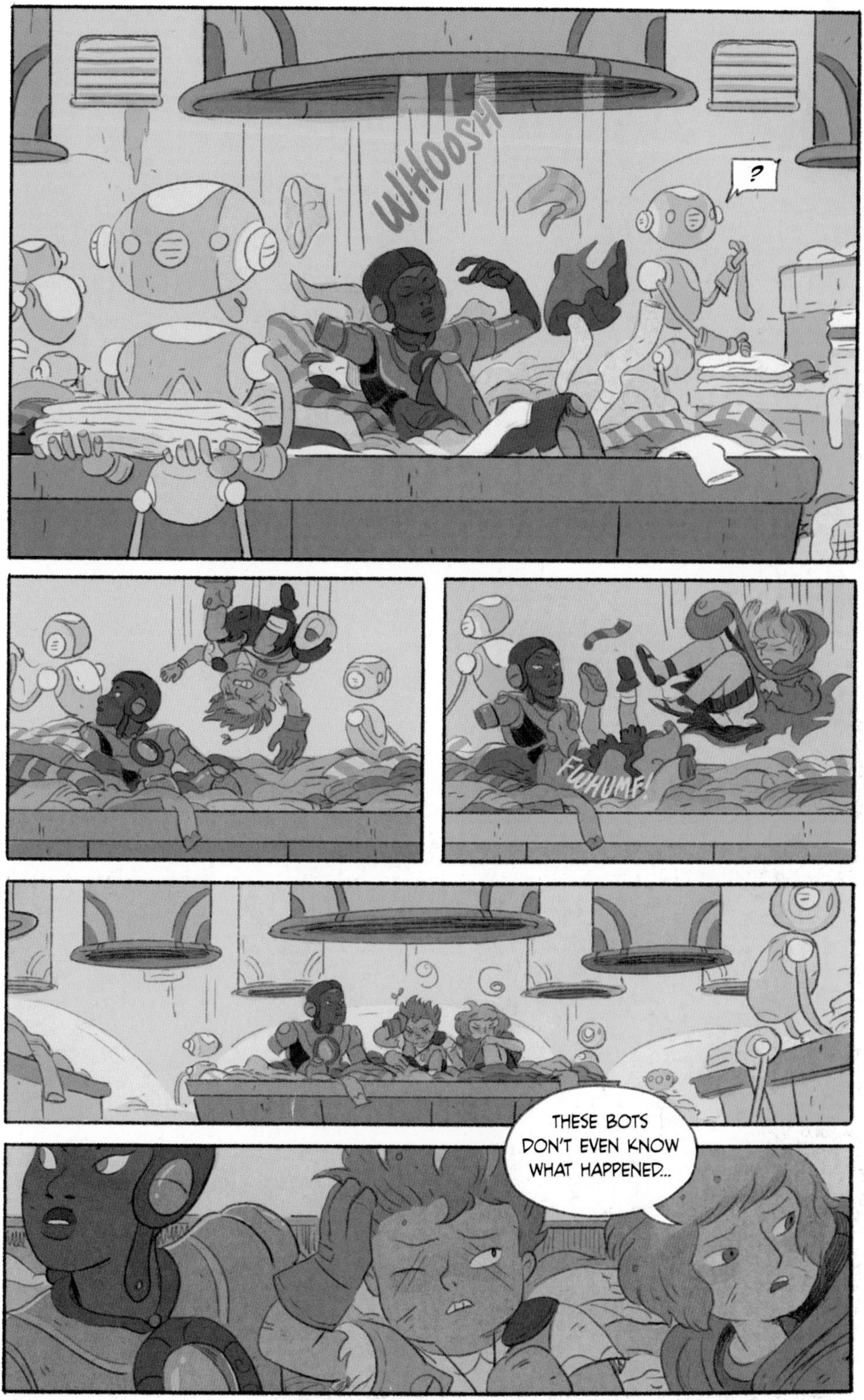
WHOOSH
?
FWHUMF!
THESE BOTS DON'T EVEN KNOW WHAT HAPPENED...

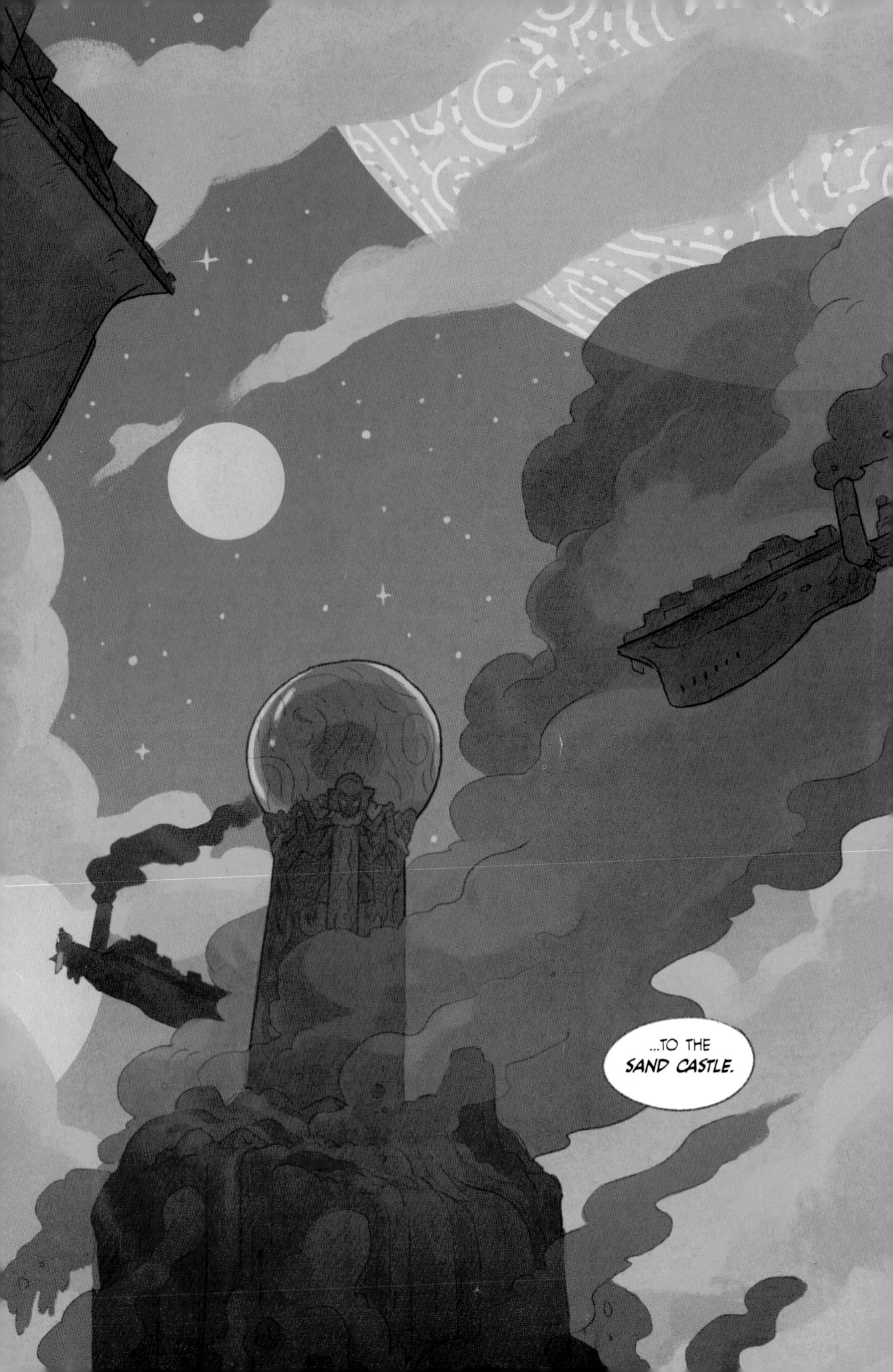
...TO THE SAND CASTLE.

Chapter 5
PASSAGE TO MAYAPOLIS

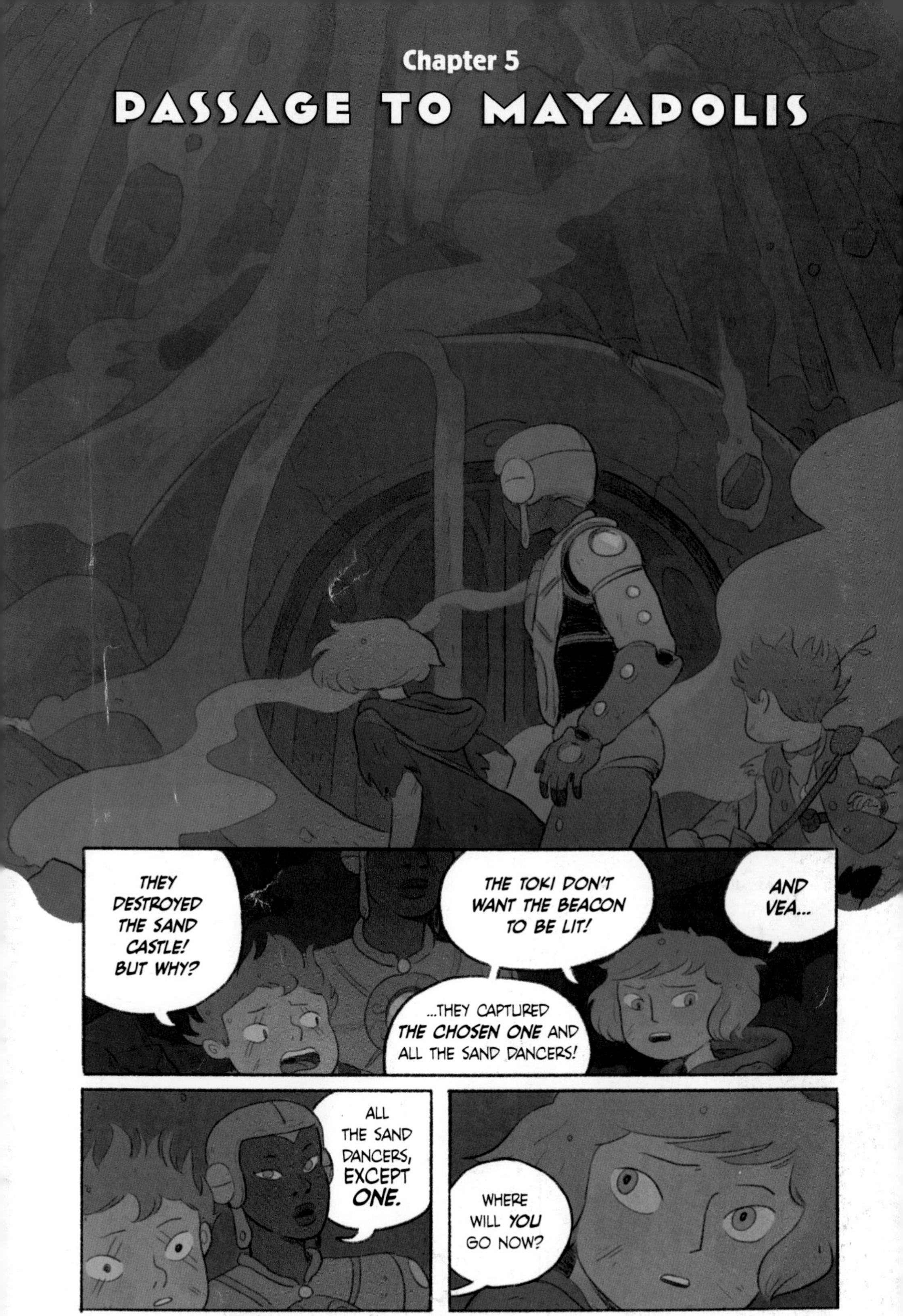
THEY DESTROYED THE SAND CASTLE! BUT WHY?
THE TOKI DON'T WANT THE BEACON TO BE LIT!
AND VEA...
...THEY CAPTURED *THE CHOSEN ONE* AND ALL THE SAND DANCERS!
ALL THE SAND DANCERS, EXCEPT *ONE.*
WHERE WILL *YOU* GO NOW?

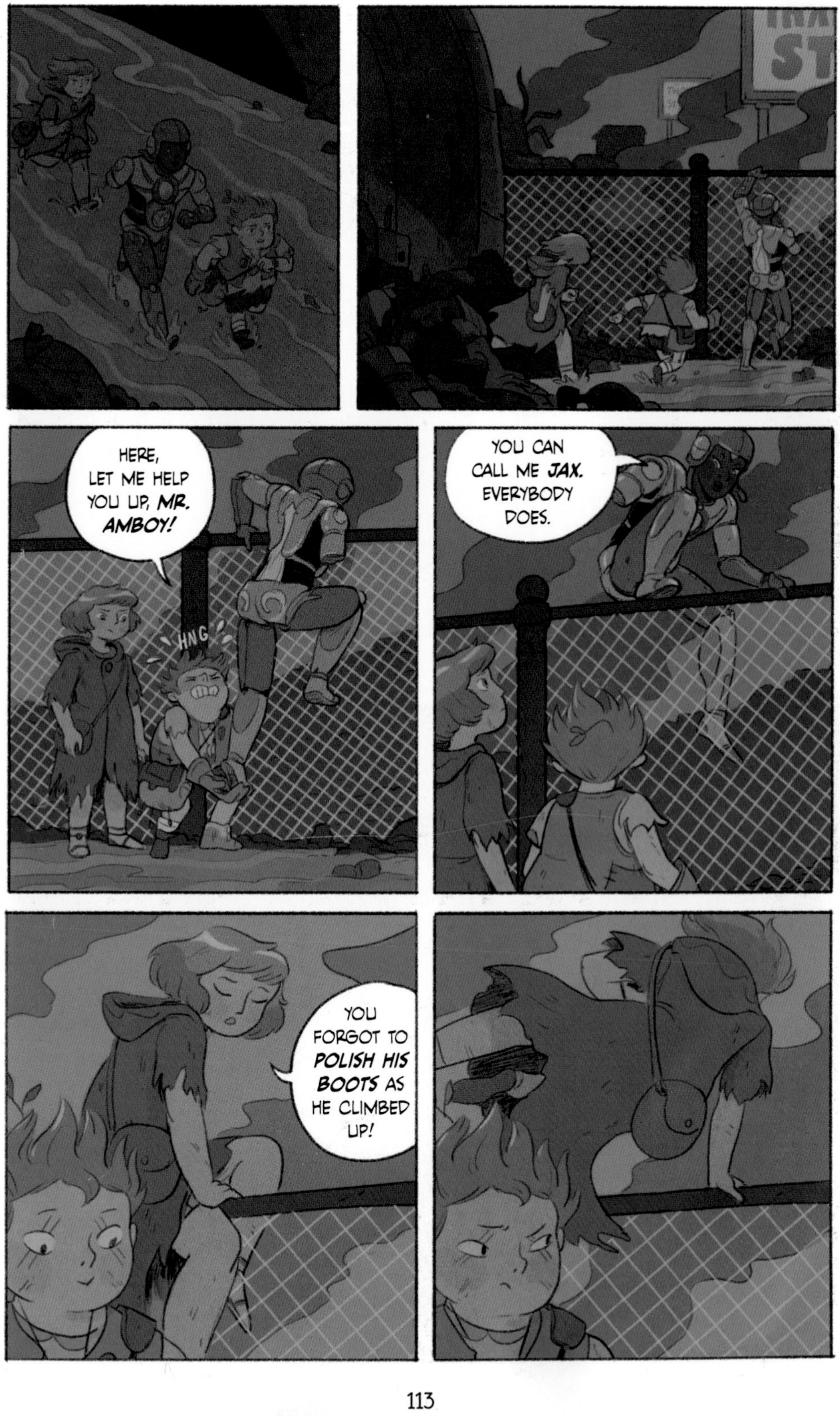
HERE, LET ME HELP YOU UP, MR. AMBOY!
HNG
YOU CAN CALL ME JAX. EVERYBODY DOES.
YOU FORGOT TO POLISH HIS BOOTS AS HE CLIMBED UP!

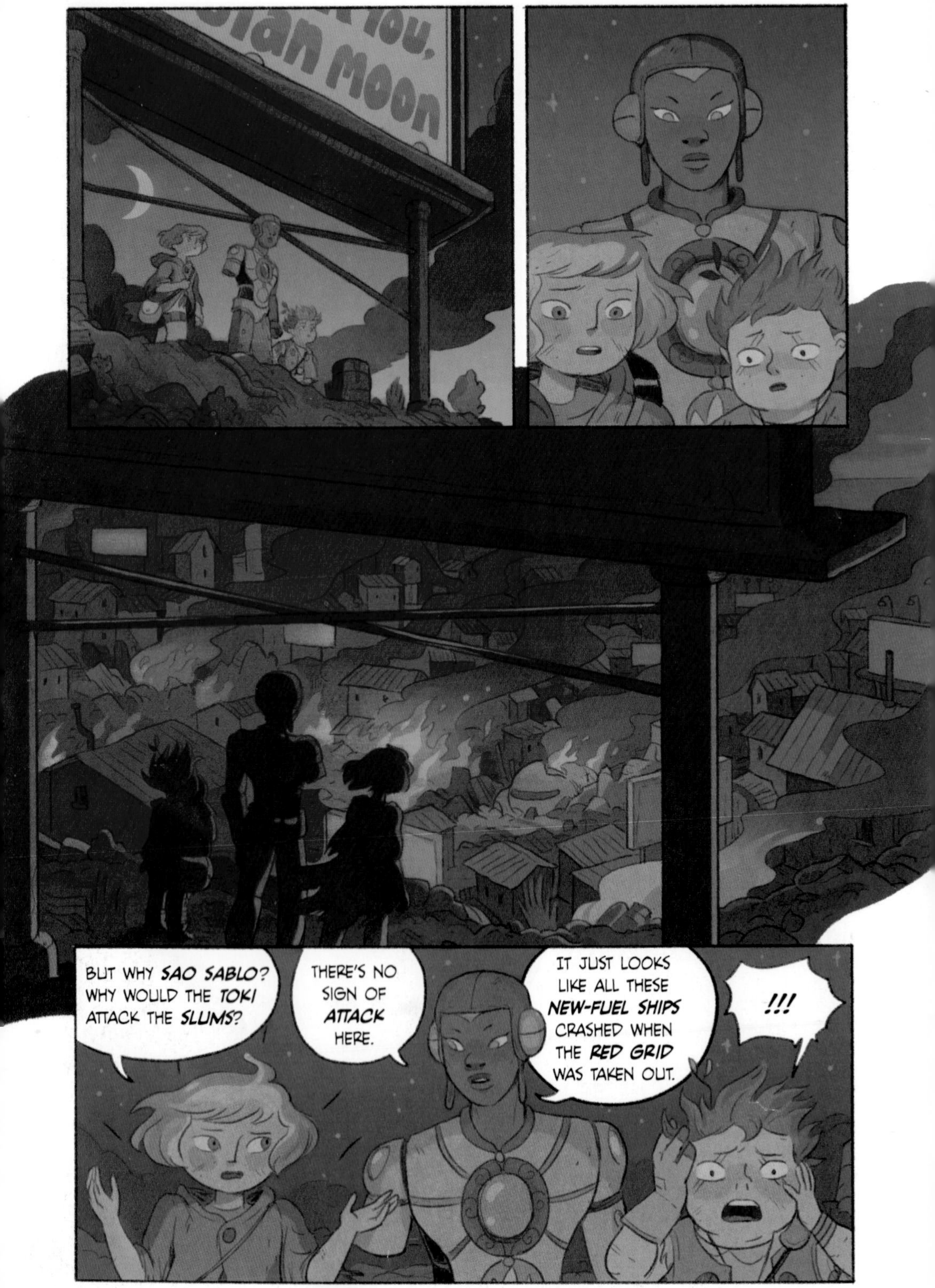
BUT WHY SAO SABLO? WHY WOULD THE TOKI ATTACK THE SLUMS?
THERE'S NO SIGN OF ATTACK HERE.
IT JUST LOOKS LIKE ALL THESE NEW-FUEL SHIPS CRASHED WHEN THE RED GRID WAS TAKEN OUT.
!!!

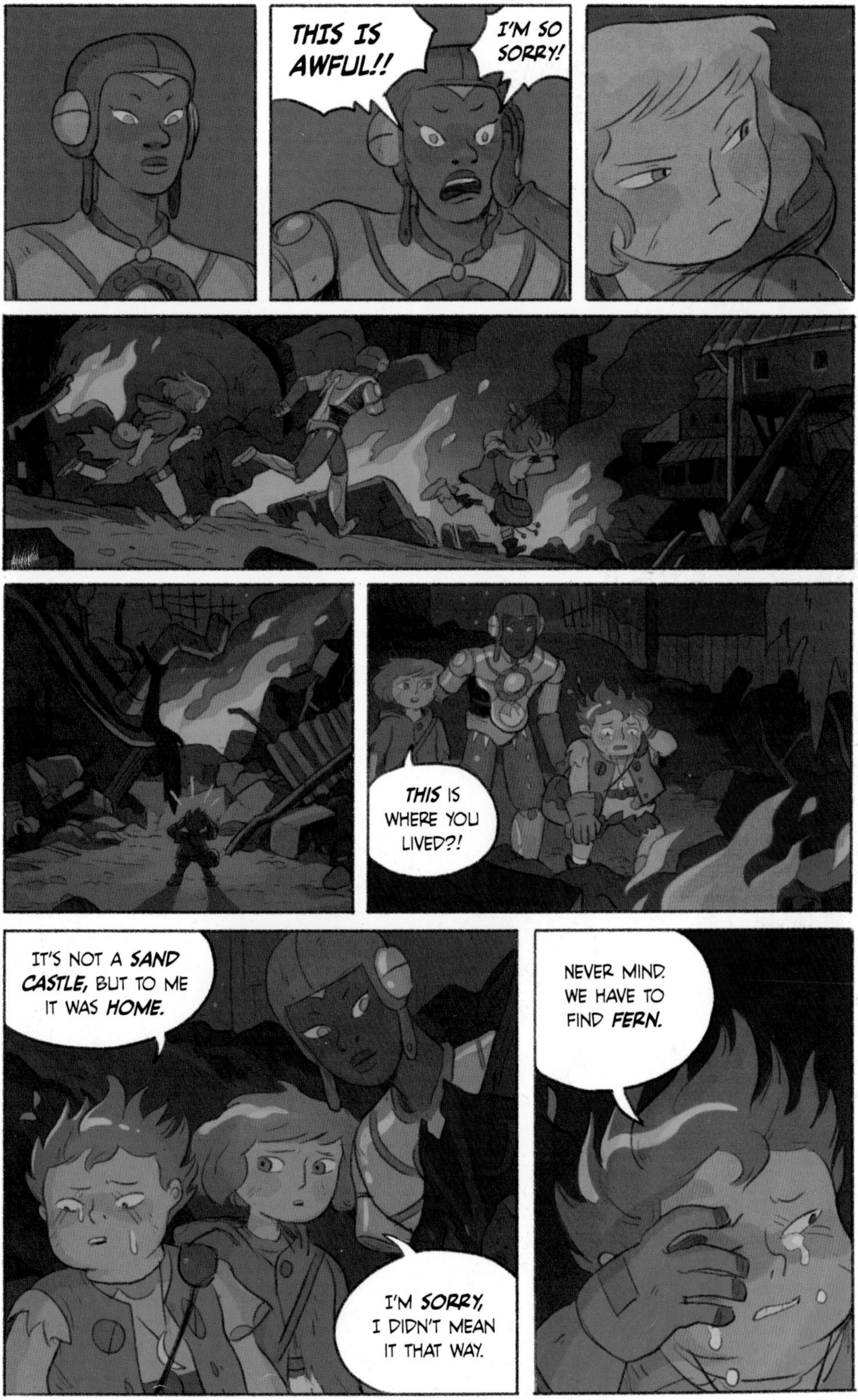

THIS IS AWFUL!!
I'M SO SORRY!
THIS IS WHERE YOU LIVED?!
IT'S NOT A SAND CASTLE, BUT TO ME IT WAS HOME.
I'M SORRY, I DIDN'T MEAN IT THAT WAY.
NEVER MIND. WE HAVE TO FIND FERN.

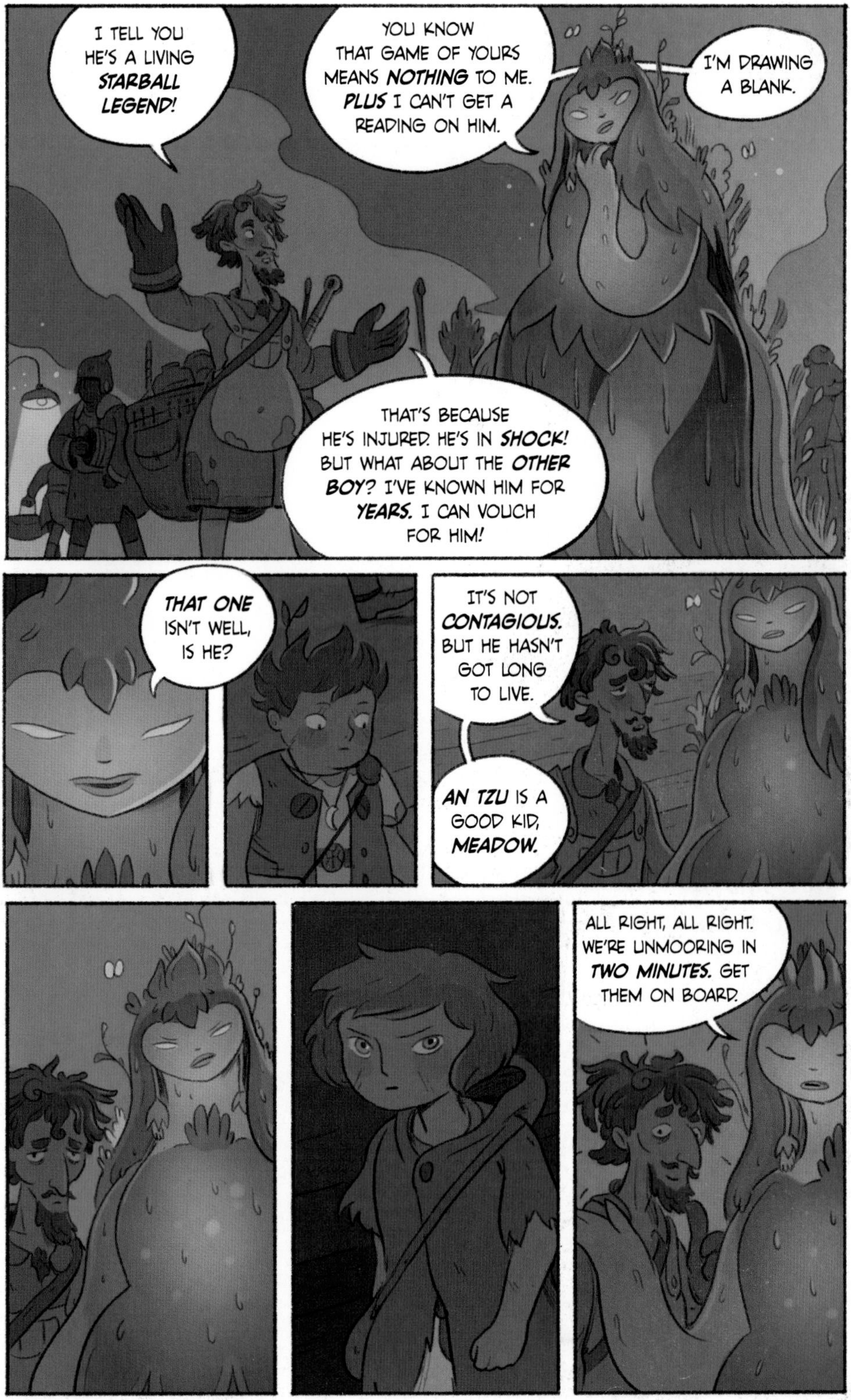
I TELL YOU HE'S A LIVING STARBALL LEGEND!
YOU KNOW THAT GAME OF YOURS MEANS NOTHING TO ME. PLUS I CAN'T GET A READING ON HIM.
I'M DRAWING A BLANK.
THAT'S BECAUSE HE'S INJURED. HE'S IN SHOCK! BUT WHAT ABOUT THE OTHER BOY? I'VE KNOWN HIM FOR YEARS. I CAN VOUCH FOR HIM!
THAT ONE ISN'T WELL, IS HE?
IT'S NOT CONTAGIOUS. BUT HE HASN'T GOT LONG TO LIVE.
AN TZU IS A GOOD KID, MEADOW.
ALL RIGHT, ALL RIGHT. WE'RE UNMOORING IN TWO MINUTES. GET THEM ON BOARD.

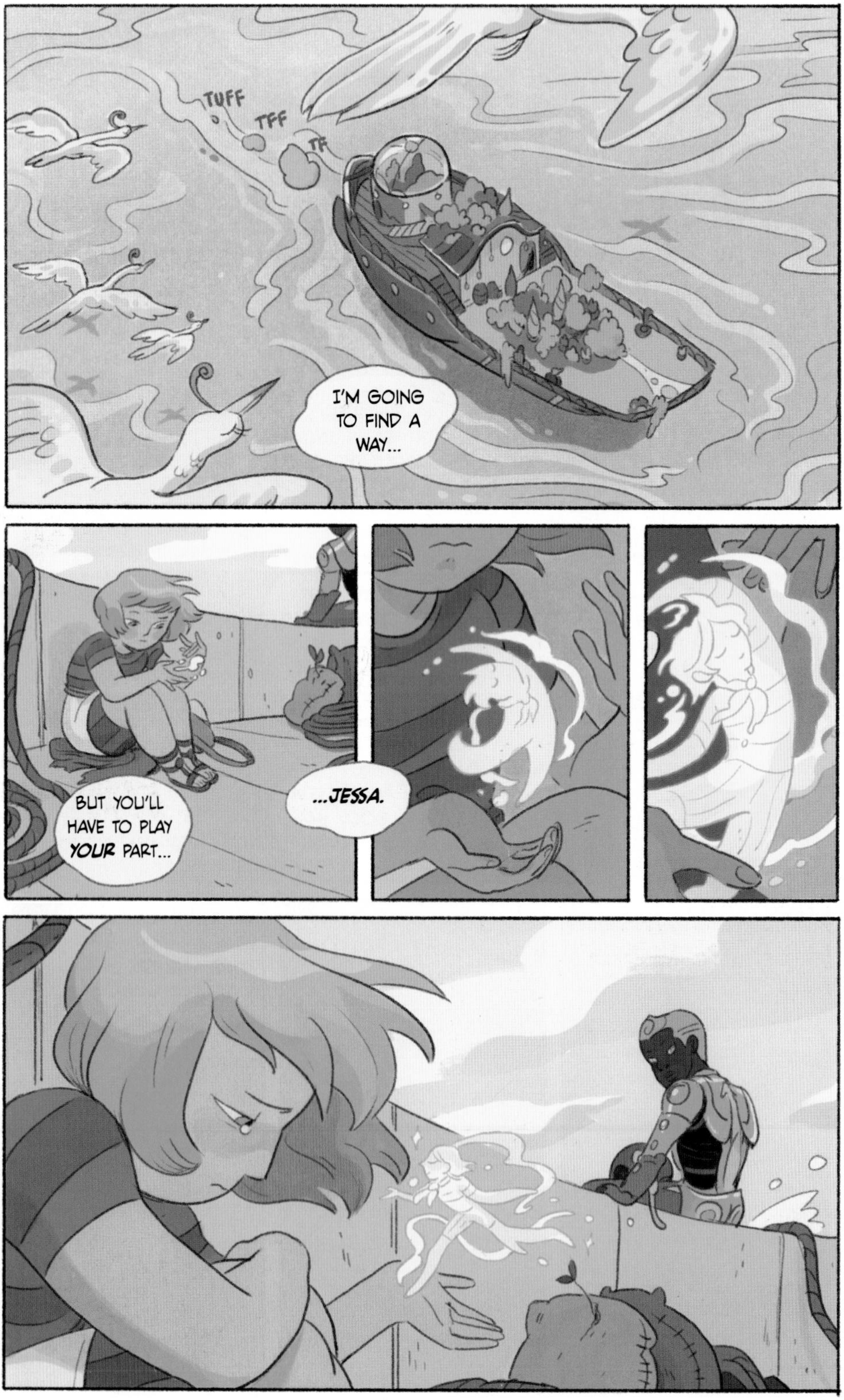
TUFF
TFF
TF
I'M GOING TO FIND A WAY...
BUT YOU'LL HAVE TO PLAY *YOUR* PART...
...*JESSA.*

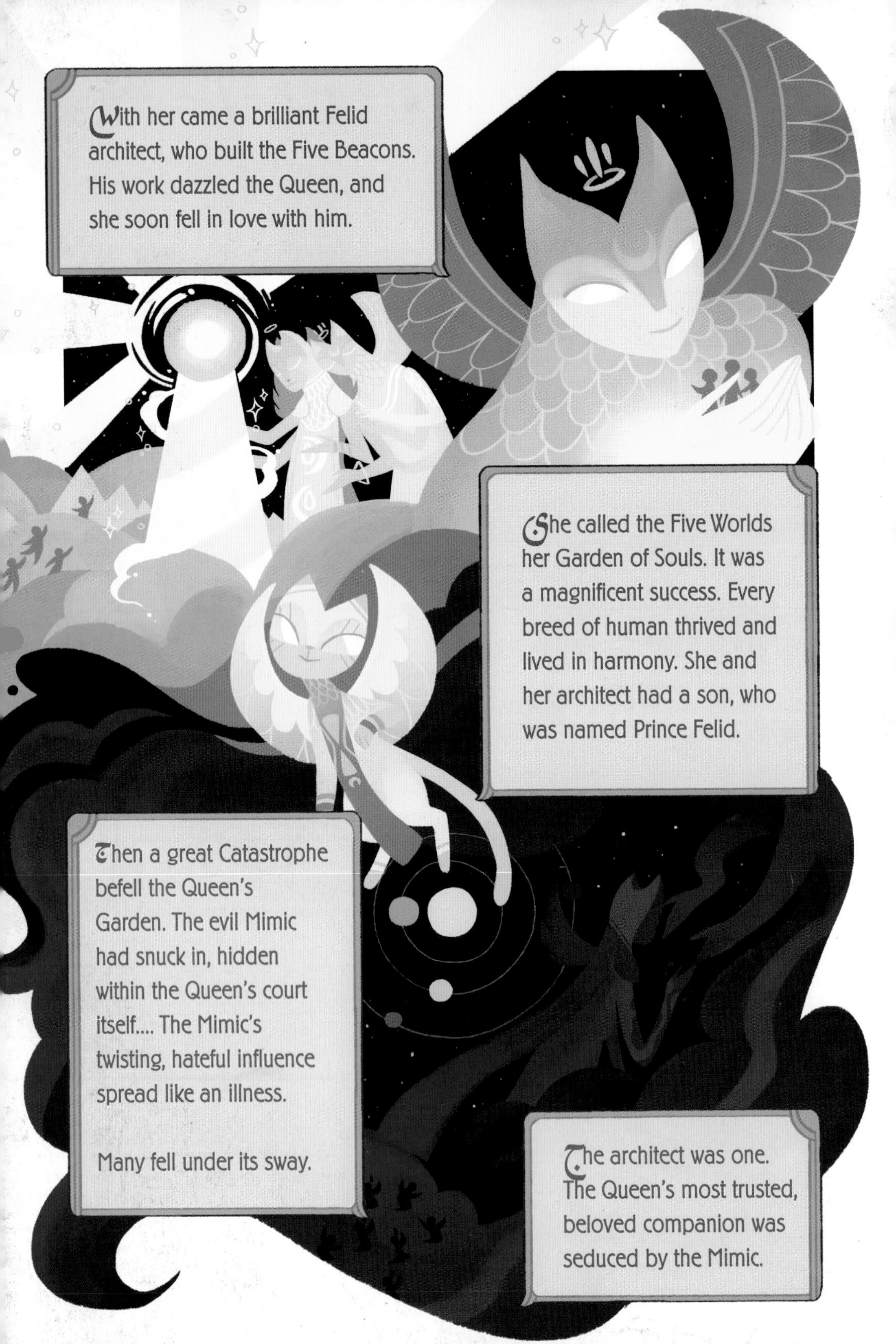
With her came a brilliant Felid architect, who built the Five Beacons. His work dazzled the Queen, and she soon fell in love with him.
She called the Five Worlds her Garden of Souls. It was a magnificent success. Every breed of human thrived and lived in harmony. She and her architect had a son, who was named Prince Felid.
Then a great Catastrophe befell the Queen's Garden. The evil Mimic had snuck in, hidden within the Queen's court itself.... The Mimic's twisting, hateful influence spread like an illness.
Many fell under its sway.
The architect was one. The Queen's most trusted, beloved companion was seduced by the Mimic.

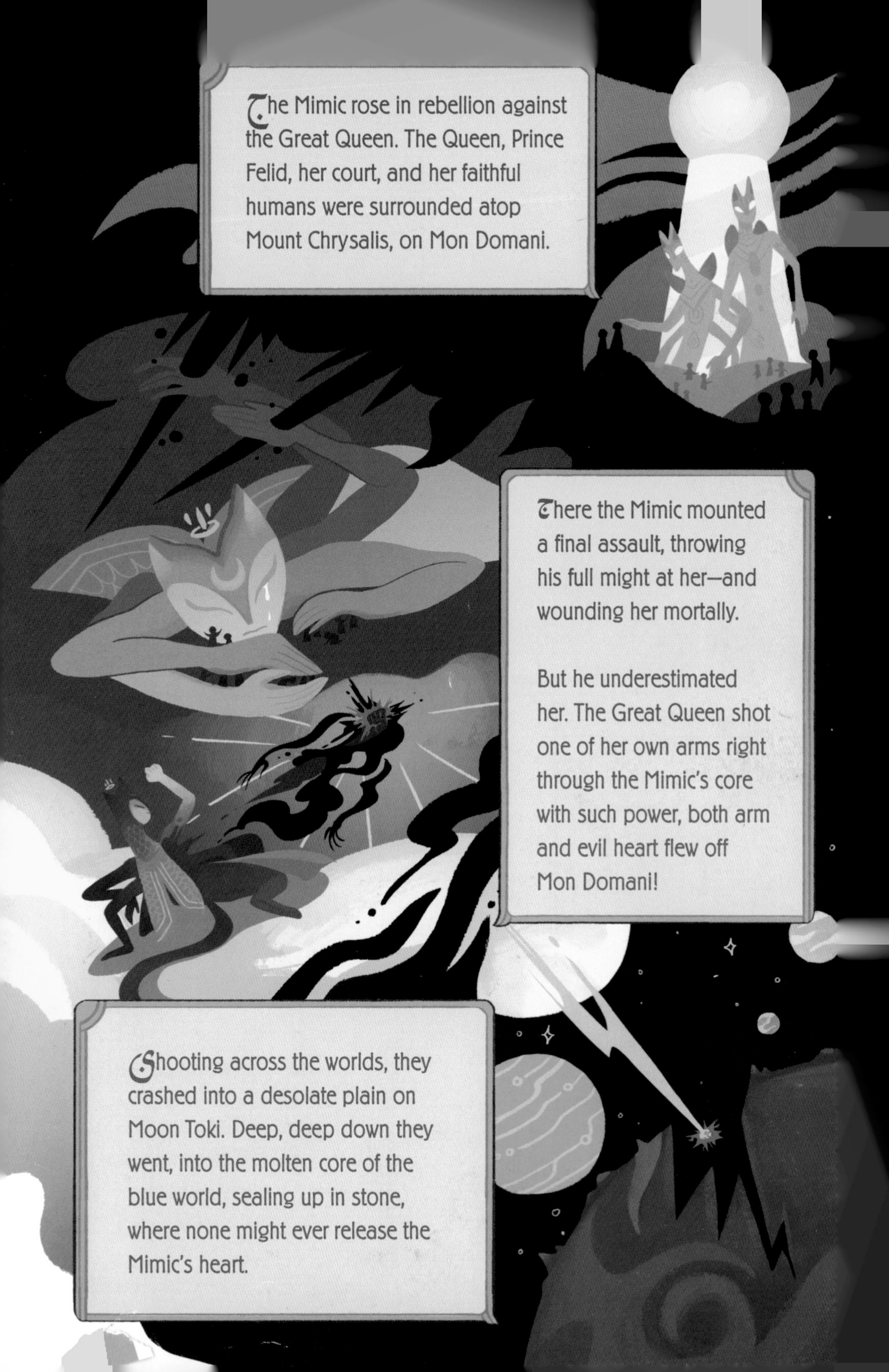
The Mimic rose in rebellion against the Great Queen. The Queen, Prince Felid, her court, and her faithful humans were surrounded atop Mount Chrysalis, on Mon Domani.
There the Mimic mounted a final assault, throwing his full might at her—and wounding her mortally.
But he underestimated her. The Great Queen shot one of her own arms right through the Mimic's core with such power, both arm and evil heart flew off Mon Domani!
Shooting across the worlds, they crashed into a desolate plain on Moon Toki. Deep, deep down they went, into the molten core of the blue world, sealing up in stone, where none might ever release the Mimic's heart.

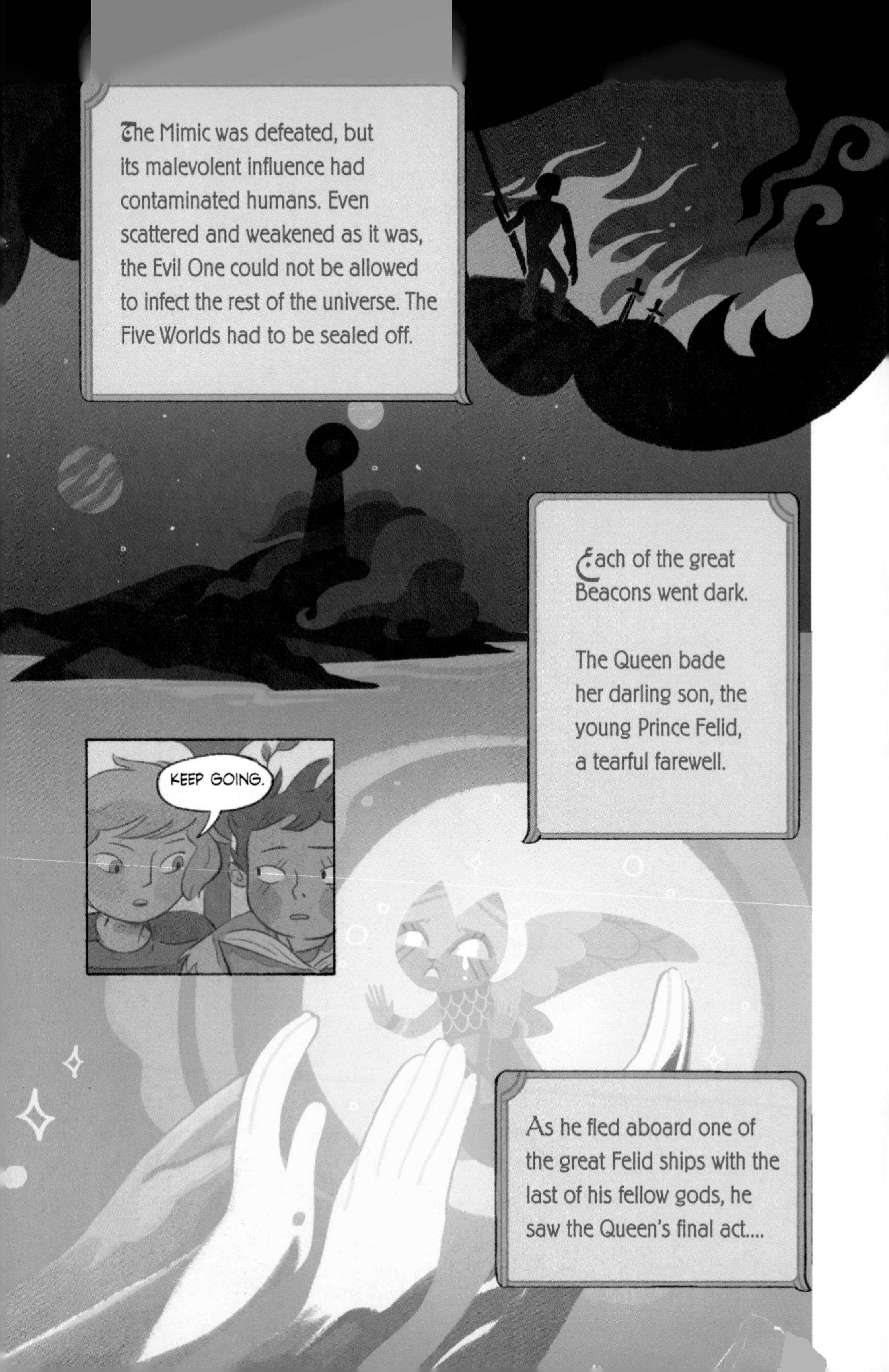
The Mimic was defeated, but its malevolent influence had contaminated humans. Even scattered and weakened as it was, the Evil One could not be allowed to infect the rest of the universe. The Five Worlds had to be sealed off.
Each of the great Beacons went dark.
The Queen bade her darling son, the young Prince Felid, a tearful farewell.
KEEP GOING.
As he fled aboard one of the great Felid ships with the last of his fellow gods, he saw the Queen's final act....

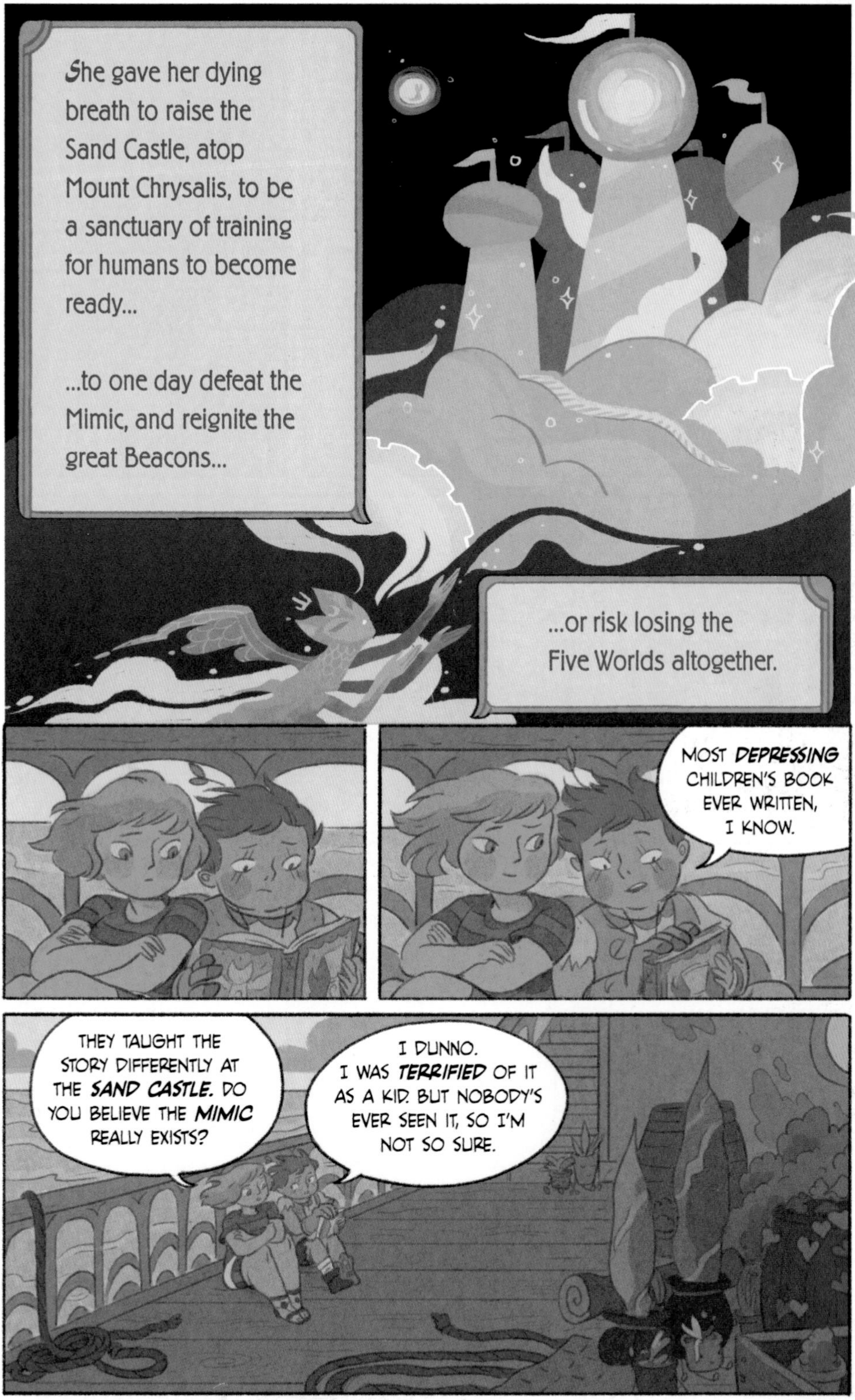
She gave her dying breath to raise the Sand Castle, atop Mount Chrysalis, to be a sanctuary of training for humans to become ready...
...to one day defeat the Mimic, and reignite the great Beacons...
...or risk losing the Five Worlds altogether.
MOST DEPRESSING CHILDREN'S BOOK EVER WRITTEN, I KNOW.
THEY TAUGHT THE STORY DIFFERENTLY AT THE SAND CASTLE. DO YOU BELIEVE THE MIMIC REALLY EXISTS?
I DUNNO. I WAS TERRIFIED OF IT AS A KID. BUT NOBODY'S EVER SEEN IT, SO I'M NOT SO SURE.

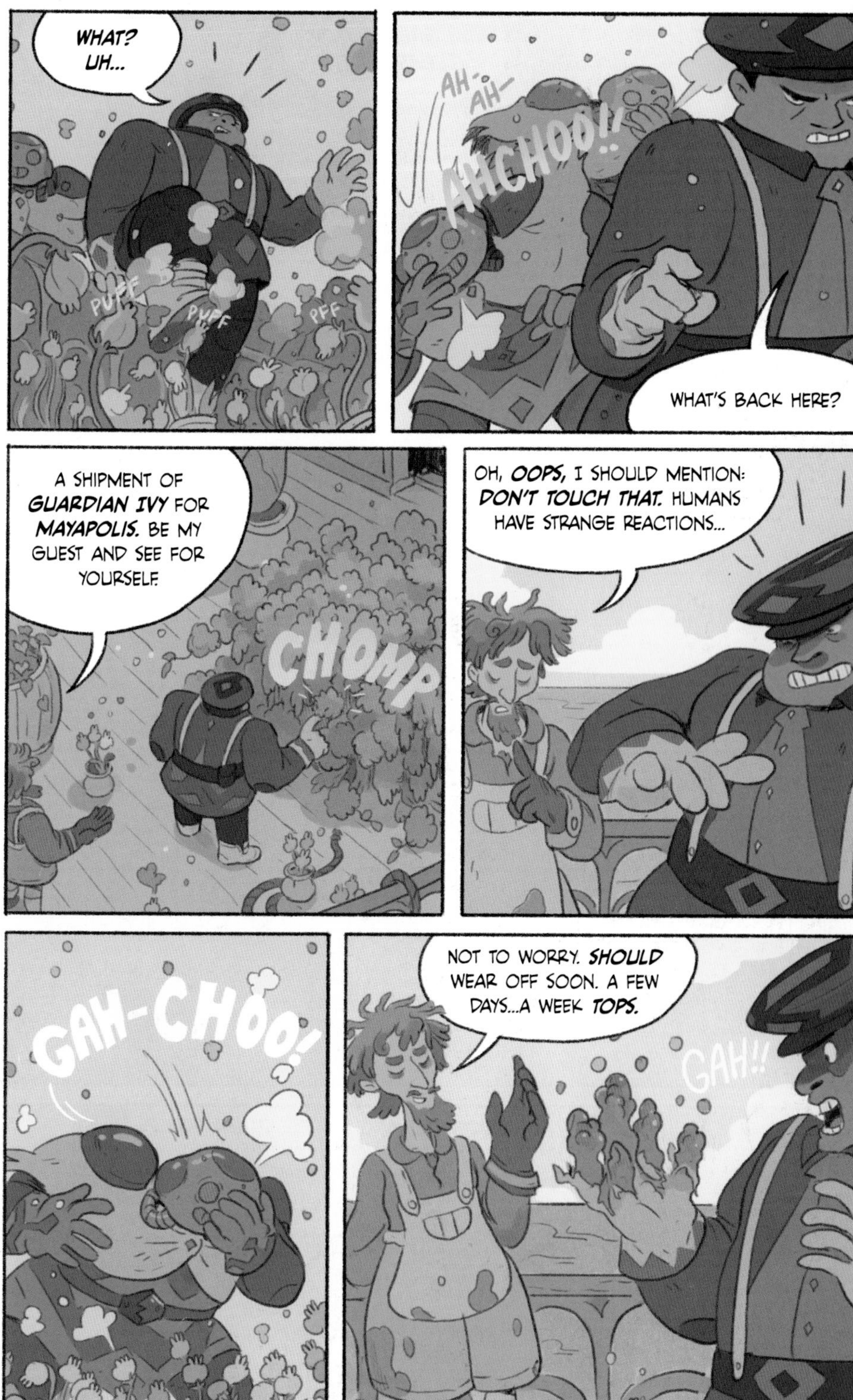
WHAT?
UH...
PUFF
PUFF
PFF
AH-
AH-
AHCHOO!!
WHAT'S BACK HERE?
A SHIPMENT OF GUARDIAN IVY FOR MAYAPOLIS. BE MY GUEST AND SEE FOR YOURSELF.
CHOMP
OH, OOPS, I SHOULD MENTION: DON'T TOUCH THAT. HUMANS HAVE STRANGE REACTIONS...
GAH-CHOO!
NOT TO WORRY. SHOULD WEAR OFF SOON. A FEW DAYS...A WEEK TOPS.
GAH!!

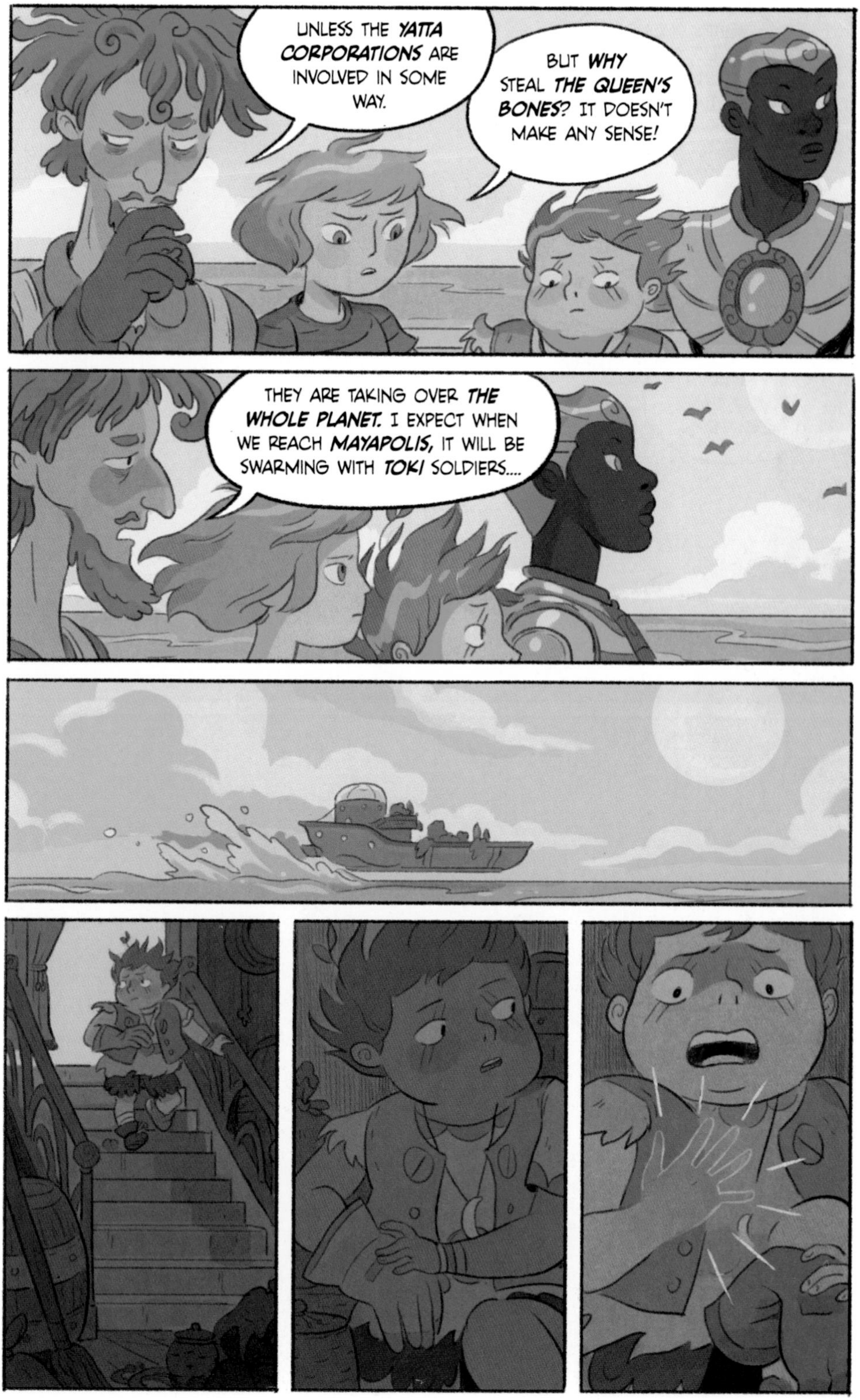
UNLESS THE YATTA CORPORATIONS ARE INVOLVED IN SOME WAY.
BUT WHY STEAL THE QUEEN'S BONES? IT DOESN'T MAKE ANY SENSE!
THEY ARE TAKING OVER THE WHOLE PLANET. I EXPECT WHEN WE REACH MAYAPOLIS, IT WILL BE SWARMING WITH TOKI SOLDIERS....

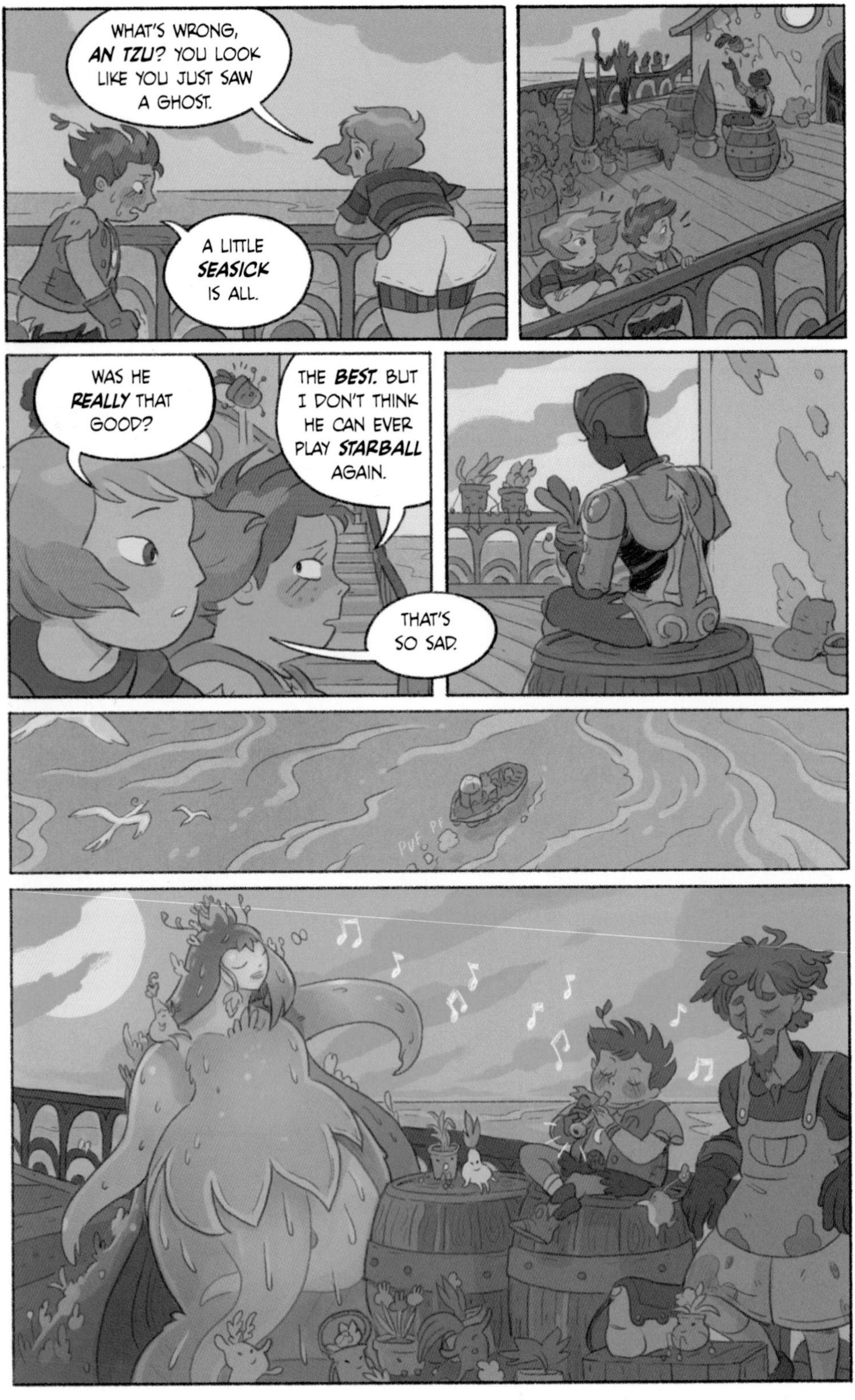
WHAT'S WRONG, AN TZU? YOU LOOK LIKE YOU JUST SAW A GHOST.
A LITTLE SEASICK IS ALL.
WAS HE REALLY THAT GOOD?
THE BEST. BUT I DON'T THINK HE CAN EVER PLAY STARBALL AGAIN.
THAT'S SO SAD.
PUF PF

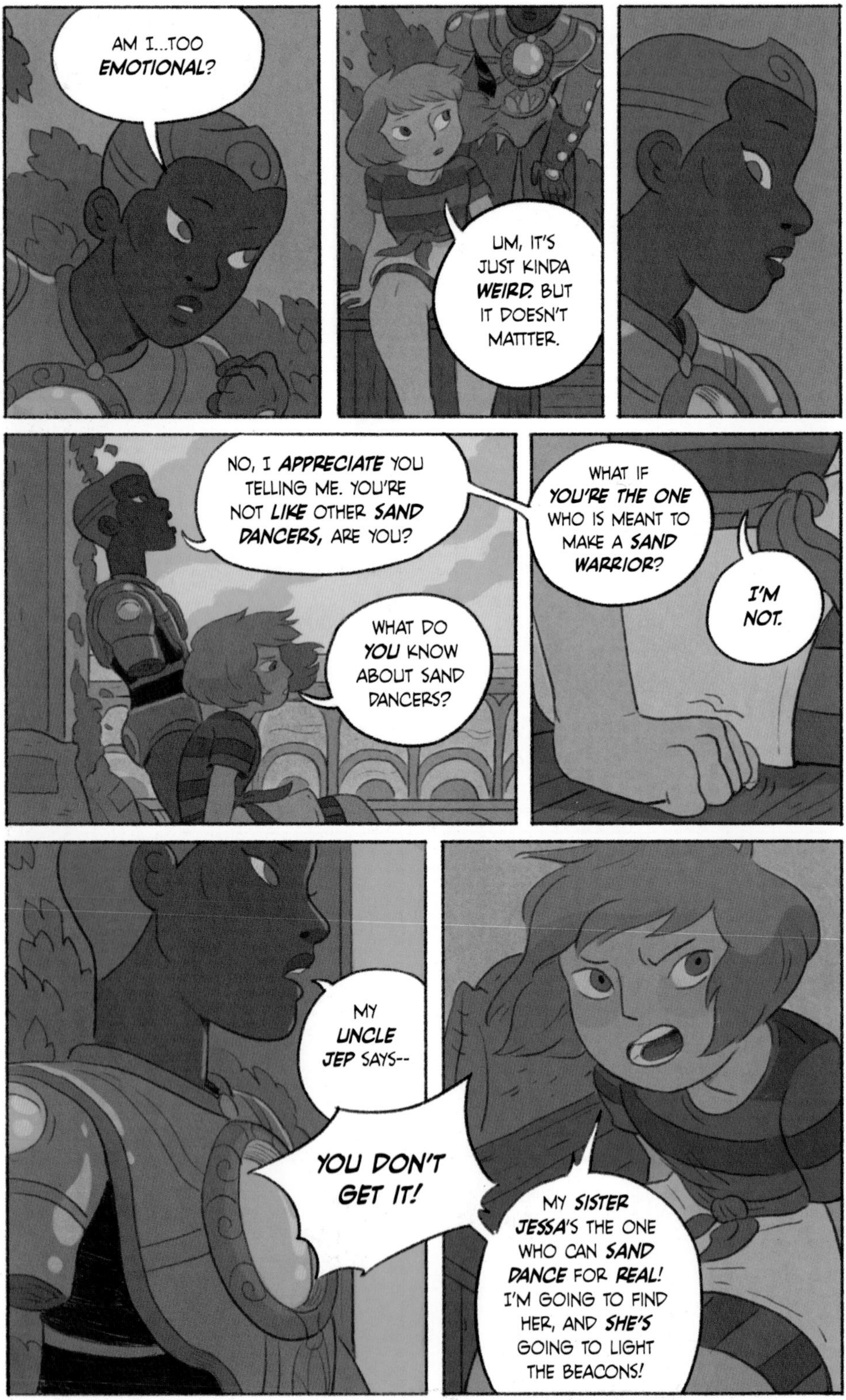
AM I...TOO *EMOTIONAL?*
UM, IT'S JUST KINDA *WEIRD.* BUT IT DOESN'T MATTER.
NO, I *APPRECIATE* YOU TELLING ME. YOU'RE NOT *LIKE* OTHER *SAND DANCERS,* ARE YOU?
WHAT DO *YOU* KNOW ABOUT SAND DANCERS?
WHAT IF *YOU'RE THE ONE* WHO IS MEANT TO MAKE A *SAND WARRIOR?*
I'M NOT.
MY *UNCLE JEP* SAYS--
YOU DON'T GET IT!
MY *SISTER JESSA'*S THE ONE WHO CAN *SAND DANCE* FOR *REAL!* I'M GOING TO FIND HER, AND *SHE'S* GOING TO LIGHT THE BEACONS!

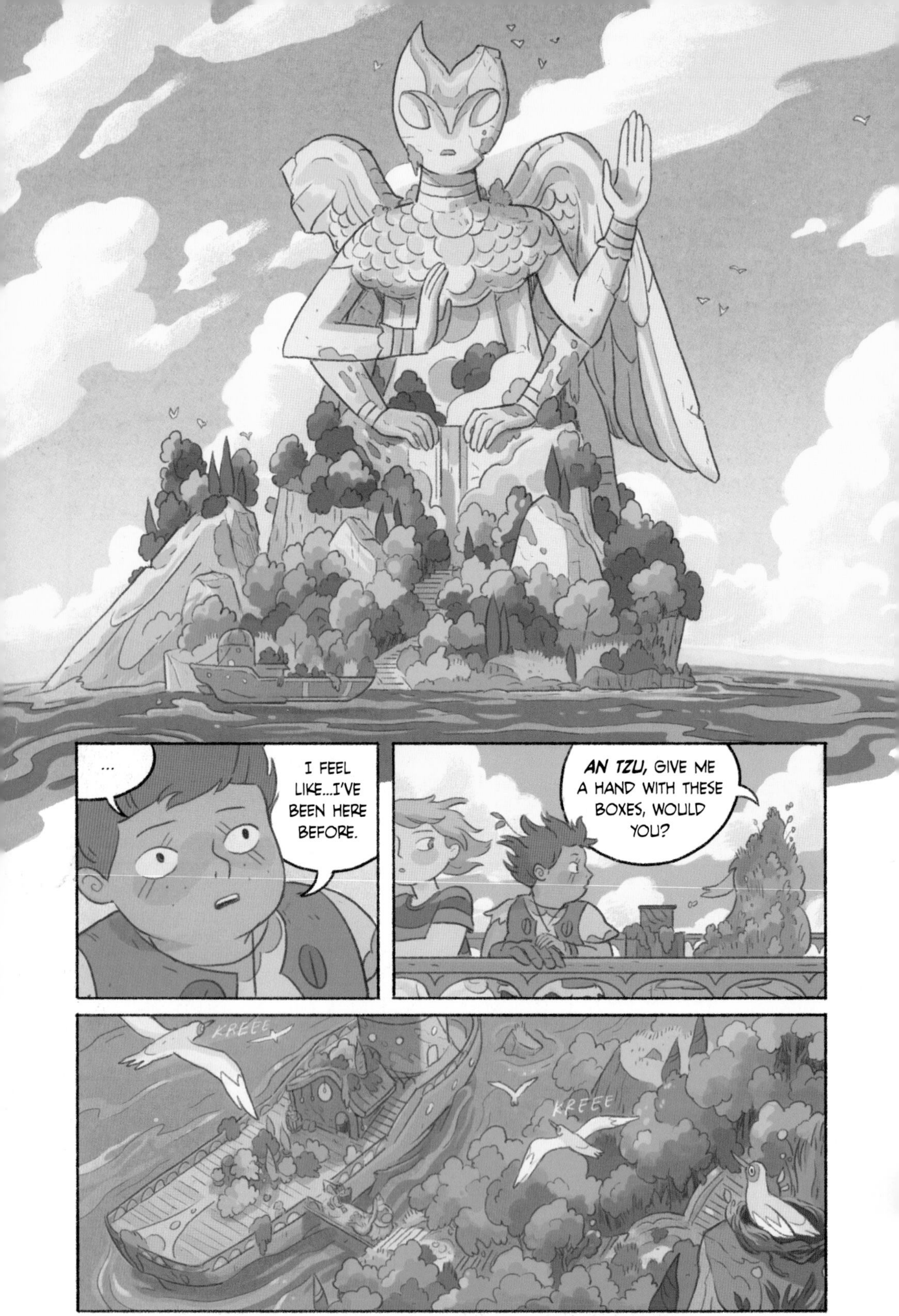
...
I FEEL LIKE...I'VE BEEN HERE BEFORE.
AN TZU, GIVE ME A HAND WITH THESE BOXES, WOULD YOU?
KREEE
KREEE

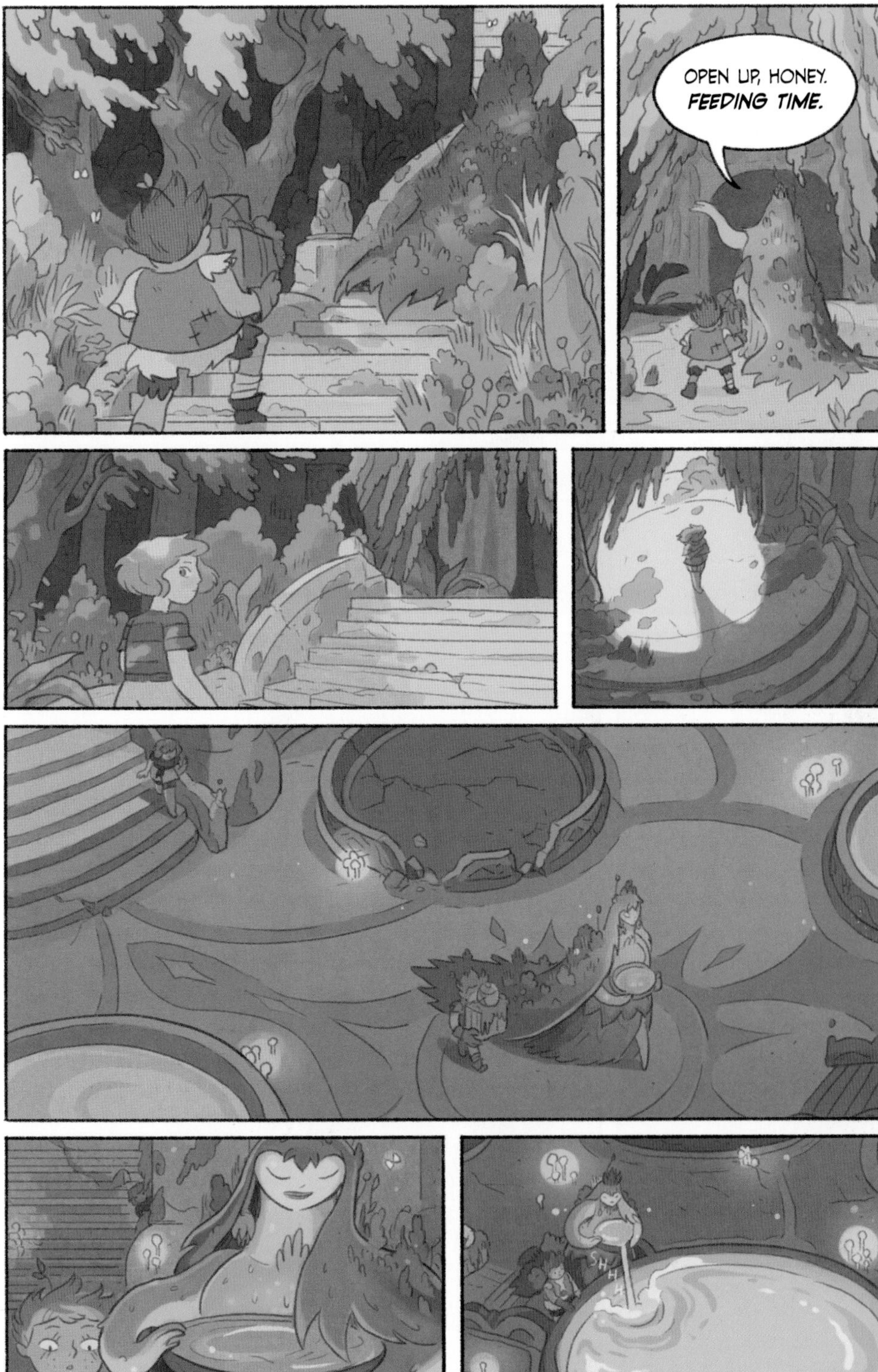
OPEN UP, HONEY.
FEEDING TIME.

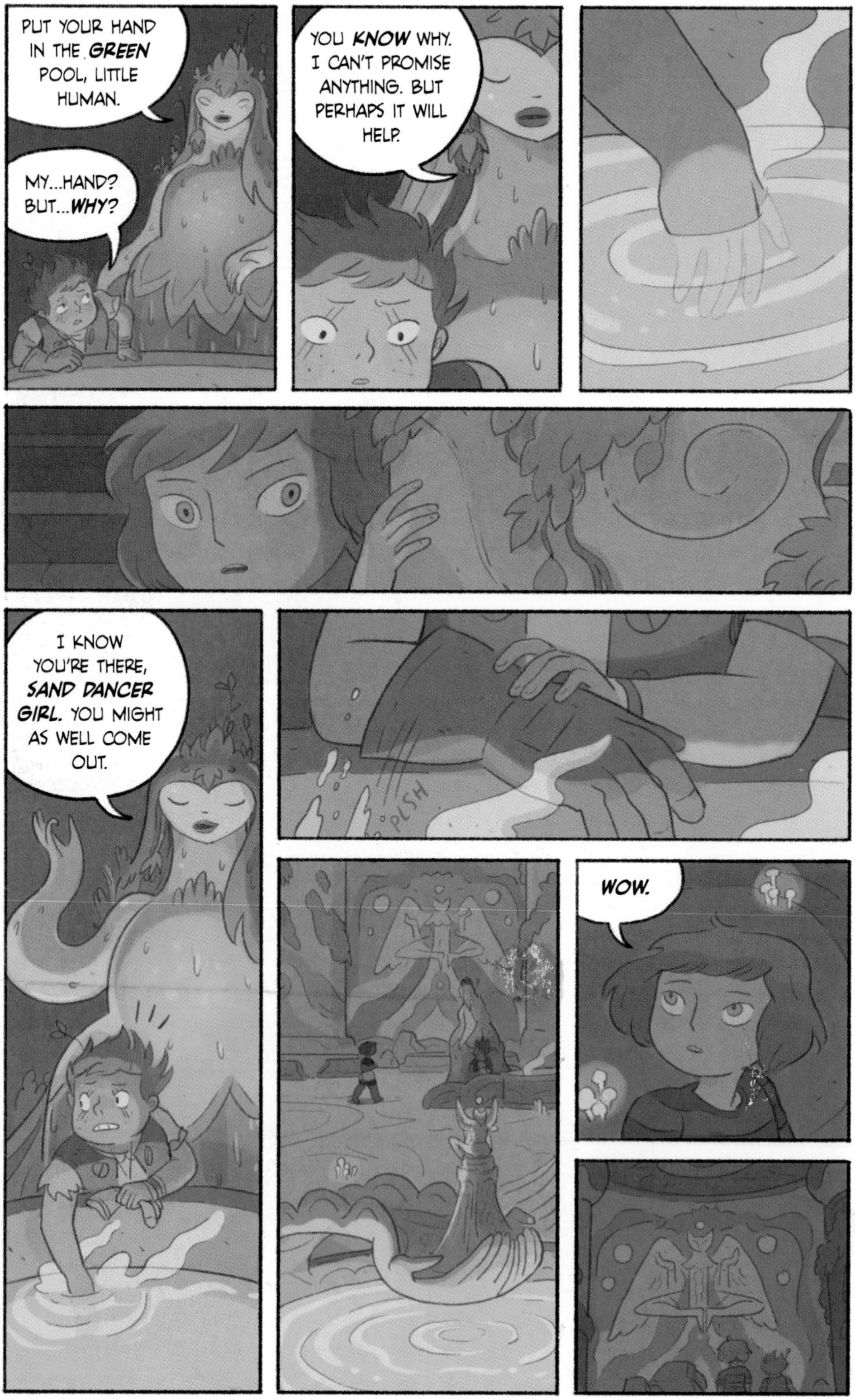
PUT YOUR HAND IN THE GREEN POOL, LITTLE HUMAN.
MY...HAND? BUT...WHY?
YOU KNOW WHY. I CAN'T PROMISE ANYTHING. BUT PERHAPS IT WILL HELP.
I KNOW YOU'RE THERE, SAND DANCER GIRL. YOU MIGHT AS WELL COME OUT.
PLSH
WOW.

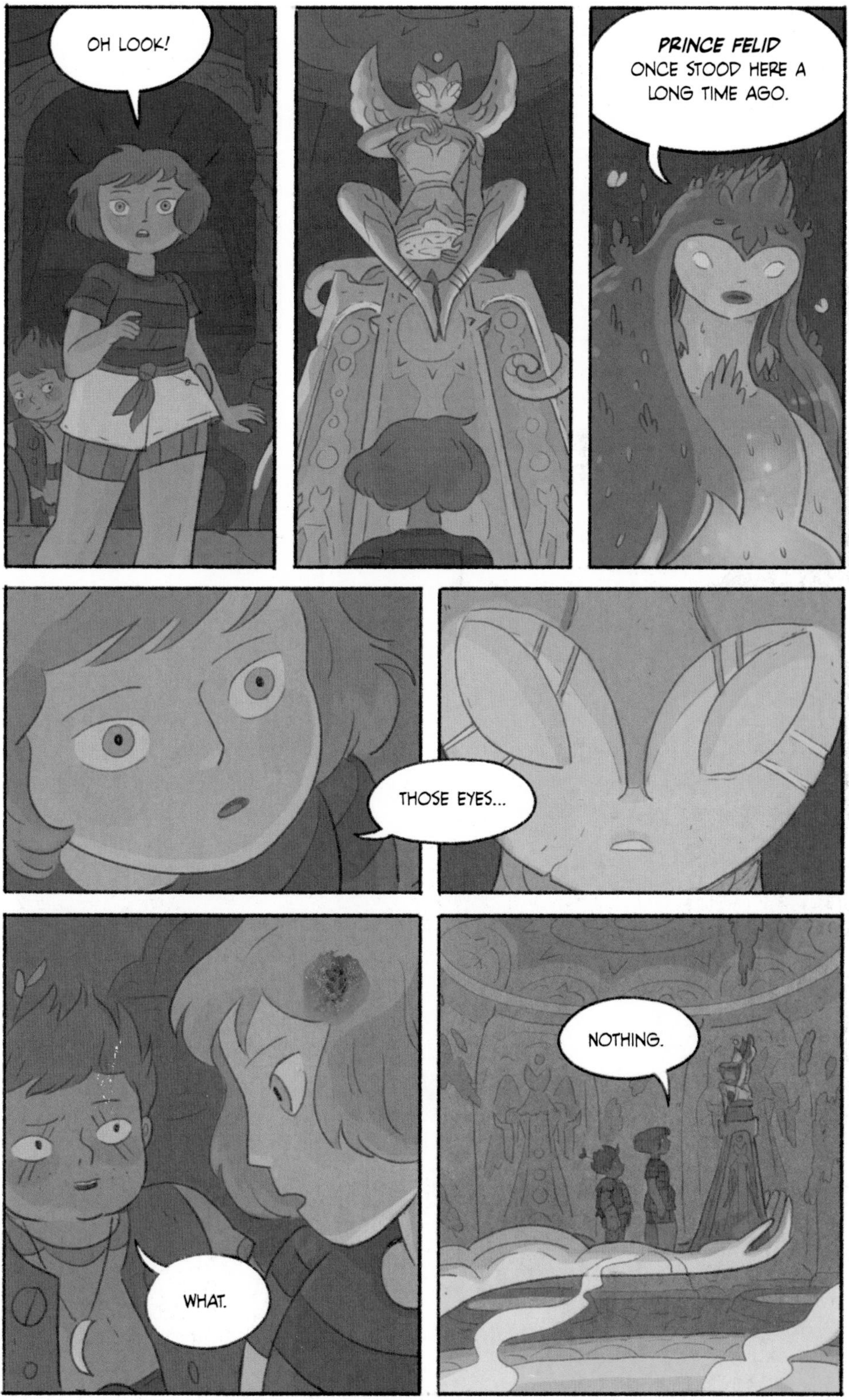
OH LOOK!
PRINCE FELID ONCE STOOD HERE A LONG TIME AGO.
THOSE EYES...
WHAT.
NOTHING.

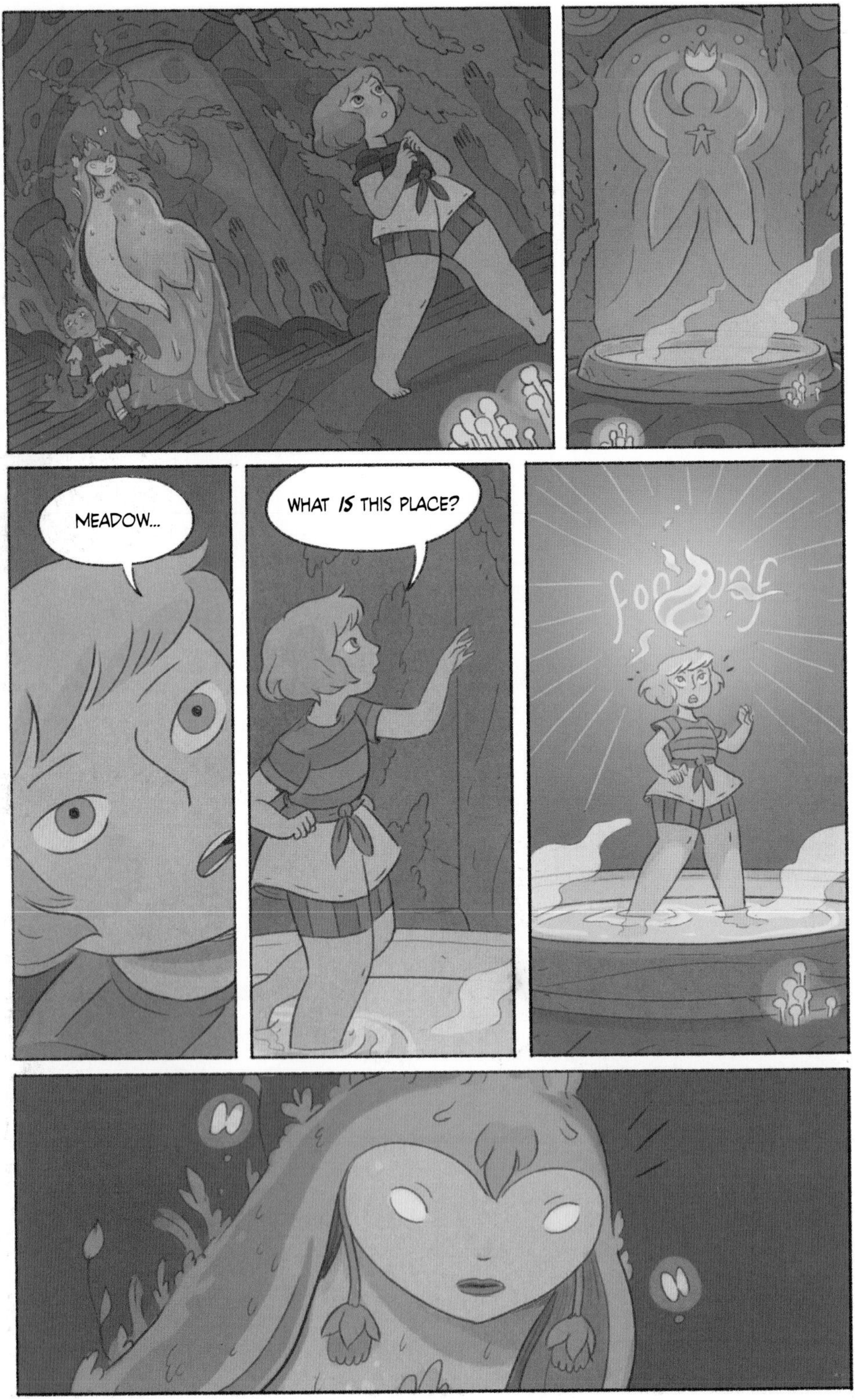
MEADOW...
WHAT *IS* THIS PLACE?

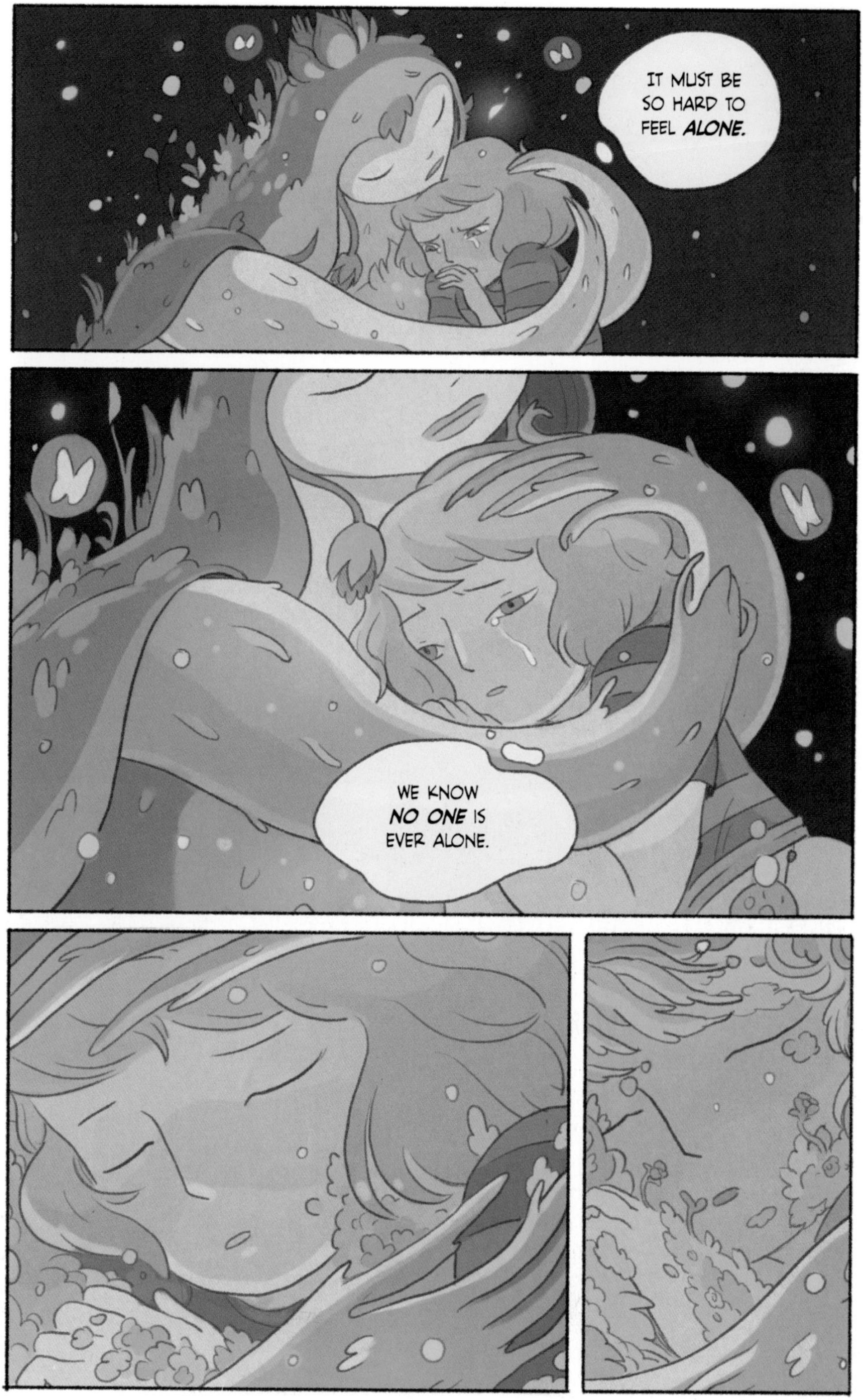
IT MUST BE SO HARD TO FEEL ALONE.
WE KNOW NO ONE IS EVER ALONE.

144

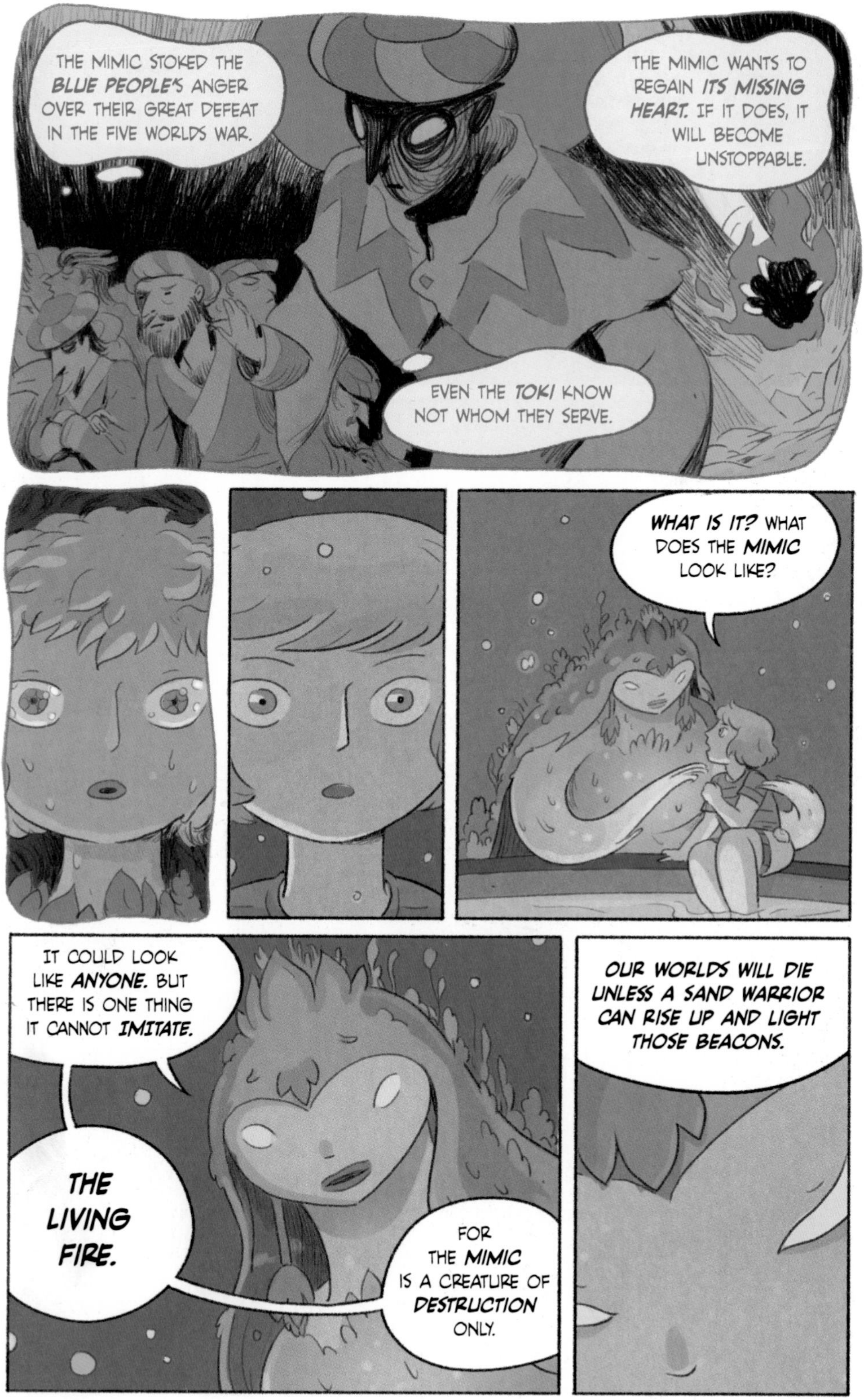
THE MIMIC STOKED THE BLUE PEOPLE'S ANGER OVER THEIR GREAT DEFEAT IN THE FIVE WORLDS WAR.
THE MIMIC WANTS TO REGAIN ITS MISSING HEART. IF IT DOES, IT WILL BECOME UNSTOPPABLE.
EVEN THE TOKI KNOW NOT WHOM THEY SERVE.
WHAT IS IT? WHAT DOES THE MIMIC LOOK LIKE?
IT COULD LOOK LIKE ANYONE. BUT THERE IS ONE THING IT CANNOT IMITATE.
THE LIVING FIRE.
FOR THE MIMIC IS A CREATURE OF DESTRUCTION ONLY.
OUR WORLDS WILL DIE UNLESS A SAND WARRIOR CAN RISE UP AND LIGHT THOSE BEACONS.

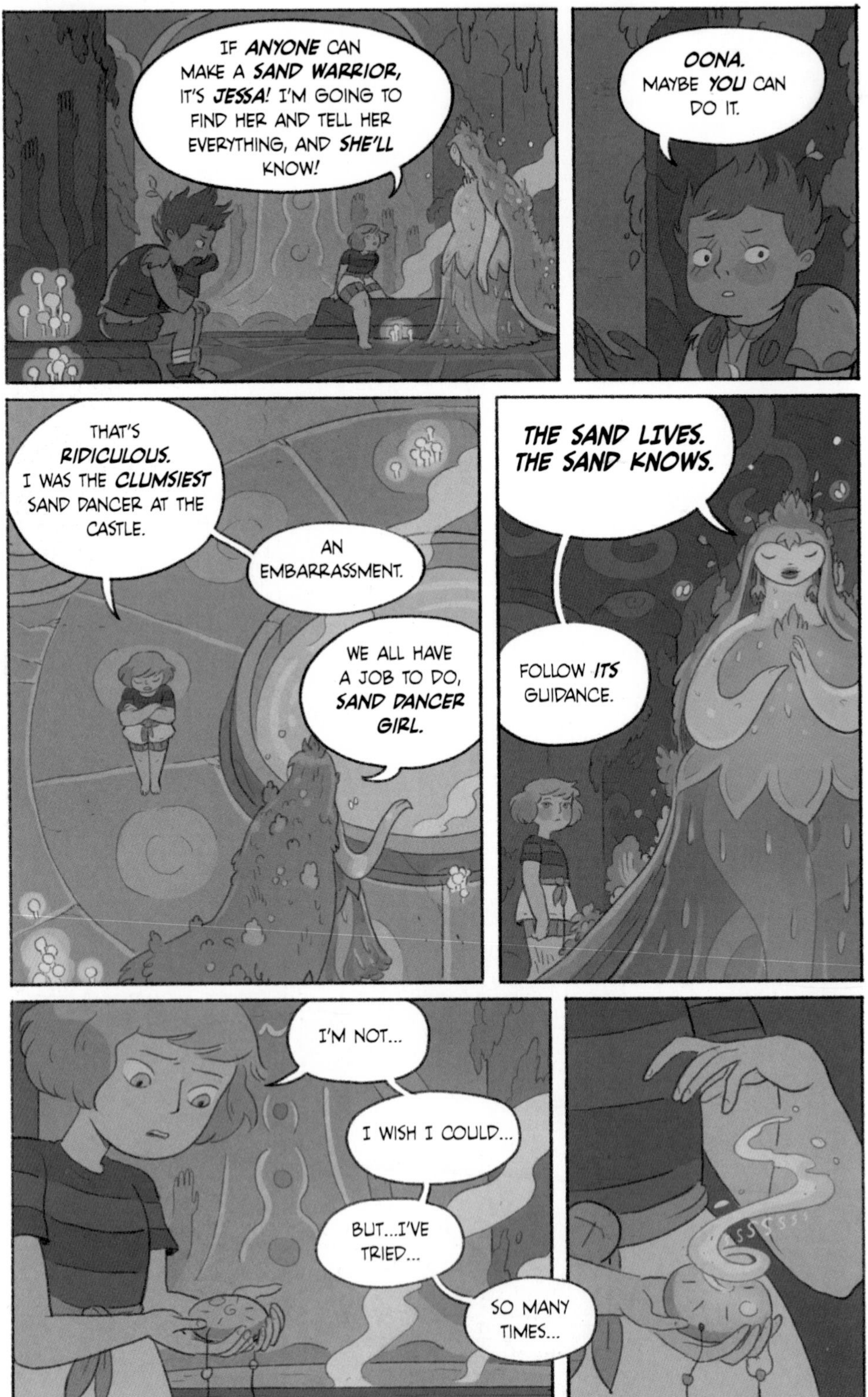

IF ANYONE CAN MAKE A SAND WARRIOR, IT'S JESSA! I'M GOING TO FIND HER AND TELL HER EVERYTHING, AND SHE'LL KNOW!
OONA. MAYBE YOU CAN DO IT.
THAT'S RIDICULOUS. I WAS THE CLUMSIEST SAND DANCER AT THE CASTLE.
AN EMBARRASSMENT.
WE ALL HAVE A JOB TO DO, SAND DANCER GIRL.
THE SAND LIVES. THE SAND KNOWS.
FOLLOW ITS GUIDANCE.
I'M NOT...
I WISH I COULD...
BUT...I'VE TRIED...
SO MANY TIMES...

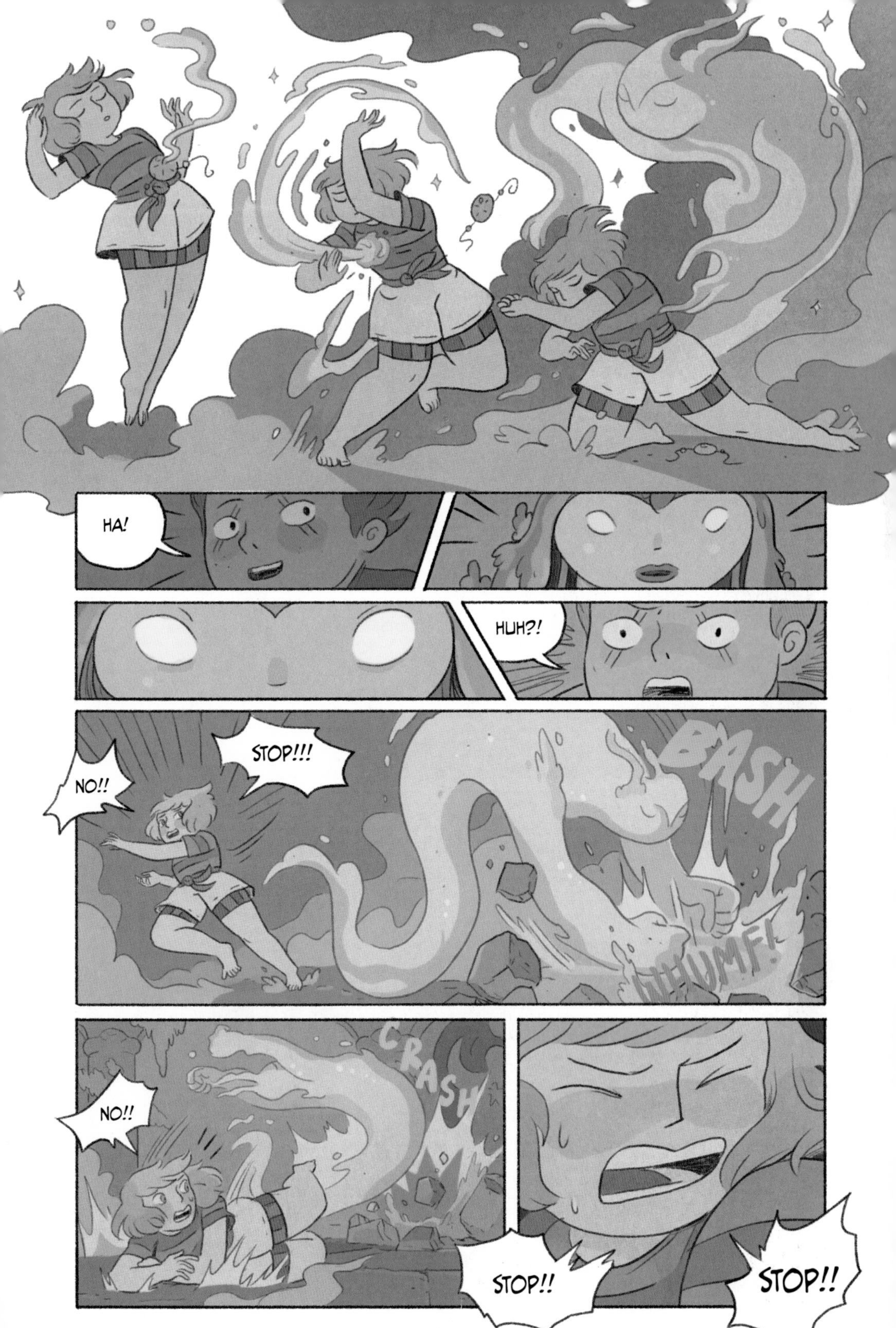
HA!
HUH?!
NO!!
STOP!!!
BASH
WHUMF!
NO!!
CRASH
STOP!!
STOP!!

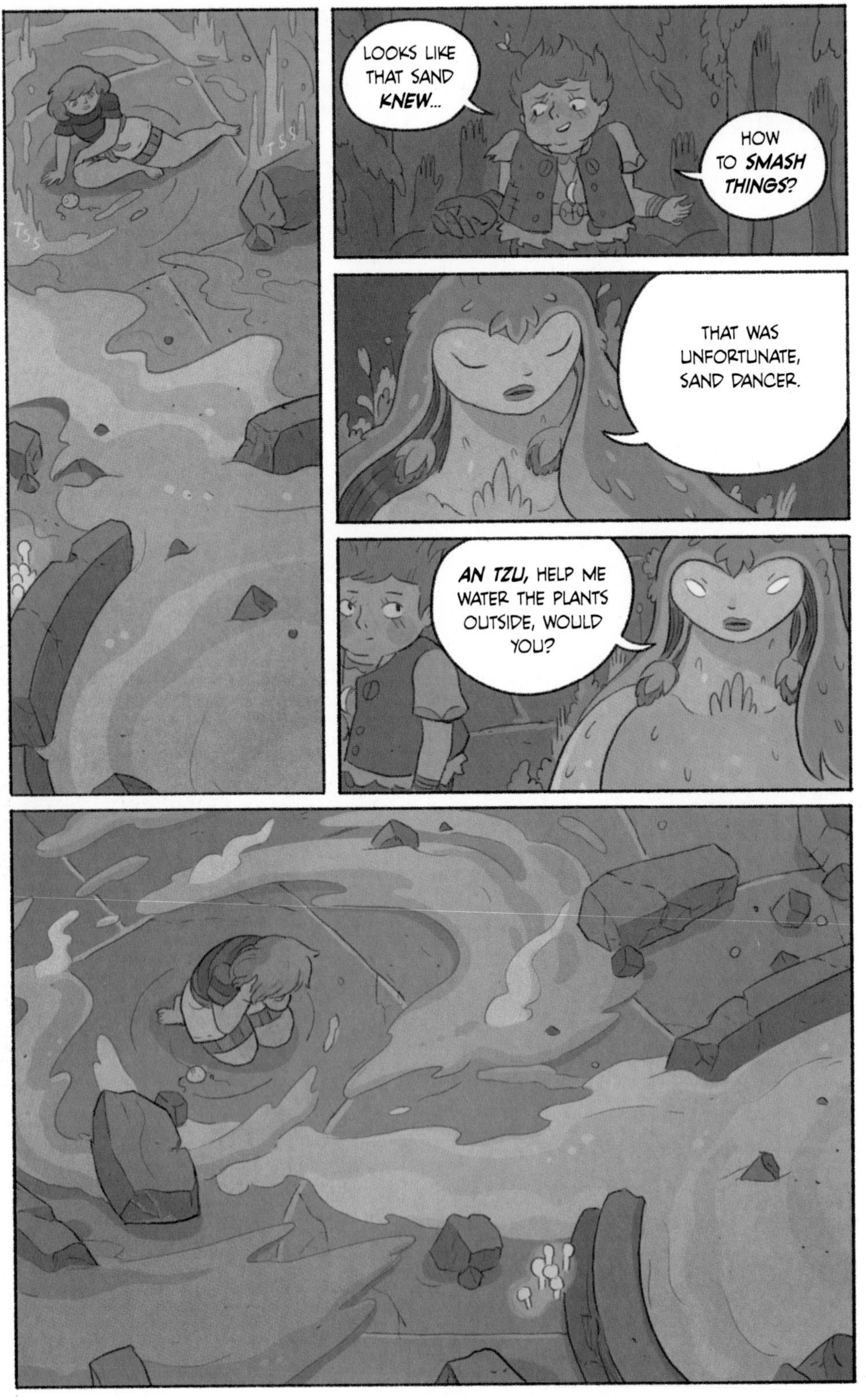
TSS
TSS
LOOKS LIKE THAT SAND KNEW...
HOW TO SMASH THINGS?
THAT WAS UNFORTUNATE, SAND DANCER.
AN TZU, HELP ME WATER THE PLANTS OUTSIDE, WOULD YOU?

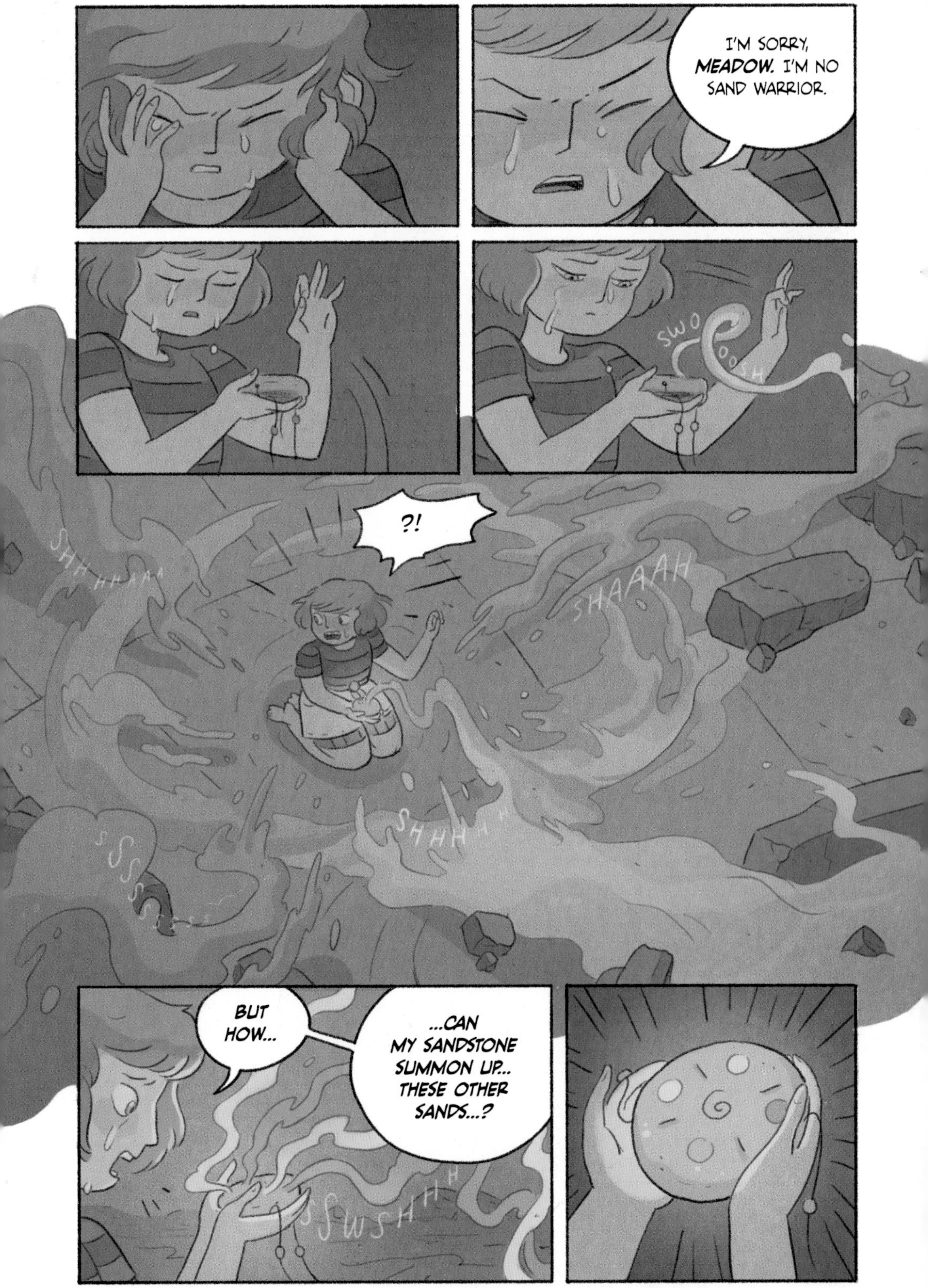
I'M SORRY, MEADOW. I'M NO SAND WARRIOR.
SWOOOSH
?!
SHHHHAAA
SHAAAAH
SHHHHH
SSSSSS
BUT HOW...
...CAN MY SANDSTONE SUMMON UP... THESE OTHER SANDS...?
SSWSHHH

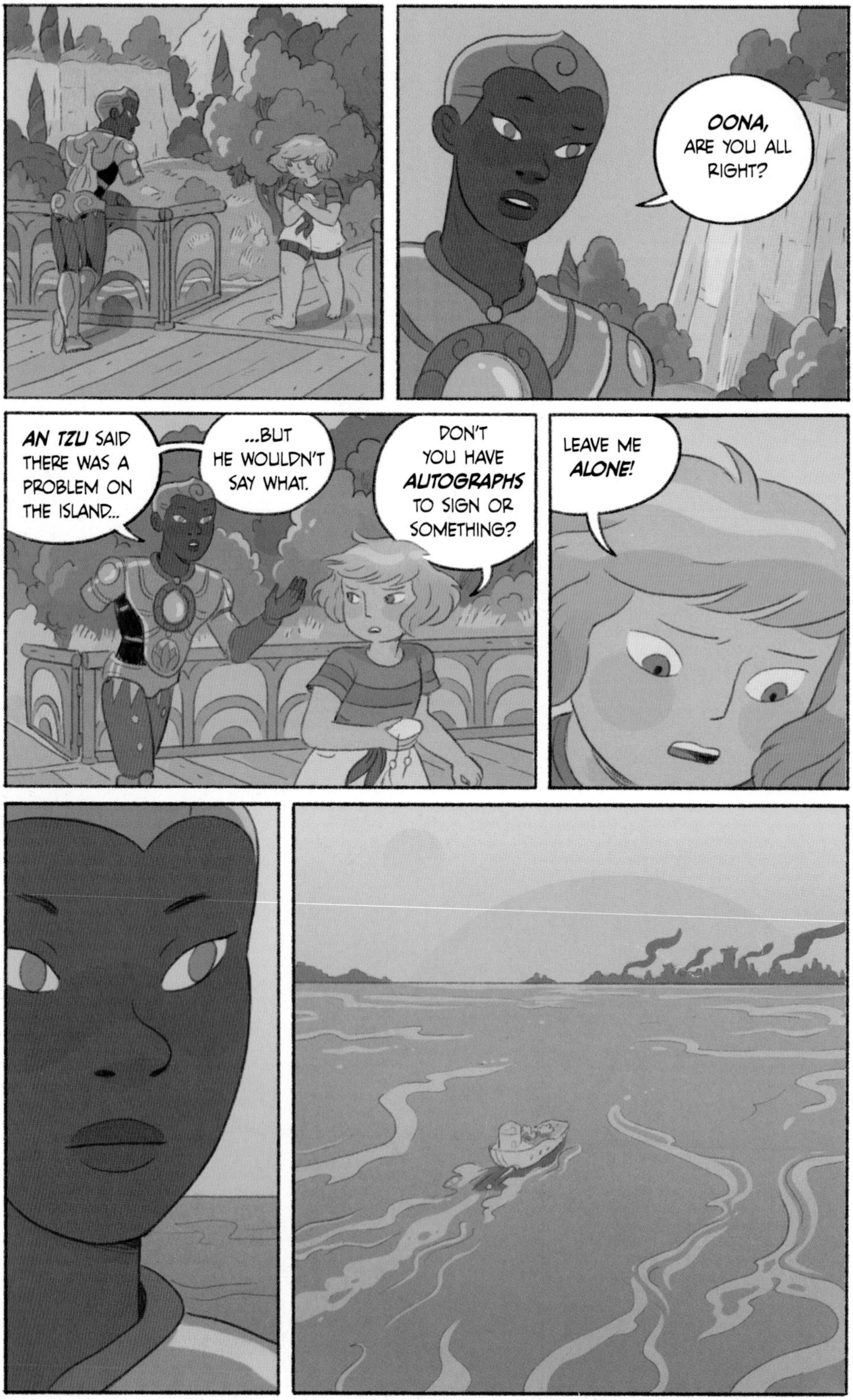
OONA, ARE YOU ALL RIGHT?
AN TZU SAID THERE WAS A PROBLEM ON THE ISLAND...
...BUT HE WOULDN'T SAY WHAT.
DON'T YOU HAVE AUTOGRAPHS TO SIGN OR SOMETHING?
LEAVE ME ALONE!

Chapter 7

THE SAND KNOWS

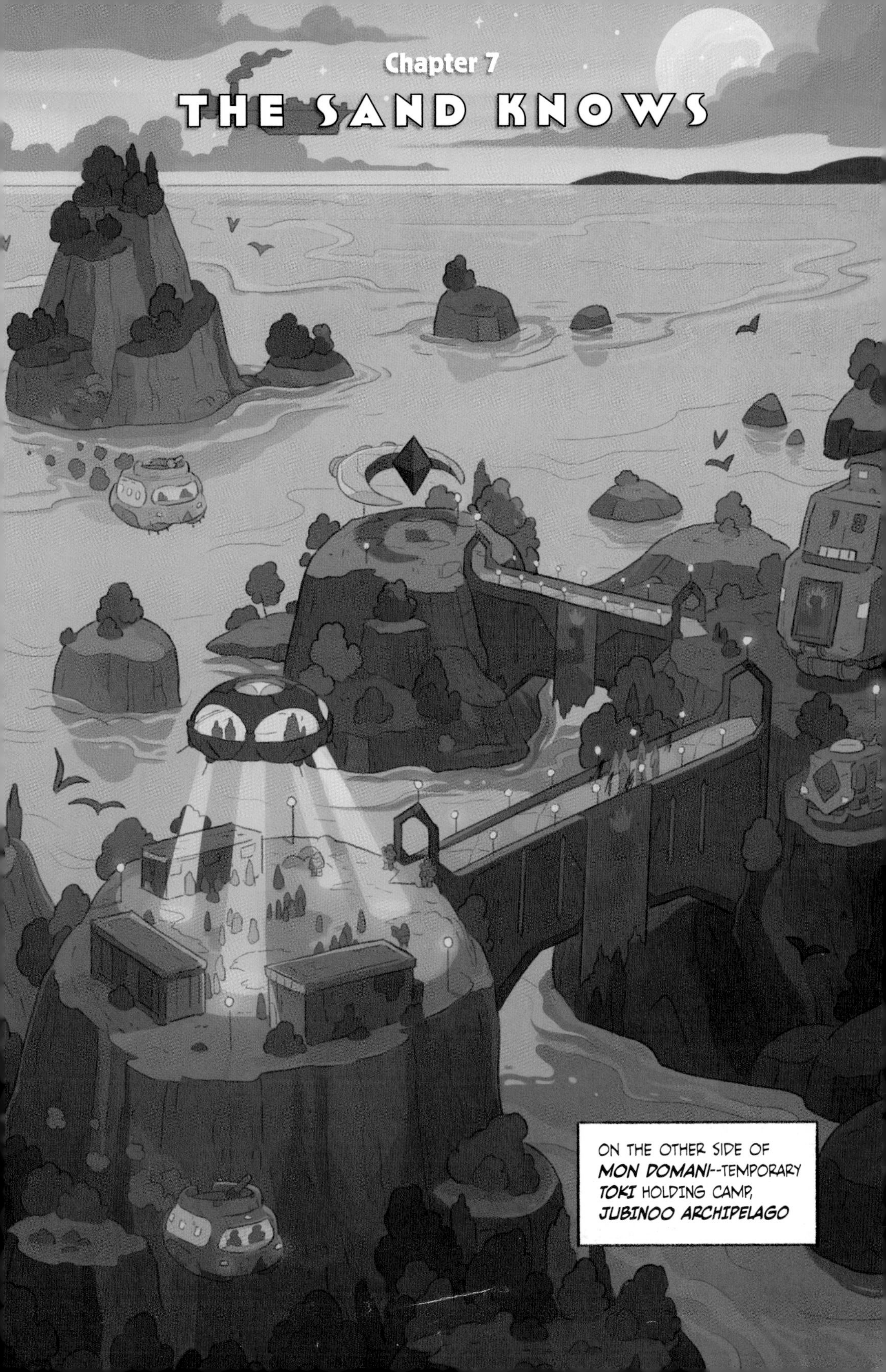

ON THE OTHER SIDE OF MON DOMANI--TEMPORARY TOKI HOLDING CAMP, JUBINOO ARCHIPELAGO

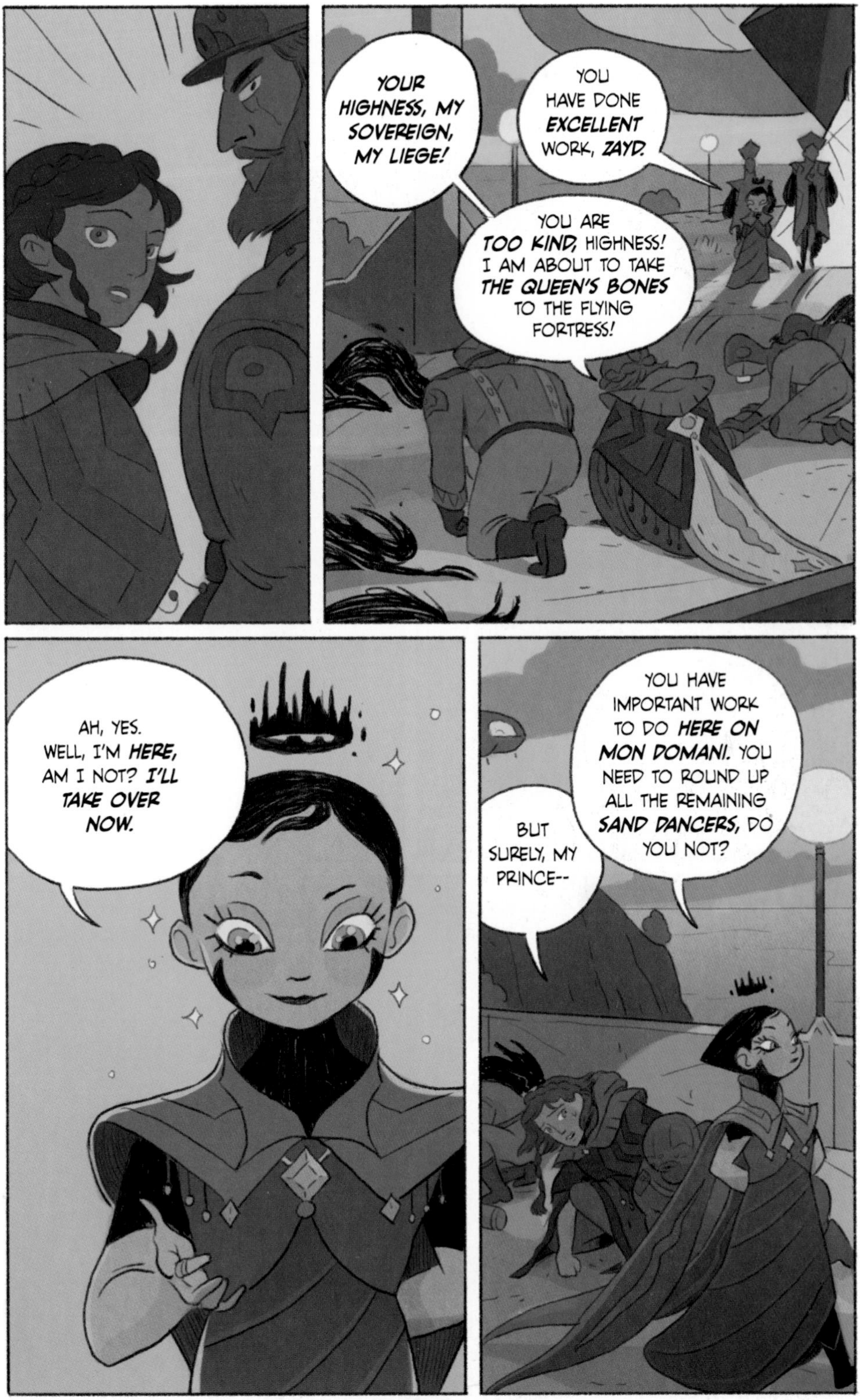
YOUR HIGHNESS, MY SOVEREIGN, MY LIEGE!
YOU HAVE DONE EXCELLENT WORK, ZAYD.
YOU ARE TOO KIND, HIGHNESS! I AM ABOUT TO TAKE THE QUEEN'S BONES TO THE FLYING FORTRESS!
AH, YES. WELL, I'M HERE, AM I NOT? I'LL TAKE OVER NOW.
BUT SURELY, MY PRINCE--
YOU HAVE IMPORTANT WORK TO DO HERE ON MON DOMANI. YOU NEED TO ROUND UP ALL THE REMAINING SAND DANCERS, DO YOU NOT?

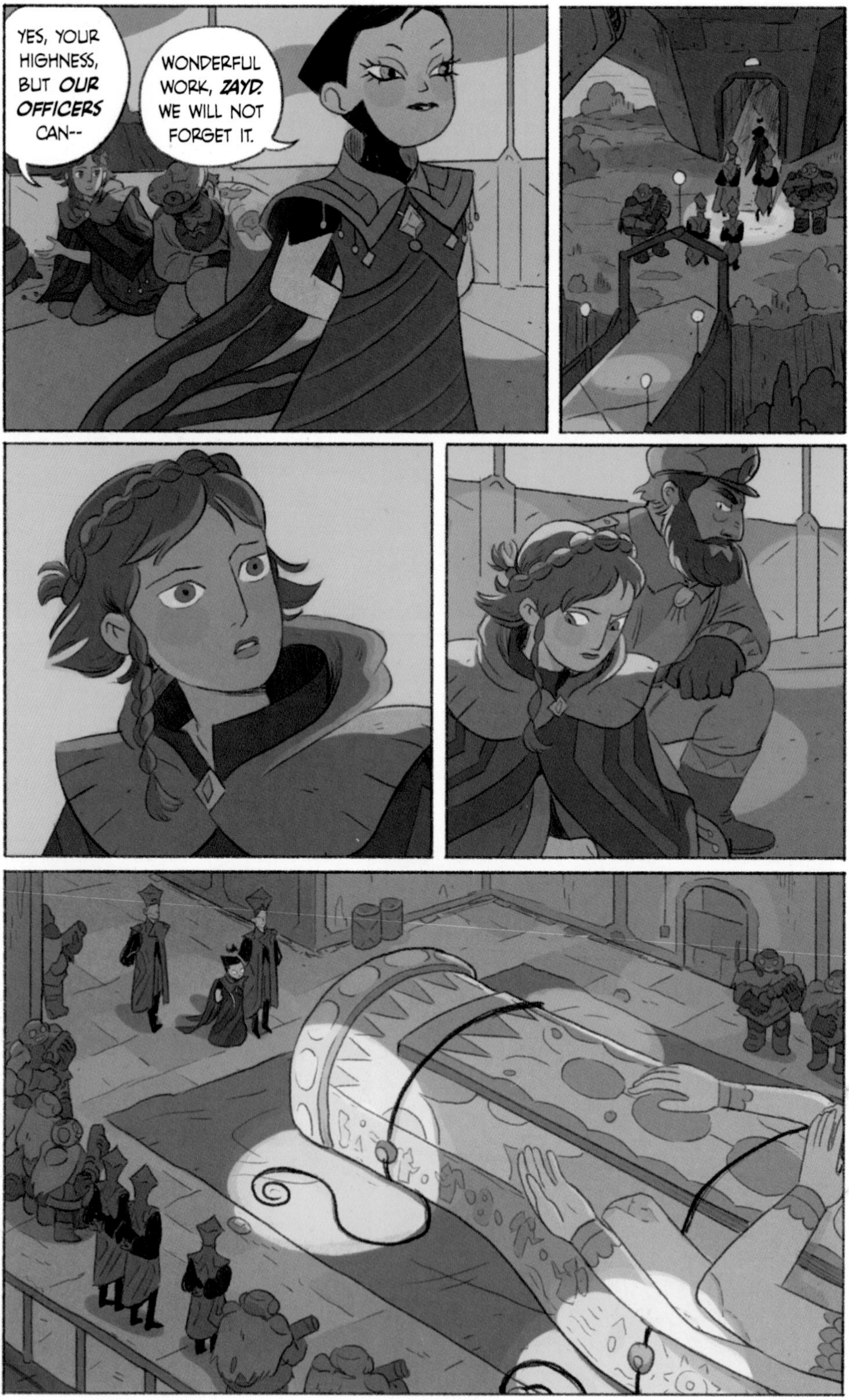
YES, YOUR HIGHNESS, BUT OUR OFFICERS CAN--
WONDERFUL WORK, ZAYD. WE WILL NOT FORGET IT.

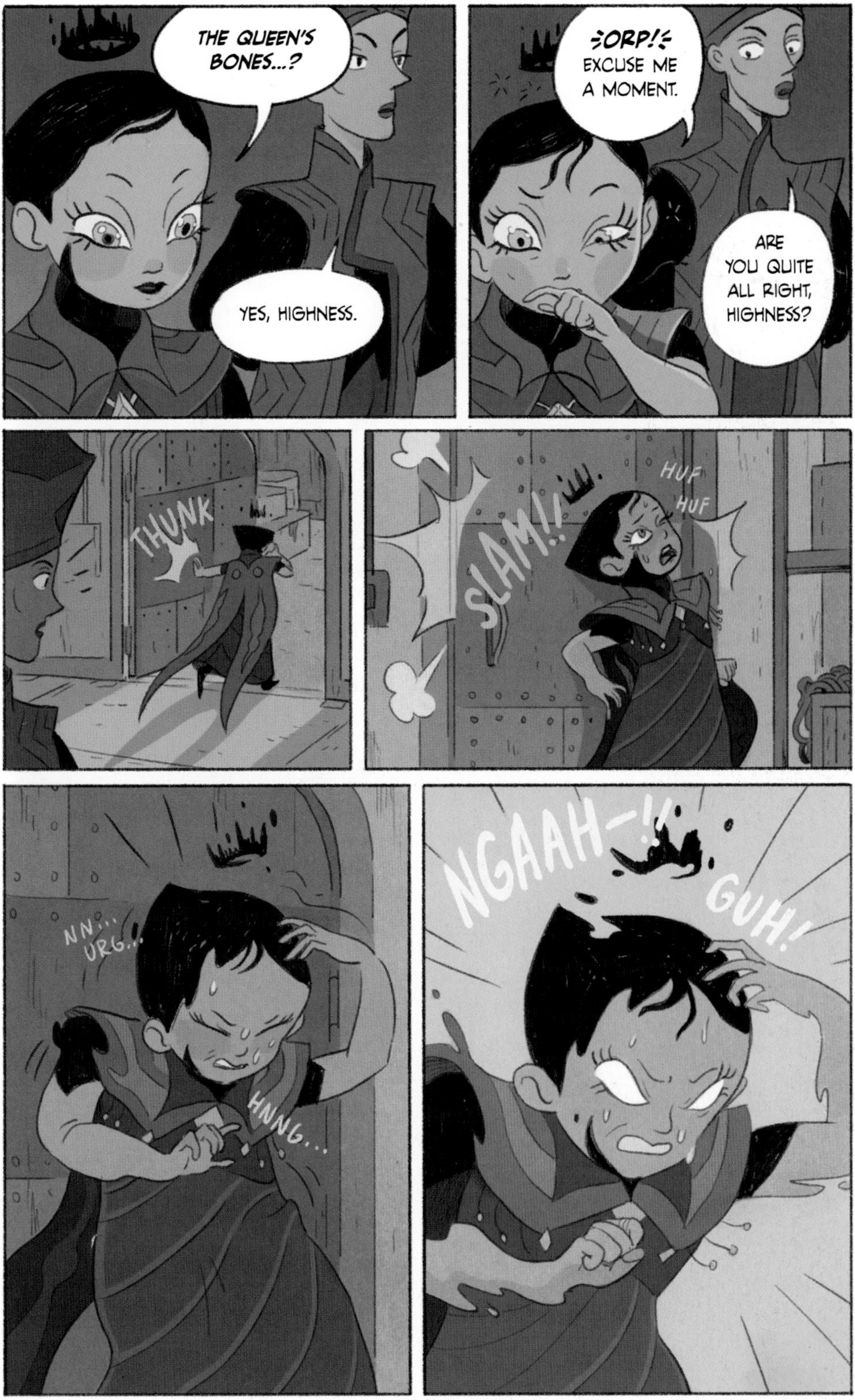
THE QUEEN'S BONES...?
YES, HIGHNESS.
ORP!
EXCUSE ME A MOMENT.
ARE YOU QUITE ALL RIGHT, HIGHNESS?
THUNK
SLAM!!
HUF HUF
NN... URG...
HNNG...
NGAAH-!!
GUH!

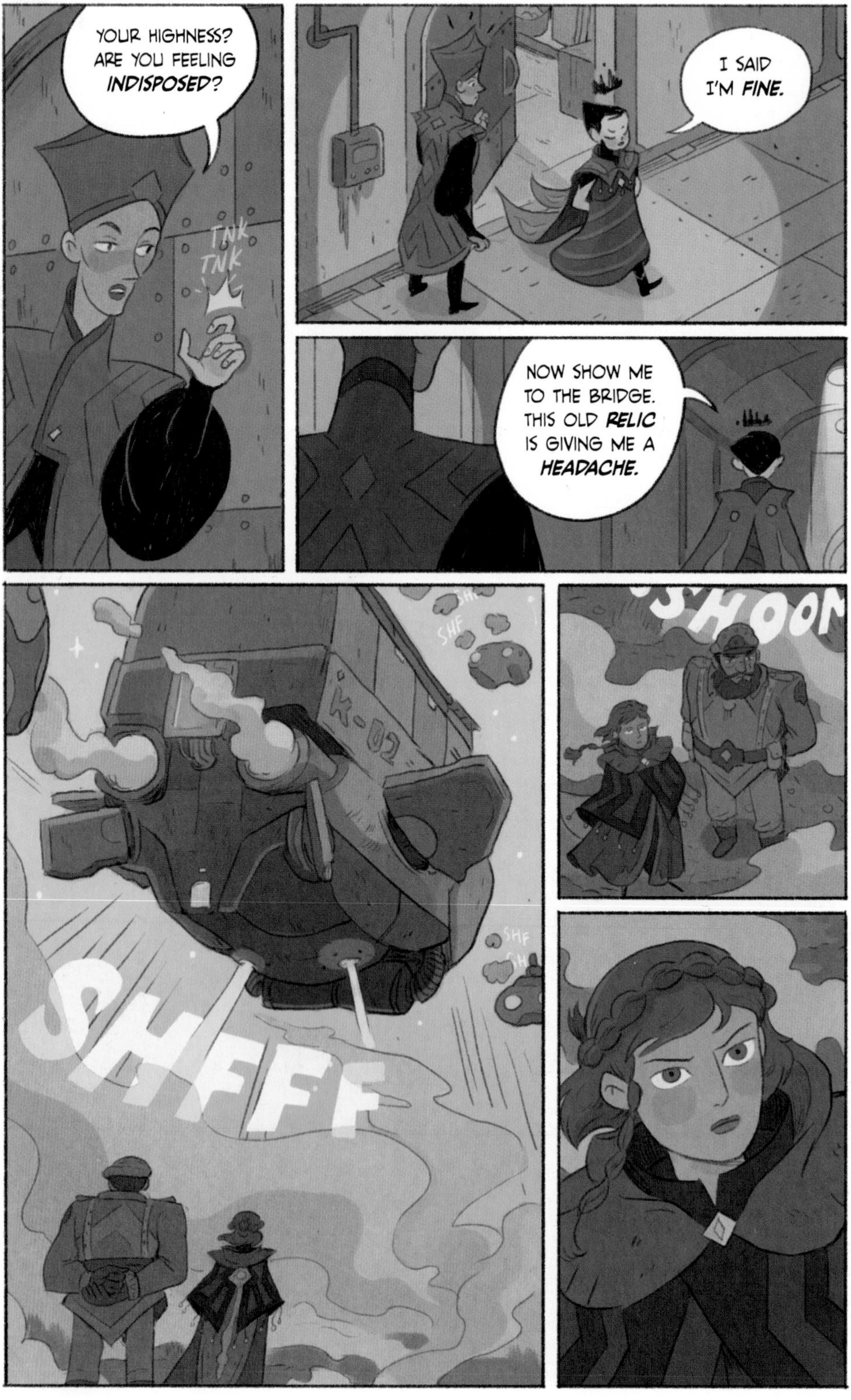
YOUR HIGHNESS? ARE YOU FEELING INDISPOSED?
TNK TNK
I SAID I'M FINE.
NOW SHOW ME TO THE BRIDGE. THIS OLD RELIC IS GIVING ME A HEADACHE.
SHF SHF
K-02
SHFFF
SHF
SHOOM

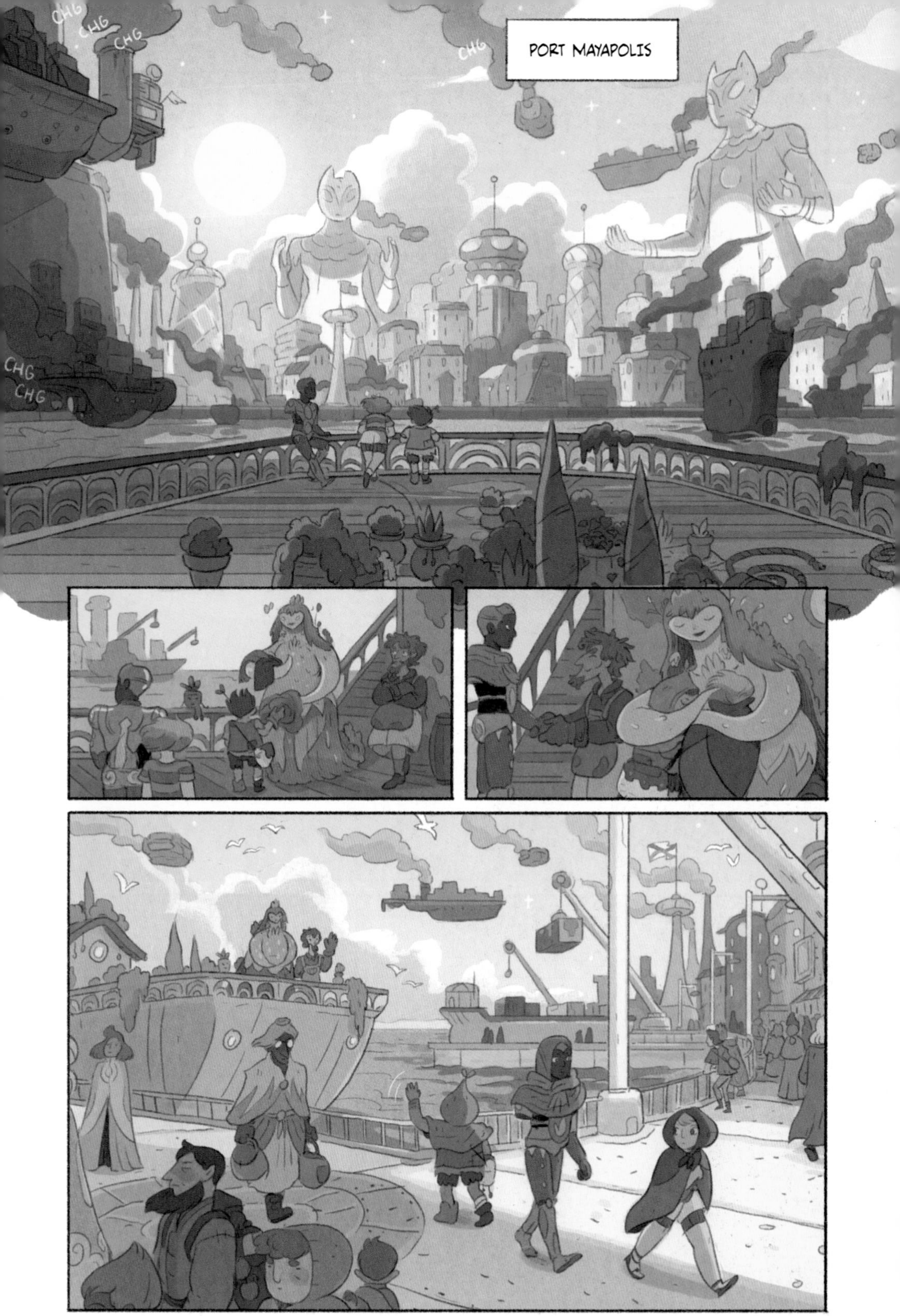
CHG
CHG
CHG
CHG
PORT MAYAPOLIS
CHG
CHG

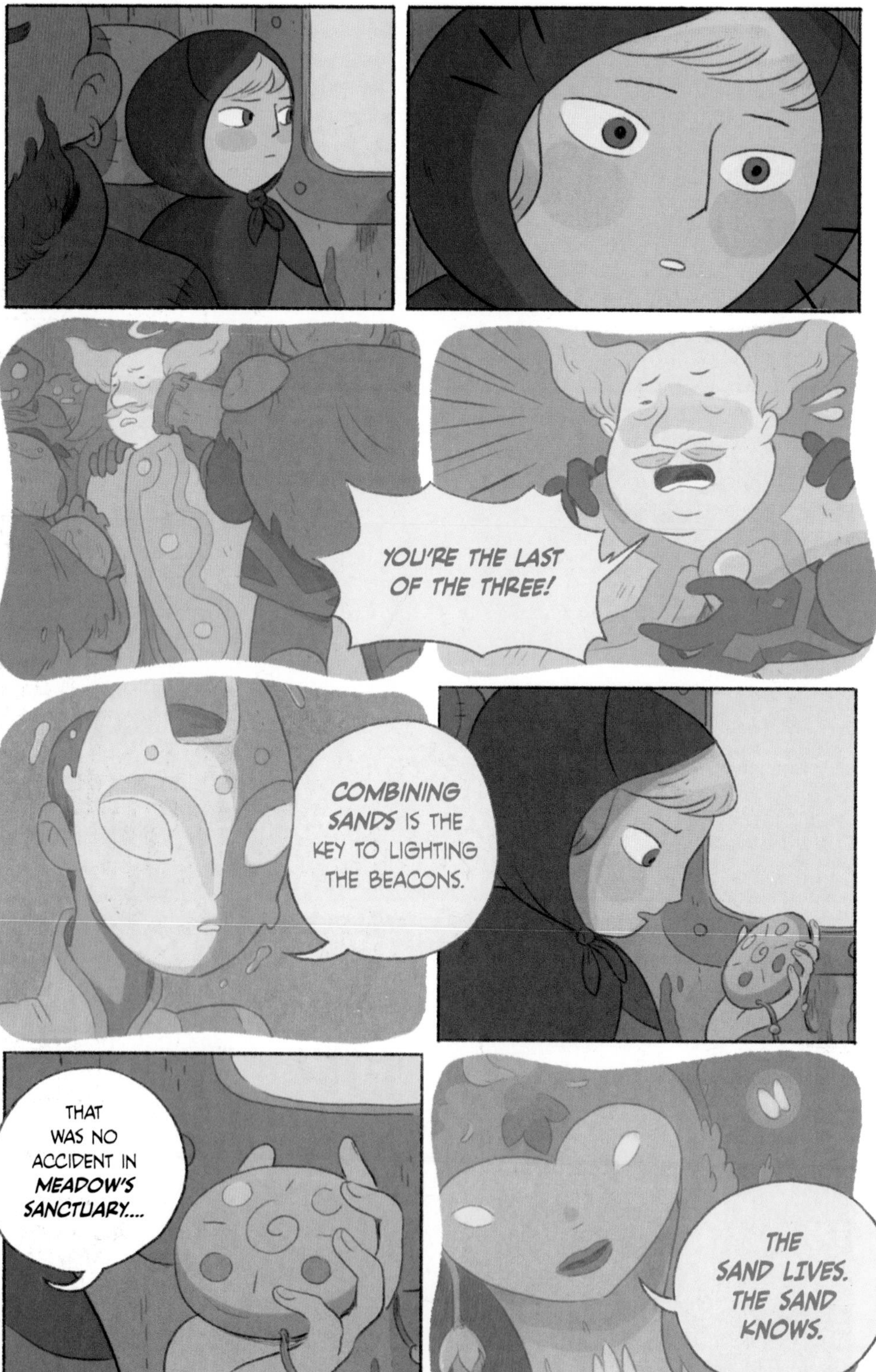
YOU'RE THE LAST OF THE THREE!
COMBINING SANDS IS THE KEY TO LIGHTING THE BEACONS.
THAT WAS NO ACCIDENT IN MEADOW'S SANCTUARY....
THE SAND LIVES. THE SAND KNOWS.

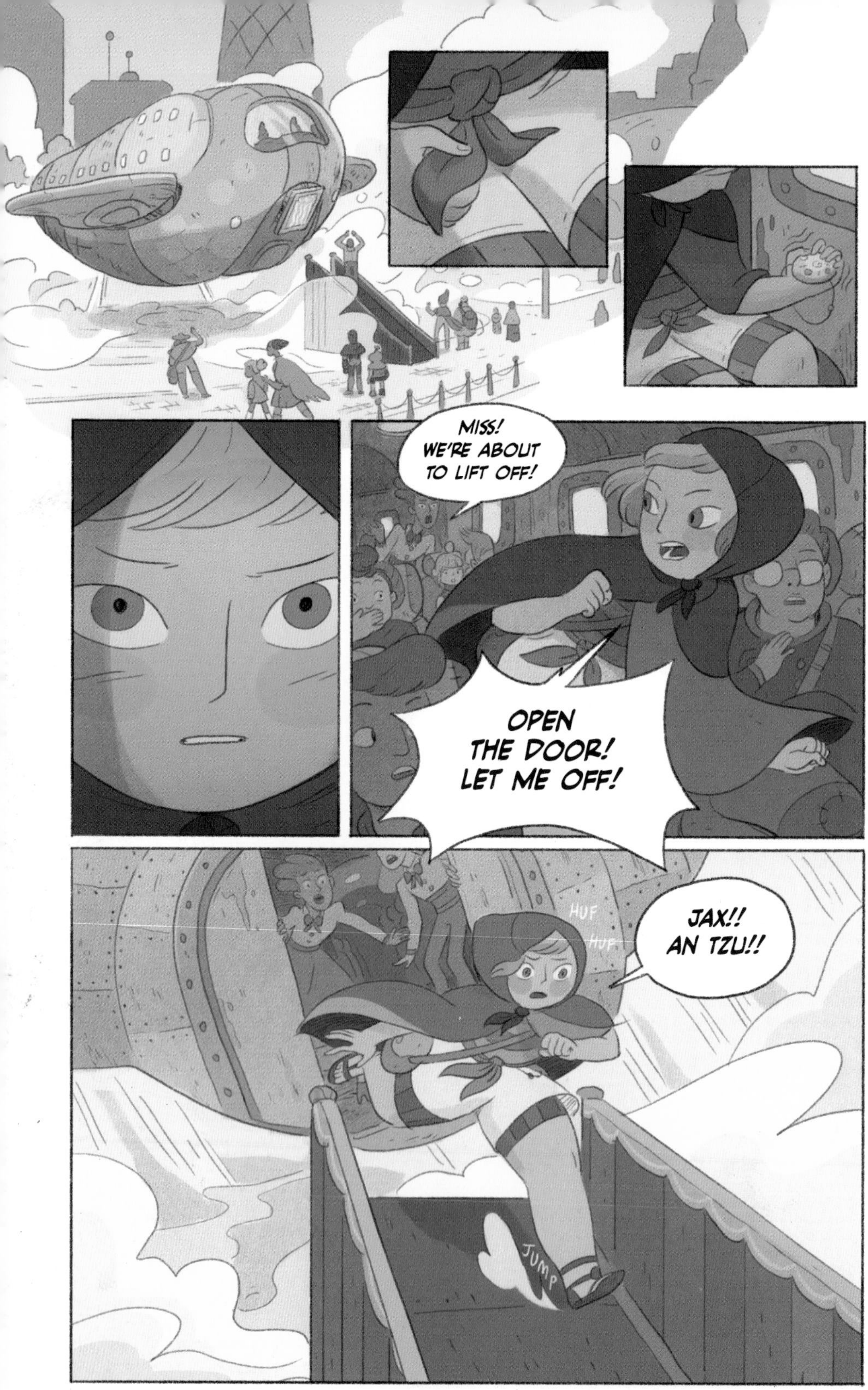
MISS! WE'RE ABOUT TO LIFT OFF!
OPEN THE DOOR! LET ME OFF!
HUF HUF
JAX!! AN TZU!!
JUMP

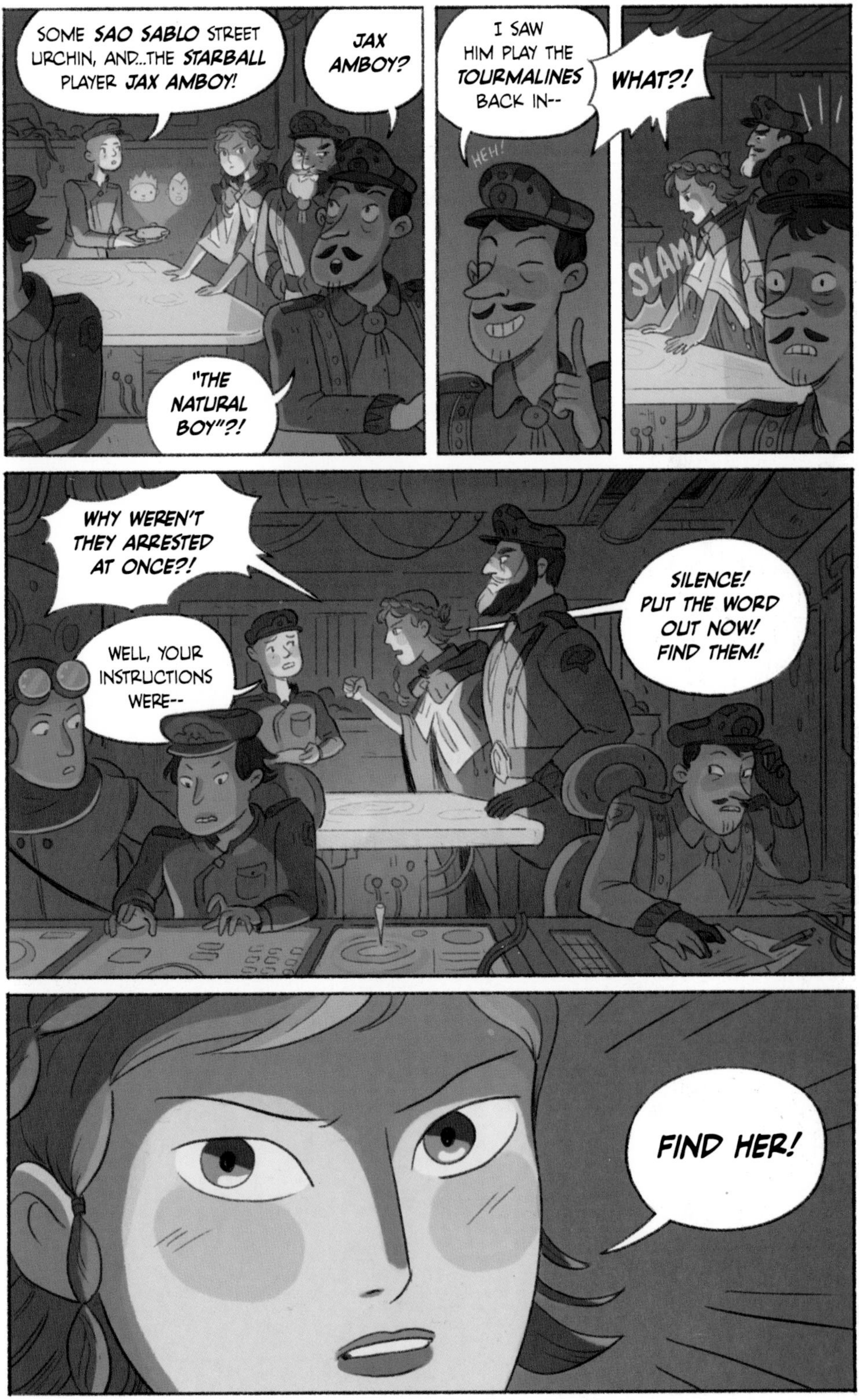
SOME SAO SABLO STREET URCHIN, AND...THE STARBALL PLAYER JAX AMBOY!
JAX AMBOY?
"THE NATURAL BOY"?!
HEH!
I SAW HIM PLAY THE TOURMALINES BACK IN--
WHAT?!
SLAM!
WHY WEREN'T THEY ARRESTED AT ONCE?!
WELL, YOUR INSTRUCTIONS WERE--
SILENCE! PUT THE WORD OUT NOW! FIND THEM!
FIND HER!

Chapter 8

JEP'S NATURAL BOY

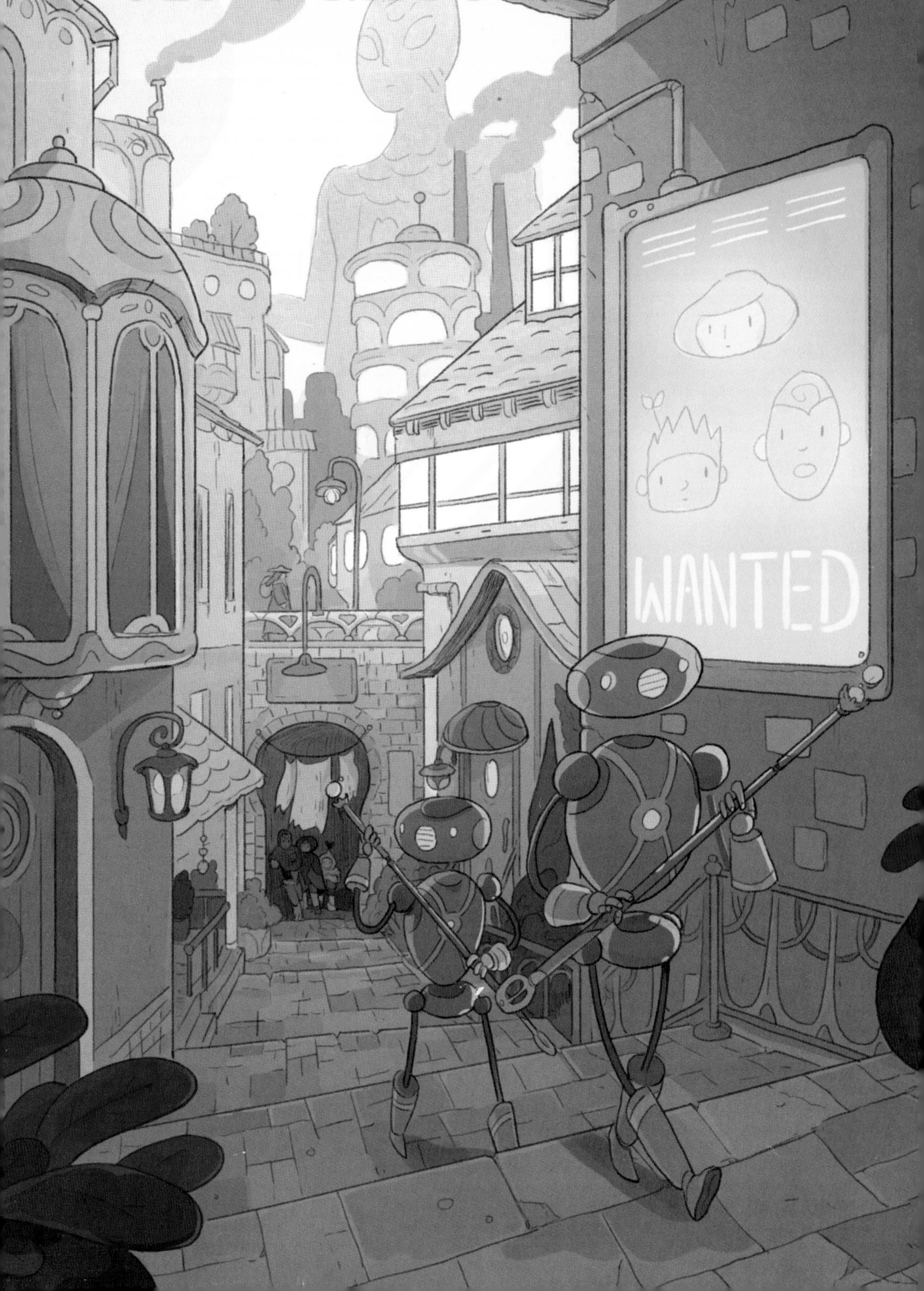
WANTED

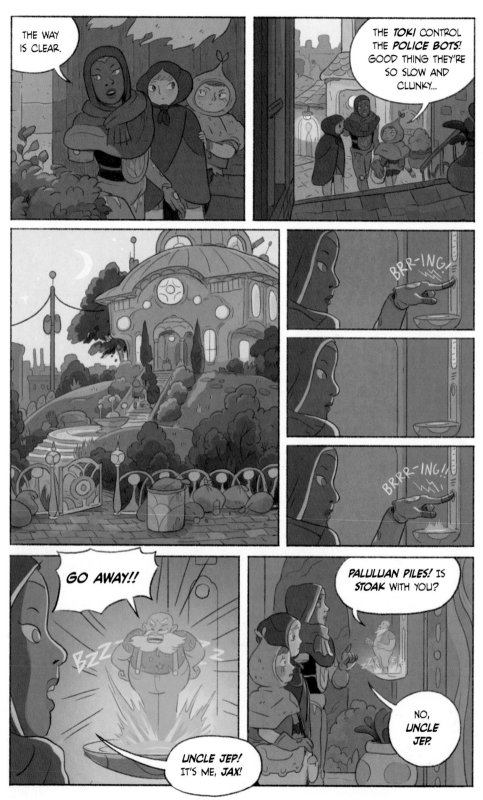

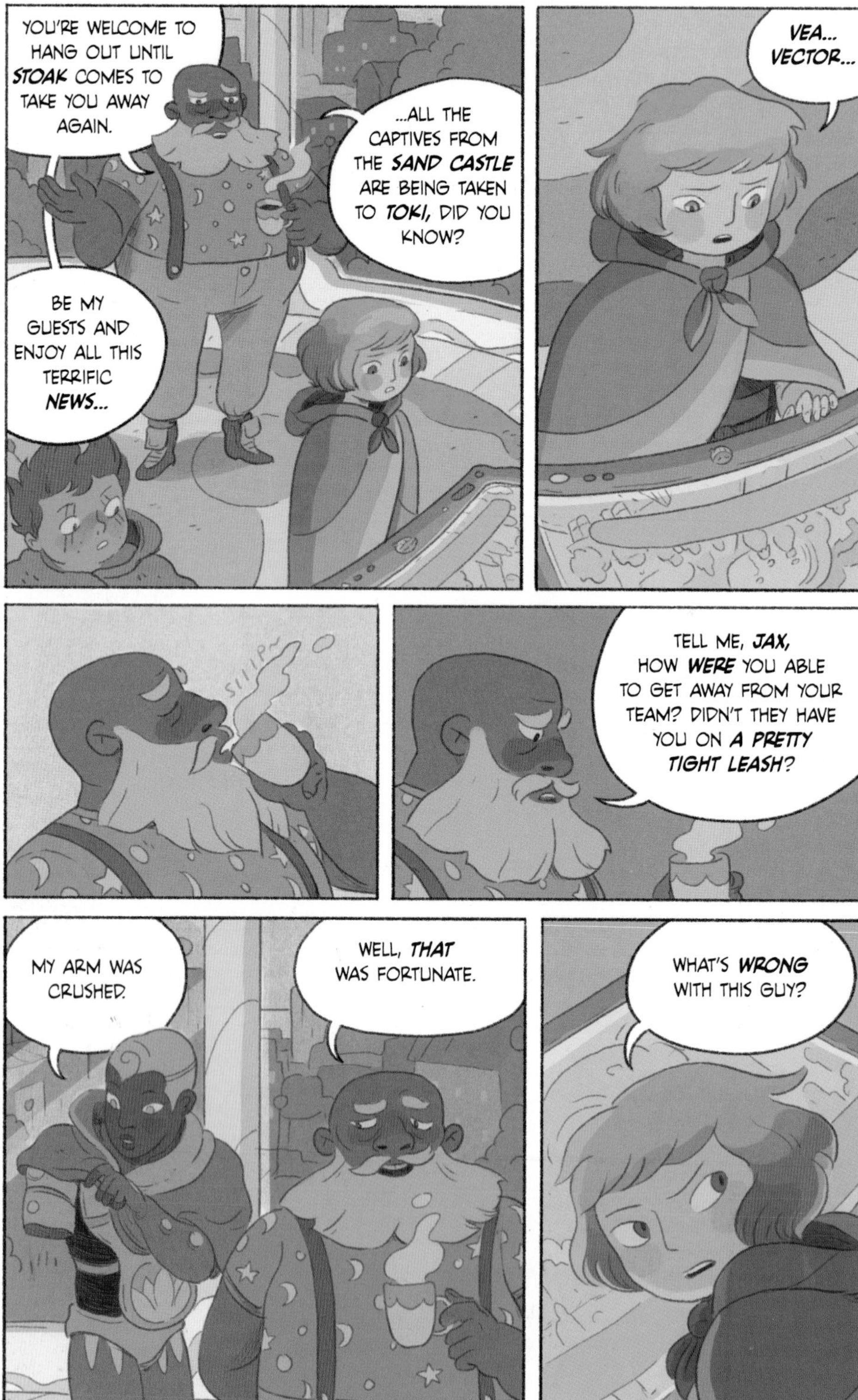
YOU'RE WELCOME TO HANG OUT UNTIL STOAK COMES TO TAKE YOU AWAY AGAIN.
BE MY GUESTS AND ENJOY ALL THIS TERRIFIC NEWS...
...ALL THE CAPTIVES FROM THE SAND CASTLE ARE BEING TAKEN TO TOKI, DID YOU KNOW?
VEA... VECTOR...
SIIIP~
TELL ME, JAX, HOW WERE YOU ABLE TO GET AWAY FROM YOUR TEAM? DIDN'T THEY HAVE YOU ON A PRETTY TIGHT LEASH?
MY ARM WAS CRUSHED.
WELL, THAT WAS FORTUNATE.
WHAT'S WRONG WITH THIS GUY?

173

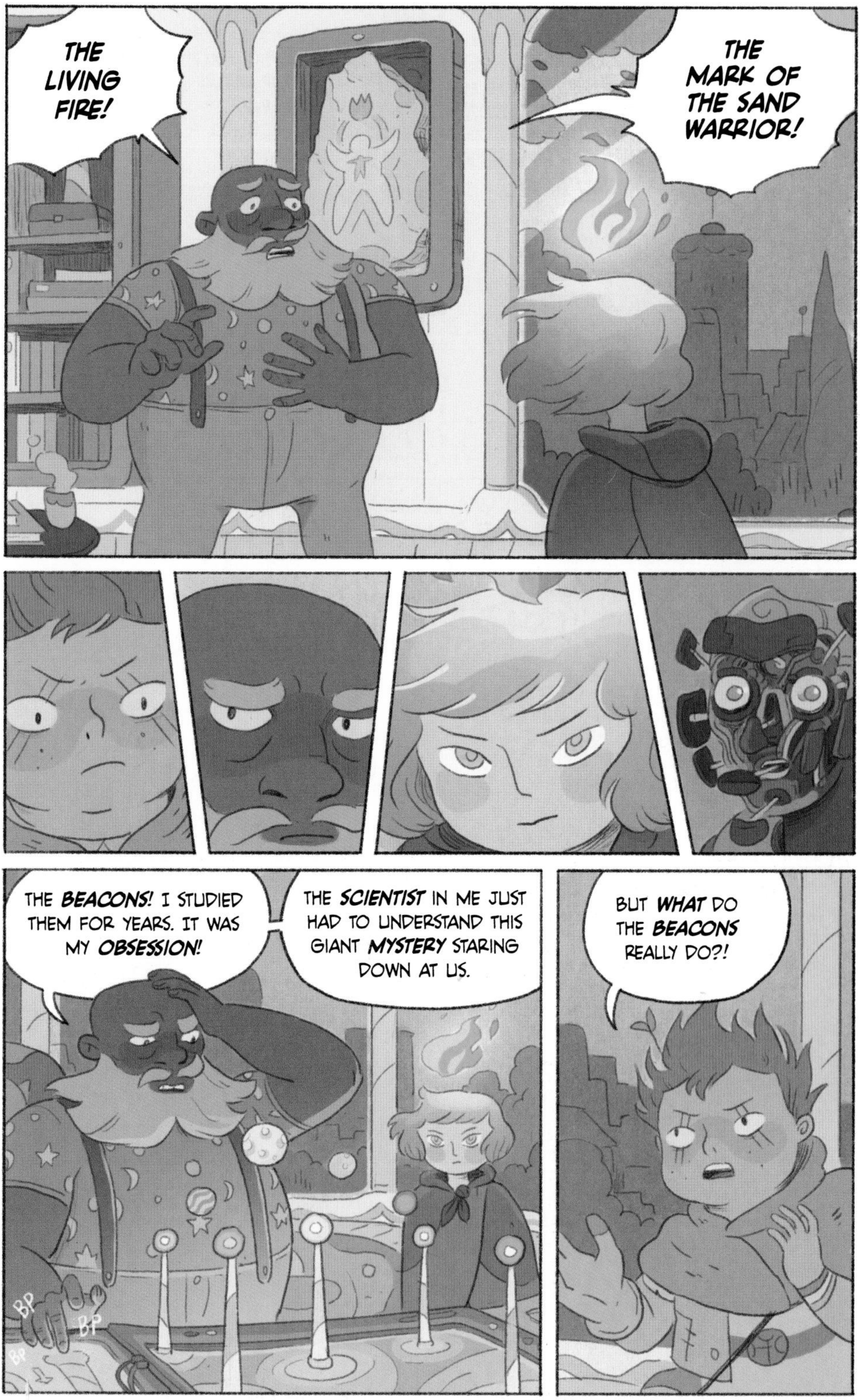
THE LIVING FIRE!
THE MARK OF THE SAND WARRIOR!
THE BEACONS! I STUDIED THEM FOR YEARS. IT WAS MY OBSESSION!
THE SCIENTIST IN ME JUST HAD TO UNDERSTAND THIS GIANT MYSTERY STARING DOWN AT US.
BP BP BP
BUT WHAT DO THE BEACONS REALLY DO?!

Chapter 9
ALTERATIONS

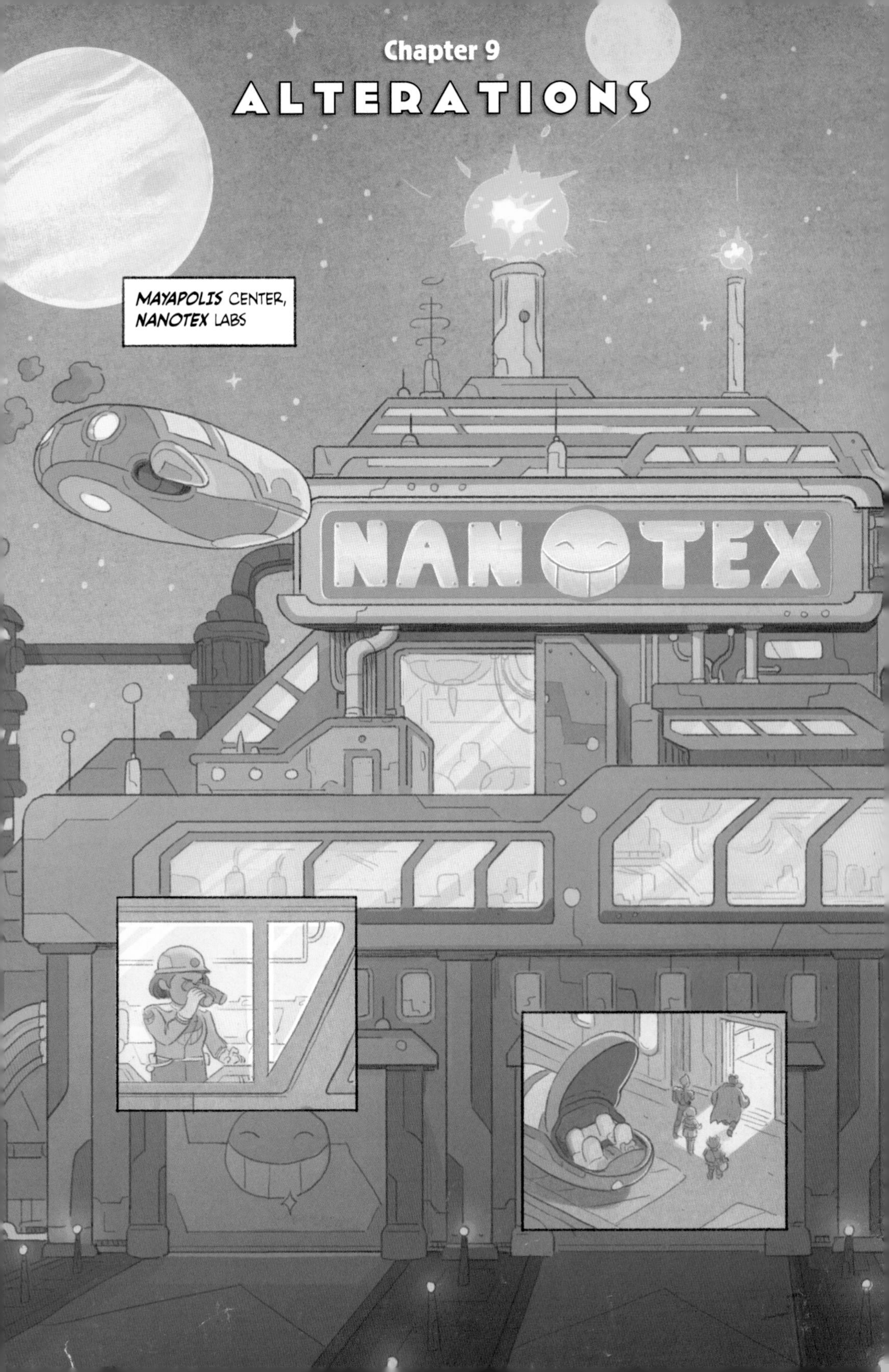
MAYAPOLIS CENTER,
NANOTEX LABS
NANOTEX

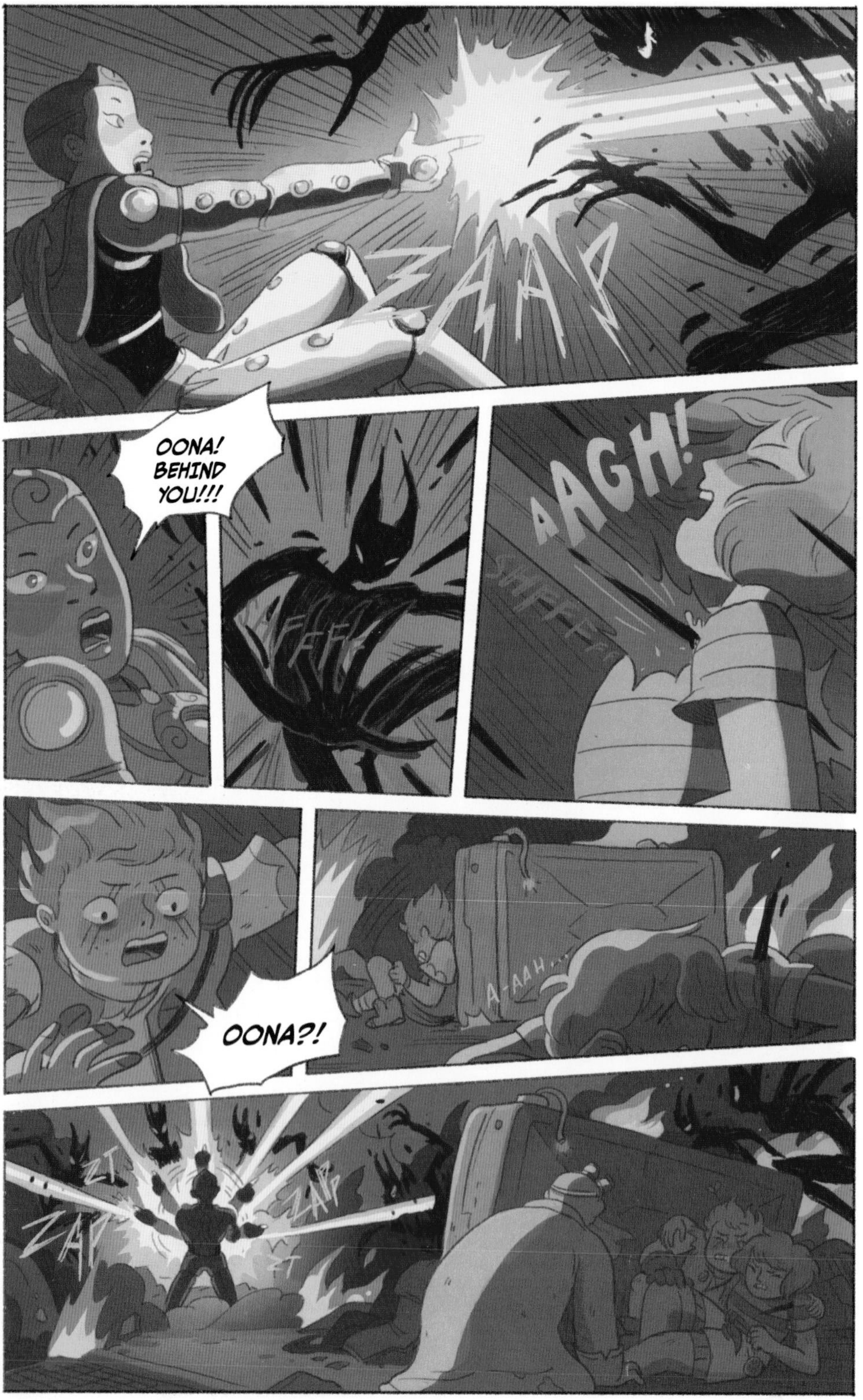
ZAAP
OONA! BEHIND YOU!!!
AAGH!
OONA?!
A-AAH...
ZT
ZAP
ZAPP
ZT

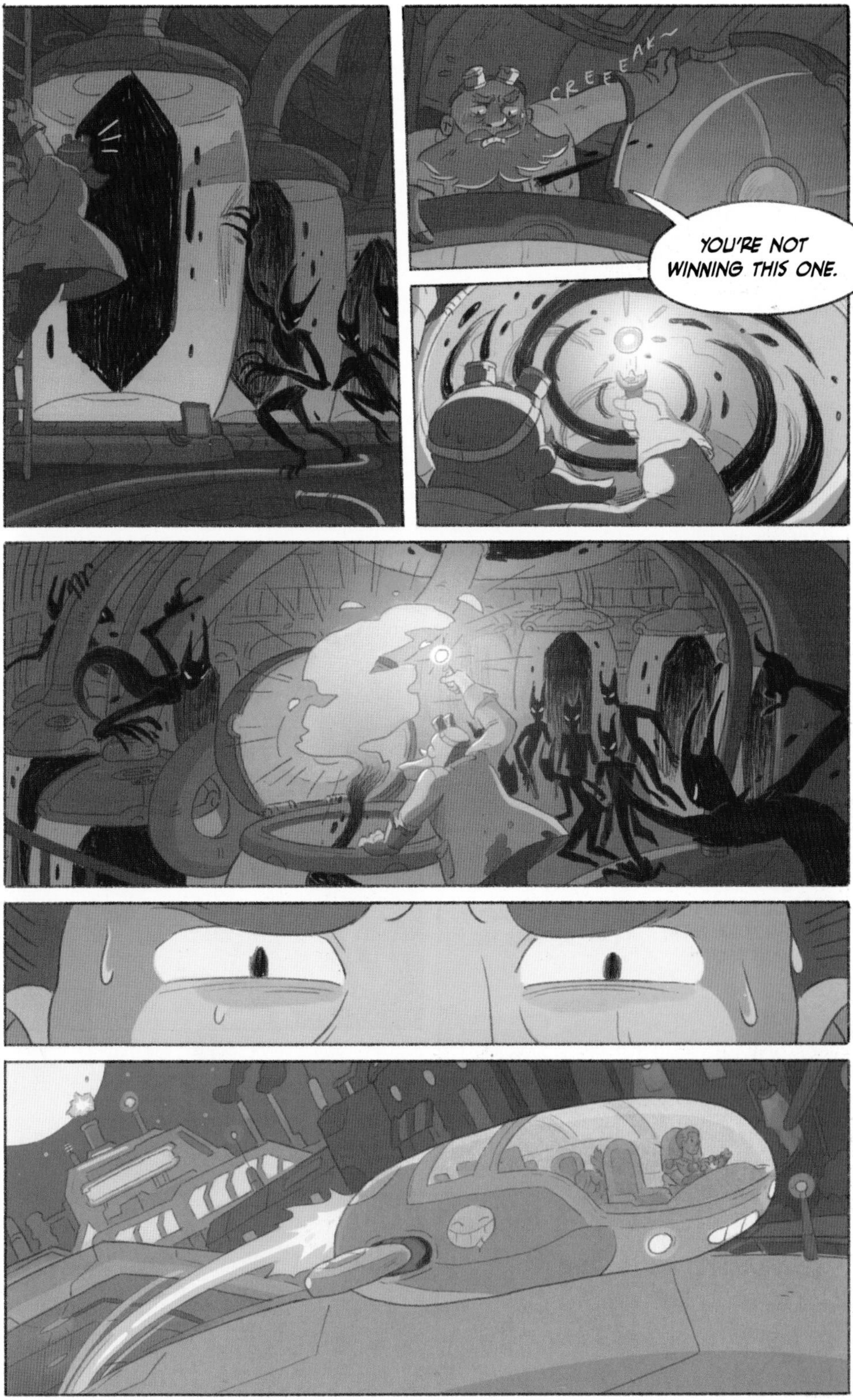
CREEEAK~
YOU'RE NOT WINNING THIS ONE.

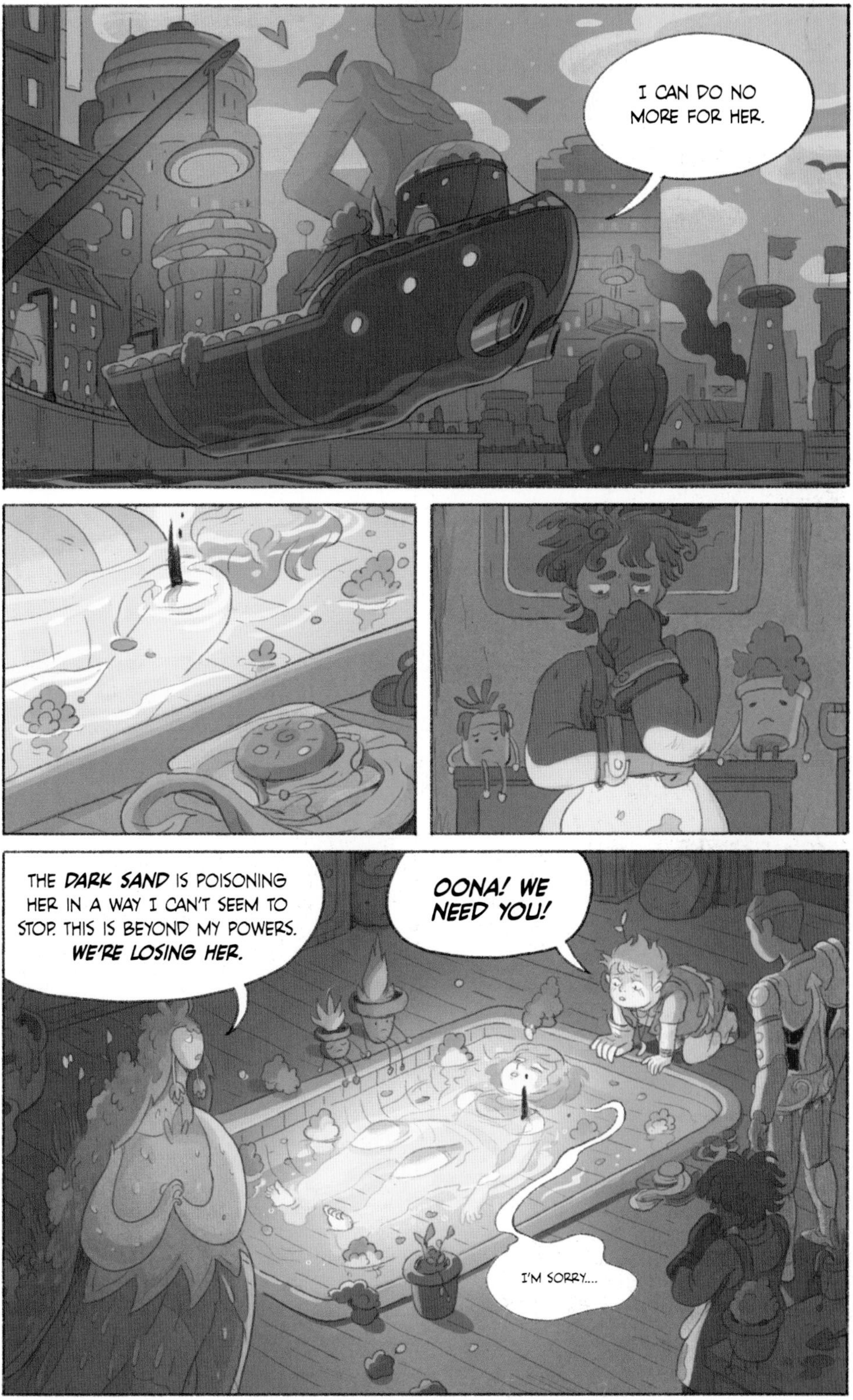
I CAN DO NO MORE FOR HER.
THE DARK SAND IS POISONING HER IN A WAY I CAN'T SEEM TO STOP. THIS IS BEYOND MY POWERS. WE'RE LOSING HER.
OONA! WE NEED YOU!
I'M SORRY....

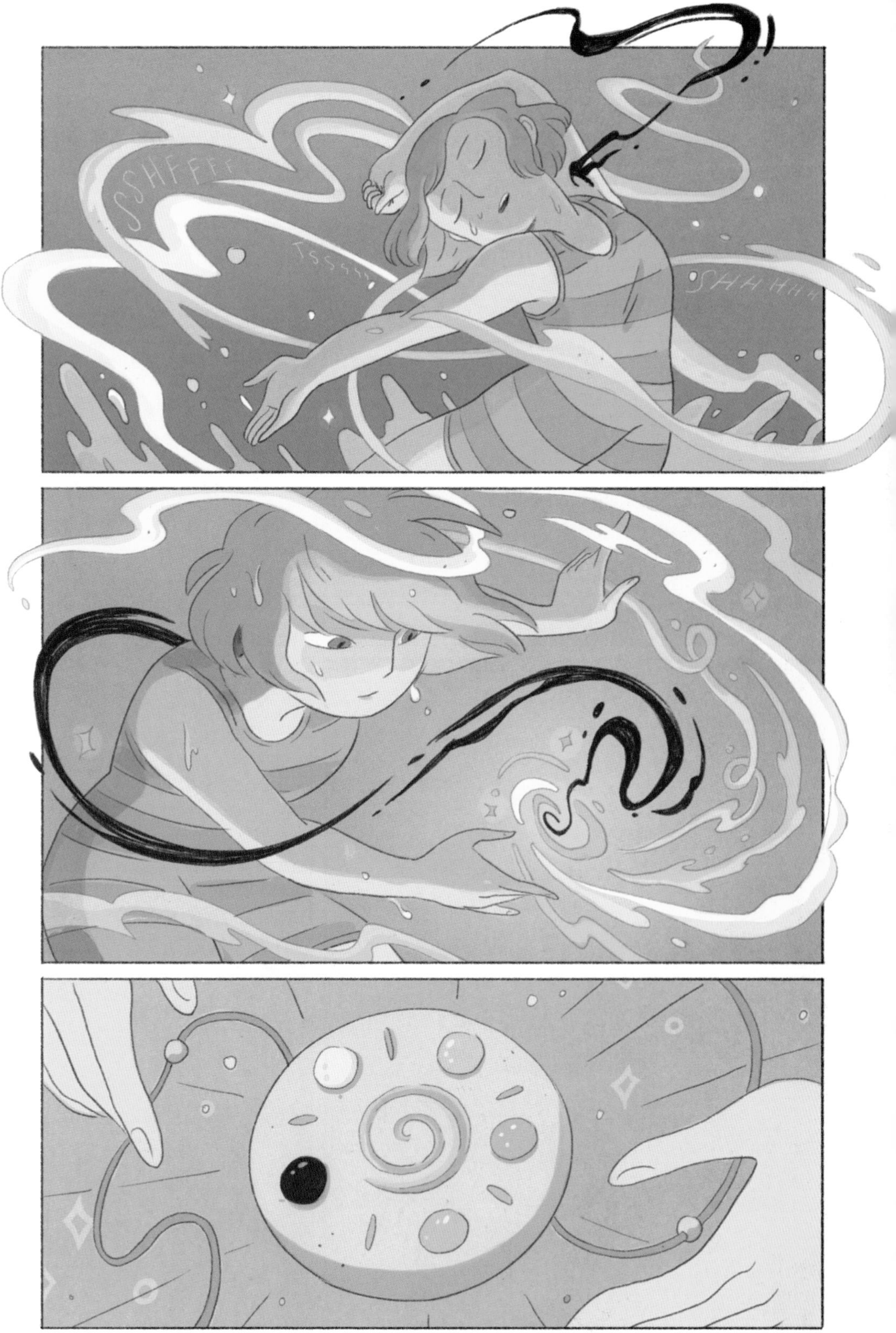
SSHFFFF
TSSSSS
SHHHHH

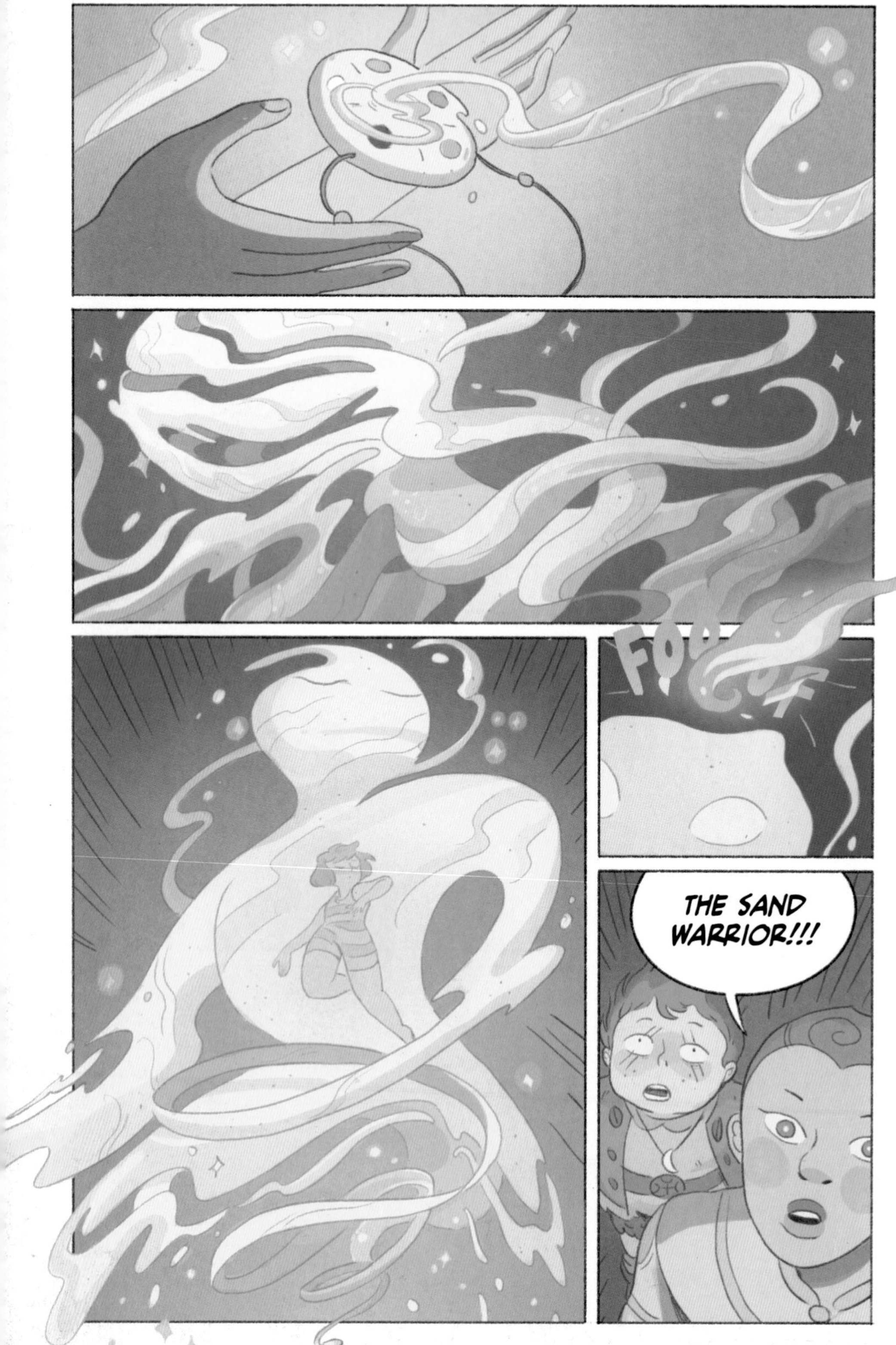
FOOOF
THE SAND WARRIOR!!!

Chapter 10
FIRE & RAIN

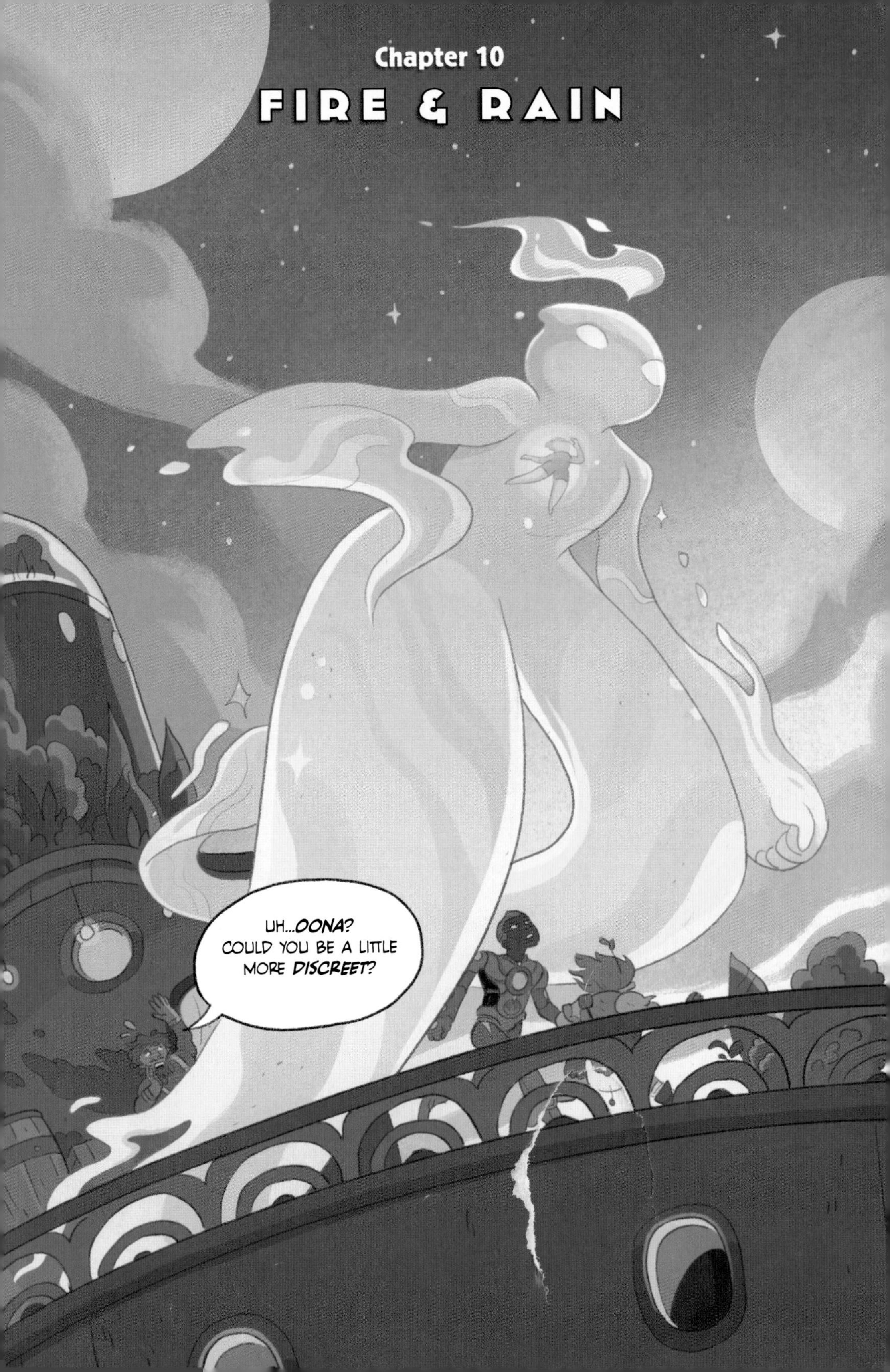

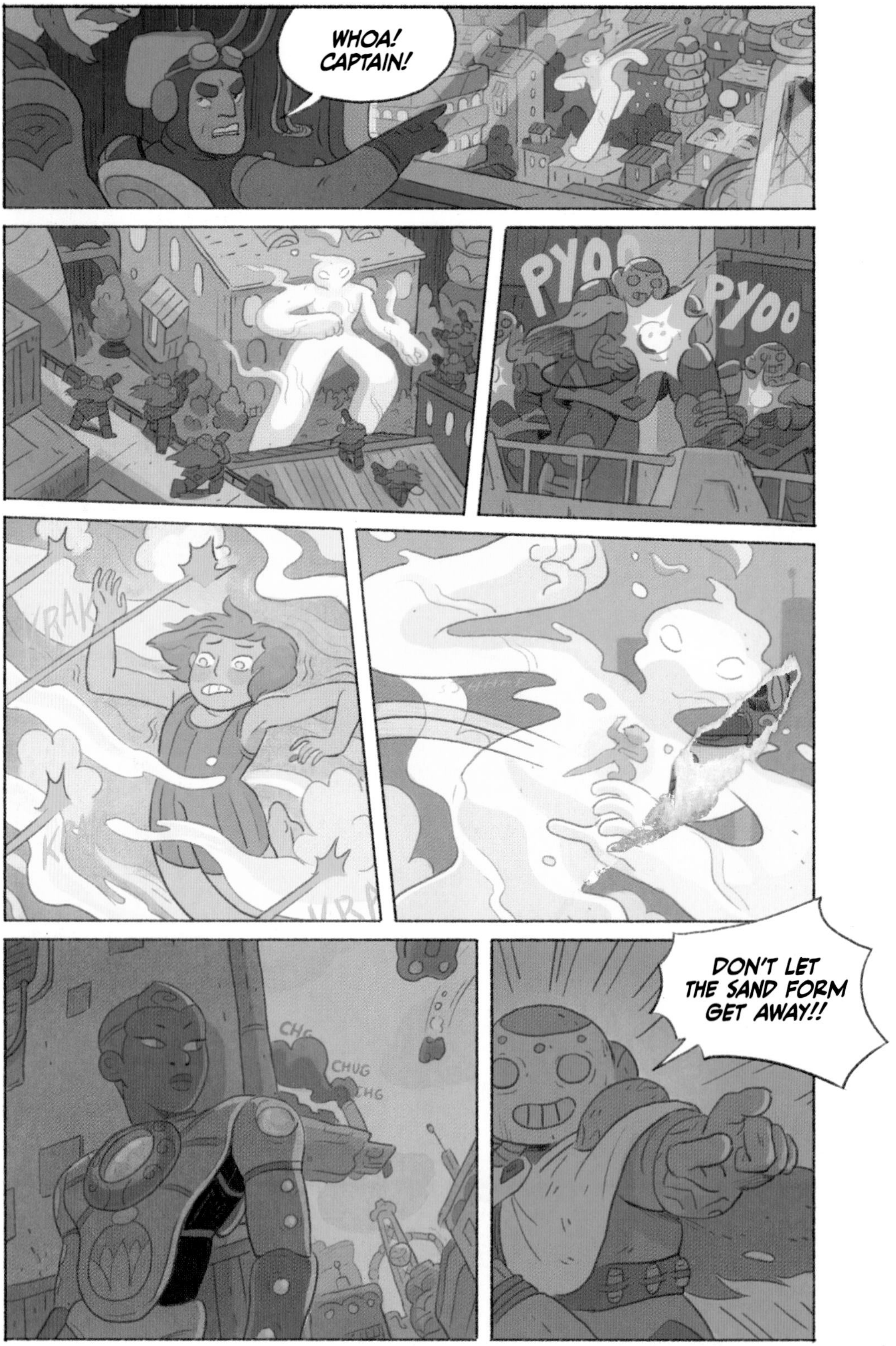
WHOA! CAPTAIN!
PYOO
PYOO
DON'T LET THE SAND FORM GET AWAY!!

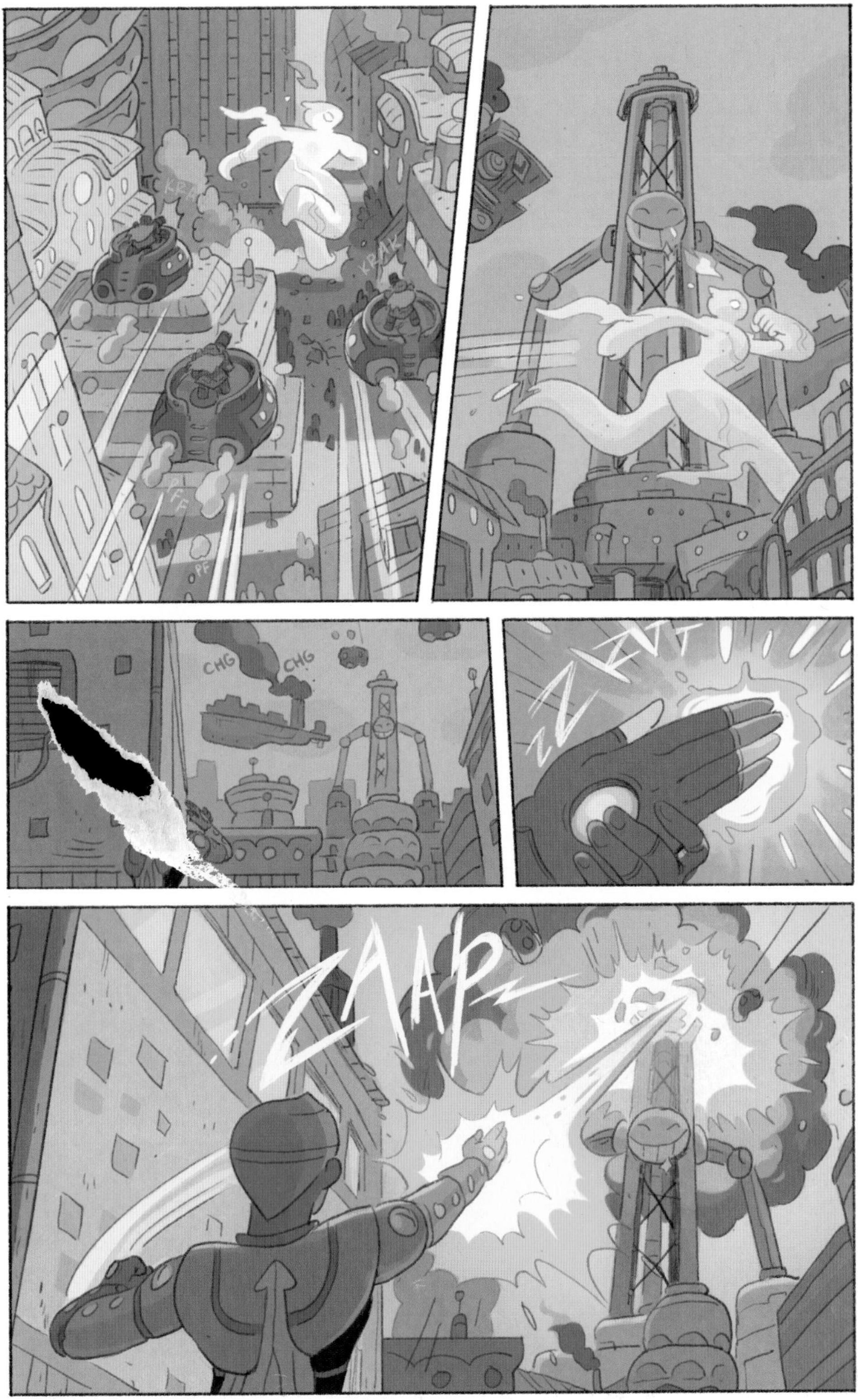
KRAK
KRAK
PFF
PF
CHG CHG
ZZZVVT
ZAAP

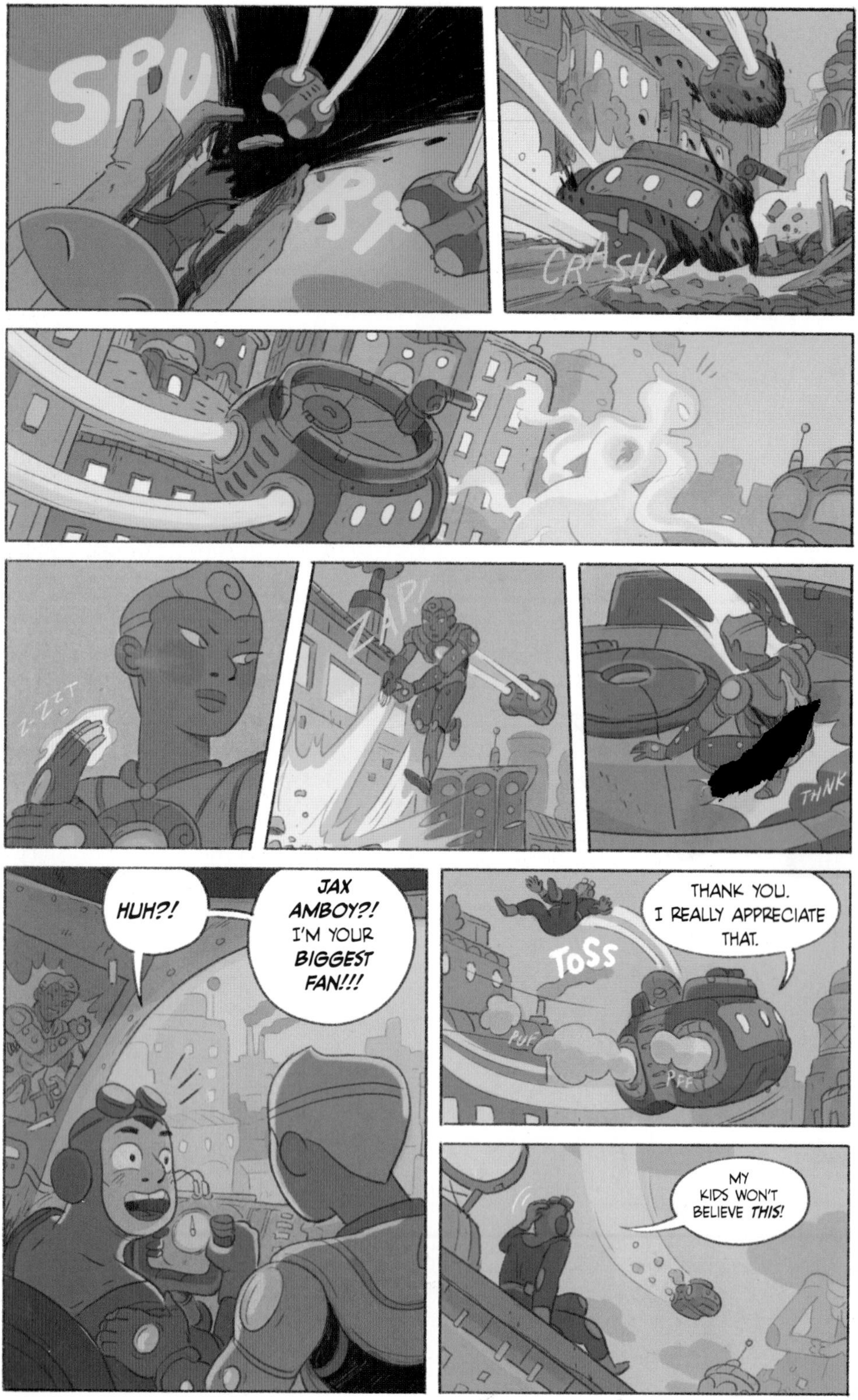
SPURT
CRASH!
Z-Z-Z-T
ZAP!
THNK
HUH?!
JAX AMBOY?! I'M YOUR BIGGEST FAN!!!
TOSS
PUF
PFF
THANK YOU. I REALLY APPRECIATE THAT.
MY KIDS WON'T BELIEVE THIS!

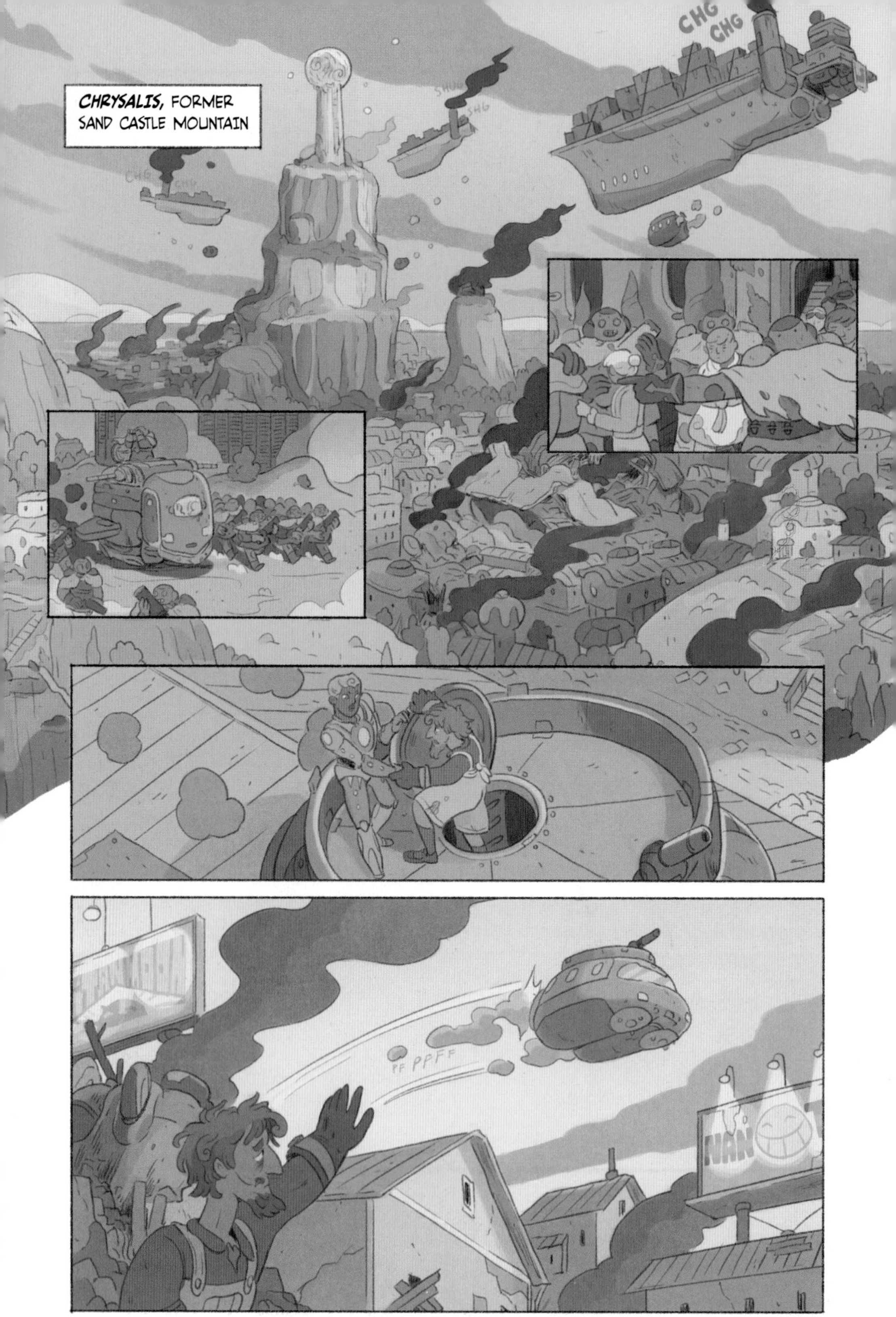
CHG
CHG
CHRYSALIS, FORMER
SAND CASTLE MOUNTAIN
PF PPFF
NAN

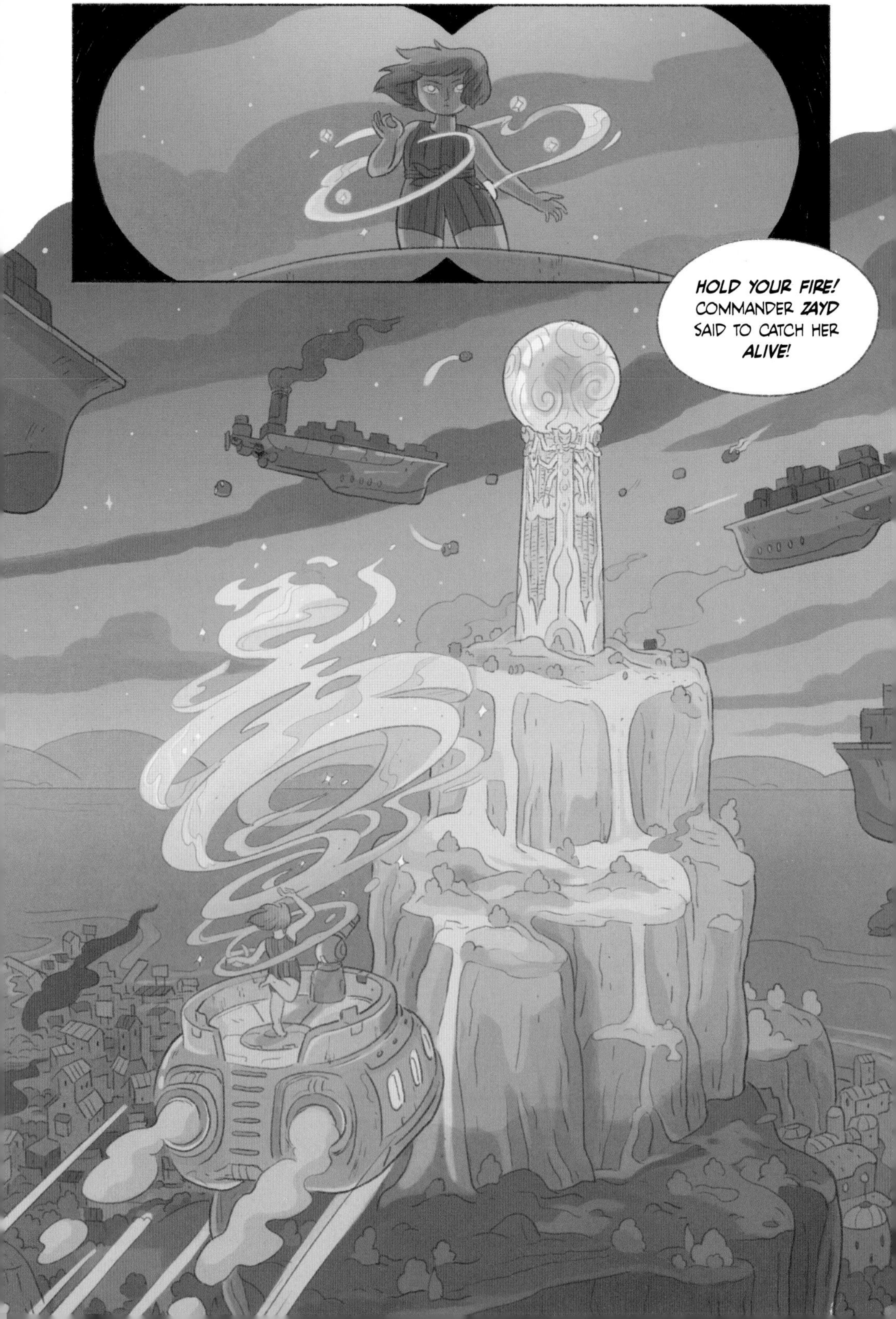
HOLD YOUR FIRE! COMMANDER ZAYD SAID TO CATCH HER ALIVE!

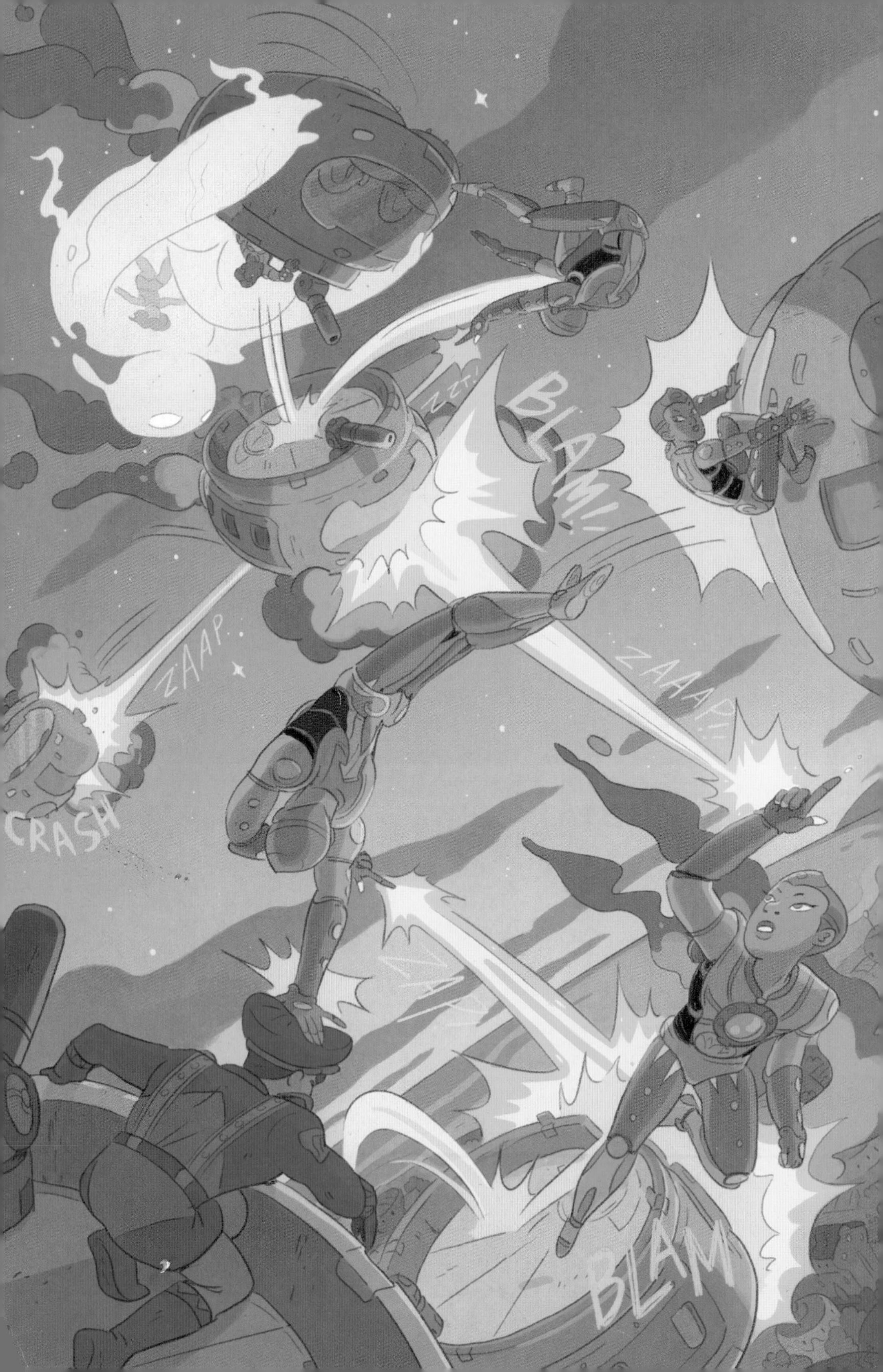
ZZT!
BLAM!!
ZAAP
ZAAAP!!
CRASH
BLAM

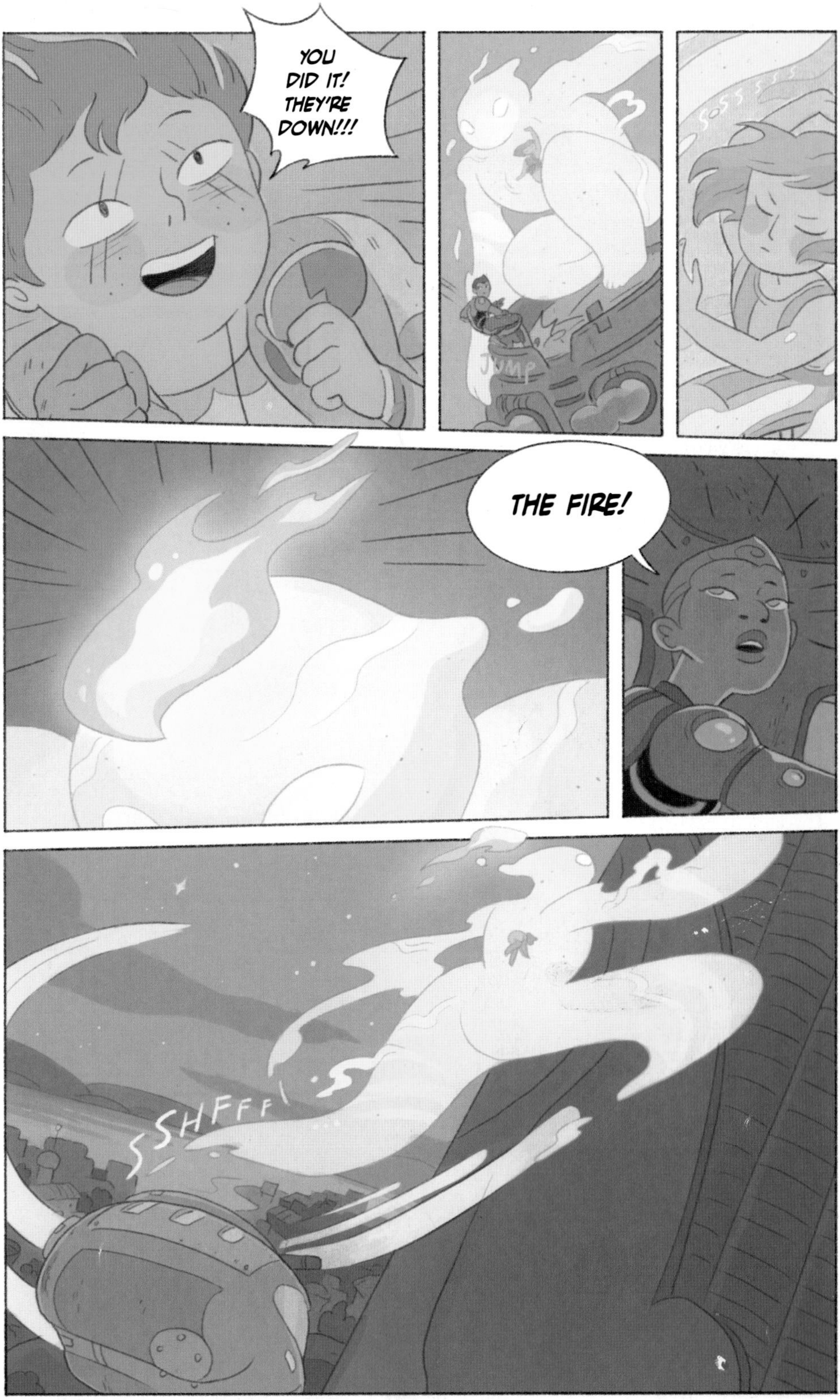
YOU DID IT! THEY'RE DOWN!!!
JUMP
SSSSSSS
THE FIRE!
SSHFFF

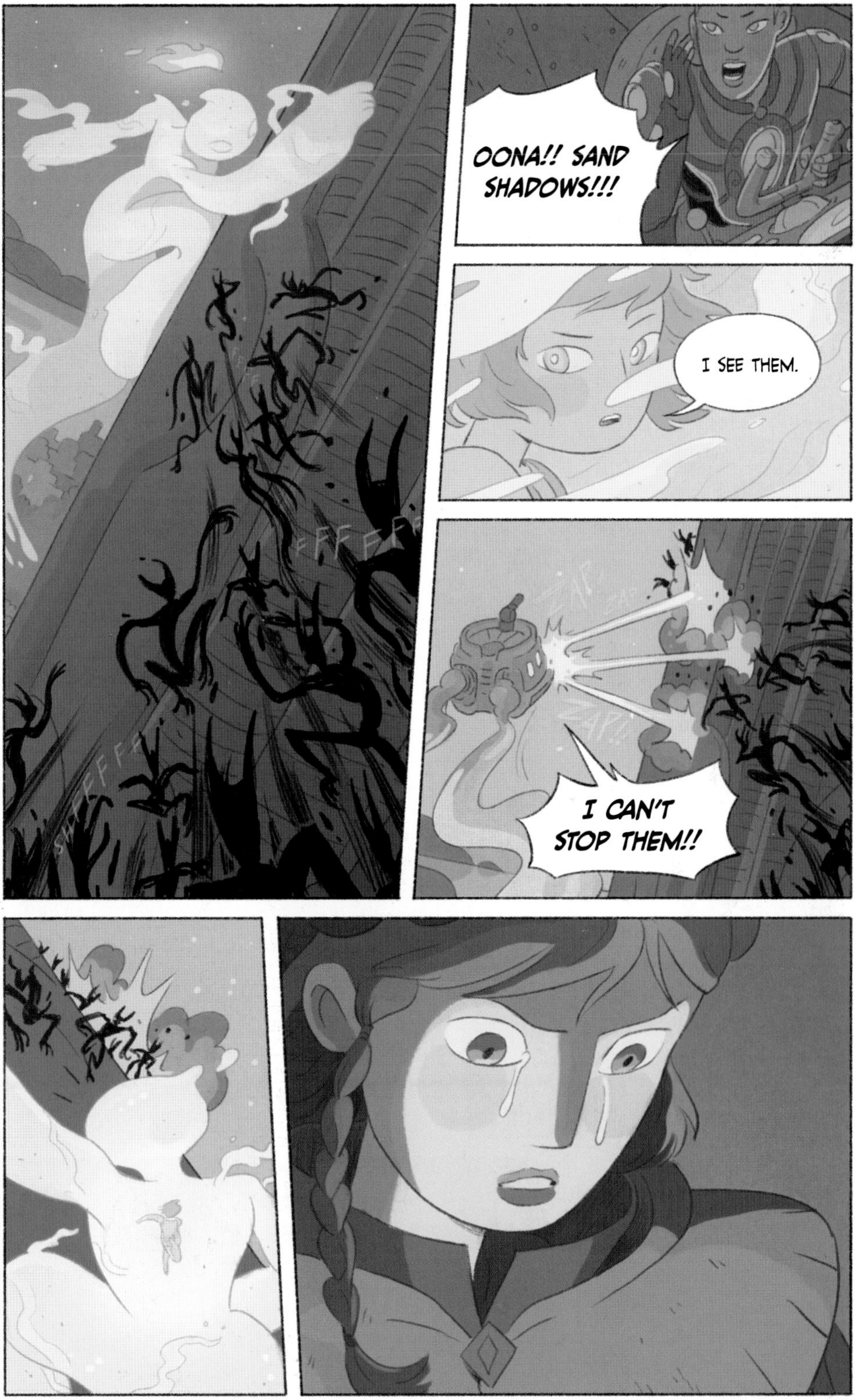
OONA!! SAND SHADOWS!!!
I SEE THEM.
I CAN'T STOP THEM!!

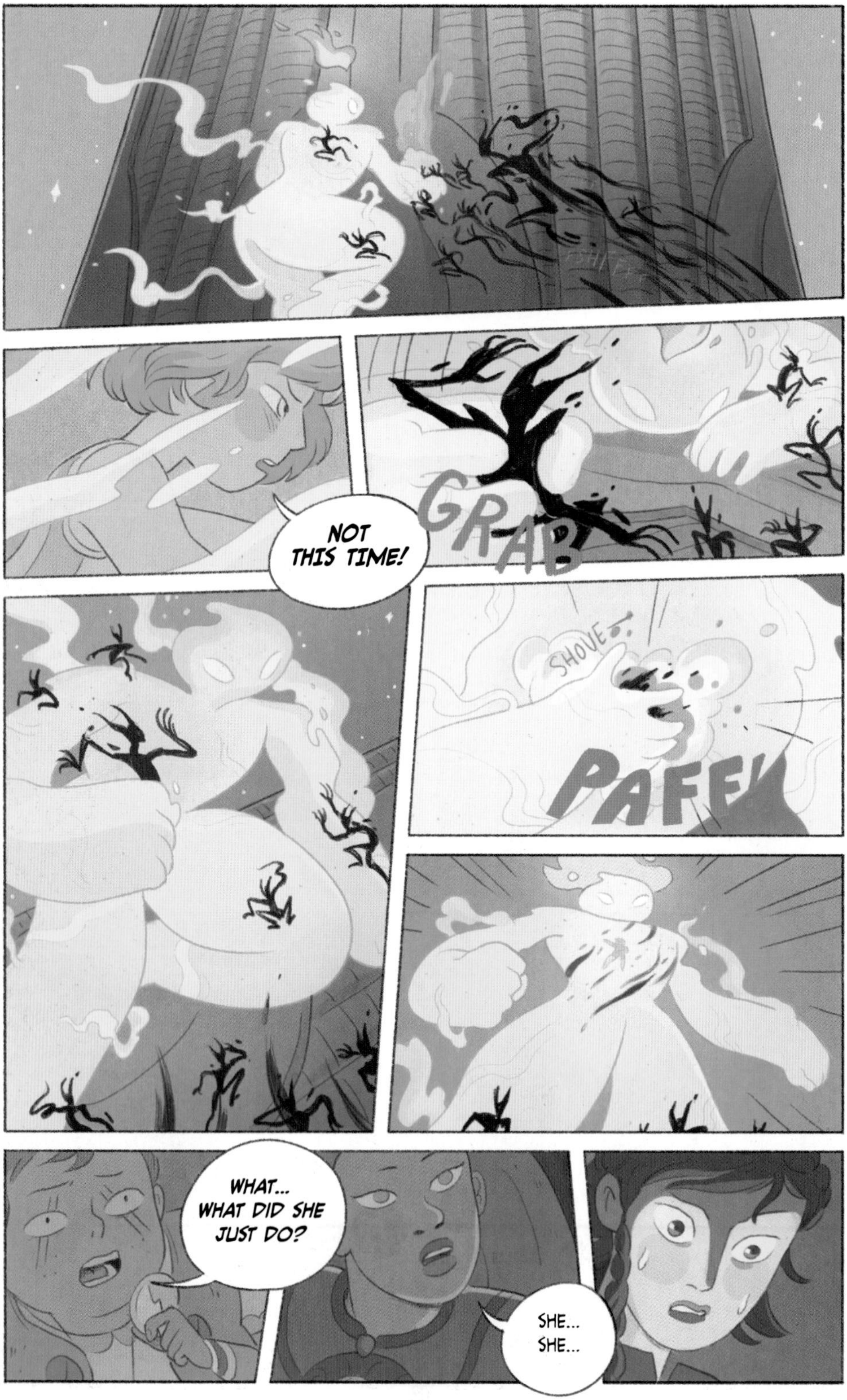
FSHFFF
NOT THIS TIME!
GRAB
SHOVE
PAFF
WHAT... WHAT DID SHE JUST DO?
SHE... SHE...

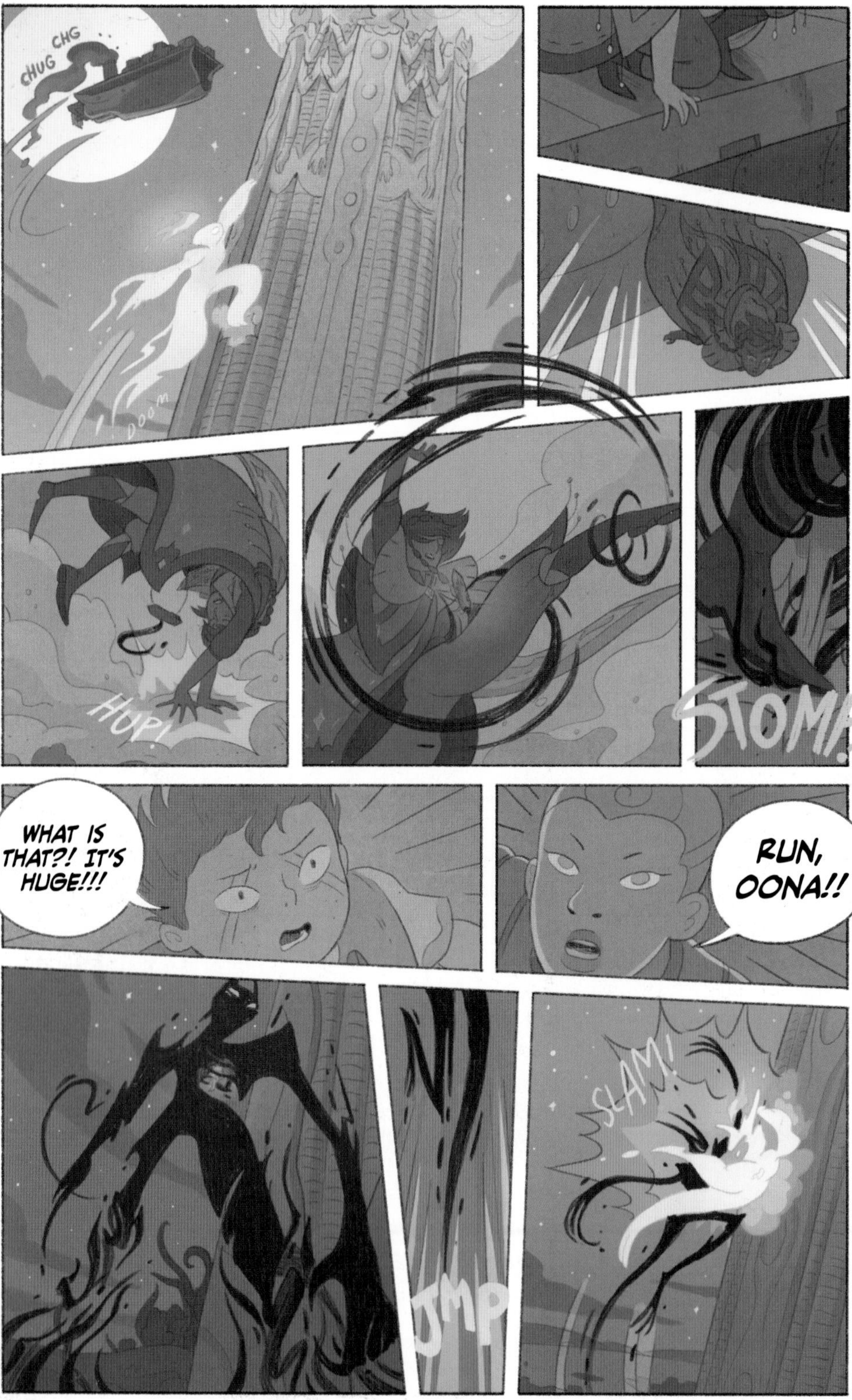
CHUG CHG
DOOM
HUP!
STOMP!
WHAT IS THAT?! IT'S HUGE!!!
RUN, OONA!!
JMP
SLAM!

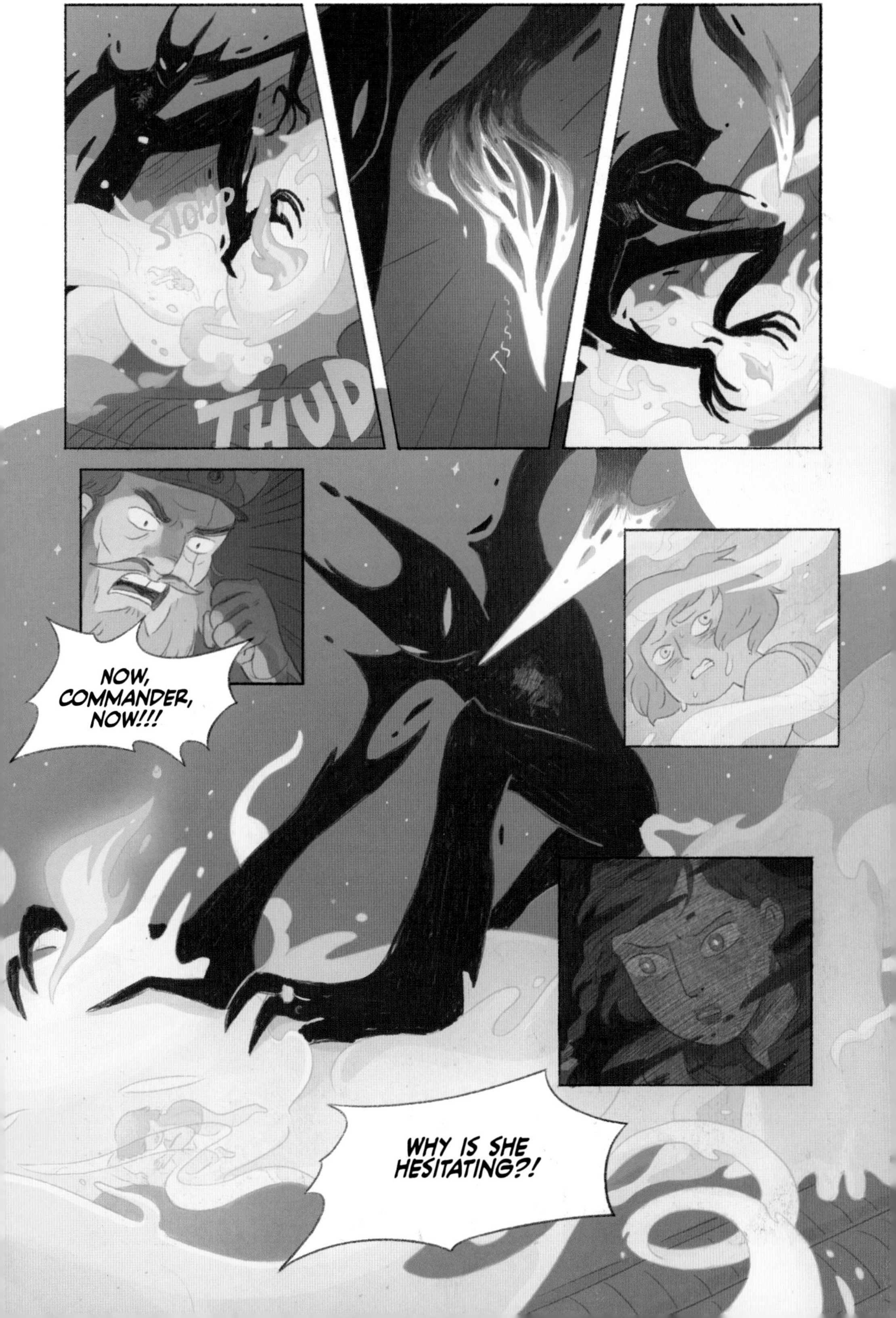
STOMP
THUD
TSSS
NOW, COMMANDER, NOW!!!
WHY IS SHE HESITATING?!

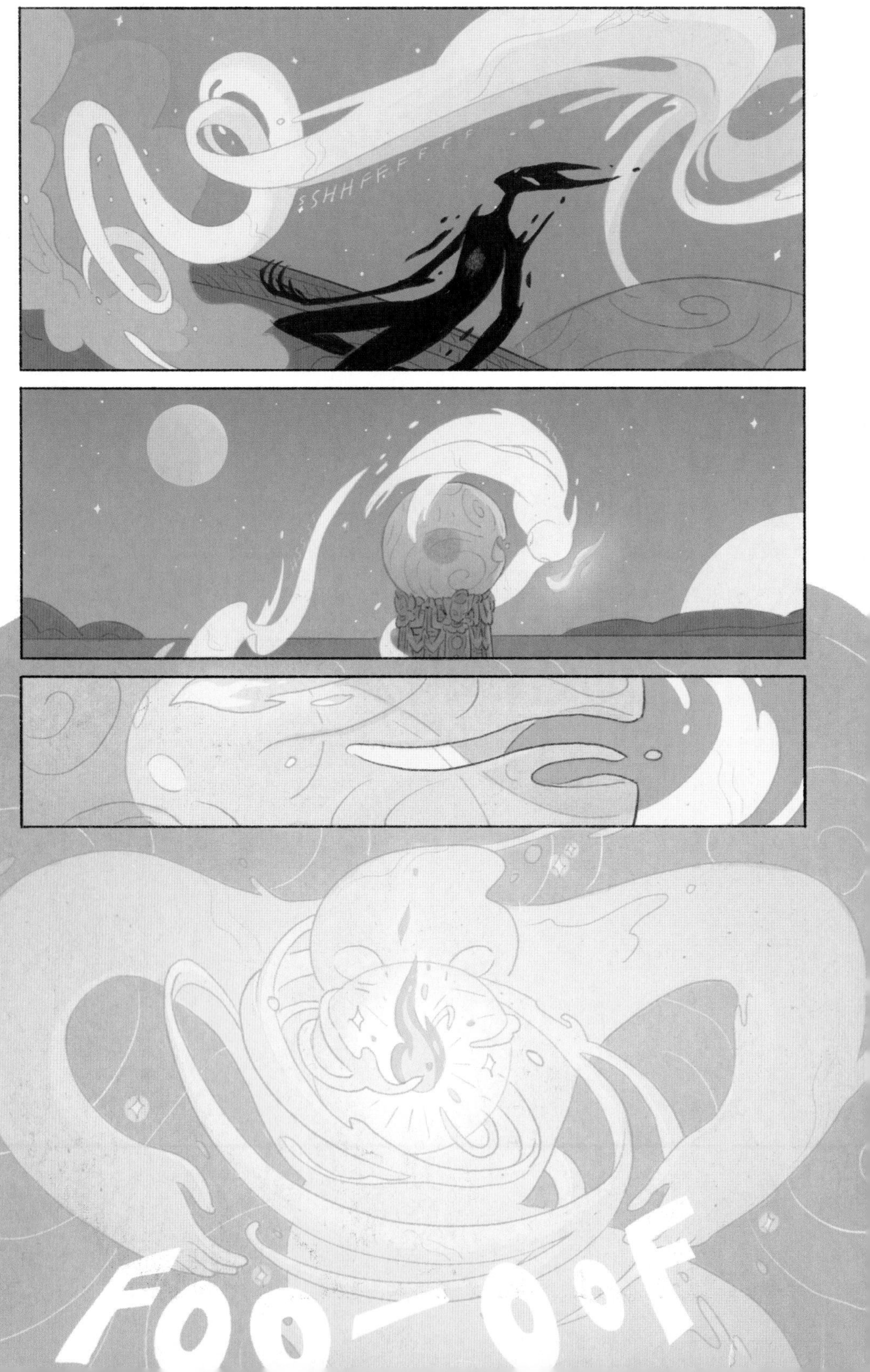
SSHHFFFFFFF
FOO—OOF

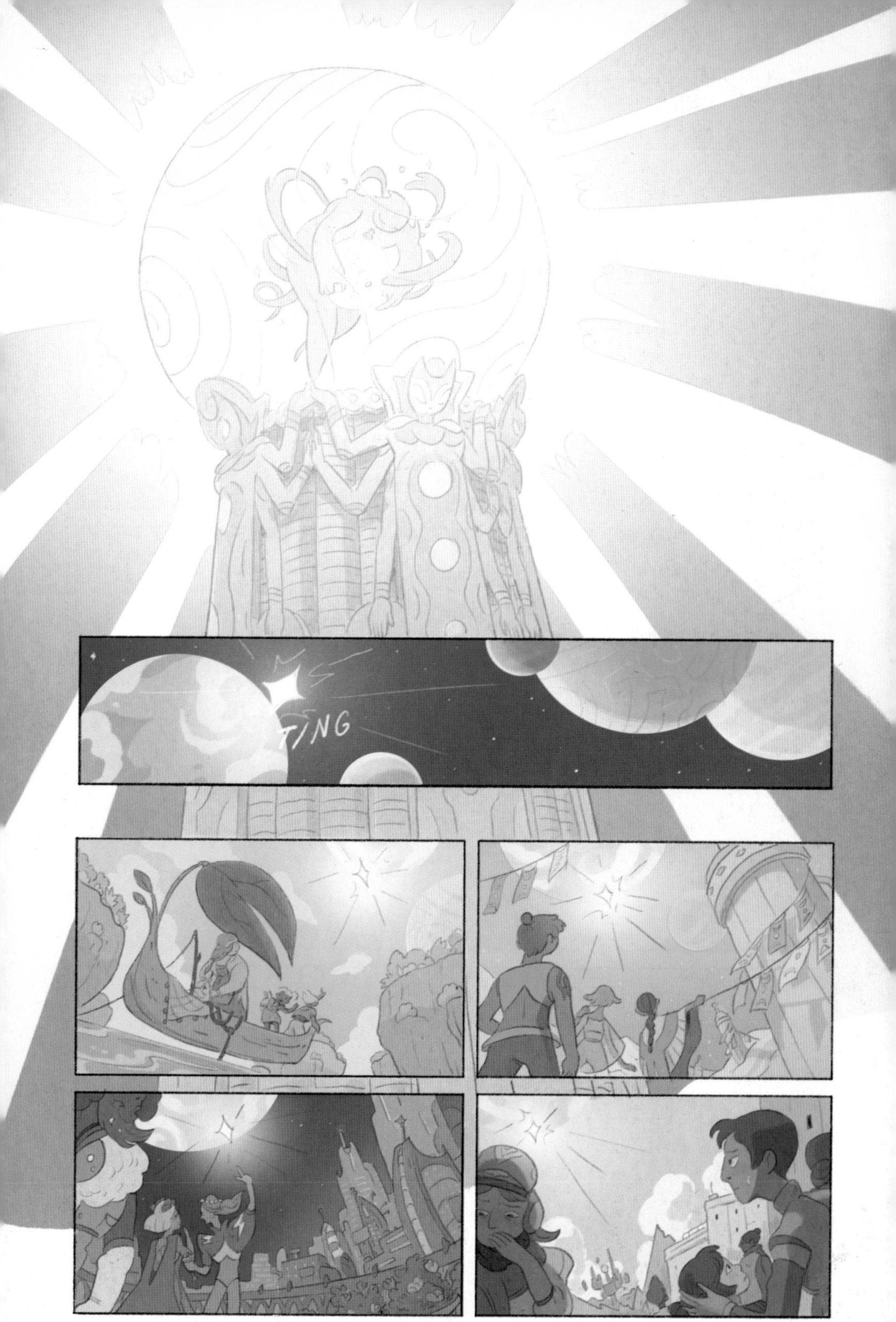
TING

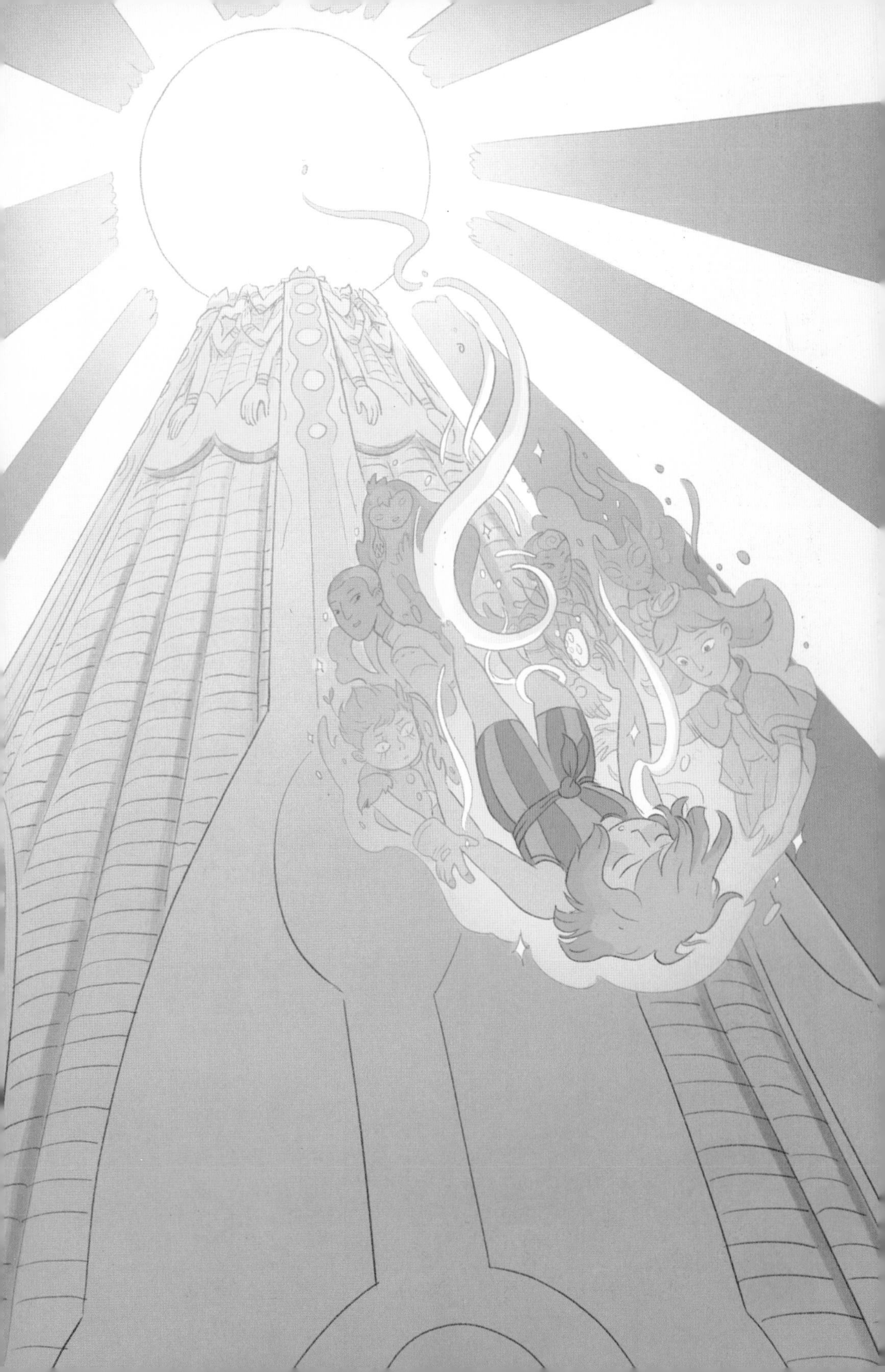

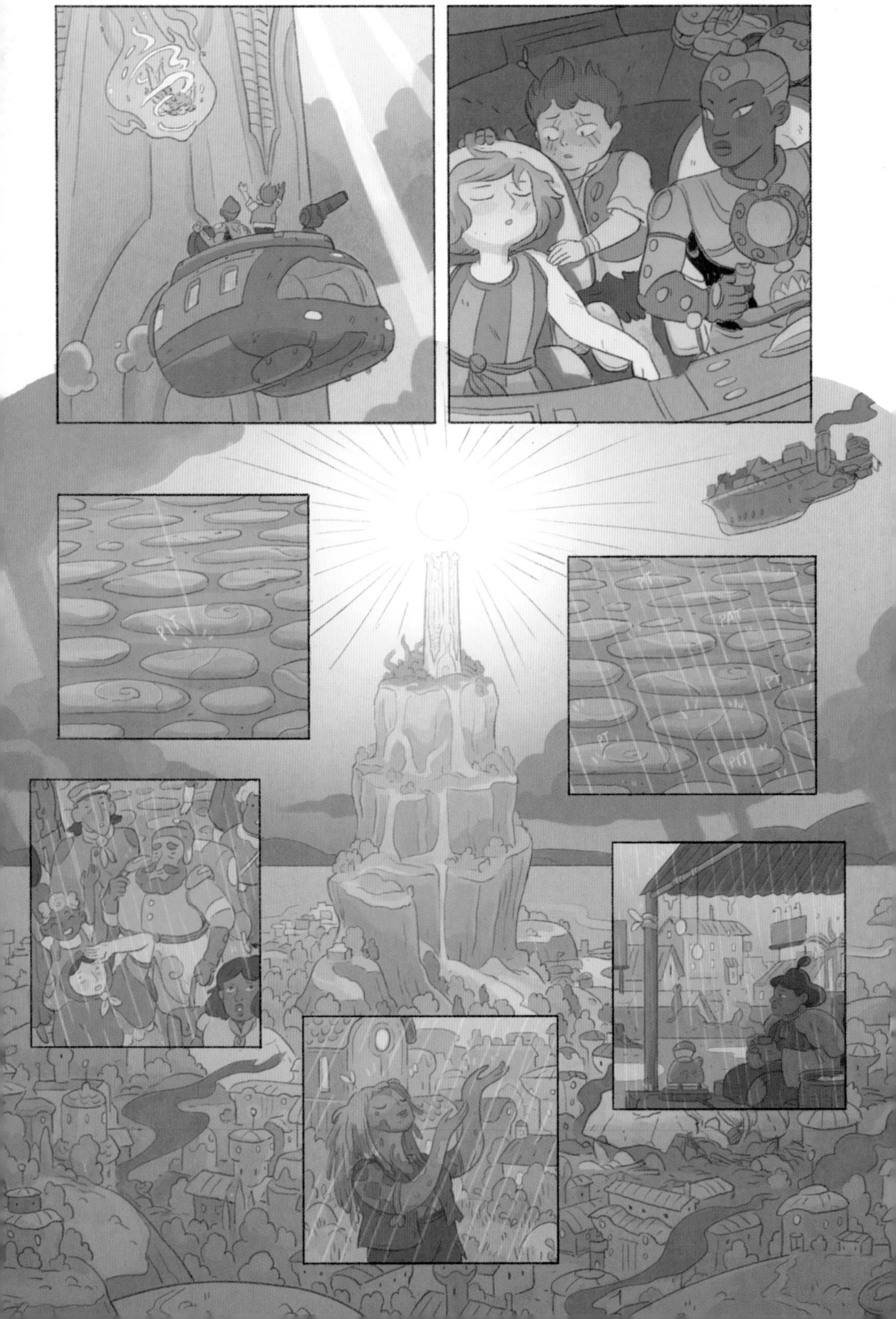
PIT
PT
PAT
PT
PT
PIT

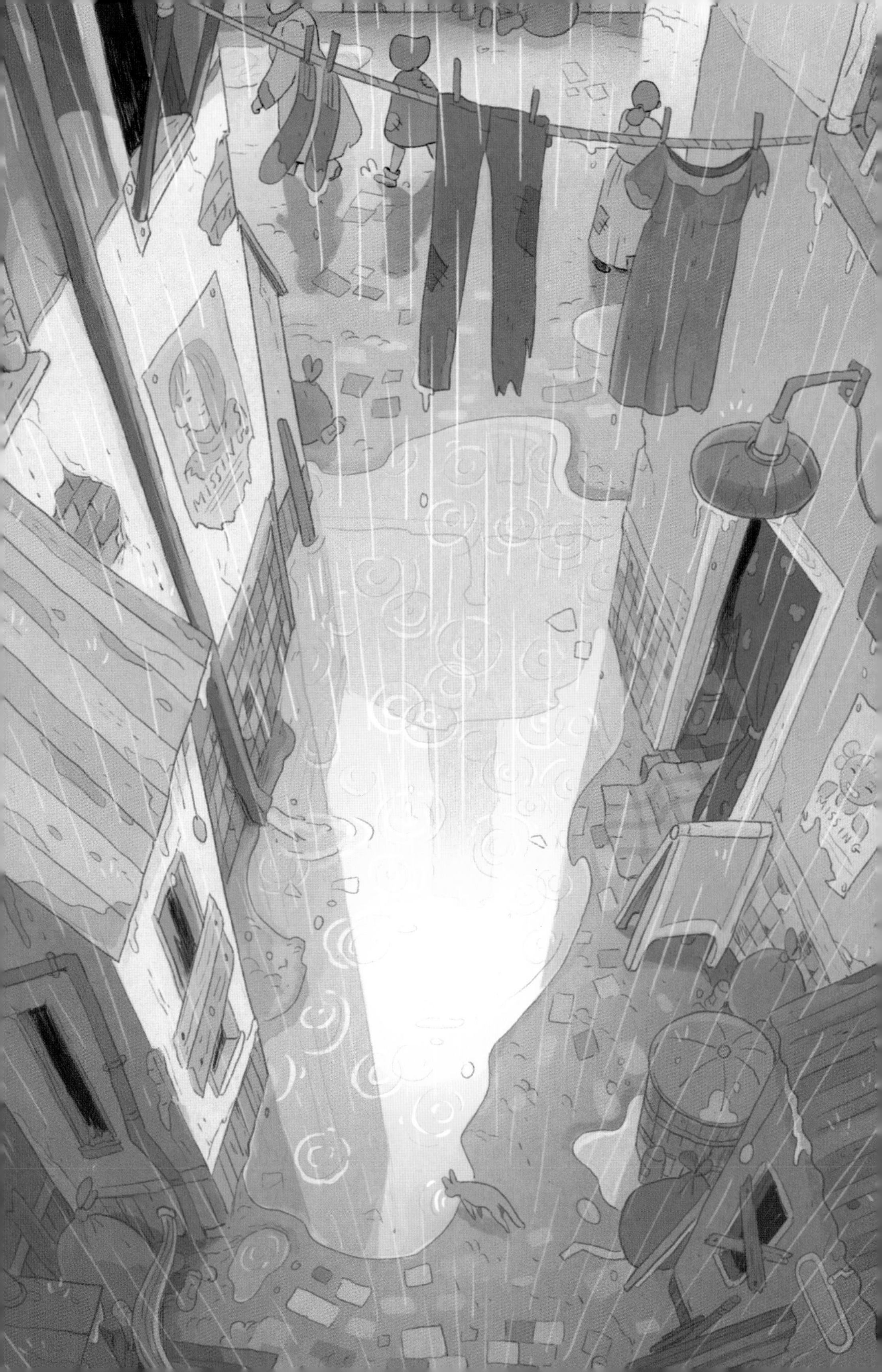
MISSING
MISSING

232

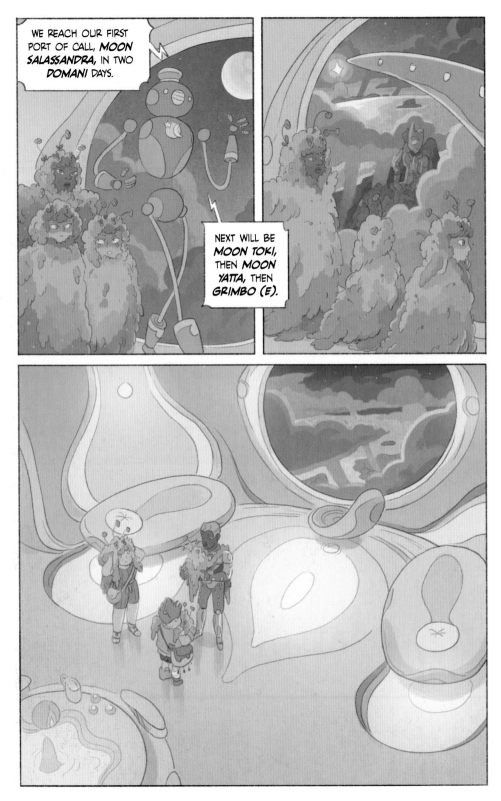

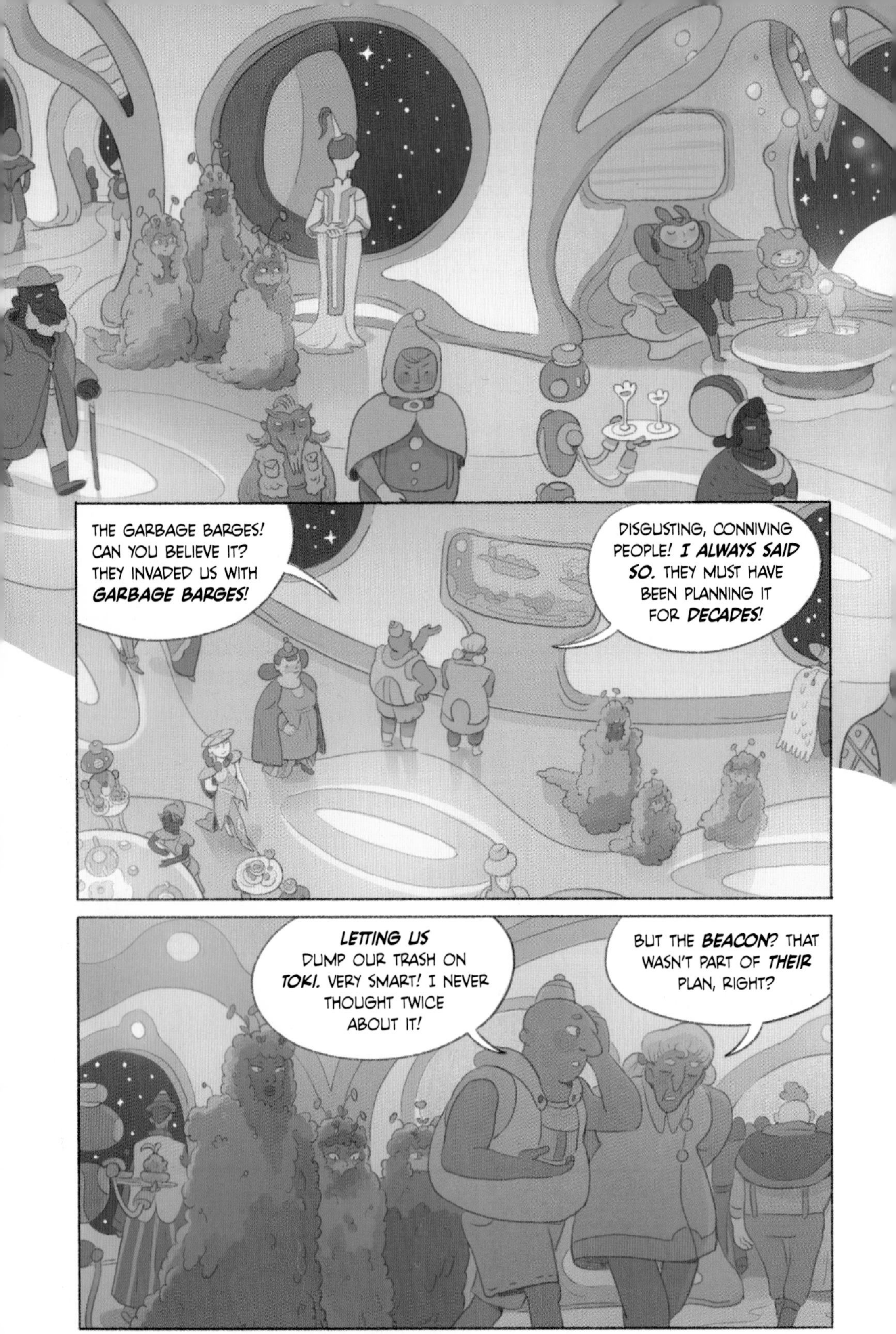
THE GARBAGE BARGES! CAN YOU BELIEVE IT? THEY INVADED US WITH GARBAGE BARGES!
DISGUSTING, CONNIVING PEOPLE! I ALWAYS SAID SO. THEY MUST HAVE BEEN PLANNING IT FOR DECADES!
LETTING US DUMP OUR TRASH ON TOKI. VERY SMART! I NEVER THOUGHT TWICE ABOUT IT!
BUT THE BEACON? THAT WASN'T PART OF THEIR PLAN, RIGHT?

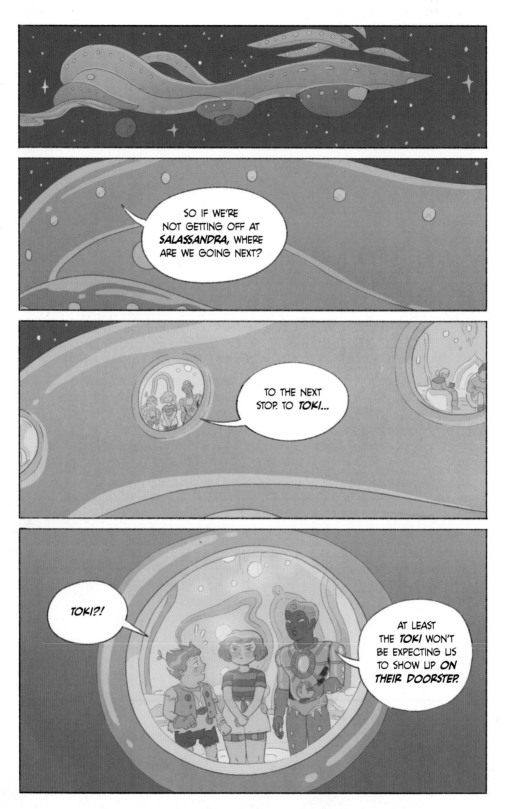

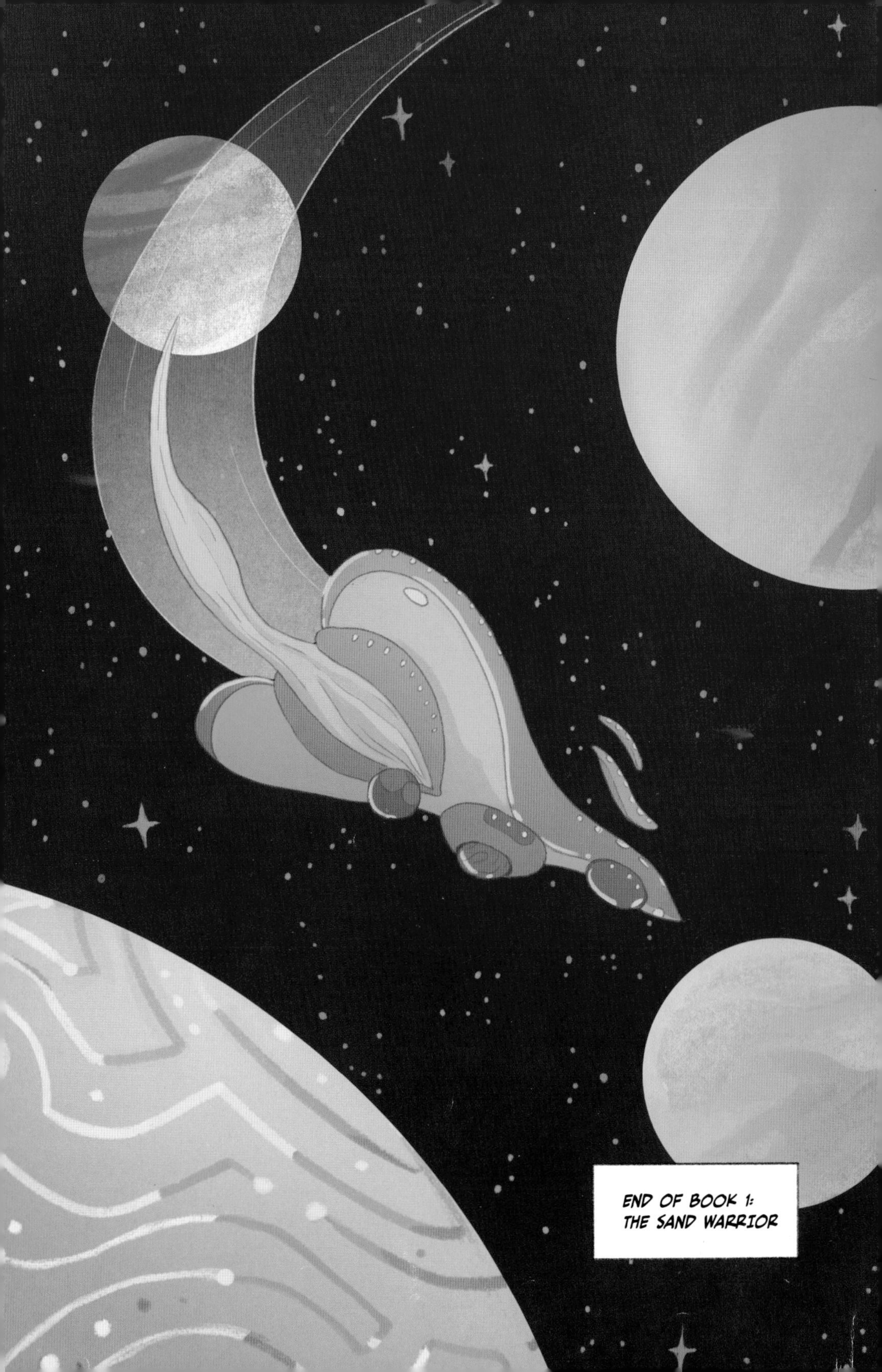
END OF BOOK 1:
THE SAND WARRIOR

To Julien and Clio—MS

To Shudan, Felix, and Elia—AS

To Mom and Pop—XB

To my friends and family—MR

To all my friends—BS

ACKNOWLEDGMENTS

Tanya McKinnon,
for support high and low, above and beyond

Our amazing Random House team:
Michelle Nagler, Chelsea Eberly, Elizabeth Tardiff, Kelly McGauley, Kim Lauber, Alison Kolani,
Dominique Cimina, Aisha Cloud, Lisa Nadel, Adrienne Waintraub, Laura Antonacci, John Adamo,
Joe English, Jocelyn Lange, Mallory Loehr, Barbara Marcus

+ Special thanks for added help, friendship & magic:
Siena Siegel, Sonia Siegel, Macarena Mata, Julie Sandfort, Gene Luen Yang,
Lee Wade, Sam Bosma, Kali Ciesemier, Noelle Stevenson, Carter Goodrich,
Moebius, Ursula K. LeGuin, Doris Lessing, Lois McMaster Bujold

Copyright © 2017 by Antzu Pantzu, LLC

All rights reserved. Published in the United States by Random House Children's Books,
a division of Penguin Random House LLC, New York.

Random House and the colophon are registered trademarks of Penguin Random House LLC.

Visit us on the Web! randomhousekids.com

Educators and librarians, for a variety of teaching tools, visit us at RHTeachersLibrarians.com

Library of Congress Cataloging-in-Publication Data is available upon request.
ISBN 978-1-101-93586-6 (trade) — ISBN 978-1-101-93588-0 (pbk.)
ISBN 978-1-101-93587-3 (lib. bdg.) — ISBN 978-1-101-93604-7 (ebook)

MANUFACTURED IN CHINA

10 9 8 7 6 5 4 3 2 1

First Edition

MARK SIEGEL has written and illustrated several award-winning picture books and graphic novels, including the *New York Times* bestseller **Sailor Twain, or the Mermaid in the Hudson.** He is also the founder and editorial director of First Second Books at Macmillan. He lives with his family in New York.

ALEXIS SIEGEL is a writer and translator based in London, England. He has translated a number of bestselling graphic novels, including Joann Sfar's **The Rabbi's Cat** and Pénélope Bagieu's **Exquisite Corpse** into English and Gene Luen Yang's **American Born Chinese** into French.

XANTHE BOUMA is an illustrator based in Southern California. When not working on picture books, fashion illustration, and comics, Xanthe enjoys soaking up the beachside sun.

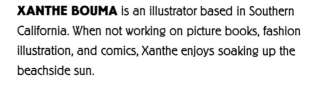

MATT ROCKEFELLER is an illustrator and comic book artist from Tucson, Arizona. His work has appeared in a variety of formats, including book covers, picture books, and animation. Matt lives in New York City.

BOYA SUN is an illustrator and coauthor of the upcoming graphic novel **Chasma Knights.** Originally from China, Boya has traveled from Canada to the United States and now resides in the charming city of Baltimore.

What will Oona, Jax, and An Tzu find on Toki?
The adventure continues in

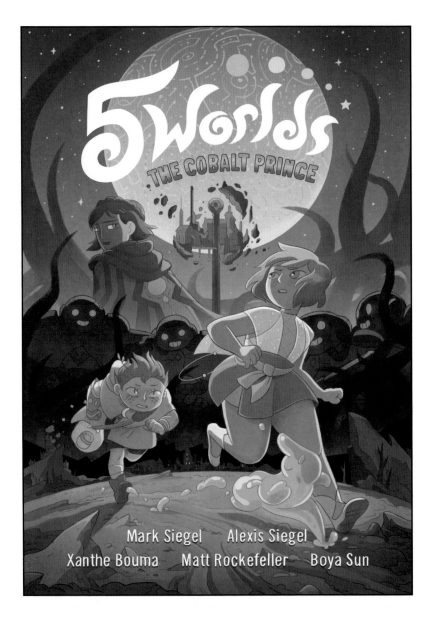

5W2:
THE COBALT PRINCE

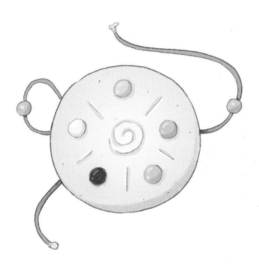